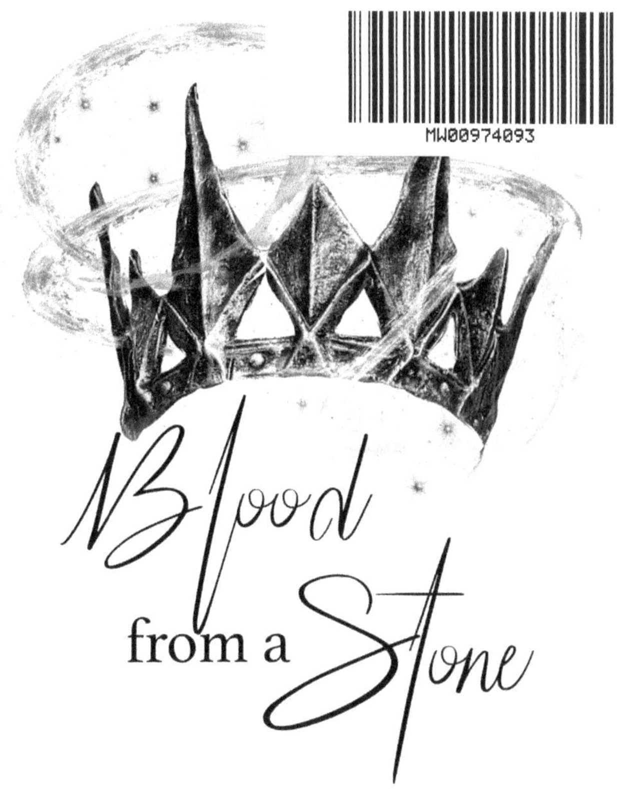

K.M. Robinson
Elle Beaumont
Helen Vivienne Fletcher
Christis Christie
J.M. Sullivan
Jessica Julien
Jalessa Bettis
Lou Wilham

BLOOD FROM A STONE: TWISTED VILLAINS ANTHOLOGY
Copyright © 2018 by K.M. Robinson, Elle Beaumont, J.M. Sullivan, Helen Vivienne Fletcher, Jessica Julien, Christis Christie, Jalessa Bettis, and Lou Wilham.

Published by Crescent Sea Publishing.
www.crescentseapublishing.com

Cover designed by Reading Transforms.
Image copyright © K.M. Robinson Photography.

This is a work of fiction. Names, characters, brands, trademarks, places, and incidents either are the product of the author's imagination or are used fictitiously. Any resemblance to actual events, locales, organizations, or persons, living or dead, is entirely coincidental and beyond the intent of either the author or the publisher.

All rights reserved, which includes the right to reproduce this book or portions thereof in any form whatsoever except as provided by the U.S. Copyright Law.

We're all the villains of someone else's story

Stories

Shattered Snow

by J.M. Sullivan

Mirror, mirror on the wall,
Who is fairest of them all?

This question from the evil queen,
Is one that ev'ry child has seen.

The queen so lovely, yet so vain,
Would ask it time and time again,

Relentless, she earned the same reply,
Until the mirror changed its cry.

And on the day she asked her query,
The mirror answered, voice so weary,

My Queen, so fair you are 'tis true,
But young Snow White is still moreso than you'

To this, the Queen took jealous rage,
And vowed to make poor Snow pay.

That's how the story goes you see,
Though everyone tells it wrong but me.

"Mara! Put that mirror away and make yourself presentable. The king is looking for a wife, not a puffed-up ninny!"

Mara blinked and pulled her gaze from the small mirror in her hand. She followed the sound of the sniping voice and looked blankly at the girl before her for a moment until her eyes cleared enough to see the hard line creased into her suitemate's forehead. Dorreen stood at the door in her best dress, scowling at Mara under a crown of elaborate curls.

"What if I don't want to be a wife?"

Dorreen's jaw dropped. "Don't want to be a wife?" She barked a mirthless laugh. "Who says this is about becoming a *wife*? The prize is becoming Queen."

Mara's gaze dropped to her mirror's reflective surface. Her dark brown eyes peeked behind loose strands of ebony framing her face before the mirror gave a faint shiver, blurring her image in a silent reminder of its presence.

"There are others who wish to be Queen, I'm sure."

A fluttering cough escaped Dorreen's throat. "Of course there are others! There are girls up and down the kingdom who would give everything they had to be considered for the king's hand!"

"Then why doesn't he call on them?" Mara interrupted, her temper blazing.

Dorreen's lips pinched, but her voice retained a proper sting as she recited Mistress Geneva's earlier words. "We do not know why his majesty does what he does, only that we are honored to be the one's he has bestowed his attention upon."

Mara rolled her eyes. "You know full well that's just the Mistress' eloquent way of saying 'I don't know and don't intend to ask.'"

"Neither do I." Dorreen tightened her jaw, then crossed the room to stand beside Mara, her voice lowered into a whisper. "But if your insufferable whining costs me the crown, I'll fix you into such a nightmare, you'll pray you never sleep again."

Mara's hands clutched the fabric of her skirts. She wasn't afraid of

Dorreen. At best, the sullen girl's power could earn her a paltry spot in some traveling faire—they were nothing compared to her own. But the king's upcoming visit followed by her mirror's cryptic message had already set her ill at ease.

"That's quite enough, Dorreen," Mistress Geneva's razor sharp voice cut the room like a knife. "My request was that you retrieve Mara to the parlor, not aggravate her into compliance."

Dorreen flushed crimson, but held Mara in her scathing stare for a defiant moment before whirling to curtsey at the school's founder.

"Yes, Mistress Geneva," she said, then hurried from the room, her swishing skirts the only sound of her fury.

Mistress Geneva placed a reassuring hand on Mara's shoulder. "Never mind, Dorreen. Stress makes her grumpy."

"Grumpy?" Mara's brow quirked as she slowly uncurled her fists from the blue satin they held captive. "I think you meant, 'becomes a pestilence'."

Mistress Geneva laughed, a low, throaty sound, that wasn't unpleasant. "You always did have a gift for words," she said. "It's what makes you such a gifted caster."

Heat rushed to Mara's cheeks, covering them in a pink tint. A small smile tugged at her lips until the herald's cry sounded, announcing the arrival of their visitors.

"Why is the king coming here?" she asked, hoping the Mistress would answer her away from the other girls. "Aside from bestowing his most benevolent attention upon us."

Mistress Geneva wore a wry smile, but her gaze was distant. "I truly don't know why he chose our lot," she said. "But his purpose is to pick one of you to be queen, and whoever it is will carry a heavy burden."

Mara's insides twisted. "Then why do you let him come? Don't you care for any of us?"

The harsh angles of Mistress Geneva's face softened as she looked at Mara. "I do." She gently swept Mara's bangs from her eyes. "But I also believe in duty. And more than that, I believe we receive our gifts for a reason. Mine tell me the king is in great need. Though I can feel the chosen queen will face incredible struggles, my gifts also bring me hope."

Her blue eyes bored into Mara before they drifted to the hand mirror resting on the table. She picked up the mirror and gently placed it in Mara's open palms. Responding to her touch, the glassy surface began to twist and swirl, but Mara glanced back at her teacher.

"Who do you think King Actaeon will choose?" she asked.

Mistress Geneva paused at the door, her shoulder stiff. She was quiet a moment before her whispered response brushed through the room. Mara's fingers clutched the cool metal of the mirror as the mistress retreated, her words echoing in Mara's ears.

"You were made for more than chasing mirrors."

It wasn't long after that Mara found herself in a silent line, itching to jump from her skin. Netted petticoats rustled under billowy dresses as Mistress Geneva's students silently strutted inside the row.

All save Mara.

Mara's ears pounded, straining against each tick of the ornate parlor clock as it counted the seconds to the king's decision. His Majesty had arrived with all the pomp and circumstance one could imagine, filling the vaulted room until it felt stuffy and small.

Actaeon was handsome enough, Mara supposed, with just enough curve to his cheek to prevent his angular face from slicing the air. His skin was ruddy and rugged, which, along with the broad sweep of his shoulders and the muscular cut of his legs suggested he spent a healthy amount of time outdoors. Although he was more than a few years older than all the girls, and tragically widowed with a small daughter, by worldly standards he was a young king with plenty of life left to live.

From the safety of the line, Mara continued searching the King, silently debating what had brought him to Mistress Geneva. The overstuffed lords and ladies seemed genuinely intrigued as well, although Mara couldn't decide if that was because of the king's choice of brides or their bewilderment at being pressed inside a country parlor like a barrel of sausages. Without her mirror, Mara could only search the king for answers. Her intent stare was interrupted when Actaeon's attention fell on her, meeting her gaze head on. A confident smile tugged the corners of his lips and Mara darted her eyes away, shamed at being caught.

"We are honored by your presence, Your Grace."

Mistress Geneva crossed the room, drawing Mara's attention from the looming monarch to Mistress Geneva's rigid back standing before them. The Mistress' words were lost to Mara, who heard nothing but the thrum of blood in her ears as a burning flush crept to her cheeks. She sucked in a soft breath and fixed her gaze on Mistress Geneva's softly swishing skirt until her lungs begged for air. Releasing her breath, she risked a glance at Actaeon, whose attention had shifted to the end of the line. An unfamiliar twinge pulled Mara's gut and she found herself wishing the king turn back before she stamped the traitorous thought away.

"Only the most accomplished girls are invited to the Academy, and of those, only the most talented are allowed to remain. We have girls of many different ages and skills and each one is incredibly and uniquely gifted." Mistress Geneva sniffed daintily, allowing her words to linger in the stuffy parlor air. "Allow me to introduce them to you, Your Highness."

Mistress Geneva's boots clicked over the tile as she led the king confidently to the end of the silent line. A tiny click lingered in the air as she stopped, leaving the gathered court staring expectantly. Mara shifted on her feet, longing to retreat to the safety of her room free from the ridiculous display. Beside her, the other girls waited quietly, with only the sounds of nervous shuffling filling the room.

The king stood beside Mistress Geneva, who had stopped at the start of the line before Khaitlyn, the youngest student in the school. The little girl quailed under their scrutiny, trembling so wildly that the ruffles of her pale pink dress shuddered too.

"Khaitlyn is our youngest scholar," Mistress Geneva pressed Khaitlyn's quivering form toward the waiting monarch. "Although her gifts are still settling, she has proven to have an affinity for several different practices. We are sure with some time, her true talent will emerge and she will be a fine enchantress."

Mistress Geneva nodded at Khaitlyn, who quickly squeaked back into line. Mara watched sympathetically as the king stepped closer to examine the tiny girl wrapped in delicate pink chiffon. She remembered the night Khaitlyn arrived at the Academy, thrashing and screaming while her parents sobbed over the broken body of her brother. It took hours for the shrieking to stop, and Khaitlyn hadn't spoken since. Actaeon knelt before her, forcing her to meet his gaze. A small fire smoldered in Mara's belly until the king gently tugged on one of Khaitlyn's loose curls and smiled.

"Very nice to meet you, Khaitlyn," Actaeon said. "I have a daughter who is about your age, a little younger. Princess Eirwen. But I like to call her Snow."

Khaitlyn's mouth rounded into a silent 'o', as she nodded. Of course, she knew about the Princess. Everyone in Mahlaydia had celebrated on the day she was born, even the peasantries on the farthest edges of the kingdom outside the Myrkur Forest. And they all mourned together when the king's beloved wife died nine years later. In a few months, there would be celebration again, when a new Queen rose to the throne.

A pang of remorse for the princess tugged at Mara's heart. Snow was only twelve. Hardly a year of mourning her mother before a new one was thrown her way, just a few years older than she. Mara shook her head to chase away the unwanted thoughts, and focused on Mistress Geneva, who had moved further down the line, leaving Khaitlyn sagging in visible relief.

"Next, we have the lady Sadira," Mistress Geneva extended her hand and Sadira stepped forward. Unlike Khaitlyn, she held her head level and looked fiercely at each of the courtiers before directly meeting the King's gaze.

"Sadira has an affinity for communicating with animals," Mistress Geneva explained, indicating to the sleek fur adorned coat Sadira wore over her leather tunic. "This is her second year at my facility. She is a skilled tracker and hunter, although she would much prefer to hibernate with the bears than skin them."

Sadira's amber eyes flashed against her dark skin as hushed laughter swept through the room. A low growl rumbled from the girl's chest, stopping the noble's laughter. Sadira's scowl twisted into a satisfied smirk, earning an approving grin from the king,

"Perhaps we can go hunting together someday, lady." Sadira smiled and bobbed a quick nod before she slunk back into formation while Actaeon pressed further down the line.

After Sadira, Actaeon waited patiently while Mistress Geneva customarily announced the rest of the younger girls—Phillida and her affinity for blooming plants; then the twins, Ahla and Ayda, who were talented in healing body and spirit.

After the youngest students were introduced, the Mistress followed the line toward the end of the row where the eligible maidens waited. Mara had to bite back a laugh as the Mistress approached Lindy. Though technically of age at sixteen, Lindy was horribly immature and addlepated. She was also the only girl in the room who wanted to be chosen more than Dorreen. With her penchant for infatuation spells, she might have succeeded—had she been anywhere other than trapped in a line. Instead, she flummoxed an elaborate curtsey, dipping far lower than appropriate while batting her eyelashes so heavily that the king asked if she was feeling well.

Mara dipped her chin to hide her shameful amusement that came from Lindy's bumbling. She let out a coughing laugh, then she raised her eyes to a shock. Actaeon stood directly in front of her. A knowing smile crept across his face and he winked, sharing silent secrets. An electric thrill ran through her, weaving a strange mix of excitement and dread around her insides, until the moment was interrupted by Dorreen's nasally whine.

"Surely His Majesty tires of this endless parade." She flashed a demure smile as if begging penance for her outburst, then took a small step toward the king. She angled her chest toward him suggestively, batting her lashes while a scandalized murmur whispered through the crowd. "You must be so very busy, Your Highness. There must be a better way for us all to get acquainted."

Mara stifled an eye roll, but free of the king's beguiling gaze, her scattered wits gathered long enough to brandish her mirror's warning.

Love and loss held hand in hand, come fast across this kingdom's land.

Actaeon nodded a polite acknowledgment and faced Dorreen, his gaze floating over her tightly cinched dress to rest intently on her face.

"And to whom do I have the pleasure of being currently acquainted?"

Dorreen trilled, and the harsh nasal tone sent bramble-thorns down Mara's spine. "Lady Dorreen," she simpered. "The eldest and most practiced of Mistress Geneva's students."

Actaeon quirked a brow toward Mistress Geneva. "Is this true?"

Mistress Geneva nodded calmly.

"She is the eldest, your Majesty, with many hours spent practicing potions." She turned her attentive stare to Dorreen, who quailed under her warring glower. "She has a solid understanding of magic; though somewhat less of an understanding of her place."

"I see." Actaeon whispered in the ear of the manservant beside him. The servant bowed and disappeared into the cloud of courtiers. Mara exhaled a relieved sigh, free of the nobles' scrutiny as the crowd whispered their selections for queen amongst each other. She hadn't even had to speak. She'd have to thank Dorreen's endless insufferability later.

A heavy footstep hushed the court as a gilded boot appeared in front of Mara.

"What is your name?"

Mara's gaze darted to meet the King. Standing before her, Mara realized for the first time how tall the king was. His chin angled toward her, lighting his face perfectly in the soft morning light. Tiny rays danced on his face, highlighting his hair and eyes with flecks of golden amber. A sharp breath caught in Mara's throat as he looked at her and smiled.

"Mara, Your Majesty," she said, thankful for the opportunity to introduce herself as she was instead of being forced to live up to the picture Mistress Geneva painted her to be. "Just Mara."

"*Just* Mara?" Actaeon's brow quirked to match the tilt of his grin.

"Yes, Highness. I am an orphan. I have lived most of my life at the Academy with Mistress Geneva."

Actaeon nodded and stepped back, studying Mara once more. He turned to Mistress Geneva.

"And this is true as well?"

Mistress Geneva stepped forward with a small curtsey. "Yes, sire. Mara has been with me almost as long as the school. The only one who has been here longer is lady Dorreen." She gestured to Dorreen, who shuffled forward with a face as crimson as her dress. "Both are fine lasses."

The King's nose turned as he observed Dorreen's simper. "But which would make a better Queen?" he mused.

An audible gasp swept the room. Actaeon looked from Dorreen to Mara with shrewd eyes. He stepped forward.

"Lady Dorreen."

The room hushed as Dorreen erupted in a delighted titter. Even with her face lit with glee, the surly lines etched in her skin remained. She stepped forward victoriously, only to be stilled by a sharp swish of Actaeon's hand.

"In what ways have you found your gift to be a boon to others?"

Dorreen's simper dissolved into a strangled choke. "Your Highness?"

Actaeon's golden eyes flashed as the trace of a smile danced on his lips. He cleared his throat, then repeated his question more slowly.

"How do you use your gift to help others?"

Dorreen's mouth gaped, resembling the carp she'd had for breakfast. "I—well, I don't know your majesty."

"I see." Actaeon hummed, then stepped to address the girls. "I had hoped to find a Queen who was able to do more for the kingdom than entertain my courtiers with cheap party tricks."

Mara bowed her head to stifle her laugh. Dorreen was often a blight, but even she had felt the sting of Actaeon's words. Surely that was painful enough for the miserable girl—there was no need for further cruelty. Once her mask was carefully fixed, Mara raised her eyes to be caught again in Actaeon's smoldering gaze.

"Lady Mara. What gifts do your talents bestow on others?"

A spark caught in Mara's chest, borne by nerves and another emotion she'd never experienced. She gasped in a tiny breath, noting the way Actaeon's stare traced her lips.

"I'm sorry to say Majesty, my gift is mine alone. It doesn't bring a boon to crops, or heal the sick, or even clean the kitchens." Her voice quailed as a low rumble filled the room and her gaze escaped Actaeon to trace over the dozens of chortling courtiers. She swallowed, then returned her attention to the king's calm stare and her resolve strengthened. "But it is the gift of foresight. Of knowledge and wisdom in times where those gifts are hard to come by. And while I cannot share my gift readily with others, I *can* pass wisdom to those who wish to receive it."

Actaeon's impassive stare twitched into a wry grin.

"I believe the lady is right." Actaeon addressed the courtiers hanging on his every word. "Wisdom is a gift; one that is challenging to come by. Words are a power all their own—with the ability to raise or destroy a kingdom with one tiny slip." The king's glance passed deliberately over Dorreen to rest firmly on Mara. "Wisdom is of great value."

Actaeon paused, allowing his words to fall heavily on the crowd before turning toward Mara. His amber eyes burned into hers as he reached for her hand.

"Lady Mara, your mistress speaks highly of your abilities, which in itself is impressive. But, a queen must not only be gifted, she must be generous. Not just to lead, but to lead by example—to lead with wisdom. Lady Mara, do not take this request lightly when I ask. Will you join my side?

The room erupted as the other girls rushed Mara in a dizzying embrace. Mara's chest tightened as the butterflies inside turned to lead, and all the while the mirror's warning echoed faintly in her ears.

Guard your heart child, protect it true; deny another joining you . . .

A dizzying fog settled over Mara as the room swirled and tilted like the glass in her mirror. She gulped a quick breath and then another as her corsets clutched her ribs. It was suddenly very hot.

"I hoped it would be you."

Cool pressure shocked through Mara's system, unmooring her

thoughts. She followed the touch to King Actaeon's hand resting over hers, cradling it in his steadying grip.

"I wanted to choose you from the moment I walked in," he breathed, filling the air with the faintest hint of peppermint. "There is a spark inside you that sets you apart like a burning flame. Even the finery of my courtiers dulls in the shine of your eyes. You are beautiful, lady, inside and out."

Actaeon smiled, different than the arrogant grin he paraded in front of the court procession—raw and genuine, with an edge of vulnerability that softened his regal features. Then, before the court and all of Mistress Geneva's school, he knelt and slipped a tear-shaped ruby ring from his pinky. He raised it for all to see, then looked at Mara, his voice even and sure.

"Lady Mara, it would be my honor and the kingdom's blessing to take you as my Queen."

Mara bobbed her head, not trusting herself to speak. The hard lines of Actaeon's face widened into a bright smile and he slipped the blood-red gem onto her finger and rose to face her. He drew her close, pressing her to him so only she could hear his next words.

"I look forward to learning much from your wisdom, Lady Mara." Actaeon's eyes glinted playfully as he spoke, his voice a low rumble that trembled through her bones. "But you must want to say your goodbyes." He brushed her knuckles with the barest trace of a kiss, before gently sweeping the hair from her eyes and leaving his hand to linger on her cheek. "I will come for you tomorrow. I'm sure you are even more breathtaking at dawn."

He withdrew his hand, and Mara's cheek prickled as cool air rushed against her burning skin. In a confident, booming voice, Actaeon addressed his court, commanding their leave. In just a few moments, the parlor was empty, leaving the blooming ice in Mara's chest as the only evidence that her life had just been changed forever.

After the courtiers stole away their pomp and circumstance and the hysteric titters of the girls finally dulled to dramatic whispers, Mara found herself in bed, tracing the gilded frame of her mirror in lazy circles. Its enchanted glass shimmered under her touch, but mercifully, it remained silent.

"Mara?" Mistress Geneva's knock was followed by impatient footsteps crossing the room without invitation.

Before she could stop, a shuddery breath racked Mara's chest and she burrowed into the pillow to hide her face. She couldn't bear Mistress Geneva's kindness. Better Dorreen and her cruelty, than the Mistress' reassuring smile. One look would bring back all the tears she had spent the last of her energy banishing.

Mara waited for the headmistress' reproach, but there was only a soft pressure on the edge of the bed as the Mistress eased herself to sit on the lumpy mattress. Silence stretched into the room, until the quiet became unbearable.

"The king will call in the morning," Mara said, her voice as dead as she felt inside.

"Aye," Mistress Geneva agreed. "We've spoken on the matter. He thinks very kindly of you."

"As kindly as he can from an afternoon parade," Mara huffed. "That's all we were. Another show for his lords and ladies, only this time, the prize was a crown."

"Did you not find his Majesty charming?" Mistress Geneva asked. "You seemed taken with him in the parlor."

Mara hesitated. That was the problem. She *had* been taken with him. In the parlor, with Actaeon's strong hands wrapped firmly around her trembling skin and the husky timbre of his voice that pierced her soul, she had been very taken with him. For a hopeful moment, she even allowed herself the freedom to believe she might have happiness with him. And then the mirror's prophecy came crashing through.

Though his love may thrill your heart, your union will be shrouded, dark . . .

Prophecy. The wisdom she had boasted skillfully enough to earn the hand of a king. That same wisdom would condemn her to an eternity of sorrow for daring to believe he could make her happy.

Rebellious tears welled Mara's eyes as dizzying emotions crashed around her, throwing her into further despair.

"I've had a vision," Mara said. Emotion tore her voice, making her words breathy and weak.

Mistress Geneva stilled. Her mouth drew a hard line as she clasped her fists, silently bracing herself.

"What did you see?"

"Love and loss held hand in hand, come fast across this kingdom's land.

Guard your heart child, protect it true; deny another joining you. Though his love may thrill your heart, your union will be shrouded, dark. For when love an enchantress takes, so much more than one heart breaks."

She let the words hang in the air, waiting until they settled to drop her gaze to her own twisting hands. "I can't marry the king."

Mistress Geneva's frown deepened. "We are more than the joy in our lives," she said sadly. "Though the king's words came from a different understanding, their meaning holds truth. He has lived his life with the assigned responsibility of royalty—and you the assigned responsibility of magic. King Actaeon may have allegiance and fame, but *you* Mara have greater responsibility. You cannot go back on that promise now; it is your duty."

"But it's not fair!" Mara cried. The panic in her chest rose as the weight of her promises tightened around her.

"Sometimes, fair requires a sacrifice," Mistress Geneva's gaze became distant. A wistful look darted over her face before the lines hardened back into their stoic arrangement. "Not everyone is equal, Lady Mara, and when duty steps in, happiness isn't always guaranteed." She patted Mara tenderly on the shoulder, then quietly crossed the room. The door creaked as she let herself out, brushing her last words with the squeak of a hinge.

"You are more honorable than you know."

Mara waited for the room to quiet, then sagged into the bed, allowing fresh tears to trail freely down her face. After the slow stream stilled, she sat and wiped her face, ignoring the mirror that lay serenely at her side. The sun glinted off its surface, and it shivered for Mara's attention. Frustrated, Mara hung it on the wall so she could glare at it while she packed her belongings. In a rage, she gathered her belongings—an entire life smashed inside a single parcel box.

All except the mirror.

She glowered at the trinket, and the ferocity of her gaze filled her with some satisfaction as she drew closer to the mirror, her voice filled with quiet defiance.

"Mirror, mirror on the wall, who's the *fairest* of them all?"

Mara glared at her reflection, her eyes flashing in indignant rage as she silently dared the mirror to speak. It was still for a moment, then a tiny shudder ran through the glass, breaking Mara's defiant posture. Her shoulders dipped in defeat, and she obediently pressed her fingertips to the rippling surface to receive the response she'd demanded.

As soon as her fingers touched the ripples, they dipped under, submerging Mara's body in ice as dark visions swirled around her, carrying shadowed glimpses of her future. All around, images swam in and out, floating close enough to taunt Mara with their existence, but shying far enough away to remain shrouded in mystery. They ebbed and flowed around her while the mirror's voice echoed in her mind, throwing her own words in low, deep stone.

Though others sacrifice much 'tis true, no soul in Mahlaydia gives fair as you."

Mara jerked back, severing the connection from the mirror. She dropped on the bed, chest heaving. Even still, cold images swirled in her head pierced through by a pair of ice blue eyes. Aching terror rolled through Mara, but having no one save the mirror beside her, Mara flung herself on the bed and wept.

Cold dread washed over Mara when she awoke the next morning. The king was coming for her. For all she knew, he could be downstairs, waiting to sweep her to the castle to live out the rest of her predetermined misery.

Mara twisted in bed, wondering how long she could hide upstairs before the mistress came for her. A loud squeak creaked at the edge of the bed followed by a shuffling thump and Mara shot up, concerned.

"Khaitlyn? What are you doing here?" Her brows furrowed as she stared at the tiny girl sprawled clumsily on the floor.

Khaitlyn flushed crimson and pushed herself to stand shyly in front of Mara. Her hands danced around each other as she watched Mara expectantly.

Mara waited, hoping the girl would explain her strange behavior, then sighed, realizing it was a wasted effort. "Has the king arrived?"

Khaitlyn shook her head and slowly extended her hand. Inside her tightened grip, a tiny chain appeared with a dangling pearl moonstone. Mara reached for the charm and as soon as the tiny rock touched her skin another vision filled her mind.

Instead of the moonstone, Mara's hand clutched a tiny baby, who looked up at her from under a shock of black hair and studied her with his golden eyes. The baby cooed and gripped Mara's thumb and she smiled as Actaeon's booming laugh filled the room before the king came and wrapped them in his embrace.

Shocked, Mara released the moonstone and the vision vanished, leaving only traces of the baby's babbles in her ears. Her trembling hand upset the chain, rocking the dangling stone as Mara gaped at it, wondering if Khaitlyn was also a seer.

"Khaitlyn, is this true?" she asked, her hitching breath turned her voice unsteady.

Khaitlyn nodded soberly, her oak eyes unwavering in their stare. She flung her arms wide and wrapped them around Mara in a tight embrace, squeezing her like a corset. Mara melted into her, touched by the sudden show of affection, but as soon as her cheek pressed to Khaitlyn's head a hollow voice whispered through Mara's thoughts.

Beware the falling snow. There is danger in its beauty.

Mara jerked back, but before she could ask Khaitlyn about the message, Dorreen barged into the room with an impatient huff.

"It is time to leave, *Your Majesty*," she said with a bitter sneer. Her eyes widened when she saw her impertinence had an audience, but narrowed when she realized it was Khaitlyn. "What are you looking at? Don't you have somewhere else to be underfoot?

Always sulking and staring—what sort of caster do you even hope to be?"

She glowered at Khaitlyn, who glanced nervously from her to Mara, eliciting another enraged groan.

"Never mind you simpleton!" she shouted, "Just get out!"

Dorreen swiped at Khaitlyn, but the girl squeaked and scampered off, leaving Mara trapped under Dorreen's withering glare.

"I suppose you're pleased with yourself." Dorreen looked from Mara to her emptied shelves and her scowl deepened. "All those pretty words of yours have finally earned you a prize. But now you must live up to them. We'll see how much your wisdom helps you then." She scoffed and turned on her heel to storm out the door. Her hips waggled in an exaggerated stride as she flipped her hair in a pompous preen. "Don't be long, my queen. We're anxious to see you out."

The door slammed behind Dorreen's swishing skirts leaving Mara standing silently, her stomach churning.

"It's not a prize, you wretch."

Mara cast one last glance around the room, and gathered her bags. She dropped Khaitlyn's moonstone into her leather pack, and gently pulled her mirror from where it hung lifelessly on the wall. Her fingers clasped the slender handle and the cool metal shivered delightedly under her touch.

"Not now," she whispered, tucking the heavy accessory deep into the folds of her skirts. "I'll show you when we arrive at the castle."

The mirror thrummed a response, its vibrations matching Mara's nervous breath. She exhaled, then before she could lose her nerve, quickly followed Dorreen's path, striding down the stairs to meet her future husband.

Mara stepped on the landing and found Actaeon waiting to greet her. She was relieved to see there was no procession accompanying him today, only his footman.

"My lady." Actaeon dipped in a respectful bow, but his gaze remained on Mara as he fixed her with a disarming grin. "Morning suits you." He reached for her hand and brushed a kiss to her palm as he led her down the remaining stairs.

A hot flush crept to Mara's cheeks, warming them against the cool morning air. She glanced at the girls gathered around the doorway, shameless in their stares.

"Your Majesty."

She bowed in greeting, vaguely wondering if she was going to spend the rest of her life in servitude to awkward formality. Actaeon followed her gaze and smiled knowingly.

"I trust you slept well?" He angled his body to face her, blocking the audience from her sight. He leaned closer, bending to conform his tall form to her petite frame, his voice pitched for only her to hear. "Of course, if you aren't, I'm more than happy to loan you my shoulder during the journey home."

Mara blinked in surprise. "I'm sure I shall be fine, Your Highness." She bit her lip to hide the wry smile his forwardness conjured. "But should needs change, your shoulder will be first to know."

A low chuckle rumbled from Actaeon's chest, sending a delightful shiver up Mara's spine.

"Then we'd best be on our way." Actaeon spoke loudly enough to make the statement an announcement and turned to face the unabashed observers before guiding her toward the door. "After you, my queen."

Thrilled titters erupted through the room as the girls extolled the love story unfurling before them. They accosted Mara with romantic sighs and glowing congratulations as she passed, leaving Mara dizzy with their giddy hugs and tear-filled goodbyes.

Finally, they made it through the crowd and past the door, and Mara followed Actaeon to the quiet of his private carriage. She sank into the soft seats, thankful for the chance to gather her thoughts. While Mara loved the girls, she had grown accustomed to practicing her art through quiet reflection and independent study. The attention currently being lavished on her was foreign, and if she was honest, made her rather uncomfortable.

Mara took a few deep, steadying breaths as Actaeon settled and the coachman readied the horses. The footman gave a final cry and the reins cracked, spurring the stallions onward. Mara glanced out the carriage window once more, waving her last goodbye. Her schoolmates bounced on their heels, arms flailing as they sent her off. She looked at each one, sealing their image into her memory. Her gaze swept over Khaitlyn's wide, knowing eyes and Sadira's prowling grin, to Phillida and her brambled mess of hair before landing on the twins and their excited, synchronized bounces. Mara even took a moment to immortalize Dorreen's scowl. It was part of her home.

The carriage lurched and Mara gave a final, trembling smile to the girls before looking back at the Academy. Mistress Geneva stood somberly at the doorway, her hands clasped tightly at her lap. Her lips moved in a hushed murmur as she followed the carriage with her gaze. She nodded at Mara and arced her arm in the formal enchantress' wave, then bowed slightly at the waist.

Mara leaned against the seat, hiding from the window as a fresh wave of tears threatened to spill free. Her eyelids pressed closed, and a warm trail trickled down her cheek.

"Do not be troubled, my love. You will see your friends again, if it pleases you." Actaeon's smooth voice lulled in her ear, betraying his daring proximity. He wrapped his hand gently around hers and drew it towards him before flashing her a devilish grin. Heat blossomed from his touch, warming her with his steady presence. Mara summoned a weak smile to meet his.

"My family," she corrected, feeling the rounded handle of the mirror pressed against her leg. She clutched it over the folds of her skirt and a small shudder coursed through her as she remembered the haunting visions it had bestowed upon her. "I only wish them to be free. "

The carriage arrived at the castle a few hours later. Even with the king's finest coach, the journey was rough. Mara's stiff bones couldn't deny the kindness Actaeon had bestowed upon her by allowing another night at home at the expense of punishing his own body with an additional two such rides. He did not seem bothered, however, as she peeked shyly at him from behind her heavy bangs. He lazed on the bench, immersed in a small book filled with yellowing dog-eared pages.

"I would have brought one for you, but I wasn't sure of your preference," Actaeon grinned as he looked up from the book, catching her stare.

Mara flushed furiously. "It isn't necessary, Majesty," she said, fumbling nervously over her words.

"Actaeon," the king corrected, setting his book on the seat. "Unless you have a different title you'd prefer," he said roguishly.

Mara's cheeks flamed as her spark of embarrassment blossomed into a blazing fire. "No your Ma—*Actaeon*." She focused her gaze on the book, staring intently at its cramped title instead of the king's teasing grin. "I have my own, my king."

Actaeon's delighted smile widened. "Then you shall have to share with me, my queen."

Mara nodded, then turned out the window to escape Actaeon's intense gaze. The kingdom passed in a slow haze, the trees and farms dusted with the final traces of winters' kiss. The castle loomed before them, growing steadily as they approached.

Despite her dread, Mara couldn't help her curiosity as she studied her new home. It was beautiful, with towering spires and elaborate carvings etched into the whitewashed stone. Bright green vines wrapped around the walls, defiantly emerging from the frosted ground to climb skyward. Though the glinting sun seemed to soften the marked stone, Mara imagined the castle was quite formidable in winter's harsh light.

A shout cut into Mara's thoughts, pulling her from her reverie as they reached the castle gates with a welcome of fanfare. A large crowd surrounded the carriage to peek at the king's new bride. Dusty children chased each other in circles, ignored by their mothers, who threw fistfuls of wildflowers while their husbands sang the traditional marriage song. They beamed at Mara as the carriage rumbled past, waving and yelling blessings.

"The kingdom is eager to meet their new Queen. Already rumors have begun proclaiming the depths of your beauty." Actaeon smiled, interrupting Mara's distressed silence. "Although, I doubt they could ever properly describe the enchantment of your eyes."

The carriage reached the castle doors and lurched to a sudden stop, sending Mara toppling. She nearly slid from her chair when Actaeon's arms tightened around her waist, drawing her back to the seat and into his embrace. Mara twisted to thank him at the same time the king leaned forward, leaving mere inches between them. The king's grip around her tightened as his gaze lingered, turning the chaste act intimate. Her stomach flipped against the reins of her corset as his voice lowered to a rumbling whisper.

"It seems you have already had quite the impact on Mahlaydia. I can't wait to see what other excitement you bring."

After Mara was shown around the castle, she was taken to her quarters. Though she marveled at the ornate tapestries and luxurious bedding, her favorite part was the adjacent parlor that served as her own personal workspace.

"You are welcome to use any part of the castle you would like to study," Actaeon had whispered in her ear, "but sometimes, it is nice to have your own private area." Mara still remembered the way his honeyed eyes lit up as she gave him her breathless thank you.

Actaeon had remained only a few moments longer to make sure she had gotten settled, then excused himself with a promise to meet her at dinner. Mara looked around her quarters, then sagged into the bed, appreciating the soft folds of fabric that enveloped against her. She nestled into the pillows, feeling like she was on a cloud. A soft thrum rustled her hip and Mara sat up to retrieve her mirror from where she had hidden it in her dress. The glass shimmered and rippled as Mara ran her finger across its surface, marring her reflection.

"We've made it mirror, our new home."

She drew the mirror closer to peer into its' surface when a soft footstep sounded at the door, interrupting her privacy. Mara whirled around, her eyes narrowed in a formidable glare as she hid the mirror's contorting surface behind her. The kingdom may have known she had magic, but they needn't be privy to all her secrets.

The servant stuttered to a stop, quailing under Mara's frown. "Begging your pardon, your ladyship, I was sent to see if you had anything you needed tendin' to." She fumbled nervously with her dirtied apron, awkwardly avoiding Mara's gaze. "I can come back if it pleases your ladyship."

Mara held her stare a moment longer, then relaxed with a heavy sigh. The girl before her was no older than she. With her pretty red hair and wide, fawn eyes, some magic and a long bath might have made her the one acclimating to the Queen's Quarters.

"No, it's alright. You just startled me." Mara offered a small smile, then glanced around her quarters thoughtfully. "Perhaps you can return on the hour?"

The girl's head bobbed eagerly. "Of course, Miss. But if you think of anythin' in the meantime, please just let me know." She pointed to a bell resting on the doorway and pulled it. Although no sound came out, there was a string attached that jumped as the vibrations travelled through it. "Anytime you need, that rings the servants' quarters. There are lots of maids happy to tend to your ladyship, but—" she paused, her eyes wide as if she'd just realized she might have said too much. She stood before Mara like a frightened deer in an unfamiliar clearing.

"But?" Mara prompted gently, trying not to vex the poor girl further.

"But," she hesitated, dropping her eyes to focus intently on her hands as they strangled her apron. "My name is Alayna." She glanced shyly up at Mara, who nodded.

"Thank you, Alayna," Mara said, earning a delighted grin. "I'll be sure to use it should I require your assistance."

"Yes your ladyship, thank you, miss." Alayna bobbed her head again and quickly backed toward the door, babbling breathlessly as she retreated. Although not nearly as petrified as she had been before, the girl continued to trip over her feet as she puttered backward. Mara watched her go, then was struck with a final thought.

"Alayna,"

"Yes, miss?" Alayna froze. Her posture became so stiff under attention that Mara wondered if perhaps the poor girl was part fawn.

"Do you know why I was fated to be Queen?"

Alayna paled, revealing a sprinkling of freckles that had been buried under her sun-kissed skin. Her hands reclaimed the edges of her apron to absently twist the corners into knots.

"I—I know the king has been lonely for some time your ladyship," she stammered nervously. "And anyone can see that you are beautiful,"

"There are pretty girls all around Mahlaydia," Mara clipped, interrupting Alayna's nervous fidgeting. "Do you know *why* the king came for me?" Alayna gulped and twisted her apron again. Mara was certain its' shape would never return.

"The servants, well, we hear more than most," the girl admitted. "People don't think to mind their tongues when we're around—our job is to be invisible, and they forget about us."

Her eyes darted nervously around the room as if searching for any other forgotten servants who might incriminate her. She gulped, then lowered her voice to continue in a shaky whisper.

"I've heard different reasons for your Majesty's betrothal. Some say the king is looking to expand his kingdom and that he wanted a foreign bride, or a wife who would add to his military strength. Others swear he was looking for an enchantress to add to his power. And still more believe he simply wants a mother for the princess." Alayna paused and her forehead wrinkled as she considered Mara for the first time. "Knowing the king, I think it is the latter," she said, then dropped her eyes as she whispered, "knowing the princess, I think there is also reason more."

Mara's brow furrowed. "More?"

Alayna flushed and dipped her head. After another sharp twist of her hopelessly stretched apron, she met Mara's gaze.

"The king is a good man. And his wife, the Queen Eifha, God rest her soul." She cast another furtive glance over her shoulder before stepping closer to Mara, her voice lowered to a sharp whisper. "But the Princess Eirwen? She's mean as the bitter wind in the winter. *That's* why *we* call her Snow."

The crease in Mara's brow deepened. She inched toward Alayna until she stood close enough to see a small soot smudge on the girl's chin.

"What do you mean?"

Alayna opened her mouth to speak, but before she could explain, there was a heavy thud on the door as Actaeon strolled in, with the princess at his side. She was lovely, with fair skin that accentuated her striking midnight hair and sapphire eyes. Dark curls tumbled around her shoulders, framing her perfect heart shaped face and matching rosebud lips. Her features fit seamlessly, creating an angelic face that would inspire any sculptor, but her stone gaze was colder than even the finest marble.

"Apologies for the intrusion, my lady," Actaeon drew the Princess forward to stand in front of Mara. "But I managed to steal the princess from her gardens and thought the castles' two ladies should be formally introduced." He tapped the princess' shoulder and she stepped forward, her lovely face drawn into a visible pout.

Beside Mara, Alayna's fidgets returned with renewed vigor. She let out a nervous squeak and dipped into a frantic curtsey.

"Begging your pardon, Majesties. If your ladyship is settled, miss, I'll take my leave." She dared a look from Mara to warily eye the princess.

Mara glanced from the servant to the princess. "Yes, Alayna. That will be all." She dismissed the distressed handmaiden with a wave. She looked at Eirwen, who waited patiently with searching blue eyes. "Thank you."

Alayna dipped into a fumbling curtsey, then rushed to the door, skirting the princess and the king on her way out. The door shut firmly behind her and Mara returned her attention to the king and the princess' blank stare, feeling strangely out of place.

"Lady Mara, I would like you to meet my daughter, Princess Eirwen." He beamed, then looked lovingly at Snow. His boxy hand rested on top of her ebony curls as he knelt beside her. "Snow, this is Lady Mara. She is going to be your new stepmother."

Snow nodded at her father, then returned her leaden gaze to Mara. Mara stood uncertainly for a moment, but when it was clear that Snow was not going to speak, Mara stepped forward and bent to meet the princess at face level.

"I'm happy to meet you Princess Eirwen." She conjured her warmest smile and offered her hand to the stoic girl. "I hope we can be very good friends."

The princess curtsied and slipped her frozen palm into Mara's hand, sending an icy shiver through her arm.

"My friends live in the garden."

Mara let out a nervous laugh, then glanced at Actaeon, who chuckled and drew the princess to him with an endearing sigh. "Snow is terribly shy and often prefers to speak to the birds," he said with a shrug. Mara nodded in understanding.

"I have a friend back home who is the same way," she told Snow.

"Ah yes, Lady Sadira," Actaeon chimed, impressing Mara with his attention to detail. "If I remember correctly."

"Indeed your highness," Mara offered a surprised smile. "You remembered."

"It is important for a husband to remember his lady's family," Actaeon said, quoting her earlier words. He clapped a hand on Snow and Mara's shoulder, forming a link between the three bodies. "Just as it is for her to remember his."

He held a moment, then released his grip and patted Snow on the head. "Thank you for coming to meet my bride, dear. You can go play in the gardens a bit longer." He kissed Snow on the forehead, then bounded from the room without a single glance back. Actaeon watched her adoringly, then turned to Mara.

"And thank you, Lady. Snow has always had her own... *unique* way of communicating. She will warm to you in time," he promised. He clasped his hands over Mara's arms, sending a rush of heat through her chilled bones. His eyes fell on hers, unravelling her with the intensity of their gaze. "How could she not?"

After a few days Mara found herself becoming accustomed to life in the castle. The largest difference was the servants surrounding her

everywhere she went. From the time she woke to when she slipped back under the covers for bed, a constant stream of people were always rushing about tending to her needs. Mara engaged in polite conversation with each of them, which soon proved tiring as she never seemed to see the same servant more than once. She supposed it had to do with the vastness of the castle, but still, Mara had never imagined the king's employ would be so great. It had little impact on Mara, save that every time she was tended to, she found herself going through the motions of yet another introduction.

It only took a week or so for Mara to stop engaging. She was never impolite, but there were far too many servants for her to keep track of, and she found that even when she did introduce herself, it only unsettled the staff more than anything. Most of them rushed to and from the rooms single-mindedly, intent on being as silent and efficient as possible.

Mara thought of this upon retiring to her room from dinner one evening. Her room, normally warmed by the large fireplace in her chambers, had been kissed by winter's chill, leaving her trembling under her blankets. Braving the cold, she summoned the staff to tend the fire and waited, shivering in her bed.

It only took a few moments for the servant to arrive. She rushed in silently, then prodded the fire to life, only pausing long enough to ensure the flames settled completely over the logs. She turned to leave and Mara thanked her, causing the girl to stumble and stare at Mara in surprise. The gawky movement reminded Mara of Alayna, the servant she had met on the first day. A pang of guilt rushed through her as she realized she hadn't thought of the poor girl once since she left. Her shame went unnoticed by the servant, who quickly caught her footing and surged toward the door.

"Wait," Mara called, and the girl flinched before turning to address her.

"Yes, your ladyship?"

"There is another servant, her name is Alayna," Mara said, hoping the girl knew her. "I need to speak with her. Please send her to my quarters as soon as you see her."

A sad look crossed the girl's features. "Apologies, lady but I won't be able to help you."

"Why?" Mara's head angled unregally. Although she was quite familiar with the word no, she hadn't heard it once since arriving at the castle.

The servant's jaw clenched, but she held Mara's gaze as she answered solemnly. "Alayna is dead, miss. She passed a few nights back. The sickness took her."

"Sickness?" Mara worried, wondering if a contagion was afflicting the castle.

The girl nodded once. "It's nothing to concern yourself with, Miss. It has been tended to."

Mara frowned at the girl's cold demeanor. "Has Alayna's family been notified?"

"Yes, Your Majesty. We've dealt with this before, and likely we'll deal with it again. Working folk are no strangers to sickness."

Mara's lips pressed together as she nodded. She imagined the serving staff would be familiar with illness and ailments after everything they tended to, but still, it pained her to think about it. She thought of Alayna and how young she was.

"Thank you," Mara said, although the girl's cool stare made her wonder exactly what she was thanking her for. "You may go."

Mara waited for the door to close, then leaned back in her bed, resolved to help the servants the same way they had helped her. As she thought, an idea struck. She reached for the mirror resting on her bedtable and gently stroked its glass. The mirror shuddered then churned, coming to life as it received her question.

Mara held the mirror, her eyes closed as she thought of her magic, the prophecy the mirror had told, and Mistress Geneva's words—*you were made for more than chasing mirrors*.

Mistress Geneva told her that the chosen Queen would be picked for a reason. But perhaps the reasoning wasn't that of kings. Maybe it was more. She repeated her question to the mirror, begging the reason she had been taken from everything she knew. As she poured her heart into the mirror, its surface continued to shift and turn until the ripples formed a steady thrum in her hand and the mirror's cool voice slowly whispered through her thoughts.

"Fated gifts and turning seasons, see you brought here for one reason,
Though dark are thoughts and dark is true, its only cure resides in you."

Mara dropped the mirror, disturbing the quiet room with the clatter of its metal against the table. She sat in bed, head spinning as she considered its words. Her gaze fell on the fire and she watched its jumping flames until sleep overtook the ricochet of thoughts filling her mind.

Within a month of Mara's arrival, the castle was ready for the wedding. Following the royal engagement, the servants scurried to scrub, shine, and decorate every inch of the open courtyard. Though the ceremony was to be held in the king's chapel, the reception, which would host all the of the lords and ladies of Mahlaydia and its neighboring kingdom would be in the courtyard itself. Each day brought a new surprise for Mara as she walked through the courts to see servants from every part of the castle rushing about in preparation. The cooks and scullery maids were constantly shouting about the placement of banquet tables and the arrangement of sweets and savories. The seamstresses and tailors, when not holding Mara captive under a cage of fabric and sewing pins, rushed around matching fabrics and stitches for the draperies that hung from the walls and ceilings. Most impressive were the gardeners. They worked tirelessly to transform the stoned courtyard into a lush garden filled with delicate trees, overflowing flower arrangements, and decorating them all with dazzling lights.

By the end of the week the whole castle had been transformed, and on the day of the wedding, it was Mara's turn. She clutched her mirror as she stood before the tailor's full-framed behemoth, staring at her reflection. A flurry of excitement surrounded her as handmaidens danced around, oiling her skin and teasing her hair while her seamstress team hemmed, stitched, and gilded the finishing touches on her gown.

Mara stood stiff as a statue while the servants continued, terrified they'd hear the erratic beating of her heart. But for all her worry, her attendants merely continued their primping, lost in gossip and giggles. She was nearly ready to feign a fainting spell to clear the room when the lead seamstress cleared her throat and ordered the others away.

"You're finished, lady," the portly woman announced. "You make a lovely bride." She bowed low before collecting her fabrics to leave. Mara watched her go, then gazed at her reflection in the oversized mirror before her.

The seamstress was right, she was lovely. The hours of attention she had been given guaranteed that. Her onyx hair fell in soft curls around her shoulders and draped to her waist, accented with sparkling threads of gold woven into her braids. The effect was lovely, complementing the delicate circlet crown they had placed over her hair. It was a simple band encrusted with a finely laid pattern of rubies and pearls to create a looping, flowered design that matched the intricate pattern stitched in her crimson skirts. The fine fabric draped her hips, billowing like a bell before cinching at the top under a wide golden band that wrapped around Mara's slender waist, making it look tiny. She twisted to see the ornate ruching in the back and the sunlight glinted off the threading, making her sparkle with every turn.

Mara clutched her mirror to her chest, its silver tones a stark contrast to blood-red hue of her wedding gown. Slowly she raised it before her, her dark eyes blinking against the solid glass before she took in a small breath and whispered.

"Fair is fair as fair can be, but tell me mirror, what do you see?"

A soft thrum swept through the mirror as its surface rippled and glided to form a vision. A picture emerged from the stilled waves to show Mara standing over a large glass case with the kingdom waiting behind her. Mara peered closer to see what was inside the case, but the surface was foggy and dim. Underneath the haze a dark figure rested, and Mara crept closer, hoping that she could just see—

A sharp knock at the door jerked Mara from the depths of the mirror. She gasped and lowered the frame and turned to address the intruder. The captain of the guard stood before her, his head dipped low in respect.

"It's time, Your Majesty," the guard said. "The kingdom awaits."

Mara nodded and gave a final squeeze to her mirror before setting it on her dressing table. She accepted the captain's arm, allowing him to guide her to the chapel while she tried to calm her nerves. Through the heavy frame, Mara heard the soft chime of the harpsichord tinkling over excited murmurs. She took a deep breath, and the sweet smell of her blood-red bouquet filled her senses. The guard rapped his pike, announcing her presence, and the crowd hushed on the other side of the chapel panels.

Slowly, the doors creaked open, revealing the chapel had been no less gloriously decorated then the courtyards. Bouquets of roses spilled out the edges of each pew lit by dainty candelabras that trailed down the aisle. Crimson draperies ran the length of the windows, laced with golden threading that sparkled beautifully in the dim candlelight.

Awed murmurs swept the room as every attendant turned and rose to face Mara. Her heart beat unsteadily against her chest, but as the harpsichord began at the front of the chapel, Mara's gaze fell on Actaeon. He stood before her at the end of the aisle, looking every inch a regal king from the intricate golden gilding woven into his black leather riding boots to the beautiful crimson cape that draped handsomely over his perfectly fitted ivory tunic, ending with the thinly banded crown with inlaid pearls and rubies to match.

Beside him, Snow completed the picture. Swathed in a dove-white dress, she looked almost angelic, with her raven hair pinned in pearls to cascade down her shoulders. Only the rubies stitched into her garments marred the illusion. Although they were lovely, the dotted jewels stood almost too-bright against the satin, spotting the perfect sheath with crimson. She stood beside her father, her hands clasped together tightly as she looked over the audience, her sapphire eyes shining against the dim lights.

Despite the excited whispers and sighs buzzing around the chapel, Actaeon's gaze was only for Mara. His carefully neutral expression slipped into a surprised 'o' before stretching into a broad grin. His countenance urged Mara forward, and soon she found herself sailing down the aisle toward the beckoning king.

The harpsichord softened as Mara approached, and Actaeon knelt and planted a kiss on the top of his daughter's head. He motioned for the nursemaid to take her to her seat and the distressed nursemaid paled before whispering to the princess with a small swallow. Snow's eyes flashed as she looked from the king to Mara, but she stepped from the platform to the pew. Dark shadows danced over her as she moved under the dim candlelight, and a cold sneer flitted over her ruby lips before they split into a cherubic smile.

Mara blinked as Snow disappeared behind the rows of standing dignitaries, then glanced around, aware of kingdom's eyes on her. By the time she looked back, Snow was seated and she had reached the king.

The pews groaned under the weight of the kingdom as the harpsichord quieted and the priest began the traditional wedding salutations. Mara focused on the priest, grateful to have the eyes of the audience on her back. Butterflies swarmed her stomach as she stood, trying to focus on the matrimonial incantation.

Unable to settle her nerves, she chanced a glance at Actaeon to see the king boldly staring at her. His body angled toward hers, revealing the dense muscles under the soft fabric of his clothes. Even relaxed, the king stood like a hunter, his shoulders taut and attention unwavering. He looked at her from under the soft waves of his charcoal hair, the gold in his eyes burning brightly into Mara's face, and warming her with a pleasant glow. Actaeon smiled and slid his hand down her arm to link his grip with hers.

A thrill ran through Mara's chest at the same time a soft murmur rippled through the crowd at the king's bold move. Even the priest looked down at their linked hands and gave a disapproving sniff before continuing his next stanza. Actaeon only tightened his grip, pulsing his hand against Mara's like a steady heartbeat. A silly grin spread across Mara's face, and she shyly dipped her head to conceal it. She listened intently to the priests' tinny voice, hoping the ceremonial adjurations would calm her chaotic nerves.

"It seems you have enchanted the entire kingdom, Lady Mara,"

Actaeon whispered, tickling her ear with his cool breath. He leaned closer, interlacing the sweet bouquet of her roses with his bold peppermint musk, clouding them in a heady scent that Mara could have remained lost in for hours. Her breath hitched as Actaeon's nose brushed against her skin, separated only by the delicate lace beading of her veil as he continued. "But none more so than I. You are stunning, lady."

He drew back, and Mara turned, ignoring the hurried titters flooding through the pews to face the king. He looked at her with such intensity that Mara felt she might be forever trapped in his gaze. She returned his stare and for the first time since she arrived at the castle, the mirror's words melted into the background leaving only Actaeon. She smiled, unabashed, and to the horrified delight of the court's lords and ladies and the absolute shock of the priest, raised her hand to rest lightly on Actaeon's cheek.

"I may be the enchantress," Mara said, "but you are a thief. You have stolen my wits and my heart, my king," She caressed his angled cheekbone with a soft brush of her thumb. "And I had no intentions of giving you either."

A soft rumble escape Actaeon's chest as his eyes lit in silent laughter. "Then a thief I am and a thief I shall stay," he said. "For I have no intentions of returning them, My Queen."

Although the mirror's premonition had led Mara to believe her wedding would be the end of her happiness, for Mara, it seemed just the beginning. Actaeon was kind and thoughtful and as doting a husband as he was a father to young Princess Eirwen. And even though her blossoming relationship with the king had thorns of its own, Mara soon found herself abandoning the mirror's caution to revel in its fragile beauty.

At Actaeon's request and to her delight, Mara's days were spent continuing her schoolwork. Though she had been deprived of her teacher, Mara had learned enough from Mistress Geneva to pursue her studies on her own. She practiced enchantments and potions, and even took to tending the servants' illnesses and ailments, which plagued the staff with alarming frequency.

Princess Eirwen would sometimes accompany her on these trips, though her unsettling bedside manner always seemed to unnerve Mara's patients more than anything. While normally the castle's attendants were happy to share a kind word, Snow's presence chilled a room faster than a winter storm.

Still, Mara allowed her to attend, even if only to please her husband. He delighted that Snow had taken so keenly to Mara, and was pleased at the chance to share Mara's gifts with his daughter. Most days, however, Mara was left alone. Despite her best attempts to connect, Snow preferred to keep to herself and spent hours disappearing into the castle gardens only to appear hours later, her sapphire eyes sparkling with mischief.

Mara's nights were spent with Actaeon. They were shy and awkward at first, but the king revealed himself to be sure and strong and gentle of mind and spirit, and soon Mara's admiration for him grew deeply into love.

Not long after, love begot love and Mara found herself with child. Actaeon ran through the castle hallways, startling the servants with his delighted cheers declaring his love for her would never end

His promise held, though her pregnancy didn't.

Before her belly could even begin to swell, the baby inside shrivelled and died. Only Mara's heartbroken cries were worse than her pain. Actaeon cradled her to his chest and rocked her through the night, until the darkness had passed and the baby was gone.

Time moved on and the ache in Mara's heart slowly subsided as she found happiness again in her work and her husband. Long summers fizzled into flourishing autumns and with the following queensharvest, came another heir. But before the final solstice, winter's chill stole him away along with the warmth in Mara's heart.

Mara yearned to speak to the mirror, but worry prevented her from seeking the solace of her childhood friend. Though its shimmering glass beckoned, Mara feared silent threats of the hidden images beneath and so, continued to suffer in solitude.

The kingdom mourned, all the while cursing the bitter winter cold that had settled across Mahlaydia, wrapping its lush lands in death. Only Snow flourished in the ice. As she aged, she grew more withdrawn, continuing her disappearances into her garden sanctuary to hide among the surviving thorns. Each time she emerged more beautiful, her black hair in tumbled tangles around her shoulders and her cheeks flushed with the bitter air's kiss, thriving in the world's misery.

Actaeon remained the same. His kindness and patience were Mara's rock, the only mooring she had from the bouts of impossible depression that threatened to drown her. Still, his steadfast presence and calm understanding weathered Mara's storms, and by the following Spring, had cut through the ice walls she'd shrouded herself in and dared her to hope.

Another year passed, and the following Spring, Actaeon filled Mara with enough love that she came with child. Tempered by her other losses, Mara held the child close to her heart and spoke not a word of her condition until she felt the child's first fluttered kicks inside her womb. Even then she guarded the secret, and only shared the news after the tiny brushstrokes inside her belly turned to full jarring kicks. Convinced by the strength of the child, Mara tearfully broke the news to Actaeon, and word quickly spread throughout the castle.

The servants tended to Mara diligently, providing her with everything she needed. Even Snow showed more interest in the child, and presented Mara with a different arrangement of wildflowers from her garden each morning. Every day she brought them, she sat and watched with interest while Mara inhaled the bouquet and sat with her for a few minutes before running out to play. It was only after Snow left that Mara would have the servants take the bouquet to the kitchens. Though she couldn't bear to tell Snow, each gift she brought contained a pungent odor that unsettled her stomach and riled the babe inside.

It was only a few weeks after Mara's announcement that the baby stopped kicking. Mara woke with cold dread that sank deeper into her bones the longer she couldn't feel the movement of her child. By late afternoon, Mara was overtaken with a violent illness that began with rolling waves of nausea and ended in bloodied sheets and fresh heartbreak.

After the loss of her third child, Mara fell into a deep depression that could not be overcome. Food and drink spoiled in her chambers as what the servants brought remained untouched. Mara was inconsolable, only stopping her shuddering wailing to gnash her teeth at the unfortunate servants that Actaeon tirelessly sent to tend her.

Handmaidens who she once befriended trembled as they traversed her chambers, scurrying quickly to and fro, changing sheets, supper plates, and daring to draw the curtains before Mara would launch into a rage, cursing them from her presence with a string of threatened hexes.

Her only console was her mirror. Day after day she would gaze longingly into it as it replayed visions of her holding her unborn children in her arms and showering them with all the love she had been denied.

At this same time a vicious drought swept through the kingdom of Mahlaydia, decimating crops and livestock alike. Fertile lands were reduced to nothing more than dehydrated ash as the sun beat the dry land with no reprieve. Once abundant storehouses were ravaged by theft and infestation leaving the people of Mahlaydia starving and looking for something to blame.

Whispers soon swept through the halls of the castle, born on the wings of hurt and fear, bearing speculation of the Queen's fault in their misfortune. Superstition and suspicion married, bringing a legion of heirs in rumors circulating hushed accusations about the Queen's rise to the throne, her inability to bear an heir, and most prominently, her strange dependency upon the delicate silver hand mirror.

What Mara had been so keen to conceal before became common gossip for scullery maids and tavern boys alike and soon all wondered what exactly it was the barren Queen kept whispering to the deviled mirror and what would happen in her next fits of rage.

Mara heard all of it and none of it at all as the mirror warned her of the kingdom's fickle hearts. But misery was her master, and nothing could pull her from the dark shadow that she wrapped her heart inside.

The king was beside himself. He had lost his children, his wife, and soon, his Queen. He threw himself into the hunt, spending hours in the forest tracking game to give to feed his people. Daily expeditions turned into overnight prowls, which soon stretched into week-long excursions, leaving Mara alone with her thoughts.

One morning, after a particularly long trip, Actaeon returned and burst into Mara's room. The sudden shot of light burned Mara's eyes and she covered her face with her hands, momentarily disoriented by the king's flurry of movement as he set upon her room. She turned her face, hiding the sallow complexion that had claimed her skin, and clutched her mirror while she waited to be left in merciful silence. Actaeon, however, strode to the edge of her bed and sat, gripping her hands in his.

"My lady, it pains me to see you this way," he said, fixing her with his amber stare. "The plight that has befallen us is heartbreaking enough without having to see my beloved wither in despair."

"Despair has no hold on me," Mara spoke softly, her voice rough with disuse. Sharp tears threatened the corners of her eyes as she spoke the words that she whispered to the mirror in an endless refrain. "Death already holds claim to everything I love."

Actaeon sagged, but sat resolutely beside his bride. He held her hand, and Mara couldn't help but notice the steady rhythm of his heartbeat pulsing through her. They sat in cold silence for a moment before the king slowly moved to kneel before her, forcing Mara to meet his devoted gaze.

"I have brought you something," Actaeon said, a hopeful smile curling the edges of his lips.

"The reach of my barrenness is infectious, my king. There is nothing in this world you can give me that will survive my touch."

Sadness ringed Actaeon's eyes, but he straightened his back, drawing Mara to sit beside him. He swept her bangs from her face to peer into her eyes. His amber gaze tugged weak threads of hope in her soul, but Mara scowled and turned away before he could break her resolve.

Actaeon sighed and brushed a kiss on her forehead. "Do not dismiss your gifts so quickly, my love. Though you may not see it through the dark, your light shines on those around you."

He crossed the room and quietly unlatched the door. Mara listened to his heavy footsteps as they passed through the door and waited, listening for the lock's click to assure she was alone, but it never came.

Instead, soft footsteps scuffed against stone until they reached the edge of her bed. Mara refused to look, hoping the unfortunate servant who had been set to tend her would retire to their next assignment, but the body just waited. Mara was about to demand their leave when the foot of her bed dipped with a soft squeak.

Incensed by the servant's boldness, Mara whirled to face them, prepared to unleash her fury. She twisted around and her glower melted into surprised shock when she saw the attendant waiting.

"Khaitlyn?"

A pretty girl stood before her with pale cream skin and soft brown curls. She was slight, and held herself with timid poise. Though the girl had clearly aged from the nervous student at Mistress Geneva's academy, there was no mistaking her striking eyes that watched with quiet curiosity, taking the toll of time.

The girl nodded and smiled, then crossed the room to wrap Mara in a hug. Mara stiffened under the sudden touch, then slowly sank into the embrace, enjoying the hint of pine that the girl carried with her from the forest and her old home. A small tear ran down her cheek as the facets of her life before the castle rushed over her, reminding her of the girl she lost.

They remained that way for a few moments, with Khaitlyn's steady presence allowing Mara to mourn. After her tears ebbed, they sat together and the young girl shared with Mara all that had happened between the other girls.

Although Khaitlyn still did not talk, the girl's talents had indeed grown and she could project her words directly to Mara. The sensation was strange as the words buzzed along Mara's brain like a nervous bee, but soon she accustomed to the feeling and the girls became engrossed in conversation. Khaitlyn told Mara everything—

the comings and goings of Mara's old friends, and the arrival of new students. Most surprising was to hear that Dorreen never left the Academy, and instead had become an assistant to Mistress Geneva, and was teaching the youngest girls. Khaitlyn herself had nearly finished her studies, and when Actaeon came requesting that one of Mara's family came to stay at the castle, she had jumped at the opportunity. Phillida has also volunteered to come, but Mistress Geneva had chosen Khaitlyn, and asked her to remind Mara that she not spend all her time chasing mirrors.

Mara smiled at that, and as she heard about the lives of her family, an invisible weight that she hadn't realized was lifted from her chest. Their conversation continued for hours, and for the first time in what seemed like years, Mara laughed with her friend.

With Khaitlyn's steady presence, the darkness shrouding Mara slowly lifted. The young enchantress took quickly to the castle and her easy manner found her suited to tending Mara as well as befriending the other servants. Soon, she began tending the ails of the castle staff, taking up where Mara's grieving forced her leave, but still she remained a constant comfort to the queen.

The only time Mara ever saw Khaitlyn unsettled was the day Princess Eirwen arrived for an unexpected visit. Although the princess never once glanced in Khaitlyn's direction, the young girl watched with apprehension as she joined Mara for her mid-afternoon tea. She stood against the wall wringing her knuckles, shrewdly eyeing Snow while she nibbled her tiny sandwiches. The visit was brief, and soon Snow excused herself to her gardens, leaving Khaitlyn to shut the door firmly behind her. Mara intended to ask about her irregular behavior, but before she could, the handmaiden was summoned to assist with the birthing of one of the castle scullery maids spiraling Mara into another bout of depression.

For the most part, Khaitlyn's presence was a great boon to Mara, and her calm and constant demeanor everyday pulled another layer of sadness from the weight of Mara's chest. Soon, Mara's appetite returned, followed by her desire to move about, then her interest in reading, followed slowly by her return to her studies. Still, she shied away from Actaeon, although it was no fault of the king's, only her shame at having been so enthralled in despair.

Khaitlyn stayed by Mara's side, silently encouraging the queen to continue her healing. Mara was grateful to have a friend, and she was truly impressed at the level of skill the young girl had attained in her own studies. Not only was she accomplished in projections, she too had acquired a talent for prophecy. Mara's gifts were still far superior and well-rounded in her studies, providing the Queen with a proficient level in healing, enchantments, and potions in addition to her foretelling affinity; but the youngest of Mistress Geneva's former scholars was clearly a talented sorceress in her own right.

Working with Khaitlyn slowly began to rejuvenate Mara's confidence. Although the pain of loss continued to plague Mara's quiet hours and memories, happy thoughts began to take hold as well. Even the awful drought that had ravaged the kingdom was soon flooded out by a torrential monsoon season, which replenished the grounds to revive the following queensharvest. Healthy crops brought healthy villagers, and soon, peace was restored to the kingdom. Carried in on the arms of Mahlaydia's prosperity, another happy event soon overtook the castle.

The Princess Eirwen had come of age. Actaeon's lovely daughter was finally able to hold court of her own, and the stunning princess had no shortage of suitors hoping for her hand. On the eve of her sixteenth birthday, the king organized a debutante ball that princes from the farthest reaches of the continent tended to hold audience with Mahlaydia's Snow.

Though Eirwen was dreadfully shy, there was no denying the draw she had on the fine young suitors. By the end of the evening four princes and even a king had approached Actaeon about pursuing court, and a brazen young duke proposed to the king's daughter outright. Although no decisions had been made, the potential arrangement placed Mahlaydia in high favor, indeed.

More balls were organized and with every soiree, Mara's spirits raised. Not long after the first month of festival season, Mara found herself once again with child. She told no one, save Khaitlyn, who found her desolate in her dressing room on the eve of Snow's crowning ball, overcome with the fear of losing herself once again.

Khaitlyn protected Mara's secret fiercely. She tended the apprehensive queen's every need and helped conceal her figure until the end of the lengthy festival season when all the dignitaries returned to their homes. With them, Wallhylm, the far east's most affluent kingdom, requested Snow's presence at their summer home. Actaeon was delighted to accommodate, and after some determined goading, coaxed Snow to agree to an extended stay. Five months later, the crown prince of Wallhylm escorted Snow back to Mahlaydia to celebrate. The kingdom's new heir, Prince Asher was born.

After the birth of the young prince, Mara didn't believe her heart could contain any more joy. Asher was a gift from the heavens and the promise that she would never forget any of her other unborn children. She doted on the tiny prince, as did the rest of the castle.

Nothing, however, compared to Actaeon. He proudly showcased the infant heir to anyone and everyone in the castle until the day the court physician finally agreed the young prince was ready to greet the kingdom. The castle set abuzz in preparation for Asher's presentation, and by midmorning, the kingdom itself was in such a tizzy Mara thought the castle walls might come down under the eager pressings of the waiting onlookers.

When the time finally came, Actaeon pulled Asher from Mara's tender embrace and held him out above the balcony for all the villagers to see. Under his tiny feet, the crowd erupted into joyful shouts proclaiming the health and well-being of the young prince. Actaeon beamed as he held his son for his kingdom to see, then gently returned him to Mara and held out his hands to quiet the audience for another announcement.

"People of Mahlaydia, it is my honor and pleasure to greet you on this day. Though our kingdom has seen its share of sorrows of late, the time for mourning has finally passed. Favor shines on us and Mahlaydia's legacy has been ensured. Queen Mara has blessed us with an heir, our fine Prince Asher!"

The crowd erupted, and Actaeon allowed their glee, a broad smile plastered over his face. But after a moment, he raised his hands to quiet the people once more.

"It is cause to celebrate indeed, but our happy circumstance does not end there. Asher is not our only delight." He turned to Snow, who tremblingly stepped to the balcony as a surprised murmur rushed through the village. "Princess Eirwen has also been bestowed a great honor. Our dear Snow has been betrothed. She now belongs to Prince Endiron and the noble kingdom of Wallhylm. Their joy is our joy, and together our kingdoms will grow in strength and friendship."

The walls shook as the village released another roar. The tumultuous cry startled the young prince, who let out an angry wail. But as Snow slowly retreated from the kingdom's attention, Mara realized Asher's fury was nothing compared to that of the princess. Snow's cold mask fixed in place, but there was no mistaking the rage pulsing from her ice-blue eyes. Mara almost reached out to her, but Actaeon stepped forward and clapped his hand on the Princess' shoulder. Snow turned to her father, and her face was clear, a perfect canvas with a beautiful smile. Actaeon beamed then returned to address his kingdom, happily allowing the princess to stalk into the castle, while Mara watched with a sense of growing unease.

The following week, Mara found herself again on the balcony before the kingdom; this time swallowed in mourning. Not three days after the prince's introduction, he had been stolen away by capricious fate. Mara had woken to find her precious son too still in his crib, frozen to the touch. Though she tried to rouse the tiny prince, he would not stir and Mara was found crumpled on the floor wailing as she clutched her beloved son to her completely shattered heart.

It took hours for Khaitlyn to move the mourning Queen, who refused to release Asher's tiny body until well after her throat had gone raw with anguish. When the handmaiden gently pulled the baby's stiff figure from Mara's broken grip, the queen went limp, as if all the life had been stolen from her as well. She slumped to the floor and laid flat on the tile until exhausted, she fell asleep.

When she woke the next morning, stiff from the hard chamber floor, her eyes flitted to the now empty crib. A single tear ran down her cheek before she stood and went to her dressing rooms, covering herself in black.

The next few days, she haunted the castle like a wraith. Her ghost-like trance unsettled the staff, and she soon found that whenever she occupied a room it was vacated as quickly as possible. Nobody consulted her on Asher's funeral, instead leaving her to mourn. Only Khaitlyn stood by her side, but after a violent lashing of Mara's temper and threats of being put out, the quiet servant disappeared to help the other castle staff.

Alone in her room, Mara devised a plan. She ventured to her study and removed her tattered potions book, paging through the dusty tome until she found the desired draught. After collecting the required ingredients from her private cabinets, she crept to her chambers to warm the kindling in her fireplace.

Soon a roaring fire warmed the base of her cauldron and the bright bubbling mixture inside. Mara consulted the spellbook for methods of application as it simmered, wondering the best way to administer the fatal brew. She skimmed the page noting this particular spell needed only be ingested—no additional fuss.

Better for her.

She stirred the mix and smiled as the rolling red liquid churned around her spoon. Dorreen had always favored affixing her potions to items, but simple was better, she decided. Imagine the ridiculousness of trying to convince someone to take a bite from a poisoned apple! A bitter laugh pressed against Mara's lips as she considered the implications then gazed into the steaming cauldron, breathing the heady hint of cinnamon lacing the mixture.

Mara gave the brew one last stir, then waited patiently as the blood red mixture simmered to a soft violet. She removed it from the fireplace, then let it cool before ladling it inside a small crystal vial. Tiny tendrils of steam wafted from the top and Mara gave a soft blow to cool the poison.

She took a deep breath and raised the glass to her lips, ready to empty its contents, until a muffled cry followed by a sharp slap knocked her hand from her face.

"Khaitlyn!" Mara's eyes flashed in indignant rage as she fumbled to grip the precious poison before it spilled across her chambers. Before she could return the vial, Khaitlyn surged forward and pressed her fingers to Mara's head.

A jolt shot through Mara as sudden images projected inside her mind. They flashed through a continuous cycle in quick, sharp bursts picking up speed until they moved so fast they all blurred together, leaving the jarring paintings stamped on Mara's brain: her arrival at the castle, dinners with Actaeon, tending to the baker's sickly daughter, who shortly after passed in her sleep, the king announcing her pregnancy to the castle, her writhing on the bed during her forced bed rest, her misery after another lost baby, and always, in the back edges of the image was Snow.

Smiling.

Khaitlyn pulled away, severing the connection before passing one last frantic look at Mara and rushing from her chamber door. Mara stood, frozen as though still trapped under Khaitlyn's enchanted touch. Muddied thoughts swirled through her mind as she tried to sort the visions apart from the terrified look on her friend's face. She blinked, stalling the dizzying images long enough to urge her into action.

Mara replaced the stopper of the tiny vial. Rubbing the deep imprint it left in her palm, she tucked it deep into her skirts and stepped toward the door to follow Khaitlyn. She had almost made it from the room, when a thought struck her and she doubled back, gently lifting her mirror from its exile before tucking it safely beside the potion.

Mara tried to force away the swelling sense of unease that rushed through her as she hurried through the corridors. A terrible crashing sound ricocheted through the halls, and Mara stuttered to a stop, listening carefully to the horrific echoes followed by a muffled moan. Cold dread swept through her and she turned on her heel, following the sound. In a few moments, she reached the winding staircase that led to Asher's abandoned nursery and froze when she saw the fractured form of her friend lying in a broken huddle.

"Khaitlyn!" Mara vaulted down the stairs to help, but when she reached her fallen handmaiden—she knew it was too late. The girl's neck twisted at an unearthly angle, her limbs folded and jutting out like the branches of a tree. Mara scooped the girl across her lap and wiped the trail of blood pooling at the side of her lip. Despair fogged her eyes, but before it could overtake her, Mara forced it away and pulled out her mirror. The tiny accessory shivered under her forgotten touch, it's surface pulsating in slow waves as Mara cleared her throat, noting the flint in her stare blurred by the mirror's shivering reflection.

"This is no sickness, mirror." She turned its face toward Khaitlyn, presenting it to the horror before her. "Tell me what plagues the castle."

Mara twisted the mirror to watch as it's glassy surface writhed to form the images of its prophecy. A tiny gasp escaped Mara's lips as she peered closer, trapped in its gruesome truth.

Tendrils of black swirled around the silver gilding, revealing a darkened room. Its walled edges were bumpy and rough, made of something besides the castle's smooth stone. Mara peered closer, feeling the cool chill of the darkened room as she crept toward a shrouded figure huddled on the floor. The ground beneath her was soft, quieting Mara's steps as she pressed on into the dark. A cold puff of air floated in her face, heated from her breath.

Mara inched closer to the figure and leaned to touch its shoulder, drawing its face toward her. Mara let out a sharp scream and pulled back, thrusting herself from the vision, but it was too late. The vacant, golden eyes of her dead king had seared into her memory.

"No!" Mara jumped to her feet, scattering the wretched prophecy into the air. She looked at Khaitlyn's lifeless body and a grim line crossed her lips as she realized what she had to do.

A desolate hush washed over the kingdom as yet another funeral was arranged. This time, for their beloved king.

The servants could barely contain their despair as they trudged to shroud the castle. The few hints of color that remained after Asher's death were washed out as Mara covered the rest of the kingdom in darkness She stood over the servants, watching with her callous stare as they completed the arrangements, matching the castle's appearance to the death that so expertly ravaged it.

"It is a wonder you are still standing, Stepmother." Snow's quiet voice startled the Queen from her dark musings. She turned to look at the bright visage of the exquisite princess. "Your *resolution* has strengthened even in the face of this travesty."

The Queen nodded gravely, noting the way the princess' raven hair twisted down her back, budded with tiny jetsam blossoms.

"Grief seems to delight in our presence," Snow continued, despondently. "And I don't believe it will be leaving anytime soon."

Mara's brow furrowed as she faced the princess in a silent question. Snow forced a smile to her lips, but it wobbled and fell. Tears pooled in the corners of her eyes, dull next to their icy blue hue.

"My beloved has fallen ill." Snow's voice broke, but the Queen could only stare.

Snow sniffled, then peeked at a nearby servant arranging a heavy bolt of fabric to layer over a large curtain. The servant saw her watching and quickly finished his task, hurrying across the room to help another pair of staff with table dressings. Snow's gaze drooped and she took in a shaky breath.

"I doubt he will survive the night," the princess' words, though soft came out in a cold growl that crept up Mara's spine. Her eyes widened as Snow raised her stare to level her with a devastatingly eerie grin. "And then I will be forced to stay in Mahlaydia."

The princess wiped the corner of her eye, dramatically pulling at an invisible tear.

"Perhaps you should add some more black to the room, stepmother," she said in a malicious sneer. "Mourning suits you."

With a graceful dip of her head, the princess retreated, walking swiftly through the castle. Mara watched as her delicate form disappeared through the castle doors, then barked at the servants to continue their tasks before stalking down the corridors to her chambers.

The Queen held her head high as she swept through the castle, fixing her furious gaze on any servant brazen enough to make eye contact. They shuddered out of her way and soon she reached the sanctuary of her room. Stale air coated her nose, but she ignored it and pressed on to her study. Her dingy potions book remained on the table, untouched since the day Khaitlyn had saved her. A thin layer of dust coated the other books on her shelves, save a large green tome with the inscription *Obscurio* scrawled across its binding. Mara ran her finger along its spine, then pulled the top of its pages, activating the lever to her secret chamber.

The space was tall, only large enough to hide prized items or—surely in the case of queens past--a surreptitious lover, but Mara's treasure was much greater.

Standing against the wall, Actaeon slept, leaning against the stone as though simply waiting for her to return. His stance was relaxed and the barest tint of a smile graced his lips—only the droop of his eyes revealed his witched state.

Mara traced her fingers down the side of his face, relishing the way his dark curls tickled the back of her hand. After the mirror's vision, she had seen to it that Snow could never find him.

Khaitlyn had known that Snow was dangerous; she had seen it from the beginning. Mara remembered the skittery way the girl acted around the distant princess. She was ashamed it had taken her so long to realize. So many people had been hurt by her ignorance. The people she had been sent to protect, and the children whose lives she had been entrusted. Furious tears pooled in Mara's eyes as a storming rage trembled her body. She stepped closer to her sleeping king and cupped his chin in her hand.

"But you, she will not have." She uttered a hushed incantation while drawing invisible lines over the harsh angles of Actaeon's face, then finished the spell with a few deft strokes of his hair. Her words settled, and the Queen paused to take in her husband's handsome features one last time.

Bottling the memory, Mara pressed a gentle kiss to his sleeping form, feeling the warmth of his lips seep into the cold that latched to her.

She drew back, watching as the glyphs she drew shimmered bright then faded into his skin before his features began to shift, marring his face until the king was buried under the darkened gaze of a stranger.

The Queen nodded with satisfaction as she noted the thick dark brows that covered the man's deeply hooded eyes that spread just too-wide across his face. His nose was no better, twisted and gnarled as though it had broken and not set right over a heavily stubbled goatee. Under the heavily altered mask, there was no mistaking this man for a king.

The time for chasing mirrors is done.

Mara's face pulled into a grim line as the man stirred, completely different from the king he had been. He stretched, then faced her with a stoic look. The Queen extended her hand, revealing a long, wickedly curved blade. Its serrated edges glinted in the dim light, but the sharp spines were the least of the weapon's dangers. An invisible enchantment coated the blade, ensuring anyone that met its kiss would feel the pain of a thousand searing suns.

"Mahlaydia has been set upon by a scourge," she announced, her voice calm and crisp. "We must find this sickness and expel it. For that, I need a Huntsman."

The Huntsman fixed her with a blank look, then slowly accepted the weapon. He blinked before returning his muddy gaze, completely devoid of emotion. Mara's heart mourned the loss of her husband's perfect golden stare, but her voice remained cool and stiff.

"Take Princess Eirwen deep into the Myrkur Forest," she demanded. "When you are certain that you have travelled far enough that no-one can hear her screams, use this blade to cut out her heart."

A confused dip formed in the Huntsman's thick brows, but his heavily stubbled jaw clenched and released, freeing Mara's nerves with an obedient nod as he sheathed his blade and stalked from her room. The Queen followed him as far as the edge of her chambers, then released him to complete his task.

It took several days for the Huntsman to return. During that time, the Queen was a terror. Her temper was so fierce that by the end of the first day, the servants had abandoned her entirely, leaving her to pace anxiously across the space between her doors and windows. She remained this way until the night her door shuddered open and through it came her Huntsman, carrying a lumpy burlap sack.

"I have returned with your request, my Queen," he bent stiffly at the waist as though unused to the subservient motion. He raised the dripping sack toward her.

The Queen fixed her mask as she accepted his offering and weighed the heart in her hand. It was heavier than she imagined, but it could have been from the weight of all her stepdaughter's sins. Her lips curled in a spiteful smile as she imagined the terror on Snow's face and the pain that wracked her body as the enchanted blade pierced her chest.

Her past had been avenged, but vengeance still remained.

"You are dismissed."

She turned from the Huntsman toward her small bedtable. Beside her mirror, the tiny vial she made waited patiently for its next victim. She reached for the bottle, but a heavy cough pulled her attention. The Huntsman stood before her, his dark eyes watching judiciously.

"Go." Mara commanded, a burning wave rolling through her as she stared at the unfamiliar face. The Huntsman's eyes widened almost imperceptibly before he dipped his head in a gentle gesture.

"As you wish, my Queen," he said, and the familiar timbre of his voice caught her. She turned to face him, her heart softening as she gazed at the man she had made. She traced her hand down the side of his face, feeling the new, rough angles in his bone structure that widened his stubbled jawline. She stared into his muddy eyes, hoping one day she could bring back some of their golden hue. She released him from her hold, then snapped her steel demeanor back in place.

"There is a small hovel on the outskirts of the castle. Remain there until I next require your services."

The Huntsman's mouth twitched as though he wanted to speak,

but the Queen spun, putting her back to him until his slow heavy steps were followed by the tired squeak of her door.

Mara let out a slow breath, as she once again mourned the loss of her king. She clenched her fist, feeling the rough burlap of the Huntsman's sack scratch against her palm. A satisfied smile rose to her lips as she pressed it to her robes and stalked back to the vial. She had Snow's heart.

Now she would watch it burn.

She placed the heart on her table, then picked up the tiny bottle and unstoppered it. Thin tendrils wafted from the top before dissipating into violet wisps as the potion tried to escape its prison. Mara smiled and raised a shaking hand over the motionless heart, ready to reduce it to ashes.

"I gave everything to protect my kingdom," she whispered before lowering voice into an even further growl. "*I* am fairest of them all."

The Queen upturned the bottle and dripped the potion over the heart. Just a few drops was all it took and the tiny violet pearls sizzled and burrowed deep into the soft pink tissue before fizzling into a sharp, audible pop.

A wave of dizziness threatened to overtake Mara as her mind was overpowered by a swarm of confused thoughts. She cupped her hands around her head as she tried to focus, smothering the chaos within. A frightened gasp tumbled from her lips as her mind stilled, leaving only the image of Actaeon swallowed inside the strange, green room. With a sharp jerk of her hands, Mara bottled the vial and shoved it into her dress before dashing from her chambers, cursing herself a thousand times over.

She had failed again.

Snow was still alive, and Mara knew where she was. She remembered the dark walls in the mirror's final vision. She had seen them before.

With a silent prayer to the gods that abandoned her, Mara wrapped her cloak around her shoulders and stepped into the biting cold. She didn't have time to notice the frost surrounding the castle as she raced to Snow's garden, a cloud of dread enveloping her heart.

Mara rushed through the garden, surrounded by the sweet smell of blossoming roses until she reached the hedge maze. A chill swept through her as she stood before the manicured shrubs looming above, their tangled branches stretching to block the sun. Inside the maze's shadow, a cold breeze rustled the leaves, revealing the unsettling quiet of the gaping entrance.

Steeling herself, Mara stepped inside the winding path, searching for Snow. The course was dizzying, but Mara continued, pushing through the twisted hedge. Her post-partum body ached under the heavy strain, but the mirror's vision streamed through her mind, urging her through the pain.

The lush hedge walls began to darken and thin, transforming the vibrant green leaves into sickly gray thorns. Mara pressed on and soon, the grassy floor under her feet began to thin until it was covered in a muddy moss. Mist enveloped her, turning the cool air sour with the stench of decay. Tiny bones protruded from the maze's spiny branches, littering the base of the hedgerow and setting her nerves on edge.

Mara crept forward until she rounded the path's final curve to a large opening, where Snow stood, staring at a huddled figure at her feet. Mara let out a tiny gasp, slicing cold air down her throat as her eyes fell on the broken form of her Huntsman.

Disturbed by the sound, the princess pulled her gaze to meet her stepmother, her rosy lips curled into a thin smile. Then, as if in a prayer, she bowed her head over cupped hands. The space between her palms glowed icy blue, and with the speed of a snake, Snow thrust them forward, hurtling a sapphire beam at Mara's chest.

The searing blue light struck, encasing Mara's ribs in ice under the burning intensity of the cold. A pained scream ripped from Mara's throat as the energy pulsed through her body, blurring her vision as she crumpled to the floor.

Darkness enveloped Mara as her body contorted in insurmountable pain. A wild scream ripped free, scratching her voice raw. She sagged to the ground, heaving as she tried to collect herself, tears streaming down her face.

Slowly, the blackness ebbed and Mara's vision returned. From where her cheek pressed against the damp earth, she could see her Huntsman's blazing amber eyes gazing vacantly while his hands clutched a gaping, bloody cavern where his heart should have been. Mara blinked, trying to will the image away, but each time her eyes opened, the Huntsman was still there, staring lifelessly back at her.

A soft footstep fell beside her head, and Mara shifted toward the sound, sending a wave of fiery pain through her. She winced and looked up to see Snow watching, her porcelain face lit with malicious glee.

"Did you really think you had won so easy?" a lilting laugh escaped the princess. She knelt and gripped Mara's hair, wrenching her neck before tossing her to the ground to stalk an agitated circle. "It might have worked, you know, had you not had so much faith in *my father.*"

A wheezing gasp escaped Mara, pausing Snow's pacing. The princess let out a satisfied huff, then continued, this time fashioning her voice syrupy sweet.

"Poor Huntsman. Cursed into an existence that he didn't want. He was so *relieved* when his memories came back. And then, confused. He couldn't begin to fathom why his devoted wife had sent him to kill his own beloved daughter."

Snow paused, her demonic face twisted into distorted innocence.

"Of course he couldn't go through with it. Instead he came up with a plan—my father has never been a brilliant man, but he was clever in his own right. The deer's heart was a fantastic touch."

She glanced disdainfully at the body of the Huntsman, sending rage coursing through Mara's heart as the princess continued her haughty speech.

"He knew he needed to find a substitute because he could never actually kill his own daughter. The bonds of love, and all that." Snow leaned toward Mara, her voice lowered into a deadly growl. "Too bad I've never had the same problem."

Another wretched cry ripped through Mara, so real and powerful that it tore her vocal cords. Mara felt the damage as her light voice dropped, and her cry turned ragged and raspy, but her rage was too real to care. She unleashed all the fury within as the garden floors shifted and shook, responding to her pain.

Snow's eyes widened as the floor underneath her rocked, but narrowed in gloating victory as Mara's power seeped out, stilling the chaotic earth.

"You seem unwell, stepmother." The princess' mouth twisted into a sympathetic pout, but her icy eyes glinted with delight. She shook her head and her devious smile crept back into place as another glowing orb sparked in her palm. "You really need to *rest*."

She hurled the spell, sending the sizzling ball smashing into Mara's damaged ribs. Mara gasped in pain as the energy spread from the hit through her chest, crushing her ribs with sheer force. Her vision blurred as the darkness threatened to overtake her once more, but the shrill keening in her ears anchored her wits.

Its faint cry sounded like Asher, piercing through Mara and urging her forward.

Steeling her resolve, Mara summoned all her strength to lift herself off the floor, wincing as she clutched her crippled ribs. Her breaths came in short, shallow gasps as her body threatened to surrender, but Mara's avenging fury reignited her strength, and with a labored effort, she straightened her back to glare at the maniacal princess. Snow's gaze narrowed in thinly veiled bemusement as she watched Mara unfold herself.

"You always were hard to kill," she seethed, bearing her teeth. "Too bad so many innocents had to die just to get rid of you," her hands crackled with a flash, another blast of crackling energy hurtled through the air.

Mara dove to the ground to dodge the deadly beam, and her ribs screamed in protest as the crumbling shards of bone disintegrated further under the jarring contact. She screamed in agony, but forced herself weakly to her feet as her whole body crackled with unbridled fury.

"You have killed everything I ever loved," she said, her voice dripping cold steel.

Snow's head fell back as she laughed. It was a harsh, wicked cackle that even now clashed with her sweet features. Her eyes slitted as she closed the distance between them, her face distorted into a furious snarl.

"And still you have the one thing I desire." Snow laughed again and stepped closer, her voice filled with derision. *"Such a pretty girl.* That's all they used to tell me. *Smile, Snow. It makes you look so much lovelier. Don't scowl so, Snow. The courts want only to see your beauty. Oh, princess, you are ravishing. You will make such a beautiful bride."* Another harsh laugh escaped the princess as she stepped closer, her gaze burning into Mara while she seethed. "All I ever heard from the day I was born was how my appearance was going to benefit some prince. Even my education was wasted on embroidery and table manners and things that would make me a fitting wife. Before I could walk, my entire future was given to someone I didn't even know. But that all changed the day *my* gift appeared."

Snow stopped and tilted her head as she considered Mara, her vicious smile deepening. "You see, your *majesty,* you were not the only gifted one in our happy little family." Her rumbling chuckle whispered across the room sending a shiver down Mara's spine. "Although it took some time for me to realize it, the day I discovered my true power, I was set free."

Snow raised her hand and another crackling orb sprung from her palm. Instead of hurtling toward Mara, this one hovered in place, a brilliant purple ball of lightning.

Panic lanced through Mara. The tension shot searing pain through her battered body, nearly upending her with a rolling wave of dizziness. She tried to take a steadying breath, and realized the damage to her lungs only allowed shallow gasps of oxygen with every breath.

She wouldn't survive another attack.

Snow let out a delighted giggle at she saw the fear on Mara's face. "Quite captivating, isn't it? I must say it has developed nicely from when it first manifested. And really, I only have you to thank."

Mara's eyes widened, but she held her gaze as she slipped her hand into the folds of her dress. Snow paid her no mind as she flexed her hand, making the electric orb spark and dance menacingly while she crept closer, her voice rising with every step.

"I really thought it had all ended when my dear mother found out about my gift. I had gotten reckless, you see. To many nursemaids with— *unfortunate*— injuries. Mother realized something was wrong, and ferreted me away. She was just so determined to fix her dear, sweet daughter. I feared I might suffocate under her desperate attention. But, mother soon fell ill."

Snow's eyes flashed, turning the deepest shade of onyx before settling into their icy blue.

"Father was devastated, of course. As was I. And while he mourned, I was left alone to do as I pleased. It was glorious--running free, practicing whatever magic I wished. And my powers only grew. All I had to do was wait until I came of age, and then I could claim what was rightfully mine."

She paused, and her lips pulled back to bare her brilliant smile.

"And then he brought you home."

Snow took another menacing step forward, leaving only a hair's breadth between them. "So more people had to die."

White fury clouded Mara's vision as all the sadness, rage, and pain she had locked in her heart unleashed. She took a bold step forward and the princess' capricious smirk fell, allowing the first trace of uncertainty to dash over her face as Mara advanced, her voice a deadly coil.

"Do you know why I was fated to be Queen?" Mara asked, feeling power sing through her decimated body. She took another step forward, and the ground began to tremble under her feet, causing Snow's cheeks to pale as the maze filled with the deafening cry of splintering branches. Mara let out a gravelly, bitter laugh as she thought of her mirror and its rippling prophecy became clear.

"Because I'm the fairest of them all."

The Queen unleashed a strangled growl as she lunged at the princess, forcing all her strength into the attack as she pulled the tiny vial hidden from the folds of her skirts. She smashed it against Snow's diabolical grin, relishing the stabbing pain that shot through her hand as it shattered, releasing the bottled toxin. Though it felt as though her hand had slipped into a fire, she crushed the vial against her mouth to administer the fatal poison.

Snow gasped, then clamped her lips to block the poison, but it was too late. The Queen's toxin had already entered her system. She thrashed wildly and the vials glass splintered into her creamy skin, staining it with lovely crimson before an agonized scream bubbled from her chest, followed by the bright liquid foaming from her mouth. Crimson frothed from the princess' lips as with one final, desperate shriek, Snow hurled the crackling orb she had conjured directly at Mara's face.

The ball writhed in the air, cascading a tail of white-hot sparks like a comet. Mara flung her arm in front of her in a desperate block, and fire erupted across her skin. The spell hit her arm, swallowing it in crackling blue energy. Vibrant electricity trickled through her fingers, mixed with the blood seeping from her injured palm to fill Mara with a pain she'd never experienced. She tried to scream, but her entire body was paralyzed by undulating waves of agony. Then, as fast as it enveloped her, the crackling electricity dissipated, leaving Mara bent over the princess' lifeless body gasping in hunched, shallow breaths.

Snow lay beneath her, a singular line of blood trailing from the corner of her lips to the gentle slope of her chin. Tears trailed Mara's face as she rose, fury burning through her like a vengeful wave, and crossed the room with slow, deliberate steps to kneel beside her Huntsman. With her good arm, she brushed a dark curl from the huntsman's face, uttering a gentle whisper as she traced an invisible pattern along his cheek. By the time her fingers had drawn the last curving glyph, the Huntsman's features had shifted back into the elegant features of her king.

"Actaeon," she growled through her harsh, new voice, feeling light-headed from her labored breathing. "I will keep your kingdom, my love."

She unclasped his cloak and pressed a shuddering kiss to his chilled lips, then fell into his chest and sobbed, the ache in her heart drowning the rest of the world.

The kingdom mourned their fallen rulers, though they never found Actaeon's body.

Days later, Mara found herself once again standing behind the heavy doors of the chapel, this time swathed in black. Muffled cries and sobs could be heard through the oaken frame, but when The Queen stepped into the open chapel, not a single sound could be heard.

The entire court held their breaths as the widowed Queen trailed stiffly down the aisle, once again to greet her king. Tears filled Mara's eyes as she walked toward the iron coffin, etched with the names of her beloved husband and son. She reached the stage to meet Actaeon again, this time to bless his resting place with a single rose and the gentlest trace of a kiss.

Mara ignored the hushed whispers as she stood and approached the secondary coffin, waiting silently beside the king. She rounded the delicate bed, tracing her hand along the surface until she reached the head of the glass case. A wry smile crept to her lips as she looked through the clear surface to the maiden encased inside. The faint line of crimson had been wiped from her lips and she appeared as if she were merely sleeping, waiting to be awoken.

The Queen scratched a long, sharp nail over the girls' face, sending a delightful shiver down her spine. The princess' lips twitched and the Queen's smile deepened as she glanced at the golden seal glinting innocently in the chapel's dim light.

"Fairest," Mara breathed. She hummed a chuckle as she returned down the aisle, her mirror clutched in her shriveled hand as she abandoned Snow's enchanted coffin to reclaim her kingdom.

ABOUT J.M. SULLIVAN

Teacher by day, award-winning author by night, J.M. Sullivan is a fairy tale fanatic who loves taking classic stories and turning them on their head. When she's not buried in her laptop, you can find her watching scary movies with her husband, playing with her kids, or lost inside a good book. Although known to dabble in adulting, J.M. is a big kid at heart who still believes in true love, magic, and most of all, the power of coffee. If you would like to connect with J.M., you can find her on social media at @jmsullivanbooks—she'd love to hear from you.

CONNECT ON SOCIAL MEDIA

jmsulivanbooks.com

facebook.com/jmsullivanbooks

instagram.com/jmsullivanbooks

twitter.com/jmsullivanbooks

ALSO BY J.M. SULLIVAN

The Wanderland Chronicles

Alice

The Neverland Transmissions

Second Star

The Rise of Ersyla

A Retellings Origin Novella

Spun Gold

by Christis Christie

I was born a blight upon the beauty and grace that is the elven world; a deformed creature that had no right or place among their society. While most babes are born to them a pearl of perfection, I held the resemblance of a newly hatched bird with colourless skin not flushed with life, and the pinched features of a hobgoblin—a nose too long, ears too pointed, and dark, bottomless eyes that spoke of the depths of the world's despair rather than the light of possibility and life.

My parents cast me out into the cold winter harshness in the hopes that the frozen fingers of Frau Holle would claim me. Instead of being pulled down into the finality of the afterlife as was intended, two trolls found my wailing form.

Those of the elven nature are known for carrying magic in their blood, and to feast upon them, for many other creatures, is not only a delight, but a way of absorbing some of that magical essence into themselves. Too frail and feeble to make for good eating though, I was bundled in a scrap piece of cloth and taken back to their dwelling in the dank depths of the earth.

There, in the subtle dimness of Grolge and Klimn's cave, I was fed and nurtured alongside other stolen chattel. The goats accepted me well enough, letting the straw of their pen act as my cradle, and offering milk meant for their own young to fill my hungry maw. I filled out quickly on that sweet offering, becoming the fatty morsel worthy of roasting on the open fire and grinding between large troll teeth as had been intended. But Grolge and Klimn were stupid beings who quarrelled over the faintest slight, and couldn't decide who should get the babe that would be but a snack to creatures of their size.

It started as a discussion that soon escalated into an outright battle that nearly destroyed the cave and left me inches from being crushed beneath Klimn's foot. In the end, it was decided that I would be allowed to grow more, and until I had reached a size that was acceptable for sharing, they would make use of me and my magic. I suppose in a lot of ways, my stunted form that was shunned by my elven parents actually saved my life. By the time I was of any decent size, barely above the head of our tallest ram, my magic had proven too useful to dispose of, even considering the quick rush of pleasure feasting on it would provide them.

With the threat of ending up spitted and roasted ever-shadowing my days, I turned into a clever survivor who continued to find new means of proving my living worth. Mortals, it turned out, are nearly as stupid as the cave trolls who kept me, and even as a small child, I found it easy to distract them so that larger cattle could be stolen to feed the abyss inside my large counterparts. Shepherds and cowherds were perhaps the easiest to manipulate, their boredom leaving them open for trickery. I laid traps, caused confusing noises and other disturbances that they couldn't help but leave their posts to check on.

After that, it took nothing to spell the animals into following me into the woods and back to the cave. With me around, the trolls barely had to lift a finger anymore, each meal walking compliantly into their awaiting arms. Of course, even simple minded creatures end up longing for more than their means, and eventually Grolge and Klimn came to the conclusion that they were not aiming high enough with my trickery. No, there was a far tastier feast to be had than Farmer Bram's prized milk cows.

I was perhaps ten years of age, still stunted in height and haggard in appearance, when the spark of new hunger arose in them.

"Oi, Rumpelstilt! Stop rattlin' those posts, you worthless pophart and come here," Grolge bellowed that morning, just seconds before the thigh bone of a calf came hurtling at my unsuspecting head.

Pain lanced through my skull that had borne many such attacks over the years, and for the briefest of moments, I allowed my eyes to close upon the cave surrounding me and just breathed. But moving at my own leisure had never been the way of life, so soon I was on my feet and leaving behind the goat pen I was attempting to mend. After a battle the previous night over Klimn picking his teeth too loudly with a rib bone, the pen had been demolished, and no one but I was going to fix it.

I didn't say anything, only trudged over to the large lump of leather and scaly flesh that made up Grolge.

"Me and Klimn, we's been thinkin', we have. We're tired of cows." In his large paw there was the head of a calf he'd cracked open and was in the process of slurping at the brains while he spoke. It was enough to turn one's stomach if you weren't used to it.

"No more cows," Klimn felt it necessary to chime in.

I felt a dawning suspicion beginning to sprout within my young mind, one I didn't want to actually contemplate, and thus did not give voice to.

"So what do you wish instead?"

In the rare times that I was left to my own devices, I had taken to watching the humans. My favourite pastime was becoming one with the shadows so that I could spy on them for hours. Other than an initial chill of foreboding, the mortals always remained blissfully unaware of the eyes in the dark. It was how I learned their ways, their behaviours, and their speech. How I saw both the best and the worst of them, and came to understand that at their most primitive, they weren't that different from the trolls, and in their more evolved form, they hungered for power—or the semblance of it.

I knew how to draw them in—how to play them.

"Man."

"Or woman," Klimn grunted.

"Or woman. But no cows, and if no human..." Grolge leaned towards me, the stench of his putrid breath strong in my nose. "Then you."

The blunt tip of his large finger tapped me in the chest and sent me reeling backwards on to my bottom in the dirt. A war raged in my head, a battle between my keen wits and the desire to roll my eyes in annoyance. Ever the same threat, without any evidence it would actually take place. Though, one could never put it past their stupidity to eat their own meal ticket.

"Fine, humans." As elegantly as possible, I picked myself up off the floor and dusted the dirt from my slacks. They were the only pair I owned, and only because I had tricked a stupid peasant boy into giving them to me by convincing him that the stolen goose I held in my clutches was a layer of golden eggs.

The trade had been well worth it in my mind.

With both trolls having made up their minds on the same thing, I had little choice but to leave in that moment and set out towards the village. One can think me heartless if they want, but I felt little sorrow for the human I was bound to lead to their death. I had not been brought up to feel any softness for them, and what I had seen of their kind had not helped any to sprout.

My legs were not of any substantial length, but still I made quick timing through the woods that concealed our cave and up into the open plains of the green fields that surrounded the local village. Here, flock upon flock of sheep grazed, their full coats as yet unshaven, resembling that of fluffy, rounded clouds, meandering lazily over the hills.

I didn't have to think of who it was I would bring back—all my time human watching had left a very clear first victim in my mind, one who, as I saw it, almost deserved the fate about to end him. Blond-headed Karl was a mean spirited boy who often taunted the other shepherds, and his crook, which was meant to aid him in traversing the hills, was more often than not used to viciously jab or beat the sheep in his flock out of his own way. Not but two days before, I had witnessed him throw another herder to the ground, land a well placed kick to his side, and then make off with his lunch. So I felt absolutely no remorse as I slipped up behind him on the hill.

"That is a tasty morsel you are eating there... if you share it with me, I will tell you where I just saw Greta Schulz bathing in nothing but her petticoat not but five minutes ago."

The boy jumped in his seat, startled into a gasp by the sudden sound of my voice whispering behind his back. The sight of me, as he leaped quickly from his perch on the boulder, was the standard one gifted to me by the general populous in the rare occasions when I allowed myself to be seen. His features scrunched in an unpleasant way, similar to that of when someone inhaled a sour scent and he scowled in disgust.

"What are you creature, and why should I believe anything that you say?"

My less-than-appealing appearance had placed some hesitation within him, but I was still able to read the desire for what I had offered in the depths of his eyes. His lusty, needy character was selfish enough to look past a suspicious nature and the potential of harm to himself, for the thrilling thought of a clandestine peeping moment in the woods. He was also just stupid enough to believe that something as puny as myself would be unable to do any real injury to him in the end.

"What I am does not matter for the purpose of our agreement, however, what I can do for you does. Greta won't be in the water for long—now is your time to decide; give up the food and find the location, or sit back down and never know. *Tick tock*, the clock is ticking. Don't spend too much time thinking it over or you'll miss your chance entirely."

What I had long ago discovered about humans was that the less time you gave them to think, and the more panicked you caused them to become, the more likely they were to make very terrible decisions without weighing the cost.

Karl stuttered and stammered, shifting on his feet before me, and then thrust the bratwurst, nestled in a lush bread roll and buried beneath juicy sauerkraut, into my awaiting hands. Staring down at my prized achievement, it was necessary to fight the desire to lick my lips. Too often my food portions were made up of whatever puny scraps were left over from the ravenous trolls, bits and pieces of half chewed veal spat from their mouth during an angry comment to the other. But this...this was a prize indeed.

"Well?" Karl grunted. "I've given you what you demanded, are you going to take me or not?"

If truth would be told, I had forgotten for the time being that he was there or that I had other things I was meant to be doing, and it irritated me to have my attention pulled away from the delight in my hands. But my life was not my own and if I came back empty handed, there was always the possibility that I could become the next meal Klimn and Grolge fed upon.

"Right, of course. Follow me, young master," I declared to him and then made a formal bow. That brought his head up straighter and chased further away any doubts resting at the back of his mind.

It then took no time for me to lead the stupid, vile boy into the woods, assuring him that Greta was just around the next cluster of trees or beyond the riverbank. When at last we came to the opening of the cave, confusion dawned in his eyes before being replaced with dawning suspicion. But it was too late at this point, and my true masters, having scented human on the winds, made their way out of the cave depths and were upon him shortly. I turned from the howls and cries, leaving Klimn and Grolge to their feeding and found a pleasant spot to sit and enjoy the meal I had managed to acquire for myself.

That wasn't the last time that I was sent out into the local village to pillage a human meal for the creatures raising me, and knowing that there would be no stopping them once the taste of blood was upon their tongues, my only hope was to convince them to leave some time between each human life taken. The last thing that any of us needed was to raise enough suspicion that the village came searching the woods, pitchforks in hand.

I became incredibly skilled in convincing all different walks of life to follow me deep into the woods, learning to read the unspoken desires on the faces of each new victim, seeing the lines of imperfection that ran just below the skin like a well-drawn map leading me directly to their greatest weakness. It should have bothered me the older I became, but instead I took pleasure in each new deception, and when that became too easy, I grew bored with it and I turned it into a game.

Giving them ways to win their freedom, but knowing that the odds I had given them were stacked too high—and yet not entirely impossible.

As the years passed, I maintained my connection to the human world, venturing to the villages on my own time so that I could continue watching from my shadows. I longed to learn all that I could about the mortals, as it was a world outside my own, and seeing as how there seemed to be no real place for me in the world of magic, perhaps I could find a place amongst them.

In the end, I learned a valuable lesson in the small village of Freudenshafen, where I first saw Lina Schneider seated on a grassy knoll, braiding alpine poppies into flower crowns to place on the heads of her younger sisters. Her copper hair reflected the light of living flame in the bright sunlight of the summer day, and her pale freckled cheeks glowed with an inner warmth that spoke of happiness and laughter.

That particular field was her favourite place to spend her afternoons, and once she had finished with her household chores, Lina would slip away from her parents' home with either her siblings in tow, or on her own. There, with her skirts settled about her folded legs, she would work on sewing, paint little portraits of wildflowers with her simple set of paints, or simply bask in the warm sunlight. For days on end, I crept into the same small cluster of trees on the edge of her field, just so that I could watch her, my breath baited and my heart pitter-pattering rapidly in my chest. Whereas with anyone else, I felt no hesitation in making my presence known, with her, I warred against doubt and fear of the unknown.

It was Lina, in the end, who made contact first. On a quiet summer day, the sun already well passed the noon-day high, she looked directly into my little hiding place, blue eyes piercing through the underbrush, and seemed to peer directly at me.

"Are you ever going to come out and introduce yourself?"

Very little in life managed to surprise me by this point, but that day, nestled snugly between two small bushes with a bed of fallen leaves beneath my body, I thought myself completely hidden from view. Yet Lina had peered through my covering and seen me anyway

—perhaps seen me the whole time. A little part of myself belonged to her that day, so startled was I to be found out by anyone, least of all my fiery-headed girl.

There was hesitation in my response—what would be her reaction to the sight of me in clear daylight, the sunshine highlighting my unsightly appearance in all its gory details, the dark, bottomless eyes set deep within my face, a harsh sloping nose that pointed too sharply, and long, elfin ears that seemed too over-pronounced, rather than the delicate pieces of art they were meant to be? The teeth in my small mouth were pointed, and my hair, which was so light blond it was nearly white, would have been lovely, if not for the greyish pallor of my flesh. I was garish in comparison to her fresh, youthfulness, and yet, I slowly crept from the underbrush to crouch in a manner that would make it easy to dart off, should the situation become too unpleasant for me.

Shock did register in her eyes as she beheld me for the first time. Up until this point, I had been nothing but a set of watchful eyes in the leaves, not the horrid little creature now knelt before her. While there was a touch of revulsion, this seemed to fade as she gazed at me, a look of curiosity and interest soon replacing it.

"Come here," she requested of me, going so far as to pat a spot of grass beside her.

Carefully, I stood to my full height, that could be no more than four feet—I'd never really thought to test this out for specifics—and then slowly made my way over to her. The heart in my chest that was typically so calm and unfazed, beat rapidly against the ribcage surrounding it.

I didn't go quite as near as she had offered, but stopped once there were roughly five steps left between us and then sat opposite her so that we were able to look into each other's eyes. Hers were as crystal-clear as a fresh brook, and a lovely shade of blue that would make the heavens above weep in jealousy. Mine, in contrast, were reminiscent of the dark, shadowy green of the forest in the places where the sunlight is but a light filter through the leaves and needles.

"Who are you?" Not *what* are you.

As of that point, I had said nothing—not a sound or gasp, barely an indrawn breath—but something about the way she posed her question loosed my hesitant tongue.

"I haven't a name, but they call me Rumpelstilt," I admitted, without elaborating on 'they.'

Those clear eyes were watching me again, flitting over my face in an intelligent manner, before lowering to take in my frame, mindful of my hands with their sharp little claws, and then back up to my face.

"Rumpelstilt? Like some form of pophart?" she questioned me, and caused a pinched look of discomfort to form upon my features. "Are you a goblin then?"

"Yes, like a pophart. And no, not like a goblin, at least I do not think." There was no real explanation for what I was. Were goblins naught but castaway elves who failed to meet the standards of a perfectionist society?

"That is a cruel name." Her words—soft and honest, filled with concern for my being, were a foreign notion.

Having never known care nor worry for myself to come from another being, I simply stared at her. Who was this divine angel gazing back at me with such tenderness and a lack of fear? She claimed a little more of me then.

"It is but a name, and we are made up of more."

"Would you care for some *maultaschen*?" From inside a pocket in her apron, she pulled a cloth bundle. Setting the bundle between us, her slender fingers swiftly unknotted it to reveal small little pastry dumplings filled with something that smelled delicious.

With good, wholesome food before me, I did not hesitate to take what was offered, and soon the flavour of savoury pork was coating my tongue and I felt a great new fondness for this thing called *multaschen*.

"Why have you been watching me? It's not polite to creep upon someone from the woods. Is that how you always behave?" She was attempting, in her best mature, young woman voice, to scold me into feeling guilty for my actions, and while I had a growing appreciation inside me for this red-haired young angel, it would take much more than a gentle voice turned firm to make me rethink my ways.

"It's better to go about my day in the shadows than be chased away by fearful lads or angry shepherds thinking I am out for their sheep."

"Well, no more hiding with me. It is far easier to trust a being you can see before you, than one lurking in the bushes."

From that point on, a strange little friendship sprouted between us, and I would flee the darkness of the troll cave to spend as much time as I was allotted in the presence of the lovely Lina. She fed me of whatever delicious treat she pilfered from her mother's kitchen, introduced me as the spirit of the woods to her younger siblings, and all in all, taught me what it was like to look forward to each new day.

For the first time in my life, I had a friend, and the notion of it sparked a new sort of light into my existence—one that made the cave I dwelt in a little brighter, and the thought of dealing with the trolls just a little easier to bear. Grolge had questioned me on different occasions about where I disappeared to most days, but humans weren't the only ones I was skilled in fooling and evading. Always, I managed to have him so twisted up in his thoughts by the time that we were done, that he would forget what he had asked me to begin with, and Klimn only aided me in my endeavours by intervening with equally confusing and incoherent asides.

But the ideal life can not last, and either I became too sure of myself and my convincing ways, or Grolge was smarter than I took him for. It was a sunny day—the sky blue and cloudless—when everything began to go down hill. After bringing the trolls a buck from the woods, I left them to their feasting and slipped into the trees, following the small path that had begun to wear from my constant travelling, and took myself off to the grassy knoll where my Lina was bound to be. She hadn't arrived yet, and so I sat in the bushes waiting, wishing to see the moment she appeared in the clearing, unaware that she was being watched, lovely and free.

As her copper head came suddenly into my line of vision, I felt the breath steal from my chest and the quickened pace of my heart, and, not for the first time I wondered if perhaps this was what it felt like to care...to love. Was this the attachment I heard so many of the mortals talking about—the thing that pushed them into foolish behaviour that embarrassed them all for the sake of wooing the item of their affection? I had thought it impossible—that I was beyond such considerations—but Lina had awoken something strange inside me.

Though I hadn't heard the crunch of leaves behind me, I was not so ignorant to my surroundings that I failed to feel the lifting of the hair at the back of my neck, as a chill of foreboding crept over me, and the large shadow chased away the sun, along with my happiness. The stench of putrid flesh and dank earth greeted me and announced the presence of the troll to my back.

"She's a pretty lil' creature, int'she?"

Grolge, apparently not as preoccupied with venison as I had thought him to be, had managed to follow the path I'd left through the forest, and found my small personal haven.

"She's just a girl," I tried to tell him, keeping my tone indifferent while a light sweat broke out along my hairline.

"Justa girl," he repeated. "I wan'er. She looks much tastier than that deer ya brought me."

In that very moment, I had entered into the nightmare of my existence—nighttime terrors made real. At my sides, my hands balled into fists and began to glow with a faint light as my magic awoke within me. However, as badly as I wanted to strike out at him, I dared not—my magic was far too untested against something of his size, and should I fail, it would mean my own death—an outcome I had been fighting against all my life.

"No."

"What?"

It had come out more firmly than I had intended, but there it was.

"No. Not her. I will bring you two others instead."

He was hesitating, and eyeing Lina with a look that did not bode well for either of us. My own appreciation for her was clearly mirrored in him, but in the form of hunger.

"Two others, and you may siphon some of my magic." There would only be one way, to open my wrist and allow him to drink—hoping that he didn't take so much that he would kill me, or become addicted to the sensation of magic coursing through him and force this upon me until he had drunk me ragged and empty.

A new hunger filled his eyes as he peered down at me, his large maw gaping in a ravenous, gluttonous fashion, and I knew then that I had him. That for today, Lina Schneider was safe from the cave trolls hidden deep in the forest.

"Magic, now," he rumbled at me, and having been left no other choice, I turned from the field with only one last longing look, and disappeared into the trees with Grolge to follow him back.

Hours later, when I was recovered enough from the blood loss, I went off to find him the two that I had promised. Mind hazy and cluttered with thoughts, I took the first two that I could find—a set of brothers that I typically overlooked due to their kind natures, but that day had already seen me sacrifice what I could for another—I had nothing else to give.

I allowed several weeks to elapse without returning to that special clearing and allowing myself to see Lina—weeks in which I feared I would lead Grolge back there, and this time Klimn would join us, leaving me unable to stop the two of them from massacring everyone present. Weeks in which I allowed Grolge to sup from my veins multiple times, using me as his living supply of magic, during which I saw a whole new sort of hell opening up before me. Eventually, I needed the light and happiness that my dear Lina offered me. So, I fled the cave and raced through the forest to our field.

She was already there upon her favourite knoll, a thick quilt spread out beneath her as she basked in the sunshine, practicing an even stitch that would make her tailor father proud. With my eyes latched on to the welcome sight of her, I didn't hesitate and ran straight into the clearing, moving as quickly as the speed of my short legs would take me, and a growing smile spreading over my face—too quickly —too distracted to notice the three boys messing about in the creek just below, waded in up to their calves with their slacks rolled up to their knees.

"Lina! Watch out!"

The shout of one of them came before I had reached her, only halfway across the field. Our eyes met across the grassy expanse, alpine poppies and long grass swaying in the soft breeze between us, and then there was naught to do but cast our eyes down the hill to where the three young males were stampeding towards me, threateningly raised sticks in hand.

Startled at this sudden change in circumstances, I came to a halt so quickly that I stumbled, bare toes catching on turf and lurching me forward so that I tumbled and rolled, the breath knocked out of me. I had barely gathered my senses to me, and the boys had beset me, several whacks of the sticks landing upon my head or shoulders before Lina's shout pierced the air, ceasing all activity for the moment.

"No! Stop, please don't do that!"

With the trickle of blood at my temple, I climbed unsteadily to my feet, trying to put as much distance between myself and my attackers as I was able to. They wore surprised expressions upon their faces, having not expected to be asked to halt their act of supreme heroism.

"Lina, this little horrid goblin was coming after you!"

"He was going to attack you, Lina, likely going for blood."

"Or something more vile—they steal children and young women you know."

She was upon her feet by this point and coming towards us all, looking like a queen in all her grace, red hair braided in a thick crown about her head.

"He's not a horrid goblin. Rumpelstilt is just a silly little creature who comes to visit with me here in the glen. He's harmless."

Silly little creature.

The boys gazed at her with looks of shock at this admission, but I had forgotten the trio of would-be heroes as a chill had spread through my form, joining the aches and pains already throbbing there. I was but a silly little creature to her, nothing but a spot of amusement in her day—nothing more than a pitiful animal to shed a little care upon when it presented itself. And yet, she had been my world.

I hardly registered the first jab of the stick in my side. The tallest boy was jeering at me in a sinister way as he spoke.

"You spend time with this thing, Lina? Look at it, it looks like it's half dead and drug itself through someone else's grave." His words were followed by another jab of the stick, and this time I reacted by stepping back a little. I should have responded or retaliated, but the world had crumbled about my feet.

"Stop poking him, Gerhard," Lina interjected.

"Did she say Rumpelstilt?" The plump boy who gazed at Gerhard waiting for cues on how to react soon added into the mix.

"Yes, Rumpelstilt. Rumpel. Rumpel. Rumpelstilt!" The shortest boy of the bunch also seemed to be the angriest, and with each announcement of my so called name, jabbed at me in a vicious sort of manner that had me lurching back in an attempt to be free of it.

Scrapes and scratches began to form on my tender flesh, the present state of my malnourishment not able to stand up to the rough treatment.

"Wilhelm, stop that, you're going to hurt him!"

"Awww, Wilhelm, please don't hurt him." Gerhard sneered in a mocking tone, his eyes had filled with a jealous light at the way Lina defended me.

He too jabbed at me, but at that point I was becoming fed up with the poking and prodding of sharp sticks into my chest and sides and grabbed at it. His and my eyes met across the stick, and we came to understand each other quite clearly. I hissed and he sneered more.

"I say kill it."

"Or at least chase it off," the well-fed one said, apparently with less of a killing streak than his comrades.

"Yes, Rumpelstiltskin, go off and rattle your little posts elsewhere, you haggard little goblin!"

A chorus of Rumpelstiltskins rang out around me, the clack of their sticks hitting against each other echoing in the open field. The trio then surrounded me, jabbing and hitting with their sticks in what had quickly become a whirlwind of noise and pain. There is only so much even a small creature can withstand before it strikes back.

"May you all be the posts with which my magic rattles!" I spat the words at them and a flash of power swept over us all.

The shout was one of anger and hurt from deep inside me, and even its true meaning was unknown to me until the shouting ceased and strangled gasps began to gurgle up from low inside each one of the boys. Their eyes widened with confused horror as fingers clawed at their faces and chests, something transpiring within that was not yet evident on the outside.

"*Donnerwetter*! Rumpel what have you done?" Lina shrieked in horror.

I had no words for Lina, and instead, I stood there watching in absent curiosity as the three boys eventually, quite literally, took root. Their booted feet sunk into the ground, as from the inside out they transformed into human shaped wooden posts, flesh hardening and splitting like an aged tree trunk shaved of its bark, shocked expressions trapped forevermore in a cast of a wooden pole buried deep into the earth. I had turned them into the very thing they had accused me of rattling.

Lina screamed, fingertips pressed into her cheeks until they were surrounded by points of white, and with a coldness that was turning my insides to emotionless ice, I turned from her.

"This silly little creature leaves you to the trolls."

She was still screaming in the field that had once been my haven and then became my torment as I walked away. I didn't bother to even look back before I disappeared into the woods. There had never really been anything true or real for me in this place anyway. My disillusioned form kept going until I was long past that village, and far away from the hellish pit that was Klimn and Grolge's cave.

I didn't belong in the fields of Freudenshafen, and I didn't belong in the cave of the trolls. Perhaps I belonged nowhere, but it was well past time I left all of this behind and set out into the world to discover whether or not there truly was a place meant for me.

They say when a man wanders the earth unceasingly, that it is not a place, but himself he is seeking, and that he can search his whole life through without ever seeing the truth of himself at the end of his days. Cast out by my own people, raised as little more than food in a hole deep within the earth, I had no way of defining the creature that stared back at me from the water's surface. I searched and I sought, but I did not find the answer to the question forever in the back of my mind. Instead, I found only more of the mortal world and the hunger and greed therein.

The more I learned of the human world outside of Freudenshafen, the more I learned of how I could control them, and bend them to my means. Hope is a very strong motivator when it comes to humans, and so long as they see what they think is a way out—even if it is but a wisp of smoke—then they will keep fighting and buy into whatever tale you spin.

As I travelled, I practiced my wiles, and with each new interaction I honed this ability to play them until I barely had to use my magic in order to be given their food, their clothing, and their gold. My magic had also grown and developed, and when I had no desire for games, I had learned to call food—and clothing—through the spaces in-between our world. I had no other person to call my own or to tie my life to, but neither was I bound in servitude and miserable obedience. Loneliness was a fair price to pay to be one's own master.

Along the way, I did think to step back into the world of magic to see if now that I was grown—though still small in stature and haggard in appearance—if I would be accepted due to my cleverness and experience. I had, in my own way, created a different sort of trickery and magic that was uniquely my own. So I travelled for decades, exploring other kingdoms outside the one of my birth, hoping that now I could step back into the place I had been cast out from, and found instead that the snobbery which had been the cause of my abandonment was still very much alive and indeed, universal.

Magical beings such as elves and fairies live for eons—sometimes indefinitely—if no harm befalls them. No one wanted to take in a young, deformed creature that would cast a dark shadow upon their legacy. It did not matter where I went, or whom I sought out, I was not welcomed by the ethereal beings who were formed in shapes of perfection and loveliness. I was reviled and shunned, not welcome in any part of the magical kingdom unless, it was with the other dredges that sought only blood and flesh. Eventually, I made my way back to my homeland—if I were to be alone, better that it be in a land that I knew and understood.

It wasn't my intention to end up near the royal city of Potsdamburg, but when I found myself nought but a morning's ride outside its walls in the small village of Nedlitzin, I discovered I had no desire to leave. Only but a small village, it was a prosperous one, filled with quaint shops that sold many wares: sweet smelling bakeries filled to the roof with pastries and breads, milliners who sold beautifully trimmed hats and bonnets, tailors selling the latest fashions from abroad, and stores where your feet could be shod in all of the best leather. All of which received patronage from wealthy farmers who owned the surrounding fields.

Nedlitzin was also home to a successful merchant who gathered spices and oils in many lands and brought them to be sold in the King's City. Just as it hadn't been my intention to end up in this village, it also wasn't my intention to become ensnared by his household and all that took place within its walls. I found myself sneaking into the shadows left by the large towers and peeping through windows to watch his servants and handmaidens serve the young lady of the house.

Sweet Katrin, with locks of sunshine that curled about her blemish free porcelain cheeks and eyes of bright jade, was a sight for any to behold, let alone a beauty-starved fiend such as myself. Though I had seen the finest of ladies around the world, there was some unspoken thing that continued to draw me back to her. Katrin's favourite place to spend her time was in the well-kept gardens behind their home, and there, in the shade of a large tree, she would sit upon a stone bench to read her afternoon away.

When she wasn't reading, she practiced her zither, preferring to do so outside with the breeze fluttering through her locks than to do so in the study of her home. Her fingers were so nimble and quick, plucking at the strings in a refined manner that seemed effortless, until music came spilling out. Occasionally, her honeyed voice would rise loud enough above the music that it would reach me in my place of concealment inside the bushes. Her voice was something that stayed with me even after she had ceased playing, finding me in my dreams and calling me awake from sleep.

I would watch her for hours, memorizing every little nuance that seemed uniquely Katrin…the tilt of her head when she was truly enraptured by her reading, the way her lips tipped upwards at the corners when she was amused by the elderly gardener who told her tales of his childhood, and the way her eyes shone bright with happiness, but also grew pensive with emotion when she played, each habit and trait something that became written upon my mind and would never be forgotten.

I knew better than to allow yet another mortal girl take her hold on me, but something about sweet Katrin drew me in until I was the one be-spelled and enraptured. Perhaps it was the gentleness of her spirit, or how she treated even the scullery maid with respect and compassion, and though she loved her finer things—bright jewels and soft silken gowns—she never demanded of her merchant father anything. Instead, she accepted all gifts with a sweet gratefulness.

Her father, however, was a boastful man who took his claim to riches and power within the village seriously and believed that all others should as well. He bragged of his many ships that sailed along the coasts, gathering all manner of fine things from other kingdoms and returned to port with treasures untold. He told tale after tale of his trips to the seacoast to check on his fleet, and brought back proof of his self-proclaimed importance by brandishing exotic spices from kingdoms leagues and leagues away.

Despite the father raising her, Katrin seemed to remain unspoiled and it was his boasting that resulted in her imprisonment with the threat of death looming overhead, not fault of her own. The human condition is a strange thing, when even men who have no need to make false claims because their lives are already so wondrous, still feel it necessary to falsify their truth in order to appear greater than what they are. Such is what happened late one night at the local tavern, when Moritz Friedrich claimed his lovely Katrin had the ability to spin straw into gold.

A drunken brawl broke out that night, as the truth of his wild tale was questioned. Come morning, once bruises and hangovers alike were nursed, and bloodied knuckles were bandaged, all seemed forgotten, and life went on.

It was late in the summer, just on the cusp of fall when the afternoon breeze was beginning to chill, and the scent in the air promised night frosts to come when word came of the approaching retinue—horse-drawn carriages surrounded by knights, and the royal banner flying high for all to see. King Ernst had come to the village in search of the girl who could weave straw into gold.

It would seem that the events of that night in the bar, though no longer spoken of, had not been forgotten, for it did not take long for the king's men to end up on the doorstep of the Friedrich household. Moritz's vanity was so fierce that he refused to confess the truth that he had made up the tale of his daughter's ability and instead allowed Katrin to be bundled up by her maids and handed off to the King's Guard.

I watched from behind a tree as the knights handed the beautiful girl up into one of the carriages, blonde head and full skirts disappearing inside while her family and the household watched. It all happened in a flurry of action, the king having come and gone before anyone had the chance to breathe, and while they all seemed content to remain motionless and let it happen, I was not.

Having no desire to get myself into Potsdamburg by means of my own feet, I snuck quickly beneath the legs of one of the large horses, sending it into a bucking fit that caused its rider to nearly go flying, and then crawled up to cling on beneath the nearest carriage, using my magic to keep myself latched on in a small hammock of fabric. I swayed back and forth beneath the carriage, the sound of clapping hooves upon the worn dirt roads, eventually turning into the clack of horseshoes on cobblestone.

Potsdamburg was a city worthy of its king, wide stone streets filled to the brim with its citizens, all bustling and harried to get to their next location. The tall brick and stone buildings that towered over the merchants hawking their wares on the sidewalks were filled with glass windows and covered with scrolling, gold-carved cornices, braced beneath proud roofs sporting dentil moulding and lace trim.

It spoke of health and prosperity...of a king who knew how to keep his kingdom strong and with pockets filled with coin.

The city proper paled in comparison to the king's palace. The lush, green gardens began long before you reached the seemingly endless granite steps that led up to the bright, sprawling home of the king. As one neared the palace, the gardens began to break into tiered levels, the steps splitting them down the centre. Each level contained its own intricate landscape of trees and bushes, leading up to a brick wall that rose up to begin the next level, its roof top the floor of the next garden. Windowed doors sprouted from the sides of each wall throughout the gardens, giving place for leafy grapevines to take root and creep up and over.

We did not travel by way of the staircase. Instead, the carriages moved freely up a winding cobblestone road to the main doors of the palace. Hammondburg Palace, set against the green of the hill, was a bright spot of canary yellow fighting the sun for prominence. It boasted columns of sandstone that were carved into statues of Bacchants, a toast to life, love, song and drink.

As the king's retinue came to a halt outside the tall, proud doors of Hammondburg, I watched and waited. First, the footmen jumped down off the back of the carriage where they had been holding on, their golden uniforms proclaiming them a part of the king's employ. They rolled out a carpet that led from the carriage to the main steps, trailing up to the now open doors. One then placed a step at the foot of the carriage. One opened the door for His Royal Highness, King Ernst, who took the offered hand and stepped down out of his carriage and quickly made his way over the carpet and up into the palace.

Once he disappeared with only the barked command to "bring the girl", the doors were opened to Katrin's carriage, and I felt it sway above me as she and her guard moved inside, then climbed down. This time as I walked out amongst them, I cast a spell of overlooking, one that essentially made me invisible as it turned all eyes from me. It kept the horses quiet and meant that I was able to follow the guards as they took Katrin inside. We travelled down numerous hallways and up several flights of stairs, until she was lead through a door and into a stone room with naught but a bed, one single window, a spinning wheel with stool, and heaps upon heaps of straw.

Not wishing to reveal myself yet, I slipped into one of the darkened corners to watch whatever would unfold between Katrin and the king—mostly to see just how the young, blonde beauty would handle this new development in her life. Either she had wept all of her tears in the carriage ride here, or she had not yet come to fully understand the predicament she was in, for she took but a casual look about her then moved to stand at the window gazing out from the tower to the gardens below.

"What have you gotten me into, Father?"

Or perhaps she did have an idea of what lay before her in this room, with its locked door behind us and barred window. Her slender fingers reached out to curve around one bar as she peered outside, possibly looking at what it was she was saying goodbye to. For a while, she stood there simply gazing out the window, and then at last she moved to seat herself on the edge of the bed, arranging her skirts neatly. Still, I said nothing.

It was just as the sun was beginning to set in the sky, that the door unlocked and servants entered, first to light the torches on the walls, and then stepped out, so that the king himself could enter instead. Katrin came instantly to her feet, with her skirts in hand, performing a graceful curtsy.

"Your Highness," she gasped out softly, startled and breathless.

"There are strange things being whispered about you in the taverns of Nedlitzin."

"Strange things, Your Grace?" Katrin gazed up from her curtsied position, a question upon her face.

"Yes, many strange and wondrous things." With his hand, he motioned for her to rise, his eyes taking her in as she did so, curious and assessing. "How old are you?"

"I've just turned sixteen years, Your Grace."

"Sixteen years," he murmured, reaching out with his hand to pluck a piece of straw from the large pile nearest him. "Sixteen years, and you shall die at dawn if this straw around us is not spun into gold by then."

Katrin was not the only one to startle at these words, I too gave a little jerk of my head as I looked between them quickly. The girl had paled, her green eyes wide in her face with a shocked innocence that did not quite comprehend what was being said.

"Your Grace?"

"Your father has boasted loud enough in Nedlitzin that it has made its way to my own ears that you have the most magical ability to spin straw into gold. I have brought you here to do that to all of this." His bejewelled hand swept out, motioning to the room at large.

"But, Your Grace, I can't," Katrin gasped out.

"Are you saying that your father is a liar?" The king was giving her a shrewd look, one that said one way or the other a member of the Friedrich family would be losing their heads come dawn.

"What? No, of course not."

"Then do this, or at dawn, I will behead you." King Ernst's eyes glinted, dark and dangerous. Turning quickly on his heel, he slipped from the room, leaving the young girl alone amidst the straw piles.

Katrin collapsed to the floor in a heap of skirts, her clasped hands clutched to her chest as she gazed in despair at the straw all about her.

What had her father gotten her into indeed?

It was well within my power and ability to ease Katrin's fear of dying, and though I planned to go to her with an offer, it was not my intention to do so right from the start. Instead, I wished to see in what way she would handle this news. Would her despair take her over and have her clutching at her head to tear the hair loose? Would she cry until there was naught left in her but dry hiccups and ragged breaths? Or would she move to take up her perch on the bed, same as before, and simply await her coming death?

She did none of these, as it would turn out.

Standing tall, with her back straight and her shoulders squared, Katrin began to make a circle of the room. Not bowed down by her hopeless fate, as her fingers brushed over strands of straw, she totalled the entirety of the room. It was impressive to see—her grace under such daunting odds—giving me a little more respect for the golden-headed girl I had been watching for months now.

With interest, I watched as she took up a small bundle in her arms and moved over to the spinning wheel. There was a determination in her look I could appreciate in the face of such impossibility, and I moved a little closer to have a better look as strands of straw were pulled from the small bundle now resting in her lap. Pressing her foot to the treadle, she began to work the straw onto the wheel as her foot pressed the treadle to make it begin to spin.

Of course, nothing happened, unable to even get the straw to stay together on the wheel such as wool would, and yet she tried over and over again until at last her shoulders slumped in defeat, and she hung her head. I waited until her hands were over her face and her shoulders were trembling with quiet cries before I left my hiding place and moved towards her.

"You seem to be in quite the predicament, my dear."

My voice startled her, and she jumped a little on her stool. Her head popped up, and tear-filled eyes gazed at me in confusion, quickly transitioning to mild horror.

"Who...who—?"

"Who am I?" I brushed a hand over my coif of pale hair that was pulled back off my face and tied at the base of my neck with a deep blue ribbon. The way I wore it caused my long, pointed ears to stand out all the more, but I was no longer adverse to my appearance. Young in years as I may still be, I had come to accept the notion that I was as I was and there was nought could be done about it. Not all the magic in the world could change that. "I am a concerned citizen."

"Are you here to harm me?" Her voice quavered with a new found fear as she continued to look at me, the foreign creature before her. I laughed a short, dark chuckle at this question.

"No, I am not here to harm you. Rather, I would like to make you an offer." I picked up a piece of straw, holding the end between a thumb and finger while pulling it through the other set of thumb and finger.

"What sort of offer?"

Tossing aside the straw piece, I pulled a small red handkerchief from the breast pocket of my little jacket and stepped towards her, offering the piece of cloth for her to dry her eyes. "The sort of offer that will save your life."

"How?" With trembling fingers, she reached out to take the handkerchief, and wiped her eyes with dainty dabs.

"I will spin all of the straw in this room into gold for you in exchange—"

"In exchange for what?" Her body straightened in resistance and she pulled back further on her stool, the hand around the red cloth tightening.

My hand rose to put a stop to the thoughts currently running rampant in her mind. "Not anything of that sort, dear one. No, I want the locket that you wear about your lovely neck."

This seemed to surprise her, and her hand lifted to wrap about the golden locket in a defensive gesture, as if I might reach forward and tear it from her.

"But this has no value to anyone but me."

"Well...not quite true. The gold is worth a pretty penny, but more importantly, I want it because of the value it has to you."

It was a delicately crafted piece—all filigree flowers making up the lid to it, allowing just a hint of what lay beneath to be seen through the gold work. Once one opened it up, they were able to see the tiny round coriander seeds and small dried blooms contained behind the pane of glass. It had been a gift from her father, seeds from the very first ship he sent out across the sea to gather spices, herbs and oils to sell back here. I had heard firsthand Moritz telling the story to Katrin, of how these seeds had been of the first handful gathered for the voyage, and he'd put them aside for safe keeping. The blooms had come off the first successfully cultivated plant in their own garden, grown from seeds that had been in that handful. Now she bore them all around her neck, carrying the sweet memory of her father's first success, and she one of his most lovely treasures since.

I wanted the necklace, not because of its monetary value, but because of the familial meaning behind it, because there was so much of their pride in their name and their power wrapped up in that little gold locket.

She was hesitant, I could see, her eyes narrowed at my admittance of why I wanted it, and the words of refusal were upon her lips, formed there in the pursing of her mouth while her fingers remained tight about it.

"Think carefully before you refuse—it is the locket or your head. Either way, the piece will not be staying 'round your neck."

A visible shudder made its way through her body at my words, and I watched the emotions play across her face. She was a prisoner of the king, and there was nothing else she could do but hope that the little goblin-creature before her was actually capable of what he had said.

"I want proof first."

Her words made me smile and feel a little proud of her. Even at this desperate time, she was not fool enough to take me at my word. I simply bowed my head in acceptance.

"My Lady." I gestured to the stool, signalling the need for her to rise so that I may take her place. "If you would be so kind."

Katrin was quick to hop up from the stool as I stepped near her, the rustle of her skirts adding to the sound of her hurried footsteps across the wooden floors. With a touch of dramatics, I flung out the tails of my coat and sat upon the stool. Pulling the stool up a little, I leaned forward to check on the wheel before me. The bobbin was already slid into place on the flyer and I reached out with my fingers to check that the whorl was set. My fingers travelled along the drive band that led from the wheel down over the bobbin and whorl. It seemed adequately taut, and I slid it into the proper position on both. I moved my foot to the treadle and worked it up and down, watching the bobbin spin freely inside of the flyer, and I knew that I was set to begin.

"Would you bring me the blanket from your bed?" I was given a suspicious look at this request, but eventually she complied, and picking it up, brought it over to me.

Of course, she stopped far enough away that we both had to stretch in order for me to take it from her hand, and I offered her a pointed look in return. She wasn't winning me over with this behaviour, and of anyone, I was in the best position to help her—something her father certainly hadn't done by allowing her to be carted off, rather than confess to his lies.

Once I had the blanket, however, I paid her no heed. Picking at the edge of the knitted piece, I was able to get a loose strand of thread and pulled a length of it free. Snapping it off with my teeth I threw the blanket back across the cell to land haphazardly onto the bed. From the corner of my eye, I saw Katrin move to pick it up, fold it, and then lay it back upon the end of the bed. Perhaps she was just looking for something to keep her hands busy. I didn't care.

With thread in hand, I looped it around the bobbin and ran it along the guide hooks before feeding it through the orifice at the end. Once all was set, my foot worked the treadle yet again, as I tested the pull of the bobbin, which needed only a little adjusting of the tensioning screw down below. Still ignoring Katrin, I leaned down and picked up the little bundle of straw that had fallen from her lap in her rush to flee from my approach. Pulling strands free, I looped the thread around the ends of it, and whispered words of magic to the straw in my hands, telling it to bind to the thread. As my foot worked, and the treadle rocked up and down, the wheel spun.

The cell was filled with the creek of the wooden spinning wheel, and I could feel Katrin's eyes upon me as straw went into one side of the orifice, and came out the other as a string of gold thread to be wound around the bobbin within the flyer. After I had done a couple of lengths, my foot paused, and I reached out to stop the wheel from spinning any further.

"Is that enough proof for you?" I asked her, turning on my little stool to gaze at her, a brow raised over one dark eye, mocking her earlier disbelief.

Katrin stepped slowly towards me, her eyes firmly latched on to the bobbin, and as if unable to help herself, she reached out to brush fingertips along the golden thread wound about it.

"It truly is gold, isn't it?"

I simply nodded to her words, my eyes staying on her face. There were so many emotions working over her features once again—

disbelief, awe, but most of all, relief. Without further hesitation, her hands reached for the chain about her neck, and she carefully lifted it up and over her head. Turning to face me, perhaps meeting my eyes for the first time since I had revealed myself, she held the locket out to me.

"We have a deal."

"Good decision."

I took the locket from her, and just to prove a point, slipped it over my own head and then dropped it inside my shirt so that it would rest against my heart, a medal of my victory in this moment. I had taken a prized possession, but she would keep her head.

"Now go away, I have work to do," I demanded, brushing her off as I set out to spin the heaps and heaps of straw within this room into gold for a man that had not earned it, and likely did not need it.

Katrin backed away, moving across the room to settle upon the bed with her skirts arranged neatly around her, and her hands clasped in her lap. I felt her eyes upon me as I worked, and though I wasn't keen on how those tables had turned, I dealt with it for the time being. Hours trickled by while I sat there at the spinning wheel, often times only the creak of the wheel itself and the soft whirl of the flyer making any sound in the room. Periodically, I would change the position of the thread along the guide hooks to fill up other portions of the bobbin, and once it was filled, I would set it aside to be replaced with a fresh bobbin from the empty stack, and waiting, at my feet.

The work was unceasing, and even for a magical being such as myself, it took a toll on my body. Yet, I did not stop until every last piece of straw within the room had been spun into gold, adding to the pile of filled bobbins on the floor. It was just before dawn when the wheel stopped spinning for the final time, and I dropped my hands to my lap. Twisting my shoulders a little to pop an aching place in my spine, I then stood up.

"As promised, one room of straw spun into gold."

Surprisingly, Katrin had not fallen asleep the entire time, though there had been a couple of moments during the night when the soft noises of the wheel seemed to almost lull her and I thought she would nod off. Instead, she had taken those times as a sign to move to the window for fresh air, and gazed out over the darkened kingdom below. Though she wasn't doing the work herself, it had seemed she wanted to see it through to the end.

"Thank you for what you have done for me. You have saved my life."

"Nonsense. We had a deal, and I always keep my word." I patted the locket resting beneath the linen of my shirt and jacket.

A silence fell between us, during which I gazed round the room, checking each crevice and corner for a stray piece. I saw none.

"Dawn is fast approaching and your king will return. Sleep while you can, my Lady." I gave her a bow, more for the dramatics of it than to pay any respect. As I did so, I backed up until I was in the shadows and able to call up my spell to hide myself from view.

Katrin gasped as I disappeared, looking around her to see if I might have moved quickly into another area of the room. When she could find me nowhere she sighed, pressing a hand to her cheek as she dropped down onto the edge of her bed to sit and wait. Soon, the king would return, and his judgment of her fate would be made. As for me, I settled down into a corner to rest for the time being, I would be there to see King Ernst's thoughts on his findings.

The king's reaction did not live up to anticipation. Just shortly after sunrise there was the scrape of a key in the lock and the heavy wooden door to the cell groaned open. Two of the King's Guard entered the room first, with King Ernst coming just shortly afterwards. Once again, Katrin stood to her feet at his appearance and offered a curtsy. Not even sparing her a glance, his dark brown eyes swept the room over and finished up on the spinning wheel with its stack of bobbins beside it on the floor.

From the shadows, I watched the king cross the floor so that he may stoop down and pick up one of the bobbins. The newly dawned sunshine filtering through the window glinted off the gold thread wound smoothly around the piece, and he twisted it back and forth so that he could watch the sun play across it.

"So he spoke true."

Katrin didn't respond, she simply remained standing there silently with her hands clasped before her. Her eyes followed him though, watching as he walked casually around the room with the bobbin of gold thread in his hand.

"See she is fed," he said to his guards, and then walked quickly to the door. "And collect those bobbins and bring them to me." The king's dark head of hair and broad shoulders disappeared outside the cell. The tallest of the guards stepped forward to gather up the bobbins. Soon enough, they too were gone, and Katrin was alone in the room once more. I watched her shoulders slacken with relief as she dropped down to the bed.

Katrin was left there for some time, her body and fortitude eventually gave out on her and I watched as she curled up on the small straw filled mattress and fell asleep. While I waited along with her, curious as to what His Highness would choose to do with her now that the deed had been done, I called forth food for myself—a trick I had developed while travelling the world over, and which I found to be much easier than talking someone out of their food. I thought about the kitchens down below and pulled some cheese and a leg of duck through the space between and into my awaiting hands. The cheese was rich and fragrant. I nipped it down in large bites before turning to the juicy duck leg. It would seem there were some benefits to residing within the king's home.

I had eaten the bone clean by the time the cell door opened once more and a servant girl entered with a tray of food and wine for Katrin. She woke in a groggy state, fingers rubbing at her eyes as she sat and fought to gather her bearings. The girl didn't say much. Instead, she set the tray at Katrin's side on the bed then fled quickly as if she might be attacked if she stayed longer than what was necessary.

What did they say in the palace below about the girl locked upstairs?

With careful movements that spoke of her groggy mind, Katrin picked up a piece of bread on the tray as well as the bowl of stew they had brought to her and began to carefully eat. Even locked away in a cell she was still a lady of substance and grace. Having set aside my own crumbs, I watched her as she ate—the small bites, the slow chewing, the way she did everything neatly despite the fact she had no idea there was an audience.

Once she had eaten her fill and washed it down with some wine, Katrin placed the tray on the floor, curling back up to sleep a little more. It was perhaps just past the dinner hour when the door was opened once more and Katrin was woken from her sleep by two guards who came to gather her.

"Am I going home?" she asked, her blonde hair in disarray from her sleep and her cheek still red from where it had lain upon her hand.

"The king wishes for us to take you elsewhere."

"What? Where elsewhere? Where are you taking me?"

Watching this unfold with interest, I stood to my feet, brushing hands along my trousers to clean away any dust. Katrin was close to weeping as they pulled her from the room and I was able to easily follow behind them entirely unnoticed. We didn't have far to go before we were in yet another cell, this one larger than the last, and also filled to the brim with piles of straw. In the centre of this room sat a spinning wheel accompanied by a stool, and beside them, was set a pile of empty bobbins waiting expectantly.

So, it was to be assumed that the same request was going to be made of her that night as had been made the night before. The remainder of Katrin's questions went unanswered as she was left in the new cell and the door locked behind the guards. The girl stood in the middle of the room, an entirely new look of horror upon her features as it became clearer to her that thanks to my actions, the king believed her truly capable of spinning gold, and with no way of contacting me, would not be able to give the king what he so very much longed for.

King Ernst, it appeared, had a keen sense of timing, for just when her horror had settled enough to make Katrin truly distraught, did the click of the lock sound and His Grace stepped into the room. Her legs failed her and no curtsy came, this time the king was greeted with nothing but the bow of her head.

"How are you finding your new lodgings?"

"I thought...I thought I would get to go home."

"Until I am done with you, you are home," the king responded, his hands came to rest upon his hips as he gazed about the room like a man surveying a newly acquired piece of land. Pride and victory shown within the depths of his eyes.

Katrin remained quiet, as there was not much to be said in opposition to the king.

"It is my desire that you once again spin the straw before you into gold." He looked to the ashen-faced girl wringing her hands before her skirts. "And if you do not, I will have your head instead."

He had not even left the room this time before she dropped down to the hard little bed in the corner, her face buried in her hands. "Please...oh please."

I decided to be kinder this time, more time would only make her more distraught not desperate, and I had no desire to sit in the shadows listening to her sobbing when instead I could be moving forward with the great deal of work that I had to do. Leaving the shadows I came to stand before her once again.

"Was that *please* for myself, or for the king?" I questioned, my eyes upon my nails as I picked at a hangnail that had formed during the hours of my work the previous night.

Katrin gasped, her head lifted free of her hands to gaze up at me, green eyes wide with surprise and a newly forming glee.

"You've come back! But...how?" She glanced about, looking for the evidence of my miraculous entrance into the room somewhere in the corners.

"I have my ways. You've been crying. Why?"

"Because, though what you did for me last night was kind, the king wants it to be done again, only now there is more, and I am still unable to spin gold from straw."

"Hmmm," I murmured, tapping a finger to my lips. "You do appear to be in quite the bind once more, don't you?"

"Will you help me again kind, Little Sir?"

I glared at her a little as she referred to me as little sir. I was more than aware of my diminutive stature, there was no need to vocalize it.

"Your ring."

"Pardon?"

"I will spin the straw once more in exchange for the ring upon your hand."

We both looked down to her right hand where a large square cut ruby rested upon her slender finger. The ring was yet another piece that she never took off, a remembrance of her deceased mother who had left her when she was but a young girl. The ring had been the piece Moritz had used to propose to Aline all those years before. Shortly before Aline Friedrich's passing, she had removed it from her own hand to slide it into the small palm of her daughter, telling her to wear it for her, always.

Katrin's right hand clenched into a tight fist while her other hand came to cover the ring over. Looking up to her face, I saw the way her bottom lip trembled with unshed tears and unspoken words. She did not want to part with it, even less than she had wanted to give up her locket—but that was why I wanted it so greatly.

"Very well."

The next action took some effort on her part, and I watched, as her chest swelled and her shoulders raised with a deep breath that seemed to help her in tugging the ring off of her finger. The hand that held it out to me, palm up, with the red jewel gleaming upon it, trembled with emotion. It was a tender sight, and would have moved me, had I felt any remorse in removing this piece from her life.

Mortals were better off without their attachments to small, insignificant items. Pieces that could easily be taken or lost and yet made their whole world crumble as if they embodied the memory or the soul of the person they were meant to represent. The only thing that truly mattered was the length of our memory and what we held onto within us concerning a particular person—what they had been to us or what they had done. Upon my soul, I bore the marks of all those I had revealed myself to. I remembered each glance, every shudder, and all the sharp inhales of horror. I did not require the aid of a piece of jewelry to carry those things with me, nor did Katrin need this ring to take the memory of her mother with her throughout her life. She would be better, stronger, if she chose not to carry her heart on her hand, but instead kept it safe within herself where no one could take it.

Without hesitation, I reached out and took the ring from her hand, lifting it up between thumb and finger, I angled it back and forth to watch the sunlight reflect off the surface of the red stone. It was a beautiful piece, befitting a Lady, not just the wife or daughter of a merchant. I slid it onto my finger, letting it wink its presence upon my index so that it would be there with every gesture and motion.

Our deal struck, I turned from her, and took up my seat upon the stool before the new spinning wheel. My actions were similar to the night before as I checked it over, except that this time, Katrin brought me the thread without me having to ask. I nodded an absent 'thank you' to her and then continued on with the process.

The room had almost doubled in size, which meant that the amount of straw I needed to spin in the same amount of time was a great deal more. It would require faster work and a lot more magic than had been necessary the previous night. It was, however, not a deed I was unsuited to—I worked best against the odds.

This time, Katrin paced, unable to sit still and simply watch as the night wore on. The straw piles diminished in a steady manner, but to anyone on the outside looking in, it looked like there may be some doubt whether or not the task could be accomplished in the time allotted. I was not fearful of the outcome, but then it was not my head at risk of the chopping block.

To her credit, she did not utter any of this doubt or dismay and left me to my work, choosing to express her worry in the steady pacing around the room. The annoyance of it eventually grated on my nerves however, and I grumbled my irritation.

"If you need something to do, be of help and bring me each new bundle of straw when I run low, but do stop that incessant pacing before I go mad."

From that point on, the evening passed far smoother and with less annoyance felt on my part. When at last the final bobbin was filled, and I was able to cease my work and stand, the sun was still an hour from rising. I stood up and stretched out my back, before turning to Katrin, who by this point had taken a more relaxed pose on her bed.

"The task is once again complete, my Lady, and you may rest easy." My bejewelled hand motioned to the bed, indicating that she should lay down and sleep. "Your life is safe for one more morning, may the king's greed not require more of you."

Katrin didn't speak this time, conflicting emotions fought for prominence in her eyes and I don't think that she was capable of forming words in that moment. I saw relief that the deed was finished, perhaps a little thankfulness for my aid, but also hate for my demands, and fear for what the morning would actually bring.

Without another word, I slipped from her view and into the shadows. This time however, I did not stay in the room, but opened a hole in the wall through the space in between and stepped through out into the hall. My curious nature was getting to me, and I wished to investigate what actually was on the horizon. It didn't take me long to find the answer to my question, for down at the end of the corridor was a bigger room—a bigger room with triple the amount of straw.

The king's greed was not yet at an end.

The king did not deign to grace Katrin with his presence this time around. I was there in the wee hours of the dawn to watch his guards enter the cell, and gather up the numerous bobbins of golden thread, leaving the girl with little more than a glance from their eyes. It left her fearful, and instead of returning to sleep, she drew her legs up to her chest to sit huddled on the bed. Her position did not change when the servant girl entered to bring her meal. Instead, she sat staring at the spinning wheel in the centre of the room—a symbol of her imprisonment, and a hateful reminder of a fate which was no longer within her own hands, but held in the greedy, uncaring clutch of a man grown cold from his own power.

I would have liked to question her then, to understand what was truly going on inside her mind—but that would have broken the rouse that I left between visits, and I did not want her aware that I was present for all the happenings taking place inside these walls. So I remained silent in the wings, watching the fear crawl beneath her skin until it was almost a tangible presence in the room with us.

She startled when the door eventually opened and the guards returned to fetch her once more. I was fully aware of where they were taking her and what awaited her at the end of the corridor—another room, more straw, and another threat of beheading—but what was there left for her to give me in exchange for spinning? This had been the thought milling in my mind over the course of the morning.

"Please, I can't keep doing this! I simply want to go home. Will you speak to the king for me?" It was sad to see a proud young woman brought so low that she clutched at the sleeve of a guard and begged for his aid in dealing with the king.

She appealed to the wrong man, however. The guards were nothing more than puppets whose strings were pulled and plucked by His Grace. Shaken off with little thought, Katrin was left alone yet again, in a larger room with even more straw.

The door had no sooner shut, than it opened once more. Instead of a servant or even the king, Moritz Friedrich stepped into the room, his leather boots clicking on the wood beneath them.

"Papa?" came Katrin's shocked exclamation and then she launched herself into his awaiting arms. Her face buried into the crook of his neck and shoulder, I watched as the girl sobbed, clutching onto the form of her father to ensure he was not going to leave her any time too soon. In return, Moritz held his daughter tightly, his arms about her slender form and his own face pressed to the top of her head.

"What are you doing here? I wanted so badly to see you...but I wanted to go home. Are you now their prisoner as well?" Finally, she lifted her tear streaked face to gaze up at her father, distraught at this new thought.

Moritz, in a calming manner, lifted his hands to cup her face between them, smoothing away her tears with his thumbs.

"I am not a prisoner, and neither are you." His words brought a frown to her face.

"But-"

"Katrin, do you not realize what you have done for us? I spoke what I thought were drunken words of falsehood when I boasted of your abilities in the bar that night, but I had no idea it was the truth! Why didn't you ever speak of this to me?"

"No, Papa, I haven't— " Moritz was not truly listening to her, too swept away by the possibilities that arose with this new talent.

"But you have, and you will again." He nodded firmly, eyeing her with determination.

"You don't understand. I can't do this, I haven't any more to give."

"Well you must find it. Whatever has given you this magical ability, you must find it again. You will be queen, my darling."

"What?" This time Katrin froze, and I watched the way her eyes widened with this announcement.

"The king called me here to the palace to speak with me. If you do as he asks and spin this final room into gold thread for him, he will make you his queen. Queen Katrin! Think of what you can do for your family—what pride and accomplishment you've brought us. Do this and all will be ours—you a throne, and my grandsons will rule this land."

I could see the thoughts racing through her mind, the way she paused to contemplate his words. Could she want this, to marry the man who had pulled her from her home at but a moment's notice, and left her locked away for three days now—the man who had now threatened her life not once, but twice? It seemed, even to me, a ghastly and humiliating thing to ask of the girl.

"I don't know that I can." His hands tightened upon her face, and he angled her chin up so that he could lean in closer, his eyes firm upon hers.

"You must. As a family we need this, and there is little alternative. Do whatever you must to give the king what he asks, do you understand me?"

Such is a father's love.

Katrin nodded her head subtly. "Yes, Papa."

"I love you." Moritz pressed a kiss to her forehead, then released her, and stepped back.

"I must go now, they didn't give me much time. I have faith in you Katrin, I know that you can do this."

His steps had taken him to the door and he rapped upon it with his knuckles. Katrin was shaking again, her hands clasped before her, turning white as she watched the door open to her father, and his form stepping through it.

"I love you Katrin," he repeated. "Make me proud."

The door closed on his words, and yet again, it was only the two of us alone in the room. I wondered if this would be the end of it, would they leave her to her work, or would the king manage to show himself? This question seemed to be upon Katrin's mind as well, for as she sat down, there remained a strained tension in her body. She looked to be waiting for something, or someone.

We did not have long to wait.

King Ernst entered the room in a flourish of capes and jewels, filling up the room with his presence. Katrin, who I had half expected to simply remain seated this time, stood to her feet, and offered the king a full curtsy once again, followed by a softly murmured "Your Grace."

"Your father was here, and I presume he has told you the offer that I have made?" He swept his cape aside and rested a hand on his hip as he gazed at her.

"Yes, Your Grace, he has."

The king nodded his head, jaw set with intent and a grand purpose that I was sure made all the sense in the world to him—justifying your actions comes very easily when there is no one who can oppose them. King Ernst strode towards Katrin and took her pale hands into his own, clasping them in the manner of an intimate lover.

"Then you know, I plan to make you my bride, my queen." I watched him release one of her hands so that he could reach up and gently tuck a strand of her hair behind her ear. "I ask only one thing from you."

Katrin was spellbound, whether from pleasure or from terror, I could not be certain—but the display made my own stomach roll. There were a few choice words tossing about in my head that I would use to describe His Royal Highness and none of them were regal.

"Nothing more than I have asked of you before. Show how true your love for me is by spinning the straw in this room into gold thread and in the morning I will announce our betrothal."

The only response Katrin seemed to have for this was a subtle nod of her head, though her skin had taken on a sickly pallor.

"You make me very happy in this, Katrin, you will make a beautiful, and dutiful wife."

"Thank you, Your Grace," she whispered to him.

"But I expect obedience, know that, and if you should choose not to finish this room for whatever reason..." he said, his words drifting off deliberately. King Ernst shook his head, eyes levelled upon hers. "The outcome still stands, and instead of a wedding, there will be an execution."

If it was possible for the girl to turn whiter, it happened, and her eyes widened to a shocking size.

"And neither of us wants that, do we?" The tone he spoke to her in was condescending, turning her into a small child that needed to be spoken down to.

Slowly her head shook, concern creasing pale brows. King Ernst was wholly unaffected by this obvious sign of outward distress, and lifted her hands to his lips so that he could press a kiss to the curve of her knuckles. Her hands were then released and he stepped back.

"You have a great deal to do, I will leave you to it. Do not disappoint me, Katrin."

Once again, the tread of boot steps crossing the floor sounded, and the heavy door was opened to allow the king to pass through into the hall. After the loud click of the lock sliding into place echoed around the room, I leaned against the wall to wait. It would be interesting to see how long it took for her to crack this time.

She was a mess of emotions—of that it was easy to see. Her hands to her cheeks, Katrin sat down on the edge of the small cot, staring across the room at the spinning wheel with a sort of hatred and fear that I had rarely seen in someone's face.

"Friend...please come to me again," her plea was whispered softly, but I heard it nonetheless.

I should perhaps have joined in on the speed at which things had been happening today, but I moved only on my own terms, and as she called to me, I contemplated. I would free her if she but asked me. I was certain there was a reasonable exchange we could settle on in return for me opening the wall and helping her slip out unseen.

I did not fear the anger of her father or even the king when the knowledge of her absence became known—but I needed her to speak the words for herself, to ask that she be freed from this upcoming marriage. That was how magic worked, and though I was free to do as I pleased, there was still a magical contract that formed during these exchanges. I gave magic in return for fair trade, but first the bargain had to be struck. Having settled on what I was willing to do, and at what cost, I slipped from the shadows into her view.

There was an expression of relief awaiting me in her gaze as her eyes landed upon me. I saw the release of a held breath and how some of the tension slackened from her form.

"You beckoned?" I commented, then began a slow trek around the room.

There really was an absurd amount of straw in the cell, and I was relieved to think that I wouldn't need to deal with all of it. She and I had been through this twice already, and I could have prodded her more to speak, or saved the both of us the trouble and simply announced what was going to happen—but that was not how this worked.

"I need to beg your help one last time, though I have nothing to offer."

Once she asked to be released, I had a number of ideas in mind for what she could give to me, of that I wasn't concerned.

"Let me make a guess, you wish for this room to also be spun into gold?" I said it expecting her to tell me no, and ask for rescue instead.

"Yes."

"Excuse me?" I wasn't so sure I had heard her correctly.

"I need for you to spin this room into golden thread as you have the past two nights."

I gazed at her, a stupefied look upon my face.

"Are you certain? There is nothing else you wouldn't rather ask for?"

Katrin paused, words on the tip of her tongue, and I waited for her to gather her wits about her and ask for help in escaping.

"I think...I would very much like to be queen."

"What?" I shouldn't be surprised at the process of the human mind—or their ability to look past horrors to shiny new things—but there you have it, I was surprised. Shocked she would allow the man who had threatened her thrice now to take her to wife, all for the sake of a crown.

"I wish to be queen. I know I haven't anything to give you now, but the king has promised to make me his queen, and if you do this for me I will have many things I can give to you."

"Of course, think of all the new gowns." I shook my head, disappointed in her. I had come out here with a plan to set her free and already settled on what pieces in her home I would take as my payment. However, things had now changed. Instead of seeking her freedom, she was asking to be permanently chained to the black hearted man who sat upon the throne.

I twisted on my foot, my fingers stroking along my chin as I contemplated what I would take. There was a spark in my dark green eyes as I spun back to her—a spark that was turning quickly into a fire.

"Very well, if it is queen you wish to be, then I will spin this straw once more for you and in exchange you will give me your firstborn child."

"What?" It was her turn to doubt that she was hearing correctly.

My eyes narrowed on her, and I could feel my lips forming a bit of a sneer as I stepped towards her. "I will spin this straw into gold once more so that you can keep your pretty head and marry your king. In return I want to be given the firstborn child that is conceived through this marriage."

It was the one thing I could not acquire for myself, and if I were going to do this, that was my price.

"I can't...that is not something that I can promise." Katrin gasped, a hand at her throat as she stared at me with suspicion and horror.

I shook my head at her and moved to lounge on the stool. "Don't give me that look, I don't plan to eat it." Just to make a show of how at ease I was—it wasn't my neck on the line—I picked idly at a tooth with my pinky finger.

"But I can't give up my child."

"Of course you can, parents do it all the time." Mine had.

"But— "

"Do you want to die?"

"N-no."

"Then make this vow now, and I will spin this straw and hand you over the crown. Then, upon the birth of your first child, I will return at sunset to claim it. You will give me the child without complaint or resistance."

Our eyes met across the expanse of the room, warm sunshine filtered through the window to the left of me heating the straw and filling the entire room with the strong scent of it. Minutes ticked by, during which I am sure she weighed diamonds and tiaras against the love of a future child, or the idea of imminent death. At last, she settled something inside of herself and responded.

"Very well, if this is my only choice...spin the straw into gold and my firstborn is yours."

I left shortly after I finished spinning the mountainous volume of straw in the third room, offering little more than a nod of my head and a reminder of the pact we had made, before I disappeared into the shadows. This time, I did not stay to see how the king received the completed task, nor did I wait to see if a formal proposal would be made. I had seen more than even I wished to—of all of them—and it was my desire to leave the palace and distance myself from any more of it.

Just when I thought I had come to understand everything that there was of the human race, these last few days occurred and opened my eyes to all new forms of disgust that was to be felt over them and their ways. So I removed myself from society, to the safety of my small cabin in the woods on the outskirts of Nedlitzin. It wasn't a grand affair, but for a home I had built for myself, it was pleasant enough.

Cool in the summer, warm in the winter, with a roof that didn't leak, and floors that were dry, it was more than I had been given in the early years of my life—best of all I had to share it with no one. Though, as I thought of it now, the little cabin I shared with only myself would need to be reworked if I were to be bringing a child into the home. I knew that it could be years, but I would need to be prepared. The small kitchen that was adequate enough for myself would not be suitable for me to prep meals for a human child. I would need to add cupboards, and a place for an ice chest to be installed. Perhaps another window would be of importance, as the space was a little darker than I had realized before. While I was used to a lack of sunshine, most humans seemed to enjoy a great deal of it in their places of habitation.

Of course, another bedroom would be necessary as well, a small room off of the warm living space where the stone fireplace was built into the wall. It was a happy little fireplace, with rocks I had hand picked from the riverbed and stacked upon themselves until there was a mantle and chimney creeping up the wall. The cabin wasn't much, but I thought I could make it into a happy enough home for myself and the child I would be bringing to raise here.

As I had expected, it was only a matter of days before the announcement was spreading around the city and villages proper that the king was to be wed to a beautiful village girl from Nedlitzin who had performed miracles for His Highness. The villagers were ecstatic, and as I slipped back into the town, winding my way through back allies and down back streets until I was able to get into the places I needed, I listened to the talk in passing. The fact that it was one of their own—not a lady of nobility, but a merchant's daughter—seemed to please the people. Katrin, it seemed, would be a queen of the people.

When the wedding finally happened, it was a monstrous affair—days of festivals and celebrations throughout the city. Her dress was an occasion all of its own, yards of satin and lace that had been imported from the far reaches of the globe, and with a train so long and heavy it required six handmaidens to carry it down the aisle for her. They were married in the cathedral as all royal wedded couples are, and once their holy vows were spoken, a carriage transported the king and his new queen throughout the city with a parade following in their wake. It was an ostentatious show of wealth and power that left everyone with something to say for weeks.

Against my better judgement, I was there, seated upon a sill in the clerestory to see the entire production. Watching, as the large cathedral doors swung open to reveal Katrin in her ivory gown that paled in its beauty only when compared to her own. Her golden hair was caught up from her face in a large braided crown that made its way around her head, and was woven with greenery and flowers. I had not seen anything as lovely as she was in that moment—young, fresh, and still filled with the new bloom of life that belongs to young women before they have come into their prime.

While the ceremony itself was long and dull, it was Katrin I remained focused on, she carried herself with a presence of mind that was impressive for someone of her age, and it was my thought that King Ernst may not break her in the end. Her voice rang steady and true as she repeated her vows, and there did not seem to be any hesitation in her actions as she stretched out her hand for him to slip the wedding band upon her finger. It would seem, she had fully committed to this new position in life, and was prepared to be the steadfast woman at his side who did not falter.

Queen of them all—thanks to gold thread she had not spun. Queen, thanks to a lie woven in the darkness of a tower cell.

I didn't stay to watch the days of feasting and drinking that followed, extravagance and excess was a human trait that I did not need more proof of. Most creatures that live, take only what they need to survive, or what they need to prepare for the coming winter when rations are low and food scarce. Humans however, ate more than what they needed, then threw away the rest. They took more than was their fair share, and saw nothing wrong with this bad habit. King Ernst was the most guilty of this tendency. Throwing celebrations, that while they brought pleasure to his people, wasted precious resources and sometimes left people without, once all was said and done.

After the exuberance of the wedding, and the celebrations that surrounded it, Postdamburg settled into a quiet state and winter fell upon the city. I remained in my small cabin in the woods outside Nedlitzin, steadily finishing things around the cabin that would make it more hospitable for a child, and also keeping an ear open for any news that an infant was to be expected.

Two years passed before the news came. It was early fall, and Katrin had just celebrated her eighteenth name day, when the cry went out through the Royal City and travelled to the outlying towns. The queen was with child—King Ernst would have an heir. Except the child wasn't meant to be his, the child was meant to be mine, and had been since that fateful day.

To ensure that my investment was being taken care of, and that Katrin remembered the promise she had made me, I ventured to the palace once again. As easily as a shadow, I traversed the hallways of the king and queen's home, passing servants with little concern. Katrin had not yet begun her lying in, when I discovered her in a small personal room where she and her ladies-in-waiting sat stitching patterns onto linen pulled taught in wooden hoops. She was not alone though, Moritz had come to visit. Moritz, looking even wealthier than the last time I had seen him.

Being the father-in-law of the king did wonders for a man's status.

Katrin looked pale, and as her father approached and knelt before her, she requested that all her handmaidens leave them for a private audience. Obediently, the women filed out until it was only Katrin and her father remaining.

"Father, I have urgent news that I need inform you of. The truth of how I spun the straw into gold and became queen, and what that has to do with my present state. It is the cause of my constant concern."

Moritz took her hand in his own and patted the top of it gently, while his other hand clasped it tenderly within his hold.

"How it was done no longer matters Katrin, not when you are now queen."

Katrin leaned forward, grabbing both of his hands between her own and clinging to them tightly, her gaze was intent upon him.

"But, Papa, it does. There was a little man with large, dark eyes and long, pointed ears, who came to me from the shadows like a house goblin. He told me that he could save me, that he could spin the straw, but made me give him first my locket in exchange. You know the one, with the coriander seeds? And the next night it was Mother's ring." She held up her hand to show that it no longer bore that particular piece.

Her father was looking at her with concern and a dawning suspicion. I could tell that his thoughts were not going in the direction that Katrin was hoping.

"Kat..." his tone was chiding, wishing to stop her before she went further.

"No, Papa, it's the truth. Both nights he spun the straw for me, that's how it happened. However, on the third night I had nothing to give him...I had come here with only what was on me and Ernst wanted me to be his wife, and you did as well. So I did what I had to. I *promised* what I had to."

Moritz was gazing at her uneasily, the spinning cogs in his mind visible, and I wondered what it was he thought she was going to say.

"Promised what?"

Instead of responding to his question verbally, Katrin placed a hand over her stomach to signify the unborn child within. His eyes dropped, and Moritz visibly jerked backwards a little, then surged forward to grasp her upper arms.

"What have you done to the child, Katrin? What are you planning? That could be the king's heir. Whatever the voices are saying, you can not do anything."

"Papa...no. I'm not—I'm not mad. I'm speaking the truth! There was a small, elvish creature that came to help me, you need to believe me, or he will come and take the baby once it's born."

I needed to see no more, it was clear that Katrin had not forgotten our pact, and that she was taking it seriously. As much as she may wish to get herself out of it, the magic of the vow was binding and she would have to give me the child when I came to collect it.

The next few months passed without incident. I travelled into Nedlitzin when I was bored and wished to be entertained by the people there, all the while keeping my ears open for the birth we were all waiting on. Occasionally, I pondered what excuse Katrin would use once the child was gone. Would she claim death, or perhaps, that the child had been stolen? It would be easier for all if she merely claimed the child had not survived its birthing.

They say that the young queen laboured all through the night to bring new life into the world and that King Ernst paced the halls outside his throne room as he awaited news of an heir. But the summer day was lovely, and the sun bright, when the bells tolled in the early morning air just after dawn to signal the birth of a new royal. The tolling was followed by the announcement that the queen had birthed a daughter—The Crown Princess of Germaine, Princess Imelda Leona Liese.

The king was wroth, the little princess was meant to be a prince and succeed him on the throne, an heir to confirm his legacy and carry on his bloodline. The queen had failed him in that respect, but I could not be happier. In my little cabin, a sweet little room had taken shape that I filled with fresh cut floral, and arranged with silks and satins ensorcelled from naive village people. Most importantly, were the locket and ruby ring that were protected in velvet boxes awaiting the moment when I could gift them to the little princess—to offer her a piece of her human life, and tell her of the woman who had bore her, and given me the family that I could not achieve on my own.

For my kind, I was very young to be considering a family of my own. Due to the long, indefinite stretch of an elve's existence, it was most common to wait until after the age of adulthood had settled upon them before considering marriage and breeding. Most often well into the first—if not second—century of life. Yet for me, waiting for the age of adulthood to be upon me was not an option. Life had seen fit to finally reward me, to bring into my path the opportunity for a child, and I was meant to seize it now.

While a disappointment to Ernst, the princess would be my pride and joy, the first creature to come into my existence who loved me unconditionally—the daughter I would otherwise not be able to have.

The king and queen may want to have a proven succession, but thrones and kingdoms were not of my concern, and I would build for myself the one thing I had always been denied. From out of this mess would come my family, and little Imelda would want for nothing. Of that, I would make certain.

I gave them until that evening before I made my appearance, slipping first into the small nursery where the babe was being kept and watched over by a wet nurse. I had already taken in a goat to aid in that part for me, just as I had supped from goats milk and grown strong, my child would as well.

She was a sweet, cherub cheeked creature—fresh white skin with the blush of new life beneath it, and a slight smattering of blonde curls upon her round head. Though she slept, she made soft smacking noises—dreaming of feedings to be had, and warm nuzzles. Leaning over the bassinet, I brushed a knuckle along her silken cheek, and felt the stirring of something within my chest. An emotion that was swelling and spreading outwards to encompass me in my entirety.

"Soon, little one, and we'll go home."

Katrin was not sleeping when I found her—not like I had expected. It seemed that she had been waiting for me to appear, and as I slipped from the shadows, she sat upright in her bed. There was a bundle of blankets about Katrin's legs and in her grasp she had what appeared to be a letter opener.

"So you have come," she murmured into the space between us.

My head nodded to the piece of metal in her clasp.

"You were expecting me, but just what is it you plan to do with that?"

"Whatever it is that I must to keep you from taking my daughter. I am surprised you've come here first, and not simply snuck off with her into the shadows you dwell in."

"Above all else, I am a creature of honour. The deal was struck between you and I, therefore you must be the one to relinquish her."

"Then I shan't do it. You may not have her, I refuse." Katrin's face had aged somewhat in the two years since our parting. She had the look of a girl grown into womanhood, and there was now a deeper understanding of the world and how it worked resting within her eyes. Motherhood, I thought, had done a lot of that, and King Ernst the rest.

"And if that be the case, you will die."

"You will kill me then, to take what you want?" Her gaze was hardened upon my features.

"No, but the vow was of a magical nature, and it is binding. Unless you have magic to break it, it will claim your life to repay the debt owed, and I will take the child anyway."

"Debt," she spat out the word, a desperation filling the newfound tension in her form.

"Yes, debt. We had an arrangement and agreed on an exchange. That is how the magic was able to happen."

Her hands pressed to her face, and I thought perhaps she was trying her best not to cry.

"I am queen now...please, take anything else but my daughter. I will give you anything else," she pleaded with me.

"I cannot. All the valuables in the land do not equal that of a human life."

Katrin flung aside her covers, and launched herself—staggering—from her large, four-poster bed, to land on her knees before me with hands raised upwards in a motion of begging.

"*Please?* I beg of you, there must be *something* that can be done instead?"

My dark eyes took her in, knelt upon her knees, her present height offered a few spare inches so that I now looked down upon her. I studied the stress etched lines upon her face, which pain and fear had wrought, and knew that in some small way I could ease her pain. Though it wasn't needful in the least—and it was well within my right to refuse her and claim the child for myself—I couldn't help but think of the sweet, innocent Katrin I had watched in her family home. The same, sweet Katrin, I would later tell Imelda of, and the way in which she had captivated me until I was forced to come forward to help her.

It was for that sweet girl of memory, that I spoke.

"I can only offer but a chance," I warned her, voice soft.

"Anything!"

"I will give you three different chances, on three different nights, to guess my name." In a lot of ways it was a trick in and of itself. My 'name' was naught but a cruel joke thrust upon me by cave trolls, rather than any true gift bestowed upon an infant—and there was not a soul left alive who knew it.

"If you should guess correctly, our debt shall be considered settled and the little princess will remain with you. However, if by the third night you have failed to guess, Imelda will leave with me as was intended." I paused to look down at her.

"Do I have any actual chance of succeeding?"

"Of course. So...do we have an agreement?"

"Yes," it was upon a pitiful breath that the agreement was released.

"Excellent, tonight we shall begin. Your first guess?"

Katrin didn't bother to move from her position, instead, she sat back on her heels and peered up at me.

"Maurice?"

"No." One of my brows lifted towards her. "Tonight's second guess?"

This turn, she took a little more time to think about it, before issuing a name.

"Gustaf?"

"No." I raised my hand and produced three fingers to encourage her on towards her third name.

She sat there for some time, and her thoughts were so loud that I could almost see her going over each and every one of the men that she knew in her lifetime, trying to imagine what names might be most suited to a tiny creature that visited her from the shadows.

"Klaus?"

I simply shook my head and turned from her, heading towards the darkened corner of the room.

"Better luck tomorrow night."

"You said I had a chance!"

I turned back to her, gazing somewhat over my shoulder, at the figure knelt in despair upon her knees in the centre of the room.

"You do, but there are a lot of names in the world, and you must choose only one."

I couldn't bring myself to feel sorry for her. Katrin had chosen her lot in life, nearly three years ago, when she asked that I turn the third room of straw into gold in exchange for her firstborn child so that she may become queen. She could have asked for anything in the world, but what she had wanted was to marry a greedy, cruel hearted man, and wear his crown.

I slept well that night, after I returned to my cabin in the woods, and rested easy all through the next day, for I had offered Katrin the glimpse of hope that she needed—though it be nothing but a poultice for an inevitable wound. Two more nights remained, but try and try as she may, Katrin would never guess my name.

It did offer me some form of amusement to ponder her behaviour today. Had she kept this to herself, or was she seeking the help of her ladies-in-waiting and any other person that happened into her room? What names would pass over her tongue this evening when I returned?

It was with this curiosity, that I returned to the palace that night, slipping unheard through the halls. As I had the night before, I went first to the nursery, gazing down at the sleeping wonder that lay nestled inside the small bed. This time, she woke, vivid blue eyes the colour of a crystal clear lake on a summer day peering up at me. She didn't startle, nor did she cry. Rather, she looked up at me in a steady manner that pierced me straight through to my core, and left me open and vulnerable.

"I will give you the world, Princess," I vowed softly, and brushed my fingers lightly over the top of her head. The soft fuzz of curl felt like satin beneath my touch, and it made my heart hurt in a way I had not yet felt. There was a frailty and delicateness to this tiny form that I had not at first imagined.

Not allowing myself too much time spent in the nursery, I went to Katrin's chambers who—seated this time at a small table with a lamp burning in the centre of it—was waiting for me. On the table before her was a sheet of paper, upon its surface were a number of names listed, crossed out, and re-scribbled. Katrin, it would seem, had been very busy.

"Good evening, Your Highness." I flourished a bow, only partially from a mocking spirit, and righted myself.

Katrin looked weary—the sign of her sleepless night worn there upon her face—which made me believe that she loved her daughter, and had no desire to let her go. Promises made easily years ago, before the weight of motherhood had settled upon her, were now weighing more heavily than she had anticipated. At sixteen, Katrin had not thought this would hurt as terribly as it did, at eighteen.

"I have no need for pleasantries. Ancel?"

Her features had never looked so fierce as they did that night, she had found a strength within her that, I think, caught both of us by surprise.

"I see we are getting straight to the point tonight," I murmured, and straightened the little forest green jacket that I wore. "No, not Ancel."

Katrin's eyes dropped to the sheet of paper before her, fingers gliding down over the names listed, perhaps with the hope that the correct one would leap from the page towards her.

"Leander?"

I snorted softly, unable to help myself. "What mother would gift a child, with this god-awful face, such a fanciful name? No."

There was a tension building once more in her shoulders as the hopelessness of this cause became even more apparent with each wrong answer. She was quiet, seeming to be lost in thought, as she stared down at her list.

"Your third name, my Lady?"

"Clemens?" she whispered.

I could appreciate the irony—a name that meant merciful. She could only hope.

"No, that is also, not my name."

I did not wait for any further exchange, rather, I turned silently to slip out of the room. It was a sign of my own hubris that I did not contemplate the desperation of a mother's love, or the extent to which one would go to protect her child. Having now spent years slipping in and out of this palace undetected, I no longer concerned myself with the thought of being seen, which was how I failed to take note of the figure following along behind me as I left the palace. Nor, did I notice as it followed me on my way into Nedlitzin, before the both of us disappeared into the woods.

It was late, and once again, I turned in for the night with strong confidence that the next evening would see me returning with the little princess so that we could begin our new life. I wasn't aware of the eyes watching me from the windows, or that they remained there in the bushes the whole night through.

Come morning, I was singing—the excitement and happiness within my form could not be contained. In just a few short hours, I would have the start to my very own dreams. The one thing that had remained out of my grasp for all of these years would soon be mine. For tonight I would acquire my own version of a family. No one could love the little princess as I could—one who had been denied love all of his existence, and had wanted nothing but. I would not wrong her, as the cave trolls had me, nor use her for my own gain. With me, Imelda would be honoured and cared for, which was more than what I could say of her human father.

The day had proven just as happy as myself, mirroring the sunshine inside me with the brightness of its sky. In the heat of the day, I worked out in the yard, picking a large bouquet of wildflowers that grew naturally around the cabin. I filled the house with them, so that the scent that greeted us tonight would be warm and fresh, welcoming my daughter to her true home.

As I worked, I hummed, which turned into a tavern song I had once heard soldiers singing around a late night fire. Eventually, the lyrics changed to ones of my own.

"Soon, soon, I'll bring you home, forever I shall be your cornerstone. And for me, you shall be the same, for they will never guess, that Rumpelstiltskin is my name."

I couldn't seem to contain myself, and like a small child I waltzed about the yard until my arms were full of flowers, continuing to sing my song to the animals of the woods. Once I had all that I could carry, I set to work scattering them around the cabin, and within the room Imelda would call her own.

That night, when I arrived at the palace, I did not stop first at the nursery—when I stepped into that room, I wanted to be able to pick her up and take her with me. Instead, I went straight to the queen's chambers, but found her not alone. This time, Moritz stood at her back, his hand resting upon her shoulder.

I gazed at the two of them in mild curiosity, did they think that when she failed to guess my name, he would be able to over power me, and stop me from taking the princess with me? I also noted that Moritz did not startle as I appeared in the room, and I wondered when he had begun to believe his daughter's tales of the small goblin who'd come to help her, when last I had seen, he had thought her mad.

"I see that we have company this evening."

"Will that be an issue? He can leave." The hand upon her shoulder tightened, a silent comment that Moritz did not agree.

"No, your father may remain."

This comment did elicit a reaction from both of them, despite all that had happened, neither of them had expected me to know who Moritz was. Had I been meant to think that this aged man was the king, and that they were presenting a united front? I doubted highly that Ernst was at all aware the presence of his daughter in the palace was up for question.

Katrin nodded to my words and pulled her slip of paper towards herself. Were they the same names as had been there before, or had she replenished the list with fresh ideas?

"Your first guess?" I prodded. I was done with the charade and wished to be done with this, she'd had her chance, now I wanted to take my daughter home.

"Hamin?" she asked, after a show of contemplation.

"No. Your second guess?" My heart was beginning to hammer faster in my chest as the moment drew nearer.

There was a longer pause this time, both of us aware that this was the last and final night, that at the end of these guesses, she would have no more.

"Anatoly?" Our eyes met across the room.

"Incorrect. Your final guess, Your Highness? And do take your time with this one," I taunted, with perhaps a sign of victory shining within my eyes.

Katrin however, had not given up, nor was she looking as defeated as I would have thought. Instead, there was a light of something growing in her own eyes, one that I could not place.

"Is your name...Rumpelstiltskin?"

"No— " Over the pounding of my own heart, thinking that her fate was now sealed, I almost didn't hear her, and was quick to state my dismissal of her guess. Only she hadn't guessed wrong, and there was triumph in her gaze, and a sick sort of victory gleaming in the eyes of Moritz. I shook my head in denial, because this was not possible.

"No?" Moritz asked, his tone telling me that he already knew the answer, and that somehow I had been the one duped.

"How?" chokingly escaped me, as the tower of hope and happiness that had built up inside me over the past few days began to tumble and crash down around me in an earth shattering way.

It shouldn't have been possible. It *wasn't* possible, but something had taken place that I didn't understand, and somehow the truth had been laid at Katrin's feet.

"Is it, or is it not, your name?" the queen demanded in a harsh, forcible tone, fingers taut upon the end of her armrest.

"Yes. It is my name."

I was desolate, lost to my own shock and grief, I paid no heed to their actions.

Moritz was almost upon me before my wits finally returned, and I realized that I was at risk for true harm—a knife drawn and aimed for my heart.

"Not today!" I shouted at him, stomping my foot viciously against the floor. The force of it rattled the entire room, and the cracking of stones sounded from beneath us as the stone tiles shattered and separated. Katrin gasped, and her father stumbled backwards, his knife clattering to the floor.

They had stolen everything from me in some rotten, foul, play-of-wits that I could not yet fathom, but I would not let them have my life as well. When the floor split fully open beneath me, I allowed my body to be swallowed up into it—disappearing into the hole to be presumed dead and gone. But instead, I fell through the space between, and landed—rather than in the grave—upon the floor in the princess's nursery.

I had not lied when I said that I was a creature of honour, and though I felt broken, I had not come here to take the little princess with me. Rather, I had come to say farewell. In a stealthy manner I made my way to her bassinet, leaning down over it, I looked at the infant who was once again awake. The sight of her was a painful arrow to my heart, and I audibly gasped for breath. The fingers that reached out to her this time trembled with emotion as I attempted to steady myself.

"Plans have changed, Princess, you won't be coming home tonight like we had planned."

I needed to go, I could hear the rush of footsteps down the passageway outside the room, they were coming to make certain I had not taken her anyway.

"But I won't be leaving you—not truly. When you look to the shadows, I will be there."

I had invested too much into this—into her—at this point and it was not something I could just walk away from. There was only so much I was willing to lose after nearly three years of focusing on little else. I leaned over the bassinet a little more so that I could press a kiss to her forehead, and in the space where my lips touched her skin a warm, golden light shone.

"Sleep well, Princess," I whispered, her bright eyes upon my face.

I slipped away into the shadows just as the door to her room opened and there was a rush of bodies filling the space—armed soldiers, Moritz and his small blade, and a frantic Katrin rushing to pull the dainty form from her bed. Imelda's cry of distress split the air just as I disappeared into the space between.

True to my word, I had left—but I was not gone.

ABOUT CHRISTIS CHRISTIE

Christis Christie was born and raised in a small town in New Brunswick, Canada where she spent most of her time either reading someone else's book, or dreaming of writing her own. Her favourite thing to dive into is an epic fantasy, or anything else magical and wondrous that really allows her imagination to take her away.

She now lives on the East Coast in Halifax, Nova Scotia where she works as an event designer, putting her interior decorating degree to wonderful use. Whenever she's not busy magically transforming venues for her clients, Christis is working on her own writing. Currently she has two projects in the works; a YA fantasy novel, and an adult supernatural short story serial.

Her other dreams consist of one day visiting Ireland so she can frolic over the hills, and owning a teacup Pomeranian she can cart around everywhere with her.

CONNECT ON SOCIAL MEDIA

christischristieblog.wordpress.com

facebook.com/christis.christie.1

instagram.com/Tiss.Writes

Becoming the Wolf

by Jessica Julien

I had the dream again. Or should I call it the nightmare. Sometimes it's hard to tell them apart anymore—maybe it's that I just don't remember what the difference is after all this time.

It always starts the same.

I see her playing by the stream, laughing as she leaps in and out of its icy waters. It was a game she liked to play, jumping in with her bare feet and standing as long as she could before they got so cold she couldn't stand it, then jumping out and falling into the sun kissed grass. I never played with her. I hated the cold, numb feeling it always left behind. But I would watch and laugh with her.

We never saw it coming.

It never even made a sound. The townspeople say you can always feel its hovering presence, hear the snapping of a branch, feel the quietness of the forest and surroundings as it approaches. We were always on the lookout, but we never saw the signs. He was like a whisper trailing the wind as it blew through the flock we protected and in an instant she was gone. I heard the scream, the crack of bone, the dragging of the body through the brush.

I wasn't fast enough.

Abandoning the sheep, I rushed to where she had been, splashing into the creek and hurrying through the wheat, following the bloodied trail that grew before me. A gargled cry faded just inside of the woods. I stopped at the edge, peering into the darkness and urging my eyes to see her. I had to save her, but the woods are forbidden for our own protection and I can't force my feet to enter. In my dream, I hear a final scream, the padding of hard steps, and a low, guttural growl before he leaps at me, reaching for my own throat. Just as his teeth sting my neck, I wake up screaming, drenched in sweat, unable to breathe.

It's my fault she's gone. I was supposed to protect her as I protected the flock. More even. Her blood is on my hands and it will haunt me forever.

I splash cold water on my face to calm my nerves and catch my breath. My parents don't come running in when I wake anymore, knowing that the screams are just the bad dreams. They tell me I'm too old to still be having nightmares—that I should move on. After all, it had been two years. Something won't let me, though. The dreams haunted me ever since. A shiver passes down my spine as I trail my fingers over the scars on my neck, the lingering reminder of my failure. No one knows why he spared me—maybe I wasn't his intended target that day, maybe I just got lucky. Some say he will come back for me, that he is waiting for the perfect moment to take me. I'm not sure what to believe.

There's a soft knock at my door.

"Come in," I call, throwing the blanket over the sweat covered sheets.

"Morning, Herrick." My father eases around the wooden door. His tall, thick frame blocks the entrance, casting a chilling shadow into my room. "Sun is up, time to get moving." I see his eyes glance at the wet pillow I forgot to flip over.

"Just about ready." I force a smile.

"Flock is up on the north hill. I need to run into town, think you'll be okay alone for a bit?" His eyes—the same warm brown hue we share—turn down and are lined with worry.

"Yeah, no problem." Quickly slipping on my shoes I take a step towards the door, but my father doesn't budge.

"I can go tomorrow—" he begins.

"No Pop, I'll be fine." Pushing past him, I grab a biscuit off the counter and take a quick swig of blackened coffee before heading out into the fields.

The grass is still dewy on my bare feet as I jog toward the far hill. I can hear the sheep as I approach, and as I climb to the top, the edge of the wood comes into sight. Even though the summer sun is beginning to shine, the forest remains eerily dark, as if even the sun is afraid to penetrate the stoic trees. I let my gaze drift over the tree line to ensure it's stillness, making sure nothing is watching—waiting—before taking my place on the large boulder that is used as the shepherds' resting place.

From here, I can see over the entire flock—they are all too busy chewing grass and leaping over small rocks to be bothered by my presence. I also have a view of the neighbors and can see Farmer Young plowing his field, preparing it for the new season. On the other side, Farmer Mayer is feeding the chickens. Everyone is working at a steady pace, moving at a rhythm with the gentle breeze and rushing stream heard in the distance.

I pick at the biscuit, tossing one piece into my mouth and another at the lamb *baaing* at my feet. She nibbles it before jumping off toward her mother. Laying my head back, I watch a single cloud drift by and let my ears do the work for now. Since there are still a few hours before I need to move the sheep down into the barn, I let my mind wander. My eyes grow heavy as images of fluffy clouds shaped like rabbits dance across my vision.

The silence woke me.

I hadn't meant to drift off, but the nightmares had kept me from a restful night and the rock is warm beneath me. Sitting up, I see the flock had moved down the hill toward home. The sun rising high enough to heat the grass more than they enjoyed. I stand and look around. Everything felt still, as if the world around me was frozen in time.

A movement catches my eye.

I turn quickly to the woods as a shadow passes in the corner of my vision. Low to the ground and large as a fallen stump, the shadow slithers out of view. I hold my breath and listen, urging my ears to pick up the faintest noise but not daring to make any myself. My pounding heart is the only sound that fills my ears. Then I hear it.

A branch snaps.

It echoes off the silence emanating from the forest. I slide off the rock and take a single step toward the sound, wanting to make sure I had actually heard it. Leaning toward the towering trees, I focus all my attention at a single point where I had caught the motion. I tell myself it could just be a woodland creature, maybe even a deer, wandering right at the edge, but I know better. Most animals kept their distance, they too know the danger that lurks deep within it. It is the same reason why we never entered them alone or unless absolutely necessary—it wasn't safe—most people never came back out of the woods.

I would have seen anything else by now. But *him*—he moves like a ghost sliding between the branches and brush and is camouflaged into the darkness.

And then I see it. A flicker. A twitch.

Taking in a deep breath, I run down the hill, scaring the flock that begins to run as well. They barrel past me, scattering and running from the danger quickly approaching from behind. Heavy steps fall behind me, growing closer. I pushed forward without glancing back, afraid of what is coming. Never waste time, always move quickly—that is how you escape. I yell with as much force as I can manage.

"Wolf!" I gasp for air. "Wolf!"

The sheep race past me and into the pen, circling and disoriented from the sudden uproar. I throw the latch on the gate and turn, seeing the neighbors drop their feed and rush towards our farm. A shadow passes over the side of the hill. He is coming—*fast*—looking for an opening to pounce, waiting for someone to make the wrong move and fall into his deadly sight.

"Wolf," I yell again, grabbing the pitchfork nearby and rushing back to where I escaped from. It was his turn to pay. His turn to be scarred and tormented. A rush of energy shoots through me as I force my lungs to push harder against the hummingbird-beat of my heart. My chest burns but I know this is my chance. After two years of waiting, hoping that he wouldn't come back for me, he was finally following through on the lingering promise of blood he left on my throat. After two years of being picked on and laughed at for my nightmares—for being afraid—I was going to prove that I was better than him. I wasn't scared anymore.

But as I come around the side of the hill where the shadow had passed, I hear a noise that stops me in my tracks.

Laughter.

I drop the pitchfork and stumble back. Two boys are rolling on the grass, holding their bellies as they chuckle and point at me.

"What is this?" Farmer Young asks, running up next to me. Sweat drips down his tanned face, and he wipes it away with the back of his hand. Farmer Mayer rushes to our side and sighs heavily.

"Boys, explain yourselves," he demands, cocking his rifle. The two boys instantly get to their feet, taking heavy breaths to try and stop their laughter.

"We were jus' playin'," the one with tight curls and teary blue eyes says through a stifled giggle. I know him and his family. We often trade furs with them in the winter for firewood. He is Nikolas Klaus, a well known troublemaker in the town and the leader of the group known for making fun of me behind my back. There have been many times since my sister's death that we've been pulled apart, fists swinging, because he wanted to show everyone else that I was weak—that he could beat me down.

"Yeah, jus' playin' is all," the other one I recognize as Brekkor Ford, the family whose house burned down this past February because he was *"jus' playin'" with a lit torch* he says. His puffy cheeks are red as a fresh strawberry, and his black hair is stuck to his forehead with sweat. A known follower of Nikolas', his right-hand man, was always there to throw the second stone. He was the beta to Nikolas the alpha.

Tears sting the back of my eyes. It was just a joke. Another silly prank. There was no wolf. No danger. Nothing. I feel my face flush with anger. Clenching my fists I take a step toward them.

"Wait until your fathers hear about this. You scared us all half to death," Farmer Young points at Nikolas and Brekkor before landing his fat finger on me.

"What? No, I didn't…" I stammer putting my hands up in defense.

"You know how dangerous a real wolf can be. Why would you go 'round pretending like that." Farmer Mayer shakes his head, turns and heads back to his farm. He mumbles foul words under his breath—ones I'm not allowed to repeat. Farmer Young follows, waddling down to his garden.

"You shoulda seen your face." Nikolas laughs.

"*Wolf, wolf,*" Brekkor mocked.

"That wasn't funny," I yell and push Brekkor hard making him fall and bounce on his own backside. Before I can catch my footing, Nikolas's fist connects with my lip, and I hit the ground hard. I feel the grass against my cheek, warm and soft. Touching my lip, I feel the hot blood on my fingertip.

"You know what they say about someone who's seen the wolf." Brekkor bends down near me. I look up and our eyes connect. "Especially someone who's been *marked.*" He motions to his throat, and my hands immediately go to the scars on mine.

Nikolas pulls me up near his face by my shirt collar. "You'll be next, Herrick, and no one will save you. You'll disappear forever just like your sister did. No one will save you. No one c—"

"What's going on?" a thundering voice rings. Nikolas and Brekkor take off around the backside of the hill, running as quickly as they can away from my father. "Herrick?" His hand reaches under my arm and pulls me to my feet. I feel his rough, calloused thumb against my cheek and his darkened eyes on my face.

"Nothing, Father," I respond bowing my head in shame. I know I am in trouble. No one cries wolf for fun in our town, no one dared. It wasn't something to joke about, but those boys had made me a laughing stock. Soon, the neighbors would tell the story of how I ran scared from "the Big Bad Wolf" and it would be the worst prank to rumor the town so far.

"Let's get you home, it's near time to eat." I see my father's disappointment as I follow him back to the house.

It always started out as just a game.

Just as I thought, the boys in town heard about the incident with Bekkor and Nikolas, heard that I had been terrified of the wolf and started making howling sounds and laughing when I walked by.

"Little Herrick, terrified of the monster in the woods." They would giggle, pinching my arm as I brush past them into the sweets shop.

My father gave me some money early this morning and told me to go into town and buy some candy.

"What about the flock?" I had asked.

"Don't worry about them today, Herrick. Take the morning off." When I hesitated he nudged me towards the door. "Go. Be a boy. Buy candy and rot your teeth out. Be home by supper though." He practically shoved me out the door, clicking it shut on my heels. I brushed the hair off my already sweating forehead and rolled up my sleeves, taking off towards the town. I take the main road that creates a perimeter around our farms and village enclosing us in a type of walkable barrier from the outside world but not against the woods that sit at its center. Everyone knows walking through the woods was the fastest way to get anywhere but we all take the main road for our own safety.

I didn't think the other kids' games are funny—who would? I didn't like being laughed at. So, after picking out some lemon flavored chews, I head down to the river where the other kids hang out during the day. A group of them stand on the bridge, dropping sticks in only to watch them float down under the bridge and appear on the other side, while the others stand at the edge with their feet in, pants rolled up high, skipping rocks.

"Oh, look who it is." Nikolas smirks.

"Little baby Herrick," another boy *coos* making a crying baby face. I chuckle sticking another piece of sour lemon in my mouth, I won't let them know how much I hated them, won't let them see the anger inside me. I lean against the railing feeling the wood pull against my elbows. Peering over my shoulder, I see the water below is just deep enough to cover your head. The last rain bringing the level up just high enough for everyone to jump in safely. We all swim in the slow current on the hottest days to take the edge off, but I know the others hadn't noticed that Nikolas never went in farther than his knees. A little known fact is that Nikolas couldn't swim—a piece of information I have held onto for just the right moment. *This* moment.

"How's the lip?" Nikolas asks, flicking my ear and leaning in closely. I feel his hot, sticky breath on me and turn to face him. A wave of anger comes over me enveloping my senses and rushing to me cheeks and I know from the amount of heat I was feeling that they had turned into a deep red hue. I don't want to let my hatred take over, but before I can stop myself, I swallow the candy, reach back and spit in his face causing him to stumble back and put his hands up. Quickly, I growl at him shoving his shoulders hard, watching as he falls backward over the wooden railing. Everyone has their limits, and after two years of torment, I have finally reached that point.

Everyone on the bridge rushes to the side, peering down as a splash cuts through their laughter. I back away, watching the boys on the ground rush into the water as Nikolas yells and splashes trying to tread water. I feel my feet hit the soft grass and take off running back toward town, the remaining lemon candy squished in my tight palm.

The game had changed. It was my turn to laugh. And I did—*laugh that is*—once the red-hot anger cooled the farther away I got, the more I laughed. Finally, I had the upper hand. Finally, I had won.

At least for now.

I know that soon he would come for his revenge, like they say the wolf will get me for his, but this time I will be ready. He won't fool me twice.

The rest of the way back to the farm I hum a cheery tune and let the soft summer breeze wash away my worries. I eat the last piece of candy as I wave to my father who is closing the sheep pen and heading for the waterspout. Grabbing the extra bucket, I run after him to help finish the chores before supper.

"Where are you off to so quickly?" The soft, mousy voice instantly draws a smile on my face.

"Ma, you're back!" I hug her tight, inhaling the lavender scent she always carries. My mother has been gone for a week visiting her sister who came down with a bad fever. Unable to care for their four children, my angel mother offered to come stay until she had recovered enough to get back on her feet.

"I am, darling. Now tell me, what kind of trouble have you been causing today?" She smiles gently tousling my wind-blown hair. When I don't answer right away, she places her hand on my shoulder and looks me in the eye. "Go. Help your father. We can talk about it later." Laying a quick kiss on my forehead, she lets me run off to help my father carry water, knowing I would give her a full confession tonight when she asked. I had never lied to my mother, and I wasn't about to start now. I'd have to tell her, but today the game had changed.

Nikolas may have been the alpha wolf yesterday, but today I have threatened his power.

Kicking off our boots, my father and I come into a house filled with the aroma of a freshly made dinner. Scents of roasted chicken and fresh bread surround my nose. I inhale deeply and fall into my chair at the table.

"Herrick?"

"Yes, ma?"

"I know you did not just sit down at my table with a dirty face and muddy hands." She didn't look up from the oven, but she knew—she always knew. I slide out of my seat and rush to clean up, scrubbing as fast as I can, and returning to the table just as dishes are being filled with steamy food.

I only get two bites in before the questions began.

"So, Herrick. Tell me what happened yesterday? Sounds like you had quite a day," my mother asks carefully as she butters a slice of warm bread. I slow my chewing not wanting to start confessing yet.

"Well." I gulp a mouthful of water. "The boys from town tried to trick me."

"*Tried* to trick you, huh?" She didn't buy it. My father must have told her the whole story he heard from the neighbors.

"You cried wolf, son. It wasn't just some prank," my father chimes in.

"They were hiding at the edge of the woods, making noises. I didn't know it was them." I lower my head into my plate as I felt the heat of embarrassment fill my cheeks. The high I had felt earlier from overtaking Nikolas faded quickly. I hear my father sigh heavily and when I look up through my lashes, see that my mother has her hand on his arm.

"It's just—" my mother begins but my father takes over in a soft tone that only makes me feel more guilty.

"We thought after all this time you would be able to tell the difference from a silly prank and the real thing. You gave the neighbors quite the fright, you know." He folds his hands in front of him as if praying I would finally learn to be a man.

"I didn't know it was them," I say, but it comes out as a whisper. "I didn't mean to. I'm sorry."

Pushing back from the table I go to my room, throwing myself onto the bed. Rolling onto my back, Brekkor's words run through my mind about seeing and being marked by the wolf. Maybe he is right and I am destined to become the next victim. Maybe I'll become crazed, running around the town screaming about invisible wolves all the time and be deemed the town dunce. Some people say a single mark can drive a man or woman insane, so much that they take their own lives. Could I really do that to myself? Could I do that to my parents after they lost one child already. Or would I let the wolf and the others continue to play their brutal games with me? Could I prove that I was better than the wolf.

I pushed the thought out of my mind as my mother comes into the room. She opens the window and looks out into the darkening sky.

"The stars are bright tonight, and there is a full moon. You know what that means?"

"No," I say even though I know exactly what that meant.

"The wolves will howl when it's at its height." She takes a seat at the end of my bed and pats my foot. "So tell me, my sweet boy, have you been having the nightmare still?"

I nod. "All the time."

A sad smile crosses her face. "You know, I miss her too. Sometimes, I even have dreams about her and I wake up thinking they were real. They make me sad. Those days are the hardest but you know what helps me?" I shake my head watching her mossy eyes mist over. "Knowing I still have you. We may have lost Harriet, but we didn't lose you both, and for that, I am thankful."

The sound of her name sends a pang of guilt through me. My heart aches for my little sister. I feel warm tears at the edge of my eyes, daring to fall down my cheek. Quickly, I wipe them away.

"It's okay to cry for Harriet, but it's not okay to blame yourself. It wasn't your fault, it could have happened to me or even your father. You know that, right? We don't blame you." She holds my face between her petite hands and looks deep into my eyes. "We love you."

"I know ma, I just miss her." I cry.

"Shh, we all do. But you must remember: no matter how hard it gets, you cannot let your anger or guilt take over and control your actions. That is how a wolf acts, and that is why we despise them—they play on our fears and use our emotions to capture us, just as the boys in town try to play with your fear and your past. But we must be smarter than the wolf. We must show him we are not scared and that we are in control. You must show them who the real alpha is...who the true leader is." Kissing my head, she leaves me and I feel the chilled night air breeze through my open window. Crawling to the edge of my bed, I see the full moon rising high into the sky. Soon, the wolf would howl and he would be looking for his next victim.

A scratching at my window wakes me.

The dream was taunting me again but the noise pulls me from the chase. I open my eyes and listen for the sound again, the lingering reminder of my nightmare still fresh on my mind.

I hear it. It comes like a tiny tink followed by a quick scrape of nails on glass. A guttural exhale causes the hair on the back of my neck to rise and goose bumps to appear on my arms. It is as if my dream was coming out into my reality. My window is still open, just enough for a fist to fit through, maybe even a little more.

My breath comes out in jagged intervals.

Loud. Too loud.

I cover my mouth with my hands as quietly as I can. I don't want whatever was out there to hear me, to know that I am awake. Counting to ten, I slow my breathing, but it catches in my throat as the scratching comes again, this time slow and steady as if it knows I can hear—like it is playing with me.

The wooden sill creaks slightly, as if pressure is being put on it. I squeeze my eyes closed feeling a prowling glare on me. *It's just a dream. It's just a dream.* I chant in my head, hoping I will wake up to the sun rising in the distance, but a quick exhale followed by four fast inhales and I know that I was in trouble.

Sniffing.

The sill creaks again. My heart is pounding against my chest, pumping so hard that I feel each beat in my ears threatening to explode at any moment.

A fast exhale through the nose.

Snap.

I jump. The window is opening. Stuck in the sun melted paint, it is forced to unlock itself and slide ever so slightly.

A low growl.

I count to five and throw myself off the side of my bed. Hitting the ground with a loud thud, I dart to the door and toss it open, race to my parents room and open their door like a tornado, slamming it shut behind me. My father jumps out of bed, grabbing his gun from the corner. My mother sits up, pulling the blankets over her as if they were going to protect her. I couldn't catch my breath. My head is spinning and I let my body slide to the floor, my back scrapes against the door. I let my eyes glance at their window.

Closed. Safe.

"Herrick?" my mother whispers.

"What on earth are you doing?" Father asks lowering the gun.

"I...there..." I gasp. "My...window..." I spit between breathes. My mother knelt beside me. Reaching up, she wipes tears off my cheek I hadn't realized were there. She runs her hands through my hair and pulls me close to her, but I push back locking eyes with my father. "Wolf," I say clearly.

He races to the door and swings it open as I scramble out of the way. I hear his heavy footsteps fall against the wood floors and him yell out to the neighbors *wolf*. Our front door opens and clicks shut behind him. A shadow passes over their window, my father's image moves quickly over the lace curtains as he makes his way to my window.

A shot echoes into the night.

"Blast you," my father yells. My mother and I exchange looks of confusion before getting up and racing toward the front door. We stand on the porch, my mother with the iron stove poker in her hand and me defenseless, waiting for my father to return. The neighbors light a lantern and appear on their porch. They heard the shot. I saw Farmer Young running toward our house, gun in hand.

"What is it?" he huffs as my father rounds the corner with Nikolas's ear between his fingers and a tail-wagging dog behind him.

"Ouch," Nikolas cries as my father shoves him onto the porch.

"Nikolas Klaus. You ought to be ashamed of yourself for scaring us half to death." My mother nudges him in the side with the fire poker.

"It was *you?*" I exclaim feeling my pulse quicken.

"It's just payback, ma'am." Nikolas rubs his side.

"Payback?" my father asks.

"Yes sir, for pushing me into the river today."

"I only did that cause of what *you* did," I spit, unable to contain my anger. It had been another joke, another prank to scare me and make me cry wolf. I shove him back and my mother grabs my arm. Farmer Young shakes his head.

"So there is no wolf?" he asks. Instantly I drop my head. I know I'm in trouble. This was the second time I had called for help when none was needed.

"Psshh." He throws his hands up. "See if we ever come runnin' again," he grumbles stomping back to his home.

"Sorry for the bother," my father calls and I can hear the disappointment in his voice as Farmer Young leaves our property.

"Come now, Nikolas, let's go tell your father where you've been tonight." I watch my father tug at Nikolas's arm and push him toward the path that would lead him to the Klaus' small apartment above their family grocery store before I stomp off to my room.

Slamming the window shut and pulling the wool blanket I used as a curtain over it, I flop face down onto my bed. For the second time this week, I've been made the fool and I swear that this will be the last time.

I keep to myself for the next few days, waiting, and watching the tree line while I guard the flock with a severe sense of want and anger. I want Nikolas to try again, to dare just one more time to get me to call wolf because this time I was ready. This time he would be the one crying himself to sleep with guilt and embarrassment.

Before I took to the hill this morning, I stole into the shed and selected a small pair of hand shears, tucking them into the waist of my pants. I won't be caught off guard again. This time I would make sure he got what he deserves.

Everything is quiet—a good quiet—the kind of quiet you expect on a hot summer day where the birds chirp happily, the sheep *baa* and play, and the trickling creek can be heard in the distance. I train my eyes on the trees, watching for any kind of movement and keep my gaze on a gradual rotation, moving from edge to edge. Sweat drips down my face from the beating sun. I swallow hard and feel the small amount of saliva push down my rough throat. My eyes begin to feel heavy. Just as drowsiness is setting in, a rustling sounds behind me.

Jumping off the rock, I reach behind me for the shears but stop just as I feel them graze my finger tips.

"Ma, you scared me." I let out a breath and put my hand on my chest. "I thought—"

"Sorry, it's just me." She smiles, petting one of the lambs that trot up to her. "I brought you some bread and water. I thought you could use a little snack and break." I take the bread and chug the chilled water, feeling the edge of exhaustion release.

"Thank you," I manage through a full bite of buttered bread. I watch my mother take a seat in the grass, stretching her feet out before her and letting the sun beat down on her pale face. Her sandy hair that mirrors mine is pulled back and up off her shoulders, but wisps of gray, unable to hide, stand out against the sunlight.

"You should go take a dip in the creek…cool off a bit." She hangs her head back, closing her eyes. "The sun feels so good today." She sighs. I toss the last piece of bread into my mouth and make an agreeable mumble returning my eyes to the woods. "Herrick," she begins.

"Yes, Ma?" I respond, gulping down the final bite.

"Go." She laughs. "The woods will still be here when you return. I will watch the flock for five minutes." Tucking her legs under her, she nuzzles a chubby sheep that approaches her. "You can still see us from the edge of the creek, we will be fine. Now go." She waves me away like a buzzing fly. Taking a final glance at the woods to ensure nothing is lurking, I nod and run over to the water's edge, taking glances over my shoulder at the flock and my mother. The cold water would feel good and help me wake up. I know it is the best option if I want to continue to patrol for the troublemakers.

Quickly, I strip off my shoes and roll up my pant legs. Dipping one foot in, the icy water forces me to pull back. I remember how Harriet used to jump right in—she never tested the water, never gave herself the chance to chicken out. The memory of her makes me smile and forget about the sun for just a moment. Taking her memory as my lead, I take a deep breath and jump in, my feet hitting the rounded rocks on the bottom and splashing cold water up on my pants.

Harriet would have been proud of me. She knew how much I really hated the freezing water.

I feel instantly better and more relaxed now that my body is cooling off. I bend down and splash water on my face, neck, and let it drip down my back soaking my shirt. When I look up, I see it.

A shadow passing behind a tree.

I blink and it's gone, but I know what I saw. Panic strikes me and I freeze in place. Paralyzed, I stare at where the shadow disappeared. It was just a flicker—just a subtle movement—but I knew.

Listening carefully, the woods take on a deathly silence. Not even the creek around me dares to make a sound when the wolf comes around. Slowly, I reach for the shears and take a single step out of the water toward the forest.

Yellow eyes find me and blink.

I step back and splash into the water. The noise rushing back as I come up for air, clawing at the sides of the creek for safety. It wasn't deep, but an even colder current hugs me, embracing me from head to toe this time, and knocks the air out of my lungs. I pull myself up onto the grass and look back at the spot where the eyes had been.

Gone.

Footfalls sound in the woods as branches brake and snap under its weight. I know that hadn't been Nikolas or Brekkor—even they were smart enough not to run *into* the woods. I know it had been the wolf. He had been watching me. Waiting.

"Herrick." My mother pants. "Are you alright? I saw you fall in. What were you doing?" She feels me over for any broken bones, cuts, or imperfections.

"Nothing, I just th—" I pause glancing back at the forest before looking my mother in the eye. "I just slipped. Didn't get my footing when I stepped out." For the first time in my life, I lied to my mother. "No big deal, I'm fine." I give her a reassuring smile.

"Oh, good." She wipes her brow clearly believing me. I had never lied to her before, but it came so easily, so naturally, that she didn't think twice about what I had told her. "Well, let's get back to those sheep, how about?" I nod in agreement and follow her back to the flock. As she says goodbye to go prepare supper, I lean against the boulder, shears in hand, watching for any more signs of the wolf.

That night, I stare out my bedroom window, watching for any more movement or glance at those yellow eyes. Knowing the wolf would haunt my dreams if I went to sleep, I continue my watch over the flock through the night, but as the grating sounds of my father's snores and small tired *baas* from the sheep reach me, they work as a lullaby that rock me into the arms of morpheus.

Harriet laughs, water splashing up all around her as her feet break the surface of the creek, her rich curls bouncing on her shoulders as she jumps out again. Icy drops hit my bare feet and I pull back in shock, only making her laugh harder, rising into a merry squeal.

I turn to check on the flock. It only takes a moment. One instant. When I look back, she is gone. Frantically, my eyes drift into the creek hoping she hadn't slipped in and hit her head on a rock, drowning in the frozen rush. She isn't there. I hear her cry in the distance and see on the other side of the creek a bloody trail bending the grass down around it.

I sprint. But as always, I can't catch her. A snap of bone shakes me. It sounds wrong though this time, like wood breaking instead of solid bone.

I shoot up breathing heavily. The sound is different, so much so that it had brought me from my nightmare. I wait to see if it would come again, lifting my head to the slightly ajar window. Outside, it is quiet, as if the blanket of night had also worked as buffer to the crickets and nocturnal nature of the dark.

Wood cracks again. This time, I know where it had come from. I see the scrambling of sheep as they push into the corner of the pen, their wooly shadows like ghosts against the glowing moon. Jumping from the bed, I grab the shears and tuck them back into my waistband and as I tiptoe quickly out the front door, snag the fire poker, grasping it tightly.

A low snarl rumbles opposite the flock. What was once a calming *baa* has turned into frightful squeals as mother sheep try to shield their young. As I round the pen, the intruder freezes, his yellow eyes catching mine. We both stop, staring each other down.

I know I should be scared.

Finally, I had come face to face with my nightmare, but in reality, I was annoyed and irate. Gripping the poker in my right hand, I feel the sweat bead on my palm. My heart is racing, skipping beats to keep up with my building rage. This was the moment I had been waiting for since he stole Harriet away from my family and he knows it. I can see it in his gleaming eyes, as if, with his one raised brow, he is daring me to come after him.

Tension builds in his back legs so quickly, I don't have time to react. He pounces on the sheep nearest him and tears a gaping hole in its side. Blood seeps out around the wool, coating it in moonlit crimson.

"No," I yell, scrambling for the pen door where the flock is pushing to find an escape. I throw the latch and they stampede past me toward the house. A lantern lights in the window below—someone else has heard the commotion.

"Wolf," I scream in warning.

As I step toward the rough brown coat crouched over the shredded sheep, he turns to face me. Blood soaks his snout in a dark ruby, dripping steadily off his jowl onto the already dirtied paw reaching in my direction. I lift the fire poker high enough so if he jumps again, it will strike him hard in the ribs or stomach. He snarls, showing his sharpened teeth and takes one step toward me.

My father is stepping softly behind the pen with a raised gun. I let my eyes flicker to him, fear finally pricking the back of my neck. Willing him to look at me but not daring to let my eyes linger too long, I raise my other hand in front of me to signal my father to stop. The motion makes the wolf stop and tip his head to the side with curiosity. I feel his gaze drift from mine down to my neck where his scars still sit from our last meeting. As if recognizing who I am, he relaxes slightly. It is the opening my father needs and he takes the shot.

"No," I yell, but it's too late. The wolf whimpers, turning sharply and lunges over the gate right onto my father. Landing hard against the ground and rolling away from the pen, my father groans under the weight of the creature, attempting to shove his face away from his throat. I run toward them, glancing at the neighbors houses in hopes that they had heard the shot and are now coming to help. There are no lights, though, or show of anyone waking.

"Get off." I stab the fire poker at him, but it is too late. His teeth have sunken into my father's shoulder, tearing the muscle away as he screams in agony. The sharp jab jars him enough to release my father but the damage is already done. Blood quickly grows into a puddle around him and the wolf, now locking eyes with me again, lets out a throaty bark that sprays warm blood on my arm.

My father inches toward the gun that now lays just out of reach of his good arm. The wolf sees his movement and brings his nose down on my father's face as if daring him to grab it and shoot. They both are injured. I see the fur darken in his hind leg where the first shot hit him.

"Herrick." I hear my mother's shaking voice as she stands, seeing my father bleeding before me. "Herrick, run," she shouts lifting a kitchen knife in front of her. The wolf sees her, realizing he is now outnumbered, howls and snaps his jaw around my father's throat. My mother screams as the sound of breaking bone cracks through our farm. The memory of Harriet ring through me—the same sound had ruined my life once already. The wolf would not win this time.

I move to stab the wolf with the shears I now have clutched in my free hand, but my mother is faster. She springs at the wolf, knife in hand, and shoves it hard into his side. They roll before the wolf ends up on top of her, the knife handle sticking out from his front shoulder. My mother turns her head to look at me, tears streaming down her face. Her eyes are wide and so much like Harriet's it pushes me back a step. They are filled with love and sorrow knowing what is about to happen next.

"Run," she mouths as the wolf snaps, dropping his head onto her throat and tearing it away in a single motion. The light drains out of her, the once mossy green of her eyes always filled with life, fades into a deep emptiness. I stand in complete bewilderment. Everything had happened so quickly.

I look between my dead father and my dying mother, torn to pieces and tossed about like rag dolls, blood stains what was once a lush grassy opening, sheep continue to run and hide in any corner they can find, and I stand there, paralyzed in confusion.

How could this have happened? Not only have I lost my sister, Harriet, but now my entire family has fallen to the blood lust of the wolf.

I spot the gun laying near my father, his hand still reaching for it in hopes of saving us all. I knew the wolf would see me if I tried to grab it, so I hold the fire poker tighter and take a single step towards him. Hearing my steps, he begins a guttural growl that grows from almost a whisper into a rumbling thunder. Covered in my family's blood, he steps towards me, lowering himself to make it easier to jump at me and pin me to the ground.

"Herrick, stop!" Farmer Young yells as he cocks his shotgun, but I ignore him, taking a step between the gun and the wolf.

"You remember me, don't you?" I spit feeling heat rise within me. The wolf barks in response shaking more drops of warm blood onto me.

His back legs tense and I move quickly. Raising the poker in front of me and moving one foot back to support the tumble, the wolf leaps and connects with the split end of the rod at the same time the gun fires.

A bone shattering howl sends a shiver down my spine and I release the weapon. Lashing out, the wolf's front paw rips across my chest shredding the thin nightshirt I am wearing. I feel weightless, as if floating on a cloud, before I feel the ground crash beneath me. His slash has knocked me over and now I lay defenseless on the ground.

Another shot echoes but misses, digging a small crater into the ground before him. The smell of fresh dirt reaches me.

My chest feels hot, like a warm summer rain has soaked into the fabric and was now absorbing the rays that escaped through the clouds. There is a metallic taste in the air. It smells like static and dirt, as if a storm were approaching, building energy to throw down bolts and thunder. I lay there, unable to move, and let the earth around me spin as if everything is as it should be.

How could this have happened? I knew to call for help when the wolf was spotted, yet no one had come in time. No one came to save my family. No one had come in time to save me, and now I couldn't even save myself.

I roll my head to the side and see the wolf crouching just feet away from me. His yellow eyes watching me, blinking slowly. A whine escapes him, his nose twitches, and a sting of agony floods me. Did I feel sorry for the wolf? I watch as his chest inflates as if in slow motion and wince. He is suffering. He is in pain…but so am I. It is his fault this happened, wasn't it? We watched each other as the sound of crickets and *baaing* returned.

I hear Farmer Young reload his gun, the ammo falling into place one by one. He cocks it and the wolf's ears perk up. Letting out a final howl, the wolf takes off toward the woods limping and leaving a trail of fresh blood behind him.

I roll over on my side and looking down, see the new marks the wolf has left. Four thick, straight wounds tear across my chest, deep and ugly, but nothing that would kill me. Not quickly at least.

Remembering the masacre around me, I crawl over to my mother. Her body lay limp covered in claw and teeth marks. I feel fresh, hot tears stream down my face. As carefully as I can, I lift her hand in mine feeling her soft skin and wrapping her long fingers around my palm.

"Mama," I cry in barely a whisper. My head feels light and stars begin to dance at the edge of my vision. I kiss her hand then place it next to her in the bloodied grass. I reach up to close her eyes but my hands are shaking and I feel the trembling begin to take over my entire body. I collapse forward onto my hands.

Without saying a word, Farmer Young kneels down and closes my mother's eyes. If not for all the blood, I would think she were only sleeping. A sob escapes me and strong, warm arms wrap around my shoulders.

"What in God's name," Farmer Mayer gasps out of breath. I look up, and see his wide eyes taking in the scene before him. Letting the barrel of his rifle kiss the ground, he runs his free hand through his already tousled hair.

"The wolf," I respond, pushing out of Farmer Young's grip and pulling myself up onto my feet.

"The wolf?"

"Yes," I snap. "The *wolf*." I feel the ground tip below me. Farmer Young reaches for me but I step back and regain my footing on my own. "The one you didn't believe me about and now look what's happened." My voice is loud...louder than I had expected but I was furious.

I can't bring myself to look away from my fallen family before me, but at the same time, it's too horrible to take in, and a tightness wraps itself around my lungs. Farmer Young and Farmer Mayer don't say anything—they are watching me with extreme caution, afraid of what I may do next.

Out of the darkness of the woods comes a sound that causes a wave of adrenaline to release the vice inside me and pulls my attention away. It slices through the quietness of night raising the hair on the back of my neck.

A howl.

Without hesitation, I push past my neighbors and take off toward the tree line. I hear them call after me, their footsteps falling behind mine, but I do not slow. My body moves without pain, without worry, without pause as I hit the forest floor in perfect stride. Fueled by the loss of my family I rush deep into the heart of the woods.

The moss covered ground absorbs my steps—I am as silent as the wolf—and as I run further into the depths of the trees, the less sounds I hear at all, as if the forest is vacant of all life except for the lone wolf who prowls beneath its treetops. I slow, feeling as though I have run in a circle until something catches my eye and I push forward. My feet take me down a small deer path about a half mile in, leading to what I hope is the wolf's den, where shadows cast by the moon dance along the treeline.

I come to an urgent halt at the end of the path as multiple pairs of yellow, grey, and brown eyes greet me. The adrenaline has my heart beating so fast I can feel the pulse behind my eyes, in my ears, and through my entire body. It's as if the world has slowed—everything blurs. I shake my head to refocus and see a wolf pack staring me down. They surround one of their own who lays motionless on the packed earth.

Something wasn't right, though. As I let my eyes drift across the pack, taking in a handful of twitching ears and sniffing noses, I notice that none of them are growling. They watch me with the same curiosity with which I watch them.

The pile of fur behind the pack moves slightly as he turns his head in my direction. What I can only interpret as shock shines in his wide eyes—shock from seeing a human daring to come into his home. His eyes follow me as I take a slow step toward him. I should be scared knowing that at any moment any one of the wolves could take me down and kill me, but I wasn't. If anything, I felt protected and calm as they carefully moved to let me pass.

As I pull closer, I see the wounds my family had inflicted on him. Deep gashes run along his side and the knife and bullet wound still ooze fresh blood. The fire poker had hit him just below the heart—an injury he would not survive. In this moment, I should feel ecstatic—gleeful even—that I had finally got my revenge for Harriet, for my mother, for my father. But as I watch the life slowly fade from the wolf's eyes, it isn't victory that overcomes me; it is uncertainty. Did I make a mistake because I didn't have all the pieces of his story? Is it *my* fault that my family is gone?

"How could this have happened?" I say to the wolf, eyes half open. "This is all your fault." But his look tells me I am wrong.

And then, as I see the wolf take his final breath, the sadness that fills his eyes as if in apology for all the hate he had caused, the guilt from all the death, the understanding in my own actions, it hits me like lightning.

It isn't his fault my family is dead. It isn't his fault—not entirely.

The pranks. The jokes. The stunts the boys from town had pulled.

Nikolas. Brekkor.

It is their fault.

I had called wolf twice before when there was no fear, no

prowling creature, no threat, and now that I had called again no one had believed me. It was too late by the time help came. The neighbors arrived too late because I had been deemed a liar.

It was their fault.

I had become the laughing stock of the town. No one believed me anymore. Because of them.

It's *their* fault.

As I lay my hand against the wolf's still body, feeling the soft fur between my fingers, I finally see the truth behind the big bad wolf. He only did what he needed to do to protect his pack, to live up to the creature the town had created him to be. He acted out of fear and anger, and now that he is gone, there is no one left to protect them. People will hear that the wolf is dead, the rumor will spread of his fall, the story of my family's sacrifice will flood the town and they will no longer be afraid of the forest.

Images of children running, playing tag, daring each other to climb higher and higher as the pack circles for the kill play in my mind and I realize that the wolf had acted as the protector not only for his pack, but for the townspeople as well, knowing that if they entered their woods, they would be killed. Maybe we have been wrong about the wolf our entire lives. Maybe creating this fear was his way of keeping a type of truce or peace between man and monster to ensure each one survived as long as they kept to their sides of the forest: the wolves inside and the people out.

I think back to the wolf attacks from the past. Was there any type of pattern, any time of *reason* why he killed if he wanted things to be at peace? I remember a few days before Harriet died, a woman went into the woods to look for mushrooms. She had been warned to stay away but did not listen and when she returned she told stories of a crazed animal that attacked her and forced her back out of the woods. The woman claimed to have taken one of them down, but no one believed her and she went insane. Then Harriet was killed.

A life for a life.

The wolves have been playing a game with the people that surround the woods and he was only trying to keep the players honest. There was only one way to keep the rules in place and that was by keeping the fear in play as well.

I finally understood. The wolf hadn't come to hurt my family, he had come for the sheep, to remind us of his presence, and we interfered. We changed the game and he acted the only way he knew.

Sitting back on my heels I look around me. Wolf after wolf stare at me as if waiting for me to make a move, to see how I will react.

I am not afraid.

As I make eye contact with each wolf I see a sense of relief flow through them as we exchange a look of trust. I understand the game now and they can see it in my eyes.

A branch snaps behind me and the pack begins to growl. Lowering themselves in preparation to jump, they all turn their attention to the path where Farmer Young and Farmer Mayer stand guns raised.

"Herrick," Farmer Young begins with a calm tone. "Back away slowly. We'll hold their attention."

I feel a laugh rise within me—a response my neighbors did not anticipate based on the shock that crosses their faces.

"*Now* you come to help me," I scoff. "And I didn't even call for it this time." I stand and step away from the alpha wolf that has fallen before me toward the barrel of their guns. The pack moves, surrounding me in a protective defense. I know that they won't hurt me, and I am not afraid that they will turn their teeth to me either.

Farmer Mayer cocks his rifle, making a petite wolf with a deep gray and speckled black coat snarl and snap at him. He points the gun at her, only enraging her more.

"Herrick, this is...suicidal," Farmer Mayer says. "These...these *things* killed your parents, you can't trust them!"

"We know you're upset, but this isn't what you want to do, child. What would your parents think of this?" Farmer Young lowers his shotgun slightly and takes a single step forward.

"My parents?" I laugh. "They're dead! They aren't thinking *anything*, thanks to you."

"To me?" Farmer Young says taken aback. "The wolf killed them, not me."

"It's not the wolf's fault. This is *your* fault." I point a blood-covered finger at him. "And *yours.*" I stab toward Farmer Mayer who spits on the ground. "If you had come when I called 'wolf,' none of this would be happening."

"That wolf got what he deserved."

"No," I shout clenching my fists. I feel the pack's anger rise with mine, their bodies clench ready to pounce. "No," I repeat in a softer tone. "He didn't. He only did it to protect his pack and to protect *us* from them. Don't you get it?"

The farmers exchange looks of confusion before shaking their heads. I sneer, taking a step back and the wolves growl deeper shifting their weight forward.

"Of course you wouldn't. That's why this is your fault." I throw my hands up in defeat, but I know now what I must do. "I forgive you but they may not." It was time to change the game. Too many people have died. Too many people now know the secret of the pack—two too many to be exact. Turning my back to the men who let my family die, I leave them to the fate of the pack.

It's the packs turn to make judgement.

I look at the pack—*my pack*—and know that we are now playing a new game. The pack will decide who leaves the forest today and who is fated to fall as their former leader did. They will pass as judge, jury, and executioner now.

With this game, we will make a new kind of fear.

"Herrick?" Farmer Mayer voice shakes with fear, but I ignore it like they ignored me, and walk into the woods in the opposite direction as the pack closes in on them.

"Wolf," I whisper, looking over my shoulder once more before disappearing into the thick brush. My steps are covered by sounds of gunshots and snarls as I make my way toward town.

I push out of the edge of the woods. The sun is beginning to rise and the town will be waking with it, so I needed to act fast. I formed a plan on my walk, talking to myself loudly in my head to cover the sounds of screams I left behind, but it would only work if I move early, fast.

I walk far around the sheep pen, taking extra caution to avert my eyes not wanting to look at the remains of my family again still sprawled about, and into what is now just the empty hollow where my family used to live. I slide into my parents room, the blankets thrown aside from their hurried attempt to save me. My mother's book sits open on the nightstand, never to be finished. My father's dirt covered boots sit at the end of the bed, never to be worn again. I cannot let myself stop and feel, though. A wolf would not let emotions stop him—they certainly didn't today. The truth is, I didn't actually feel any emotions. I felt as empty as the house.

Reaching under the bed, I feel the silky-finished sides of my mother's memory box. The dark mahogany is cold on my stained fingers as I cracked the lid and pull out the family photo and trinkets. My mother held on to everything: a snippet of mine and Harriet's first haircuts, pieces of our baby blankets, my father's pocket watch, passed down from his great-great-grandfather, and her ruby ring passed down from her grandmother. The weight of the pocket watch is heavy in my hands, heavy with the thought that I am the last descendant of this family. I slide it into my slacks and look at the stained and faded family photo.

Harriet is just a toddler. My mother holds her in her lap as she sits in a wingback chair. She and Harriet share a wide grin, their faces mirroring soft, feminine features—all except their eyes. While I share my mother's eyes, Harriet holds our father's downturned eyes that always look sad and proud at the same time. My father stands at the side of the chair with a young me before him, holding his hand. We aren't grinning like the girls, but we hold stoic smiles that show how happy our little family is. It is the only picture we ever took. I fold it and slide it in next to the pocket watch.

I finger the ring my mother couldn't bring herself to wear. It is delicate—silver, and tarnished from the many women who had worn it before. My grandmother had hoped she would use it as her wedding ring, but my mother refused to be the one to ruin or lose it. I pull a piece of string through it and loop it around my neck, taking the final figments of my family with me I walk into the kitchen.

Grabbing a kitchen rag, I soak it in water and begin to wipe away the excess blood on my hands, arms, face, and neck before removing my ruined shirt and examining the wounds. They stopped bleeding —*when,* though, I wasn't sure—but they are red and sore. I gently dab the rag over them, doing my best not to irritate them more, then wrap them with strips of fabric and tie them in place. I toss the dirtied rags on the floor and pull on a clean shirt.

I take one last look around, wanting to take in the last few memories that linger before throwing a lantern near the curtains and watching them catch fire. Once the flames are high enough, people will notice and come. There was never denying a fire being a fire, unlike a wolf being a wolf, but what they would find would not be what they expected.

I walk out of the house, this time straight to where my father's body lies and pause for an instant. I look at him, taking in the freckled face from years of working in the sun, the stubble that had begun on his chin, waiting to be shaved, and then I look at my mother. Her already pale skin was even paler, as if she is becoming a ghost right before my eyes. I bend down and kiss her forehead, as she did to me when I was young.

"I'm sorry," I whisper, swallowing down a knot that begins to form in my throat. I push myself up, glancing once more at the house that was no longer a home, beginning to light with red-orange flames, turn my full attention to my next task, and run back into the woods as the sun begins to poke above the horizon.

Crossing the threshold of the forest sends an icy chill down my spine that awakens all my sense. Instantly, it becomes colder, as if the edge of winter never left the woods, trapped within the darkened branches, stuck beneath the moss covered trees. I move forward, following the small path created by the wolves who had run them so many times before, one that I will now run, and head in the direction of town directly across from our farm. Letting the adrenaline carry me, I don't stop until I reach the other side of the woods, the opening where Nikolas's family comes to collect their firewood to be sold and traded with the rest of the town.

Nikolas was known to wander too closely to the forbidden woods and today I would give him a reason to look closely, to come nearer, to let his guard down for just an instant.

I sit on a moss covered log that bends in under my weight. I take in my surroundings, catching my breath, as the sun rises outside of the woods. The rays lift the flowers and grass at the edge of the wood, but not daring to touch the dirt or moss that lay just inside the line. It's too early for anyone to be out yet so I wait but the longer I sit the more my adrenaline falls and the heavier my eyes feel.

The damp moss tickles my nose. Pushing up from the nap I had fallen into, I see the sun has risen and can hear distant voices outside the wood. I take careful, calculated steps to not make noise not wanting to spook anyone other than Nikolas—I have to be sure it's him I am hunting and not someone innocent. Hunching down to hide myself behind the line of shrubs, I peer out into the sunlit field of stumps and trees where Nikolas and his brothers are swinging axes. The rough chopping sound is methodic and almost rhythmic. With each swing of the axe, I narrow my vision on Nikolas.

He is the youngest of the three boys, the smallest but not the weakest. I watch as he struggles under the weight of a thick log, trying to pull it on his own. His brothers laugh but walk over to help him. They are kind to him, at least from where I sit watching, waiting. I wonder what makes Nikolas so nasty, but it doesn't matter anymore, he wouldn't be a problem to anyone much longer.

Nikolas begins walking towards the edge of the woods to relieve himself. This is my chance to get his attention. I snap a branch between my hands. Nikolas turns his head toward the sound, leaning in my direction to make sure he actually heard the noise. Throwing a rock against a tree, it slaps against the bark and echoes into the silence making Nikolas jump slightly.

I grin.

Shuffling through the brush, I move closer to Nikolas. He is stepping back from the edge, peering into the darkness, trying to find the source of the sound. I know he heard my movements—I didn't even try to hide them.

"Did you hear that?" Nikolas calls back to his brothers who aren't paying him any attention.

I let out a deep, throaty growl.

Nikolas freezes. I am close enough now I can see him gulp as panic sets in. He knows something is lurking in the woods and he was taught like I was to not call wolf unless he was sure. Just as Nikolas begins to turn away, I reach out and grip his wrist pulling him into the cover of the forest. He tries to scream but I cover his mouth.

"Shut up, you fool," I rasp.

"Herrick?" His eyes are wide as he pushes back. "What —"

"Shh" I shush him pulling him down onto his knees next to me. "I don't want your brothers to hear us." He gives me an uncertain look pulling his brow together.

"I don't...I don't understand. We can't be in here." Nikolas motions to the woods around us. He stands but I grab him and pull him down again.

"Listen," I whisper harshly. "You'll never guess what I found in the forest." Nikolas doesn't say anything. "I found him."

"Him? Who?"

"The wolf." I smile.

"Psh, no way."

"It's true. I found him and I killed him." I make a stabbing motion. Nikolas smirks shaking his head but then he looks at me, really looks deep into my eyes and a change of opinion transforms on his face.

"Prove it."

I got him.

I motion for him to follow me. He hesitates, looking back at his brothers to make sure they won't notice his absence, then nods and begins to follow me without question until we get to our destination.

We slow down trying to catch our breath. The run is both long and tiring having to maneuver through the trees and we walk the rest of the way on foot until we are through the opening at the very center.

"Oh my—" Nikolas starts.

"I told you." I shrug as if it's no big deal that there is a large wolf laying in the blood stained opening.

"How did you *do* this?" He smiles as he kneels down and pokes the corpse. I don't answer him, I am looking around as if for the first time and taking in the den before me.

The clearing itself isn't huge, maybe wide enough to fit my entire flock of sheep and some horses. It is circular and surrounded by lush trees that reach high into the sky. The opening is lit, but not bright, from the sun streaming in through the top and as I look closer I can see the blood trails smeared across the dried grass. None of the wolves are here and neither are my neighbors. I don't remember seeing the blood before, but now it is everywhere. Dripping from the side of the trees and low branches it glistens and I know it is fresh. Splatters hit leaves and flowers on the edge of the trail, their delicate white and yellow petals now tainted with fresh crimson.

My gaze drifts over Nikolas who looks up and past me. I see his eyes go wide as he tilts his head and squints. "Are those *bones?*" Nikolas stands quickly almost tripping over his own feet to get a closer look. I follow his line of sight and notice that under a bush a crisp white item sticks out against the green and red.

"Oh gross." He covers his mouth. "It's definitely a bone." He nudges it with his foot. "Man, look at all this blood! What is this place? Is this the wolf's blood? Did you do all this?" Finally, he turns and looks at me.

A sly smile creeps onto my face.

"Not all of it, no. It's where the wolves live and most of this wasn't here when I left." I motion to the bone.

"Wolves?" He gulps. "Like more than one? Wait." He thinks. "*Most* of this wasn't here...what does that mean?"

I watch as Nikolas's face turns from intrigued and excited to concerned and fearful. "My family is dead." I said flatly.

"What?"

"My mother. My father. Dead. They're both dead."

"Did the...the wolf kill them?" he asks as if accusing me of drawing their blood.

"Yes. The wolf killed them and we hurt him. Now he is dead."

"W—We?" He gulps.

"The neighbors came—chased after me as I went after the wolf. We ended up here. I'm the only one that left, though."

"Herrick, I—"

"He killed them because of *you.*" I interrupt.

It's his fault.

I begin circling him, just as the wolf would a sheep, waiting for the chance to jump and take his prize.

"You did this," I say to him.

"Did what? *Kill them?* No, no way. Herrick, you know I would never—" I'm behind him, kicking the back of his knees, forcing him to the ground. Nikolas's knees crash into the dirt and he falls forward on his hands. I step on his back and push him all the way down into the dirt, his arms buckling under my weight.

"You're a bully, Nikolas. Because of your silly pranks, my family is dead," I growl. "Do you understand the intensity of *your* actions?" I pause, waiting for him to answer, but he doesn't. I remove my foot and step back. Nikolas doesn't move, though.

"I forgive you," I say in a soft whisper.

"W-what?" He tilts his head toward me so I can see the tears in his eyes.

"I know you never meant for my family to die—at least I hope you aren't that heartless—and that you truly believed what you did was just harmless pranks." I watch him stand slowly and brush the dirt off his clothes. Behind me I hear a rustling of leaves as soft steps pad closer. Nikolas wipes the tears with the back of his hand and sniffs and I feel the energy of my pack heat around me.

"I'm sorry, Herrick. I honestly never meant—" He gasps as the wolf pack appears out of the surrounding trees snarling in his direction.

"Apology accepted." The wolves begin to close in, I see the black speckled one lick her blood-covered snout. "But you have to understand that your actions had deeper consequences than you thought. You killed their pack leader and for that I can not give forgiveness for. You'll have to persuade them." I turn and walk between two charcoal colored wolves that begin to bare their teeth and growl at Nikolas.

"It's a new game, Nikolas. 'jus' a silly prank'," I mock. "But this time the rules are made by them." I motion toward the pack. "If you win, you get to leave the forest. If you lose," I pause and laugh slightly. "Well, I'll let you see what happens if you lose."

"You can't be serious," he says with a shaky voice as a wolf gets closer to sniff him. He freezes in place as the moist nose touches his pant leg, inhales, and growls quietly.

"As serious as calling *wolf*," I reply, not turning to face him. I continue forward, heading to the last place, the last person, I needed to speak to.

I see him standing on the bridge throwing rocks into the river—probably waiting for Nikolas who will never show. He hasn't noticed me yet standing on the far side of the small field that leads from one side of the bridge to the woods. I take a moment to review my plan, then set off in a fast run, breathing hard.

My feet stomp onto the wooden bridge, startling Brekkor who throws his hand over his heart as if I had just stabbed him.

"Brekkor," I gasp.

"Holy hell, Herrick. You gave me a heart attack," he laughs shaking off the fright. "What are you doin' runnin' around like a lunatic?"

"You." I take a deep dramatic breath. "You have to come with me. It's Nikolas, he's in trouble."

Brekkor looks at me, taking in my disheveled hair, frantic wide eyes, and the urgency in my voice, and furrows his brow.

"What kind of trouble?"

"I'm not sure but I saw him run into the *woods* not long ago. Do you know *why* he would do that? *No one* goes in there," I speak fast and do my best to emphasise my need for him to follow me.

"He wouldn't do that," he says, but his face lets me know he doesn't believe his own words.

"I swear to you, Brekkor, I saw him. I tried to stop him. I ran right into the woods but I lost him. They're so dark and he runs faster than me. I couldn't catch him. I went as far as I could before hearing screams and I ran to get help." I watch Brekkor's face change as he begins to imagine the horror his friend may be facing. "I can't go in alone, it's too dangerous. I need your help. We can save him."

Brekkor considers my story, my need, and the frantic nature of the whole situation before nodding once. I take that as my cue to lead and race off back to the forest I so recently left with the final piece of my plan trailing behind me.

Before we reach the wolf den, we hear Nikolas begging and crying. I hadn't expected to hear him, he shouldn't be alive. The time it takes to run out of the woods to the bridge and back gave the pack plenty of time to pass their judgement. I can tell by how much light is streaming in that the sun has moved enough that at least thirty minutes had passed, yet it seems they hadn't made their final decision.

We both slow and look at each other, listening carefully for his wails to reach us again. I am breathing heavily and I can hear Brekkor take quick, short breaths, wheezing in an attempt to fill his lungs.

"You okay?" I ask noticing how pale he had become and the sweat dripping down his face.

"Yeah," he says with a deep inhale. "Which—" A piercing scream cuts him off and sends us both running toward it and as we enter the frenzie, I see Nikolas in the center of the pack.

I was right, he is still alive.

Nikolas is on his hands and knees, shaking and whimpering. Soft cries reach us and Brekkor sucks in a sharp breath. One by one the wolves turn their heads toward the gasp. I feel Brekkor grab my arm and I know he wants to run but that he is also afraid—as he should very well be. His hand is sweaty and trembling on me, but instead of turning to run, I take a step forward. I feel the pressure of his fingers pull me back for only a second before they vanish completely.

A pit forms in my stomach at the sight of Nikolas. He looks up, tears streaming down his face, leavings tracks in the blood and dirt that now cover it, and his eyes beg for help. His clothes are torn and blood seeps through an opening on his arm, shoulder, and chest.

My loss is his fault—but this loss will be mine.

Have I let the game get out of hand? Is this really what I wanted? I didn't want him to suffer, I want him to be judged fairly for his crimes. The pack has taken it too far. I open my mouth to speak, but a large, light gray wolf snaps his jaw at me as if in challenge—he is daring me to try and save Nikolas.

"What do we do?" Brekkor whispers behind me. I glance over my shoulder and see that he in fact didn't run away, he is staying, wanting to protect his friend. Stepping forward to penetrate the circle, the wolf reminds me that Nikolas's fate is not mine to decide. He snaps at me and I step back.

My heart pounds against my chest and although I have forgiven Nikolas clearly the wolves have not. I wonder too if they are saving him to prove a point. Maybe this is their way of showing me that I shouldn't forgive so easily, that a life is due where a life is taken to keep balance.

"I'll...I'll go get help. Your farm isn't that far." Brekkor speaks behind me.

"You can't," I say through a clenched jaw, fighting back the tears that sting the back of my eyes.

"I'm a fast runner—"

"You *can't*." The snarling wolf is still staring me down and I do what anyone else would be terrified to do—I turn my back to him. I lock eyes with Brekkor who is looking at me as if I have just transformed into a wolf before him, and maybe deep down I have.

I hear the pack move behind me and I feel their energy rise sending a shiver down my spine.

"You can't because its *gone*," I tell him.

"What do you mean *gone*, Herrick? I don't understand." He shakes his head, watching me carefully. I see him shift his weight back and I move mine forward.

The growling gets louder behind us, growing like a distant thunderclap rolling in.

"My home is gone, Brekkor. My home, my family. All gone. The wolf came for the sheep but took my family instead. They died because no one came to help me. I called wolf and no one came because of Nikolas and because of *you.*"

"Herrick, I...I'm so sorry." His chin quivers and tears shimmer in his eyes. "I didn't...we didn't mean for any of that to happen." He motions between himself and Nikolas who is watching, unmoving, from behind the wall of wolves. "It was just a joke—a harmless prank. No one was supposed to get hurt." He looks over my shoulder at Nikolas and speaking to him repeats, "No one was supposed to get hurt!"

A wolf snaps his jaw sending a bark echoing through the woods. The sound makes Brekkor jump and I wince knowing what is about to happen.

"But people did get hurt and it's time to face the consequence for your actions." Quickly, I reach out and grab his wrist. He struggles, pulling against me yet, he is unable to free himself from my grasp.

"Herrick, no. I'm sorry. We couldn't have known that would happen. It was a game, just a game," Brekkor is speaking fast making every word a plea for his life. The pack is now barking and snapping behind me as I turn to face my challenger.

There is crimson drool dripping from his sharp teeth. I look from him to Nikolas who is watching me with a look of hope in his eyes—hope that I would save him. I lock eyes with the grey wolf and stare into the light bronze and yellow iridescence.

For just a moment everything around us seeps into the quiet nature of the forest. Out of my peripheral vision I see muted colors, blurs that were wolves swirl together like a Van Gogh painting, and I hear nothing but my own breathing and the low guttural growl from the wolf.

A buzzing sound grows louder in my head until it reaches a pitch that would make me wince and cover my ears, but I dare not move in fear that I may lose. Just as I feel like I can not take it anymore, it stops in a crash of light against my eyes. Sunspots clear from my vision, the wolf blinks, and the vague world around us returns in a rush of color and sound.

I've won.

Yet I still can't save Nikolas because as I look up and make eye contact with him, the petite female wolf jumps and tackles him to the ground. His head snaps back against the forest floor and he pushes his hands up trying to shift the wolf off of him.

Nikolas screams as the wolf howls and drops her head into his shoulder biting deep and snapping it quickly just as the former alpha did to my father. Brekkor pales next to me and continues to pull against my grip. I watch as two other wolves join in and begin tearing Nikolas apart, one piece at a time. The pack has made their decision —Nikolas has lost the game.

I choke back the bile that has risen in my throat and push forward. The grey wolf steps back, allowing me to pull a still babbling Brekkor to the edge of the circle. I swing him around me and push him between the grey wolf and a fluffy white one who is speckled with blood.

Brekkor falls on his chest with his hands under him. He recovers quickly, shoving up from the ground and stands with his arms up as if he believes the wolves understand he is asking them to stop.

"Herrick. Herrick, please. None of it was my idea I swear," he begs.

It is equally his fault they are gone.

He had listened to Nikolas. He had played the prank.

No one came because of him.

I turn to leave but something stops me at the edge of the circle. Looking back I see Brekkor, really see him. Standing in a growing pool of his friend's blood, his eyes are wide and moving quickly trying to see which wolf will move first, tears stream down his face. He is mumbling to the wolves. Mumbling to me.

"Please, stop. Stop. I didn't want to. I didn't mean to." His words cause me to raise a single hand and step forward back into the circle.

"Herrick. Herrick. Come on, this is crazy. Please, please don't do this." I shoot him a look and he shuts up, drops his head and shakes it thinking I am about to set the pack free on him. As if in complete surrender, he drops to his knees and lets his head fall into his hands. He sobs. His back rising and falling with each cry of defeat.

I hesitate and remind myself that this is my game now—I make the rules.

No one would know what happened today if I let the wolves do what they pleased. No one would understand that the woods are still dangerous. No one would learn the consequences of bullying and picking on others. *No one* would learn if I killed him.

I knew I could never return to the village—there was nothing to go back to. Nothing and no one. I have become a wolf now and I belong in the forest. I am one of the pack but I am, and will be, a new breed. They were created by a bloodline while I was created by bullying, teasing, distrust, and fear. I am the new alpha and I have the power to control the pack.

I walk up to Brekkor who is still pleading under his sobs and breathing in short, quick bursts. Stopping in front of him I motion for the grey wolf to stand by me. As if he can read my mind and understand the gentle flick of my wrist, he pads to my side. I don't take my eyes away from Brekkor's as he looks up. His gaze moves between the wolf and me.

I understood why the wolf had saved me back when Harriet was taken. He wanted me to understand that it wasn't my fault, not completely. He watched. He waited. He did what everyone expected him to and killed my sister to remind them how dangerous he was. But he wasn't greedy, he only took her, only needed *her*. He let me go.

He was the wolf who rose on the fear, the hate, the stories the town had created. And yet, he still chose not to harm me even when he could. The wolf was fair. Showing the town he had mercy he had left behind a tiny piece of hope for those who may come in contact with the wolf again, hope that I will continue to show.

"I am the wolf," I say quietly and Brekkor tilts his head to me.

"What?" he stutters shaking his head.

"I am the wolf," I tell him with a strong, steady voice. There is a deep power behind it and behind me I feel the pack breathe as one as if they are now too realizing that they answer to a new leader.

"I don't...understand." Brekkor's voice shakes as a fresh wave of tears fall from his eyes.

"I'm letting you go." My voice is gentle and calm. I see Brekkor take a breath. "You will survive this, Brekkor. I forgive you. But you must do something in return." He nods and I glance a the wolf next to me. I want to mark Brekor, like the wolf had marked me. A mark will remind him of this fear, of his actions, of his mistakes just as my mark has reminded me of the loss, the agony, and the tragedy. My beta wolf looks at me and sees the scars on my throat. His eyes soften as he turns with understanding and in a single slapping motion, slashes Brekkor's collarbone leaving behind four thin trails dripping blood. Marks that will leave behind scars.

Brekkor stumbles back grasping at his neck. Blood trickles between his fingers and down his wrist. He pushes himself back with his feet, scooting against a thick tree trunk. I move to him, kneeling down to his level.

"You will tell the story. Tell everyone about the wolf, about the pranks, about the consequences. You will fix the mistake you've made." I pause waiting for him to acknowledge and agree. Brekkor searches my eyes, looks over my shoulder at the pack then nods. "I marked you, Brekkor. I can come back for you if you don't do this. I *marked* you. I am the wolf and I have spared you."

With a single action I have continued the game ensuring the future of the pack as well as the town.

I let Brekkor go that day with only the marks to keep him honest for the rest of his life and the fear the I could come for him at any time.

"You are my voice now, like we were the wolf's. We told people how dangerous he was, how scary, how frightful and he became what we said. A monster. A killer. But you. You will tell this story. You will do this and remember that I let you go. You will make sure no one gets hurt again knowing I am always watching, always waiting, always listening, and that I can come back for you at anytime."

"What will happen to you?" Brekkor asks.

"Don't worry about me. I have a new family now."

"Herrick," he says before disappearing into the woods. "I'm sorry. About everything." With that his feet pound back toward town. I knew this time he meant it because fear brings out the honesty in people.

That was the last thing I said to him—the last thing I said to anyone. Since then I've hidden in the woods safely with my pack. My beta—the large grey wolf—and I prowl the edge of the forest keeping curious minds from wandering into its darkness. We've made appearances and left our mark behind on many farms to ensure the story and the fear of the big bad wolf continues all in hopes of keeping as many villagers alive as possible—as many wolves too. Maybe someday we will all be able to live in peace together, but for now we must live in fear to ensure both survive.

It didn't take long for stories of the massacre to spread through town. They had never had such a tragedy as this; a couple bodies, rumors of a dead wolf, a missing boy, two missing neighbors, families torn apart and tossed aside like rag dolls. It was the biggest new story in the history of our town.

Search parties were called off and the families held their funerals, weeping as each casket was buried—some resting empty. Farms were sold. People moved on but the story remained.

Brekkor did his part. He told my story and how it was partially his fault they were all dead. He took the blame and explained why the wolf had saved him.

The town believed him.

They lived on knowing that a wolf still lingered in their woods, but this time they knew not to take the call for granted and to come when help was needed.

I'll never need to call for help again as my nightmares have finally vanished. I have no more fear of the wolf returning to take me, no more guilt of my sisters death. She is safe in my memories and my family is kept close to me with the trinkets I saved. With the ring, I feel the weight of actions and am reminded that even I can be judged in the end. My father's pocket watch reminds me that things take time. The wolf waited and prowled for years to keep up his stories and the ticking clock reminds me that it is my turn to be patient. Our family photo reminds me that Harriet is resting peacefully and that her death—and my parents'—have been avenged.

Brekkor sits on his porch sipping a glass of lemonade on a warm fall afternoon. Adjusting his hat on his fading hair he wipes the small amount of sweat that had accumulated on his brow off with his weathered hands. His little girl with long wavy hair that wrap around her in the breeze is playing with dolls and his two boys who take after each of their parents, pretend to sword fight with sticks across from him. He smiles as his wife takes a seat in the matching chair next to him.

"You're just too scared!" one boy calls.

"Nuh huh," the younger one sneers.

"Scared of what?" Brekkor asks curiously.

"Of the wolf! I told him it wasn't real. No ones seen the wolf before, pa. It's just a scary story and he's being a baby." The boys stick their tongues out at each other.

"Come here boys and take a seat." He leans forward on his knees as the boys follow their father's orders. "Did I ever tell you the story of how I got these scars?" Brekkor points to his collarbone, noting each one slowly. Both boys shake their heads. "Ah, well let me tell you about the wolf because he is in fact as real as you and I."

He winks at his wife as his daughter climbs into her lap ready to hear the tale he has told many times before to young and old, friends and family, and used as a token of a cautious reminder of what happens when someone gets pushed a little too far, when someone isn't treated fairly and causes the worst to happen. A tale of games and misery. A tale of *The Boy Who Cried Wolf.*

ABOUT JESSICA JULIEN

Born in the picturesque state of Washington, Jessica Julien is an online ESL teacher to students in China, a stay at home mom, wife, and wanderluster. When not in the virtual classroom, she spends her time writing young adult novels focused on the paranormal and supernatural inspired by her love of all things dark and twisty. With her vivacious imagination, witty personality, and ability to bring sarcasm to a new level, Jessica creates unique worlds and characters that readers can't help but hate to love and love to hate.

In her free time Jessica can be found enjoying a cup of dark roasted coffee while snuggling under a blanket with a good book. When the weather is right, she hops in the car with her husband, son, and dogs to roadtrip across the country where she delights in eating red vines, drinking iced lattes, and singing loudly in the passenger seat.

CONNECT ON SOCIAL MEDIA

jjulienauthor.wix.com/author

facebook.com/jjulienauthor

instagram.com/jjulienauthor

twitter.com/jjulienauthor

Sugarcoated

by K.M. Robinson

Sweets give us the illusion of happiness, beckoning us to sample brightly-colored sugar treats and revel in their sweetness…until they destroy us from the inside out and make our worlds crumble.

"Your brother will be here soon," I remind the small girl. "You need to get into position before he arrives."

"Annika, really? Can't we just wait until we see him coming?" She heaves a sigh as she traipses back over to the container. The blonde girl lifts her foot, nearly tangling herself in her skirt.

"You need to get used to it if you're going to help the cause, Gretel. You'll be in there for a long time." I almost hope my words might convince her to walk away from this mission—killing the king is no place for a little girl. The other half of me knows that she is our only chance at ending this.

"You sound like my brother," she grumbles.

"Yes, and *you* look like him," I snip at her, grinning. "Now, in."

Gretel drops down into the barrel that used to contain flour, her blonde braids dipping below the rim. I set the lid on, leaving just enough space so that air can flow in and out. If there's time, I'll inch the lid over before Hansel comes to collect her.

I walk gently over to the window, lecturing Gretel on the importance of controlling her breathing in small spaces while I keep an eye out for her brother. Just like every day for the past three months, he should be arriving any moment from the woods after work.

Right on cue, he saunters down the path, pack over his shoulder. I duck behind the curtain before he has a chance to notice me. Scurrying over to where Gretel is hiding in the barrel by the fireplace, I bump the lid.

"Showtime," I whisper to myself. Lifting my hand, I brush back a piece of hair. In my peripheral vision, I notice a bit of flour on my hand from the barrel—I imagine Gretel will come out white as a ghost. We'll have to clean her off before she leaves so we aren't discovered.

"Annika," Hansel regards me as the door swings open. His tall frame fills the doorway, and I feel myself blush as he smiles. "Is Gretel ready?"

"You can take her home if you can find her," I reply, turning away from him. I busy myself kneading bread.

Hansel sighs heavily, dropping the bag on the ground by the table leg. I glance down as I work, but don't comment—I know he's intentionally going to leave the delivery here for me so I can work on our project this evening.

He walks around the room, quizzically appraising everything as he searches for his younger sister's hiding spot. Hansel crosses an arm over his chest, grabbing his elbow as his free hand migrates toward his chin.

"Well, she's obviously not *in* the fireplace," he muses. His footsteps are heavy and intentional. "And I know you didn't move the fireplace —I measured after the last time. She's not in the loft. You hid her under the floorboards yesterday, so I'm guessing you wouldn't repeat that."

Hansel steps closer to me before reaching up to flick the long strands of my bangs back, smirking. I consider making it look like the fireplace has moved a foot while he's busy staring at me, but I don't.

"I can't help but notice the flour in your hair, mistress baker, might that be a clue?" His nose is an inch away from my ear, and I shudder as his breath ripples against my skin. Blinking, I try to keep my composure.

"A clue that I run a bakery? Why, *yes,* however did you guess?" My words are sickly sweet. His eyes spark with laughter.

"Where is she, Annika?" he whispers quietly.

"You can come out, Gretel," I call, refusing to give him her location.

The lid scrapes off the barrel. Hansel turns back toward the fireplace, dropping the strand of my hair he was twisting around his finger. His face lights up when Gretel appears.

"Well," he drawls. "There she is. Not bad, little sister. I never would have guessed."

"Not until you tried to move the barrel," I add.

"Oh, I don't know about that. Gretel's as heavy as a barrel of flour now." He offers his sister a hand as she smacks at him for his joke. At thirteen, Gretel is the resistance's best weapon.

"You realize I have to take her home, right?" Hansel teases. "I can't take her out of here looking like she just lost a fight with Winter."

He bends down and starts brushing the flour off of Gretel's dress. The barrel was mostly empty, but everywhere Gretel brushes against the sides of it, traces of the white fluff adhered itself to her clothing. I could create the illusion of her being clean and save some time, but it would only last until they got halfway home.

"See you tomorrow," Gretel says, waving as her brother herds her out the door.

"See you tomorrow, Annika," Hansel adds in a deep voice. He tosses a look back at me, and I know it won't be long before he returns for his bag.

Once they're gone, I scoop it up and paw through the contents. Hansel doesn't mind me going through his things, but somehow it always feels a little wrong, despite the fact that he's hidden pieces of our device inside his belongings for me.

I come up with an apple in my hand, a small ribbon tied around the stem. I try to bite back my grin, but he's not here to see me, so I allow myself this small moment as I twist his gift in my fingers.

Hansel and I have worked together for years, but our mission is too important to let our feelings get in the way of what we need to accomplish. Still, the last few weeks, Hansel hasn't seemed to care. I told him it was a bad idea last week when he kissed me…that hasn't stopped us from kissing again since. It's reckless, but I've always felt Hansel was meant for me.

"Not bad," I murmur, holding the hinge up to the light when I find it in his bag. It would fit perfectly inside of the compartment. I set to work installing it before night falls and it becomes harder to see.

A few hours go by before I hear Hansel knock. I set down the tools I'm using and walk to the door—somehow this is easier when he just walks in to pick up Gretel—the formality of knocking sets me on edge. His grin does not.

"Did it work?" he asks, stepping into the shadows of the room. He scoops me into his arms, and I drop the hand I had poised to cast an illusion over the room to protect my work had it not been Hansel at the door. The moon is partially in the sky, though twilight still glitters above us.

"Seems like it." I motion toward the tall outline of a tiered cake.

Hansel's arms drag around me as he steps toward the fake pastry.

"Your father would be so proud, Annika." He tosses a look back at me. His muscles flex as he steps around the mobile hiding place I wheeled out of the back room to work on. "I know you never wanted to follow in his footsteps, but God himself had to plan to put you here in our time of need."

Hansel strides back over to me, wrapping his arms around my waist once again.

"The resistance would be lost without you, Annika. No one else has been able to get us this close to the king." The fate of our country somehow rests on two eighteen-year-olds and a thirteen-year-old-assassin.

Outside, the fireworks explode in the sky with streaks of white light. It illuminates the rooftops in the distance, round and sloping in candy-colored stripes. Walls glitter against the burst of light.

"Right on time," Hansel mumbles, leaning in to press his lips against mine.

"This joke is getting old, Hansel," I mumble, silently willing him not to stop kissing me. My breath catches as he pulls back.

"You would prefer I talk business during the display?" His smirk casts deep shadows over his face as the sky lights up again.

"I didn't say that," I mumble, his lips roaming over mine as his hands tangle in my hair. Brown locks slip from the loose bun on top of my head.

The tangy scent of apple hovers between us from the present he left me earlier, lingering on my lips as he separates them. All around us, candles grow brighter, intensifying as Hansel pushes me backward toward the table. I bump into it, dropping to sit on the workspace as I drag him down with me.

Hansel pulls back to grin, light dancing over his face as it grows even more golden. His hand reaches behind me, steadying himself as he leans back down to kiss me.

"You should learn to control that," I tease.

"You make me light up, what can I say, Annika?" His voice is low, and dangerous enough that my stomach twists up. "The lights only do what I tell them to do."

Fireworks crackle outside over the city, casting a white glow over us for a moment, mixing with the golden gleam of the candles burning brightly enough to be a raging wildfire.

"And you think letting the king's guards know we're here is a good idea—they can probably see us from the city the way this place looks like it's ablaze."

Hansel's eyes crackle and spark like the flames around us, but he lowers his eyelids, forcing himself to consider my words.

"Fine." He sighs, dousing the lights until only two glow dimly off to the side. "Happy now, mistress baker?"

I was happier when he was kissing me, but I refuse to say it out loud.

"I'm happy that I don't have to whip up an illusion to keep the guards from noticing us," I pretend to chide, ducking under his arm as I slide away from the table.

"Annika," he calls quietly. A candle near me bursts.

I turn as he illuminates the fireplace again, the last of the fireworks fading in the sky outside the window. I wander back over to him but hover just out of reach.

Glancing up, I create a crystal chandelier above us. It picks up the firelight and glitters around the room.

“And here I thought *I* was going to be the one to get us caught.” He smirks, revealing deep dimples on his cheeks.

"Well, I need something pretty to inspire me now that I can start working on the cake again. It's a good thing that hinge fits, Hansel."

“I know, but we have it now and we can move forward with our plans.” He reaches forward and carefully wraps an arm around my waist as he turns me toward where I’ve hidden the wooden cake form.

“Is she ready?” I ask, waving my hand to unveil the cake. The cloak drops from around it like a sheet, the illusion wall disappearing before our eyes to reveal the cake.

“I hope so,” Hansel whispers. “You’d know more than me. One more reason we’d be lost without you.”

“Hansel, are *you* ready?" I ask cautiously. We've been preparing for this for what seems like an entire lifetime, but now that the time is drawing near, we're all a little terrified of what could go wrong.

“I’ll save her,” he whispers quietly, but his grimace is a silent admission that he’s scared of what might happen.

“You will,” I whisper back, wrapping my hand around his arm. Sometimes, he still flinches when I touch him, as if he’s not expecting me to be so familiar with him, but he looks down to me, soft smile on his lips and lowers his face to me.

“She’ll be all right,” he says after a moment. “She’s got both of us—we’ll make sure she’s safe.”

“You’ll pull her back, Hansel,” I assure him. “We’ll all make it through.”

An explosion ripples outside. The entire house shakes under the weight of the blast. If the chandelier I created had been real, the glass would have clinked together and fallen to the floor, smashing into a million pieces. Instead, it’s the only thing that doesn’t move.

“What in the name of the king’s court?” Hansel races to the window, ground still trembling.

“What do you see?” I ask, pausing just long enough to cover the room in an illusion to conceal our secret.

By the time I reach the window, smoke fills the air, dancing in the night. Hansel douses the lights so we can see outside without interference.

My hand feels cold as I place it along the window sill. The king must have had an enemy in our sister town, but instead of dealing with it discretely like he usually does, he took down what I estimate to be half the tiny town. Thankfully it's in the opposite direction that Hansel and Gretel's home is in, though I'm sure if they blew something up, the guards will also be making the rounds to look for others to destroy.

"How fast can you finish that cake, Annika?" Hansel's voice is dark. If he's willing to speed up the timeline like this, it must be worse than I think.

"What do you know about this, Hansel? What did you see today?"

Hansel spends his days traveling for work and has his ear to the ground more than any of us. Nothing happens in this country that he doesn't have a way of learning about.

"If it's who I think it is, it's not one of ours."

My eyes close in relief. I'm horrified that someone has died tonight, but at least it's not one of our own.

Hansel opens his mouth to speak, but I cut him off. "Gretel."

He pauses, jaw still open for the briefest of moments before he closes it and nods. Hansel pulls me close, kissing me hard.

"Be safe." His voice echoes in my head as he rushes to the door. Once outside, he spins and looks at me, demanding I cast an illusion.

Shaking my head to pull myself from the fog, I arch my hand, transforming the bakery into a rundown old building. The lights go out on the outside, leaving nothing but a shadowy old house that's about to fall apart. Only the window remains for him to see me.

Hansel nods, approving of my choice. Quickly, he ducks his head and turns away, running from the bakery toward Leipden where he left Gretel in the care of his great aunt.

I wave my hand again, concealing the window from the outside.

Inside, I throw strings of lights around the room, casting a white glow over my workspace. I tear down the illusion wall and reveal the cake form again so I can work—I won't be sleeping tonight.

The king must die, and my chandelier-lit handiwork will be the trojan horse that leads to his death at the hands of a thirteen-year-old girl that acts as a guardian of death and life.

Hansel casts a worried look at me as he drops off Gretel the next morning. She rushes in, clearly having slept through the explosion—though she was farther away and it might not have made an impact in Leipden—and dances around the room.

As soon as Hansel is down the drive, Gretel drops her act.

"What happened?" she demands, taking me by surprise. "He didn't tell me, but it can't be good."

"An explosion," I answer. "That's as much as I know. I'm sure he'll learn more about it today."

"We need to move up the timeline," she replies. Her jaw twitches with nerves—something I've seen repeatedly over our time together.

"We can't exactly convince the king to change his party, Gretel," I remind her. "He's already sent word on what he wants for his cake. In a week, we'll deliver the one we made for you instead. We have to be patient, darling."

"A week and two days," Gretel murmurs, brushing back her long hair. *Of course* she would know the exact countdown—it's the day *she* might die as well. She drops her hand quickly, face hardening. "Can't we force his hand?"

"For a ball?" I scoff. "No, our plan is a good one, but we can't even suggest he move up his party or he will know something is wrong."

"I just want to get this over with." She's frustrated, and I can't blame her.

"We'll get you out of there, Gretel." My words are soft as I try to soothe her fears. "Hansel won't let anything bad happen to you."

"I'm killing the king of Candestrachen." She looks at me incredulously. "I'll do what I must."

Gretel has always been willing to sacrifice herself for the cause—better to give up a few lives and save the masses than to watch us all perish at the hands of a corrupt and unpredictable king—but Hansel and I are willing to do what we must to keep her alive. Besides, we might need her again for the next man who rises to power.

"They won't even know it's you, Gretel, I promise. You'll look like someone else entirely."

"If you can get in the door," she reminds me. Turning, she makes her way to the cake form.

"I have to bring the cake in. I'll find a way to be in the room, Gretel. I won't let you down. Once it's over, Hansel will pull you back and get you out of there."

"His lightness and my darkness," she muses.

"You have life and death, Gretel." I walk up behind her and take her long mane in my hands. Braiding it quietly, I add, "Hansel has light. He will pull you back from the darkness when you destroy King Levin. I know you don't like using death, but we're all grateful to you, Gretel."

She's quiet for a long time. I would be terrified if I were in her position. Entering the palace in a Trojan cake with the intent of killing the mad king—if anything goes off plan even in the slightest—there's no telling what the crown would do to a thirteen-year-old assassin.

"Will you at least give me brown hair like yours? And make me look older?" She places her request for an illusion to change her appearance while in the palace.

"Would you like my face too, Gretel?" I laugh.

"No, but only because they'd come after you afterward." She turns, and the braid falls from my hand.

"What's wrong with your hair, my little darling?" I prompt, hands on my hips. A smirk tugs at my lips but I try to hold it back.

"Nothing," she remarks, curving around me to walk along the wall toward the window. The girl touches a plant sitting there and it springs to life, bursting with flowers. "I just like yours better. Besides, if I'm going to look different, I should look *very* different."

"Fine, brunette it is. Now, do you intend on helping today, or are you planning on frolicking around the bakery all day growing things?"

She turns to see what else she can sprout with her touch in the cool fall weather. Before she can notice, I create a few vines as an illusion a few feet away. Gretel moves to touch them, but she can't make them grow.

I flick my fingers by my side, changing the positions of the vines. My charge turns around to glare at me. "Very funny."

"I try." I don't bother hiding my grin this time.

"You and Hansel were made for each other." Gretel rolls her eyes. She doesn't know about us yet, but if we survive the assassination, we'll have to tell her.

"Well, what do you expect, little bird? We were raised by our fathers—they were practically like brothers, so of course, we have the same training."

"Yes, *that's* what I meant," she mumbles so low that I almost miss it. Perhaps she *does* have an idea of what's going on without her.

"Come along, Gretel. I've had enough of waiting around for answers. We're going to town for supplies."

"Hansel will be furious." That doesn't stop her. She grabs a cloak from the rack by the door and wraps it around her shoulders. Bright pink tones make her hair pop, and her eyes sparkle as she looks back at me.

I wrap a brilliant blue and lavender shawl around my shoulders, the long center corner hanging down my back. The tassels tickle against my arms, but no matter what walk of life you are from, in the towns of Candestrachen, the women are meant to be seen in bright colors and ornate clothing.

My long skirt bounces around my ankles as I walk. It's a muted gray color—one that would be entirely unacceptable in town under normal circumstances, but it's best for baking in. When we finish walking through the woods, I'll use an illusion and make myself more presentable.

Gretel flicks her wrist and brings a blueberry bush back to life, fruit springing out of its branches. She pauses long enough to gather a handful of berries and pats the bush as if it were a dog. Holding her hand out, she offers me some.

I indulge, but only a few so she can have the rest. Gretel is about to save us all—she should have whatever her heart desires in the coming days.

Music swells up in the distance. Gretel sighs, displeased with the display we're too far away to see.

When we reach the edge of the tree line, I transform my dress into a brilliant gown that matches the cotton candy colors of the center of the town of Leipden. We round the corner and reach the true spectacle.

King Levin doesn't like for his people to work where he can see them. Anyone trapped inside of the city centers is forced to create a spectacle for the king and his guests to see, as if the entire country were one big festival. People like Hansel and I who live outside of the town limits were given permission to work, but the poor souls inside still had to provide for their families without any source of income—we help however we can, but it's still not enough.

Young men sometimes sneak out to live with relatives in the woods while the women stay behind to cover for them using their flashy dresses to catch the noblemen's eye in the streets as they bustle about, pretending to be happy. When Hansel and the others find the ones that escaped, they put them to work, giving them a place to belong and a way to help their families back in the towns.

Gretel falls behind me just slightly, her now-vibrant dress bouncing with each step. She stays behind my elbow as she follows me through the streets.

"Good morning, Annika," a voice calls. A friendly hand waves as the gentleman pushes a cart through the town. I wave back, offering a smile.

I make my way to the miller's shop to order more flour. While I have enough to last through the assassination attempt, I need to make it look like business as usual. The miller's shop is far enough away from the flour mill that I imagine it's difficult for Bauer to run his job, much less help lead the resistance.

The buildings loom over us, looking down on two young women making their way through the streets of Leipden. Each tower on every building is striped with a different color, winding its way around the pointed precipice of the roofs.

Bold magentas and orange tones dot this section of the town, mixed with bright whites like a twisted mint. Perhaps it's unfair of me to compare everything here to a candy world, but when one's entire life revolves around baking and creating confectionary delights for royals and peasants alike, one has little else to compare the bright world too.

We pass a row of brightly designed fireworks meant for later this evening. I secretly wish Gretel's powers extended to turning inanimate objects into duds so we could have one night of peace in the skies.

Turning, I allow my hand to scrape over the embossed edges of the building at the start of the street. Each groove is familiar beneath my hands. From the corner of my eye, I see Gretel do the same.

A group of young girls runs by us, clad in bright yellows and blues. They spin, laughing as they run down the street. Their mothers have taught them to have fun with the king's little games, but when they're older, they'll learn the truth of their prison.

A bell dings above me as I guide my charge into the miller's shop. Bauer looks up from his place behind the counter, a streak of flour runs across one side of his forehead.

"Ahh, young Miss Annika and her apprentice," he regards us. "What can I help you ladies with today?"

"The King is coming!" someone shouts outside. Bauer tosses me a worried glance but hurries around the counter on his bad leg. Gretel and I pick up our skirts and step out of the door before the miller—I can't let the crown see our secret child-weapon.

In the streets, people are busy lining the walkways, ready to put on a show for when the king passes by with whatever dignitaries he has hanging on his every word today.

Lights flicker on down the length of the street. Despite being trapped in Leipden, the people have developed a system over the years to help each other out. A lookout sounds the alarm when a member of the crown's guards come close. Lights are turned on only when necessary, and the people crowd into the streets. When possible, a few slip away into the darkened corners of a shop to be productive while they can.

Everything sparks to life as if we've all been in the streets celebrating all day. Men raise their glasses and women dance as voices fill the air with rehearsed lines.

I tuck Gretel behind me, using my tall frame to block her. Bauer sidles up next to me, leaning on my arm for support as he too covers Gretel from sight. He reaches up to swipe the flour from his face, jostling his light brown hair in the process.

The parade files past us, led by guards in brightly colored uniforms. Should anyone ever attack Candestrachen, there will be no hope for us—subtlety is not the king's strong suit and his guards are more easily spotted then the women's dresses.

A cart wheels by—Hansel would be fascinated by how they power it. A short man sits in the front, guiding it down the roads as an engine quietly hums beneath him. We don't have access to all of the technology the king has, but Hansel has ways of finding things we aren't supposed to have.

A woman in royal blue raises the shout, and we all follow, watching the vehicle move.

"A blessing to King Levin and to Candestrachen!"

When the third round of cheers dies down, the king leans out of the red, white, and yellow cart. He waves his hand, tousling his dark brown hair—if I didn't know any better, I'd say we could be twins...if I were a decade and a half older, that is.

Music fills the air as musicians dive into song—it doesn't matter which one. A group of older women starts singing, swaying together in unison. I raise my voice with them, knowing I need to blend in as I croon about the magnificence of Candestrachen. Gretel sings behind me but stays hidden.

The king eyes us all as he passes by, a calculated, jovial grin on his face as he points us out to the man seated next to him. The lights on the miller's shop behind me flicker in bursts of bright colors, painting light over King Levin's face—his father before him was handsome, and one could even argue that Levin was a sight, but the blood on his hands has stripped away every last shred of humanity I could ever find in him.

He locks eyes with me for a moment, focusing on my face. My muscles go stiff with the shock of his gaze but I force myself to smile, and I sing—his death is coming, and I will be glad for it.

"You know what color we're missing here?" The king shouts to his companion. I hold my breath, knowing what's coming. "Red!"

The cart wheels down the street and around a corner. Terrified, people run around buildings hoping to catch him on the other side—if they're in his presence, they're safe.

Several guards in the back stop, prepared to carry out his coded orders. We didn't put on enough of a show for his guest, and one of us will pay the price.

"Go," I murmur, pushing Gretel back toward the door. I step back, not turning away from the street, trying not to draw attention to our escape.

Bauer grasps at Gretel, catching my arm by mistake. Four, five, six steps and we're at the door to the shop, and he pushes us in, closing it behind us.

The street erupts in our wake as men and women try to avoid the guards—whomever they catch first will be the one to add red blood to the streets. Stifled screams fill the air—it will be worse if the king hears our cries from the next street over—but those near the guards can't help but call out in fear.

"Annika!" Bauer tries to keep his voice down as he shouts at me.

I wheel around to find him pointing to a hidden compartment in the wall. I suppose I don't need to find a place to hide Gretel after all.

"You too," he hisses, grabbing my arm to force me into the compartment. I start to argue, but I know he's right. For as much as the resistance needs Gretel, they need me too—at least until next week. "I'll be fine."

Once inside, the panel slides shut, concealing us from view. Through a small hole, I can see Bauer hiding behind his counter, ready to act as if he were the only person hiding in the miller's shop should the guards choose his establishment to disrupt.

I add a secondary wall in front of ours, preventing the guards from finding the secret panel, should any of them be smart enough to look.

"*Don't*," Bauer warns when he notices. I drop my hand, taking his advice not to hide him—if anyone saw us come in and they don't find anyone, they'll tear the shop apart and find us all.

We all have to make sacrifices for the cause.

Gretel presses up against me, also trying to see through the small hole. I wave my hand and add a second one to allow her to see what I see.

Minutes pass by. The waiting is the hardest part—possibly even harder than the small pop we hear five minutes later. Somewhere, someone has been tied to posts with a small explosive device attached to them, only big enough to tear them apart when it goes off. Blood is splattered, coating the area red as onlookers cry tears of sorrow and relief. Soon, somewhere new will be painted red with the blood pooling on the ground as the guards finish their assignment.

I drop the illusion, and Bauer releases us from the small hole in the wall. I climb out, pushing and pulling my skirt into place as I stand. Worried, I quickly change the colors and styles of our dresses before we leave the miller's shop.

"What do we know?" I ask, trying not to sound shaken. I smooth back my hair, knowing at least part of it has toppled out of its bun.

"The explosion last night?" Bauer asks. "Not much, I'm afraid. I was waiting for Hansel to come tell me. I'm afraid we have much to worry about, though."

He loops around to stand behind his counter, as if ready to take my order. I lean forward onto the countertop as he scribbles on a pad.

"Are you ready?" he asks, head still down.

"We will be."

"I'm ready," Gretel chimes in, furious over the events of the morning. "He will pay for this."

"Gretel, this is not a mission of revenge," Bauer snaps. "If that is why you are doing this, I'll pull you out right now. We are preventing further loss of life; that is all."

"Yes, Bauer. I know. I'm sorry," Gretel hangs her head. "It is for the greater good—for the future lives."

"We can't change the past," Bauer concludes. "You *will* save the future, though, Gretel."

He swings back to me, dropping the conversation. Gretel may be the key to stopping the king, but she's still a child, and it amazes me how some of the resistance treat her as one.

"Take her home, Annika, and do not come back here until it's time for the delivery," he instructs. His implication is clear—I messed up by bringing her out this close to the assassination attempt.

Bauer hands me a bag of flour, softening his gaze. One side of his lips tick up—an apology for being harsh. I take the flour from him and hand it to Gretel before resting a second bag on my hip.

The streets are back to bustling when we exit the shop. Gretel's green dress is a startling difference to the pink one I had created for her earlier, but I need her to look drastically different. I'm not sure if the king will remember me when I journey to the palace next week, but I certainly hope not. I'd change my hair if I could, but enough people know I'm the baker that if I showed up without my signature brown locks, they'd know something was wrong.

Music trickles its way down the streets, calling for us to join the celebration, but we avoid it. Instead, we follow the main street laid with colorful rocks until we can turn onto a side road that leads back to the woods. Gretel knows to keep quiet until we enter the trees, but I purposely take the long way, knowing we won't run into the remnants of whatever poor soul painted the town red this morning.

"Are you okay?" I ask as soon as we are concealed in the tree line.

The illusions drop around us, and we stand in our muted clothing again, the only signs of color left back on the town rooftops that peer through the tops of the trees.

"Bauer seemed angry," she comments.

"Bauer is always angry."

"Not with Hansel," Gretel corrects.

"That's because *Hansel* plays by the rules," I remind her.

Gretel stomps off, leaving me to trail behind her. The trees rustle on the wind and Gretel waves her hand, leaving a trail of bright green leaves where dying ones had once clung.

A gasp stops us.

Turning to the right, I search the bushes for the source of it. Throwing my hand out, I add illusion leaves to the ones Gretel gave new life to, creating a wall of greenery between us and the voice, as if the wind had blown them to cover their sight.

His uniform is green, covered in designs of white, cream, and yellow—the guard nearly blends in with the foliage. He staggers back, eyes wide.

"You're a witch; a magic woman." He collides with a tree.

"Whatever are you talking about?" I adopt a fake cheery tone as he takes in my altered appearance—an old, haggard woman. "Are you all right, sir. When we found you, you looked like you had hit your head."

"Don't approach me, woman!" His hands claw around the back of the tree as if he wants to pull it out by the roots and throw it at me. "Your kind has been banished for decades—they don't exist here anymore."

"Sir, I don't know what you're talking about." Another step toward him and the apprehension on his face slips away. He grasps his weapon and aims it at me.

"No!" A scream tears from Gretel's lips. She throws herself on the ground behind me, her hand stretching out just far enough for me to see in my peripheral vision, and the entire forest twists.

Trees burst from the ground, while others rearrange themselves, moving from the roots. Vines drop from branches, while bushes spring up around our feet. A wall of massive trees separates us from the guard.

Instead of fighting to reach me around the bark, he turns and runs toward the town. We're in trouble.

"Gretel, change the forest," I instruct. I drop my illusions as she grows new paths all around us, changing the way to the bakery to make it nearly impossible to find.

"He'll go to the king about this," Gretel says from her place on the ground. She summons more plant life, hindering the man's way back to the palace.

"We need to get back, Gretel, hurry."

I scoop up the bags of flour we both dropped and pull her off the ground. I start running, but with the changed landscape, I'm not even sure we're headed in the right direction.

The ripple effect travels before us, the forest quietly changing as Gretel's summons moves throughout the woods. I slam to a halt as a new tree presents itself in our path. Turning, I pull the little girl around it, taking a different route.

I hear the voices before I see them—men.

"Do you have any idea where to go?" one asks.

"This isn't right, the path should be right here."

"Are you drunk, my friend—spent too much time out last night?" a third calls jovially, enjoying the confusion. He slaps the second man on the shoulder loudly. Perhaps *he* is the one who spent too much time out last night.

"Something isn't right." I recognize the fourth voice—Hansel. This must be his team. Then I realize I know the other voices as well.

"Hansel!" I shout as we step around the tree blocking our view.

His head whips around to me. All of the boys are carrying large sacks on their shoulders. Pickaxes and other tools are attached to the belts on their waists. Hansel's eyes widen as he takes me in.

He stalks over to me, grabbing my elbow to spin me.

"Get us home, Hansel," I whisper before he can speak.

"You did this?" He looks to Gretel.

"Get us to the bakery," I demand again, knowing we can explain later.

"Boys, we're officially off duty. Come on," Hansel calls, waving them over.

His team surrounds us, and we set off in the direction we believe the bakery to be in. Gretel's ripple slows, transitioning quietly into the world we know as we get close to the bakery.

Hansel's feet pound into the ground alongside of me, clearly frustrated as I quietly explain what happened. The muscles in his arm are stiff as I collide with them as we walk.

The bakery is a tall, two-story building with high ceilings downstairs, perfect for creating my confections. The dark brown tones of the wood are highlighted by pops of aqua blue and cream, my father's homage to my late mother. Whereas the towns are covered in decadent architecture, out in the woods, we are more understated with our buildings, only adding color at the king's demand.

Hansel takes the stairs two at a time and Gretel, and I struggle to keep up. The team of six waits outside, watching for anyone who might be coming our way.

I wave Gretel off as I follow Hansel to the back wall near the stairs. The little girl mills by the fireplace as I create an illusion wall between us, shortening the interior of the house by ten feet.

Anger rolls off Hansel in waves, and as I turn, his face softens with worry before slamming me into the back wall. His arms go around me protectively, caressing my waist while his lips move against mine —not the conversation I was expecting to have, but I much prefer it.

"Are you okay?" His lips catch on mine as he tries to speak between kisses.

"Yes," I mumble, words catching against his skin.

One hand quickly reaches into my hair, working his fingers between the strands. I wrap myself around him, holding his back with one hand, the other palm cradling the back of his head just above his neck.

I can hardly breathe as he crushes against me, worry written on his face as he pulls back with a wrinkled brow.

"What were you thinking?" he whispers harshly, chest dragging up and down against me as he struggles to catch his breath.

"I was ordering flour from Bauer," I protest. I run my hand along his arm, hoping to soothe him. "I was trying to keep up appearances. I knew I'd need next week to finish the cake form, and we need to create all of the pastries for our cover story before that happens."

Hansel tips his head forward to learn against my forehead.

"Annika, what would have happened if we had lost you?"

"Bauer and I were going to protect Gretel."

"Yes, but I'm asking about *you*." His hand twists in my hair that is now fully released from the bun I had wound it in. It cascades down behind me, tumbling to the sides.

I pull him toward me, pressing his chest against me as he cocoons us against the wall. His sister is only a few feet away on the other side of my magical wall, and his team is only on the other side of the door, but I don't care—neither does he. His voice is hushed as he speaks, but actions are louder than any words and Hansel's movements are saying a great deal.

My back moves away from the wall as I lean forward to kiss him, our lips colliding and parting furiously. His arms reach around me and for a moment, I think he might pick me up and carry me away to a safer town far away from Candrestrachen. My fingers slip around his suspenders, and I'm careful not to let them snap out of my fingers as I pull him closer. He grins against me, laughing so quietly that it flutters over my skin.

"I will not lose you, Annika," he responds to his own question. "You're too important to the cause and too important to Gretel and me."

"You'll be just fine without me if it ever comes to it." I sigh—if I could stay hidden behind this wall with the people I care about for the rest of my life out of the sight of the king, I'd be happy.

His hand comes up to my chin, tipping my face up to look at him. His eyes are intently focused on me as I gulp air. His shoulders sag with each breath, and I realize we should have pulled apart earlier.

"Don't sugarcoat this, Annika. We can't lose you." Hansel is frustrated, but I don't back down.

"I'm a baker—sugarcoating is what I do, or haven't you ever tried my palmiers?" I snap back. I regret bringing his favorite dessert into the conversation, but I'm not going to tolerate him saying I'm being too soft about this. I'm not the important one here—the focus should be entirely on Gretel.

I should bake him something later as an apology—maybe my peanut butter fudge that he loves so much.

"We have to go back out there," I inform him. I'd pull away if I could, but he still has me trapped against the wall.

"Is Gretel okay?" he asks reluctantly. As he takes his arms from around me, I realized he's had me up on my tiptoes this entire time, supporting part of my weight as we kissed. I feel heavy without him holding me up.

"I think she's scared about all this, but she's not wavering."

"What about the woods?"

"The guard scared her—she reacted out of fear. She did the right thing changing the forest, but I think upending everything like that unnerved her a little."

"It will be easier when she only has one task to focus on and not changing an entire landscape."

"Speaking of, how are the locals going to get around now?"

"Most of them stay out of the woods, so it's really just our teams," Hansel says, thinking it through. "I'll come up with a signal so we know how to find our way back here."

I nod, trusting him to handle the situation. Hansel has always been a problem solver.

"Annika, I think Gretel needs to stay with you until this is over. We can't risk her traveling now that we're so close."

"You don't think they'll notice you traveling without her? We can't afford questions. They'll notice you coming and going without her even if you *don't* live in town."

His hand grazes mine, fingers wrapping around mine slowly before pulling away. Hansel holds my gaze and brushes back a strand of hair. I tip my head toward him and rub the back of his hand with my cheek.

He sighs and pulls away. Reaching up, I wrap my hair back into a loose bun making him smile.

"I'm going to make a trail of lights," he informs me, stepping back. I follow him.

"They won't notice that?"

"Blinking lights," he corrects. "Electronic fireflies. They won't have any idea."

I consider the merits of his idea. If he creates a path of tiny devices that flicker like an insect, people who pass by won't know. No one will stand for prolonged periods of time to watch for a trail, nor is it uncommon for an insect to land on a bush and stay there for a time. It makes sense. If anyone can get access to technology for that, it's my co-conspirator.

"That's brilliant, Hansel."

"I save all my best ideas for you and the mission, Annika," he teases. "Gretel will stay here with you tonight—don't argue. I'll take her home tomorrow after I set the trail in place."

"You mean *after* you figure out how to get home." His back is turned to me, but his head twitches to the side as if he started to turn back to me.

"Another reason she's spending the night here—I don't know how to get her home safely yet. Just start your baking project early since you'll have the extra help. It will cover for us in case things get busy over the next few days and you can't make your stockpile supply to use as a cover."

Hansel nearly walks into the illusion wall, trusting me to take it down in time. If I didn't want to kiss him again soon, I'd let him walk into it, but I need his face to stay intact if I want to taste his lips again. I wave my hand and the wall drops as he raises his voice.

"We have a plan," he announces, brushing back his hair. I hope my own mane looks all right—he would have told me if it hadn't because he doesn't want to give away our secret any more than I do.

Gretel turns, jaw locked. Two of Hansel's team members stand in the bakery, looking annoyed. One uncrosses his arms, letting them fall to his side while the other raises an eyebrow.

"What exactly is this plan?" asks the one who was clearly just pretending to be drunk. Aurik has always been unique.

"We're marking the trails tonight, boys. We'll come back tomorrow. Annika will be babysitting."

"What?" Gretel shrieks.

Hansel motions for the guys to leave the bakery and they oblige, turning on the heels of their work boots. They leave bits of dried mud in their wake for me to sweep later.

Few people know Gretel is the key to the rebellion's success—it's too dangerous for people to know. As far as most people are concerned, Gretel is just Hansel's kid sister and responsibility since his father died. Aurik and Brahms know, but even so, some distance is kept.

The fierce little girl marches up to her brother, not letting on how tired she must be after rearranging an entire forest.

"Why am I being left here?" Her long blonde bangs fall in front of her face, and she pushes them back harshly.

"I don't know how to get home, which means it's not safe to take you out. Annika needs your help tonight anyway to work on the food supply for your alibi. I have a feeling next week won't be kind to us."

"Hansel has to concentrate on building firefly bots anyway," I inform her, touching her elbow softly. "He's going to light the paths so we can find each other."

"Just do what Annika says," Hansel directs his sister. He hugs her quickly, tossing a glance at me. He mouths, "Sugarcoat it."

He eyes his sister before he pulls away—she doesn't need to know how difficult her handiwork has just made our lives.

Hansel is worried, and I don't blame him. So much could go wrong over the next few days.

"They won't even think to look here, Hansel," I promise. "It will be safe."

I twirl my hand in the air, coating the entire outside of the bakery in bright colors. Hansel laughs from the drive outside when he turns to see my handiwork, the team members mercifully already in the woods. Sculptures of candy wrap around the columns of the porch—everything Hansel's sweet tooth has ever craved over the years. The top of the bakery now has points like the buildings in the cities—mine drenched in what looks like whipped cream and pink frosting. Chocolate drips from the shutters coated in rainbow colored sprinkles found in only one shop in the entire kingdom. The door is covered in melted green and white peppermint, leaving the steps transformed into rows of salt water taffy lined with lollipops.

I've sugarcoated the world for Hansel and Gretel…at least for now.

"Could you flirt any harder?" Gretel mumbles next to me once her brother is out of sight. I whip around to face her. "I'm about to kill a king, Annika, you think I don't notice the things around me? Conjuring up all of Hansel's favorite sweets was a clear and definite message to him. Now, take it down before anyone else sees."

"Just for that…" I reply. Instead of finishing, I transform the interior of the bakery into a candy wonderland. The banister on the stairs twists into swirled rainbow candy canes, and a lavish sculpture protrudes from the wall with every treat imaginable. A chocolate fountain streams in the corner surrounded by a base of butterscotch candies. Macaroons and truffles line the fireplace mantle.

"I'll forgive you," she replies, "but only because I love macaroons and I know you have some real ones in the back."

I smile, leading the way after making sure the door lock is secure. She glides behind me gracefully—she'll be a force to be reckoned with when she grows up.

"We've got fudge to make tonight, Gretel."

"Oh lovely, more bribes for my brother."

"*You* like it, too," I remind her, tugging on a few strands of her hair. "We've got a lot to create tonight, so I hope you aren't tired."

"Considering we haven't had lunch yet, I guess we're in for a long day."

A rock clicks against my window, waking me. The floor is cold as I set my feet down—the fire must have gone out downstairs. I've only been asleep for two hours, so it shouldn't have gone out so quickly, but perhaps the draft quieted the flames.

I reach for my cloak, tucking the hood up over my hair to help with the chill. A few long strands of hair tumble out from behind the fabric and I don't bother to tuck them back.

Hansel is standing below the window, poised to throw another pebble. I rest my hand on the window, and he drops his arm, knowing I've seen him.

I hurry down the stairs to let him in. The embers from the fire still glow in the blue-toned night. Only the moonlight illuminates the house now.

"You kept the candy, I see." He greets me with a smirk as he brushes past me to come inside.

"Only for you, Hansel."

"Where is Gretel?"

"She's still sleeping," I reply, closing the door.

"I'm here." Her tiny voice bounces off the walls in the early morning hours. She glides off the stairs, also wrapped in a cloak.

Hansel moves his hand, and the fire ignites once more. Another flick of his wrist and the candle bursts into flames too. A small light on the side of the room comes on, allowing us to see more easily.

He eyes me as if to say, *you really should watch tha*t, but I'm in no mood for his judgments. Hansel's gaze sweeps over to Gretel. Catching sight of the mountains of pastries we baked in the hours since Hansel left us, his eyes grow wide. Tarts and scones fill the table where we left them to cool. A few extra pies sit on the stools, though the rest are in the back. Cookies sit in baskets on an open rack off to the side, while rolls and sticky buns rest in containers waiting to be moved—we were too tired to transport everything into the back when we went to bed at two.

“Did you get everything done?” He asks, looking at Gretel.

“Mostly,” I answer.

“Good.” He nods, all business. “We need to go.”

"It's four in the morning," Gretel complains, yawning. "You couldn't have just left us until morning?"

“No, Gretel, I couldn’t.” Dark shadows pass over Hansel’s face. “The king’s men are out looking for the witch that transformed the woods. If they found you here out of place, you both would have been detained for questioning. You and I have to go home *now* before they discover we aren’t there.”

Gretel's face pales in the candlelight. Hansel turns to me and scoops up one of my hands.

“You need to remove the illusion.”

Startled, I raise my hand in an arc, dropping the façade outside. I had already removed it from the interior of the house as we worked because we needed more space to set the things we were baking. Hansel squeezes my hand before dropping it.

“Shoes, Gretel.” He nods to his little sister’s feet. She turns, rushing back upstairs to collect her things.

“Will you be all right here alone, Annika?” It’s sweet that he’s concerned.

“I have to be,” I reply. I don’t have a choice. “Will you two be okay out there?”

I'm terrified the king's men will find them as they make their way back to Leipden. Their poor aunt must be beside herself.

"The course has changed, Annika, but there are still ways to get to and from the palace when this is all over. I know the way to you—I've lit the path. But here—" he holds out his hand, waiting for me to open mine, "—use these wisely. They're bots. They'll follow you wherever you go."

Tiny yellow lights blink in my hands, the same size as a firefly. I close my fingers around them.

"Once you activate them, they'll hover every hundred feet on their own until you run out. If you run out, they're programmed to move on their own, spacing themselves out further. If anything happens, Annika, and you need to run, these will let me find you."

Hansel is brilliant. I shouldn't be so shocked.

"Yours are yellow—I figured that would be the least likely to be noticed aside from the green ones I made for Gretel. Mine are a light blue."

"You had time to create these *and* mark the trails?" I ask skeptically.

"Well, *some* of the trails. This was more important." Hansel shakes his head, tossing his blond locks. "It appears some of Gretel's force is still at work and occasionally the boys have witnessed a tree moving. Most of it is farther out, mind you, but these were the only way to find each other if we have to."

"Oh, great," Gretel mutters, coming down the stairs. "I can't even handle an escape plan—are you *sure* I'm going to be able to kill the king?"

"You'll be fine," we both protest at the same time.

Gretel yawns again, fighting against only getting two hours of sleep. I like to think I'll be able to crawl back into bed once they're gone, but I know I'll be wide awake, worrying.

"You know the way home?" she asks.

"Yes, we just follow the blue trail." Hansel waves for me to follow them out into the yard. I slip on a pair of dainty slippers before stepping out onto the porch.

The grass is wet with early morning dew. Mixed with the cool weather, it soaks through my slippers, piercing my skin painfully. I'm grateful Gretel has boots on for the walk home.

"This way," Hansel says, leading us to a tree.

I wince as I follow behind them—I despise the cold weather, even when it hasn't fully arrived yet.

"See that little dot there?" Hansel points. I watch for a moment, seeing nothing. Then, a tiny blue glow appears down the path. A few seconds later, another blue dot glows so far away that I can barely see it. "That, ladies, is what you're looking for."

He takes a firefly from Gretel and shows us how to activate it. He has Gretel test it out, walking back toward the house. Once she reaches the porch, she returns to us, several lights still in her hand. Hansel demonstrates how to call the robotic creatures back to us before wrapping his arm around his little sister.

"Stay safe," he warns me. "Gretel and I will be back in a few hours."

I nod, waiting for them to leave but Hansel refuses to move until I'm standing in my doorway once again. When they slip out of sight, I lock the door.

Knowing it's a waste of my time to try to sleep, I set to work hiding the evidence of how Gretel and I spent the last twenty-four hours.

The sun is up, glistening off of the rooftops in the distance when Hansel and Gretel return. They're dressed brightly—Gretel bound in a deep red dress with laces up the front, and a navy cloak wrapped around her shoulders and Hansel outfitted in three different hues of dark green.

I noticed them through the window as they exited the woods, but look up when they knock, keeping to our usual routine in case anyone is watching. When planning to assassinate a king, paranoia is called preparedness.

"Good morning," I greet them, brushing back part of my hair. I feel woefully underdressed standing next to them. "What's all this?"

"The king's guard was out in full force this morning." Hansel's voice is deeper than usual as he drags a hand down his face. "You should change, too, in case they come this way."

My shoulders sag, but I move my hand out to transform my wardrobe into an illusion to match theirs.

"No, Annika. Change for real. You may need to hold other illusions in place should anything else happen."

I grimace—with an illusion, I can get dirty while baking without ruining my fancy clothes, but if I use real fabric, anything I drop onto it could be damaged. Crossing his arms, Hansel doesn't take no for an answer.

Gretel moves about the room, preparing for work as I turn and make my way to the stairs. If I have to be put out, I'm going to make a point of it.

My parent's room is large. When I first moved into it last year, I didn't know how to handle all the extra space, but I had wanted to be close to them and this was the only way I could think of to do it. Of course, as the new owner of the bakery, it was also expected, and should any of the king's guards ever inspect the house, there would be far too many questions raised if I was still in my childhood room.

I slip into a dusty pink dress, draping a light-colored fur over my shoulders. Pulling my necklace out from the collar of the dress, I let it rest on my chest as I navigate toward the stairs again. Hansel's eyes widen when he sees me.

"The ball is *next* week, Annika," Gretel jokes, snickering.

"Yes, but who doesn't like baking in furs, darling?" I retort, shaking my head playfully.

"I didn't mean you had to dress for town, Annika," Hansel adds, shaking his head.

"You made a good point, Hansel—we don't know what might happen later today, especially once the king starts to investigate the forest. Anyone could stop by."

"And *you* were being snarky," he muses, smirking.

"Of course." I wave him off. "Go to work, Hansel, something tells me you're going to be busy today."

Hansel angles himself toward the door, walking slowly. "Keep an eye out for the boys today."

I nod. If any of Hansel's team shows up today, it means something bad is happening. If he's worried enough to tell us to actively watch for them, we'd better be extra vigilant.

"Well, that's new," Hansel says from the door, looking out from under the porch. Gretel and I scurry over to look out of the doorway with him.

In the distance, nearly blocked out by the blinding light of the still-rising sun, something floats in the air. First one, then five, then enough that it could be a cloud if it weren't for the sun piercing through them, destroying the illusion.

"Are those…lanterns?" Gretel asks, squinting to see.

"Those are definitely lanterns," Hansel responds. His hand quietly bumps into mine.

"But those aren't ever sent up until night when the people can see them," Gretel whispers, realizing something is off.

"Stay in the house today." Hansel frowns, moving toward the steps.

"Wait," I call, turning to run back into the bakery. I hear Gretel say something to her brother as I pick up a small bag of the peanut butter fudge we made for Hansel last night. She brushes past me as I hurry onto the porch again.

Hansel raises an eyebrow, quirking one side of his lips up. He runs a hand through his hair as I approach him.

"I forgot to give this to you earlier." I hand him the candy.

"I give you apples, you give me fudge," he muses.

"We all have our different kinds of sweets, Hansel."

"Just like we all have our different kinds of gifts," he teases, finishing my thought. "But not all of us have those."

"Not all of us have sweets, either," I remind him quietly. "Don't let those go to waste."

"These won't even make it down the path, Annika, and you know it." He grins, untying the ribbon holding the bag closed. "You spoil me, woman."

Hansel hands me the ribbon that matches my dress. I close my fingers around it, unsure of what to do with Gretel a few feet away in the house, likely watching through a window.

"Be careful, Annika. We don't know what's happening out there anymore. If you think anything is going wrong, get Gretel out of here and I'll find you." He pauses a moment before sighing. With a quick glance to the house, he turns and saunters off toward the woods.

Back inside, I set the ribbon down on the table. Draping the fur over the back of a chair, I instruct Gretel to sit by the window behind the curtains and watch for anyone coming from the woods. I'm less worried about the morning lanterns for the moment than I am for possible intruders.

I turn my attention to the wooden cake frame while Gretel keeps watch. I carve an intricate design into the wood for when I place the fondant over it—it will save me time on the design later. The wood scrapes under my knife, filling the room.

Gretel sighs loudly, nearly making me jump.

"Bored?" I ask playfully. I reach up and brush a piece of hair out of my face with the back of my wrist.

"How is the cake going?" she asks in a monotone voice to make her point. I giggle quietly.

"Well, they won't know it's not some elaborate sugar creation until after the fact," I reply. "Honestly, I'd like to get the fondant on and just get going with this."

I look up in time to see her cringe and realize I shouldn't wish the assassination—and her possible death—to come faster.

"Annika." Gretel's sharp voice tells me she hadn't been reacting to my comment.

"What is it?" I drop the tools I was using, flick my wrist to put an illusion over the half of the room where the wooden cake sits, and rush to her side.

"Bauer," Gretel murmurs. "This can't be good."

It feels like my internal organs drop inside of me like when I jumped off that cliff into the river as a child before King Levin took power. Air fills my mouth as I remember to breathe, gulping in oxygen.

"Go to the back, Gretel. Get the cake and go." I drop the illusion so the girl can move our secret weapon out of sight. The wheels drag against the floor as she pushes it away.

I rush to the door, opening it as Bauer hobbles up. He clutches at the neckline of his coat that falls below his knees. Stone blue makes his dark hair stand out.

"Bauer?"

He thrusts two large bags of flour at me. I fumble to catch them before they hit the ground. Straightening, I follow him inside, flour bags in my hands. Setting them on the table, I wait for his gasping to stop.

"What's happening?" My voice sounds hollow even to me.

Bauer starts to shake, breathing deeply. As he leans back, I flick my wrist toward him, rolling my fingers gently as if I were shooing a fly away from a freshly baked roll. A tall stool materializes behind him, catching him as he sits.

"Has anyone been here today?" he asks.

"No, just Hansel and Gretel."

"Where is she?" Bauer's brown locks fall in his face. Soft wrinkles form around his eyes and crease his brow from years of wear.

I nod to the back. Gretel steps out.

"We have to go," Bauer informs us, standing to his feet. His voice loses its wavering tone. Was this an act?

"Those lanterns were the start of something, girls, something bad."

"You're not really suggesting we leave, are you?" I ask, horrified.

"We can't leave you where they can find you," Bauer protests, looking less winded.

"What is going on, Bauer?" Gretel asks, crossing her arms over her chest. "We can't leave. If we do, how will we get me into the cake and delivered to the palace? Annika can't just abandon the bakery."

"What about the cake?" I ask, glancing at the back wall.

"Hansel and I will come back for it, but if anything happens to Gretel, all is lost. We can always come up with a new plan, but not without the girl," he confronts me. "We need to get you both somewhere safe."

"Where is that?" I demand, hands on my hips. I know Bauer would never move us without a reason and if he's willing to risk this plan, he must be exceptionally worried.

"Closer to the palace."

"Excuse me?"

"What?" Gretel speaks over me. "We can't be there until the ball. It's still days away."

"The king's guards will be scouring the towns, we can't move closer. Our ticket in is the cake—we have to wait until we take it to the palace for the ball." I frown.

"The guards aren't going to know who is bringing the king his cake, nor will they know where the baker appeared from. As long as *you* show up with the cake, everything will be fine, Annika." He puts his hand on my back and turns me toward the door.

"What do you know that we don't, Bauer?"

He sighs but continues to push at my back, propelling me forward.

"The king is searching for us. He's looking for rebels. Somehow, word has been spreading that a plan is to be enacted before the ball—rumors, as far as I can tell, I don't think we have a traitor—but he's scouring the cities looking for us...for *you* and for *her.*

"He's already searched the towns around the palace, and his men are branching out. If we can get you safely beyond the perimeter as it comes toward us, you'll be safe until they've completed their search."

"And if they find the bakery empty?"

"They won't, Annika, we'll make sure one of us is here. The guards don't know better unless they grew up here and knew your father. Even then, we should be able to explain it away. We just need to make sure you two are in the palace district."

Gretel looks nervously at me as we step outside and Bauer closes the door behind us. "We need to go."

I trust Bauer almost as much as I trust Hansel, so I swallow back my argument and take the steps down to the dirt path. The trees seem to swallow us as we step into the woods that are now completely unfamiliar to me.

A bird chirps loud enough to make Gretel jump, and she moves closer to me as we walk. Bauer limps along beside us at what must be a brutal pace for him, but he doesn't stop.

"Does Hansel know about this?" I ask.

"Not yet, but he will as soon as you're safe. Our next mission will be to rescue the cake."

I tap the fireflies to life, and the first takes its place to guide Hansel to find us—I won't risk him losing us should something happen along the way. Gretel notices me and nods.

"The lanterns this morning were some kind of signal, weren't they?" I question as the trees block out more of the light. Each leaf rattles as the wind picks up enough to blow my hair in front of my face. Reaching up, I pull it from the messy bun I'm wearing so that it falls to help prevent me from getting chilled.

"I'm afraid that was my fault," Bauer admits. "I was on my way from the mill to the shop and I saw the guards. I overheard their plan and knew I needed a way to get some attention.

"Our people all saw it—anything out of the ordinary makes them vigilant—but it also kept the guards distracted long enough to make it to a few of our key players to warn them. I came straight here as soon as I could find a way to escape without being noticed rushing from the town.

"Quiet now, girls," Bauer warns us, suddenly sensing something. He stops walking, straightening both of his knees. Dropping his voice, he adds, "We need to run."

Grabbing Gretel's hand, Bauer launches forward, no longer limping —yet another of his façades. We crash through the bush, nearly colliding with a tree we forgot had recently moved.

Everything blurs around us as we stumble over the underbrush. My foot catches on a tree root, nearly sending me toppling forward. Gretel's long, blonde hair trails behind her as she leaps nimbly over tree roots and fallen branches.

Behind us, I hear the guards' voices calling to each other. After a moment, they catch the noise we're creating as we trample through the woods in the distance and follow us, quickly gaining speed.

"*Gretel*," I call. She reaches for my hand so I can steady her as we run.

"Are you sure?" Bauer asks, wrenching himself around so he can assess our enemy.

"Is it her?" a guard yells.

"Do you honestly think a witch can run that fast?" another calls in reply.

"Oh, well, this is lovely," I grumble. "Time to give them a witch."

Gretel drags her hand across the rough bark of a tree as we pass by it. I'm sure it hurt, but she doesn't cry out. We pass another, and she darts her hand out again. The tree immediately begins to move, and I catch it from the corner of my eye as I pass it.

Unlike the last time, Gretel isn't transforming the forest. Her touch is merely coercing the trees to form a wall behind us, corralling the king's men away from us.

A firefly leaps from its place on the small pouch attached to my belt and darts toward the bushes. It blinks once before it disappears behind a bush left untouched by Gretel's commands.

I consider telling her to touch the ground and affect the roots of all the plants in the forest again, but Hansel and the others have already worked so hard to navigate the trails—it will be hard enough for him to locate us now and the line of trees is giving us a temporary reprieve from the chase. Still, we don't slow.

A bird cries out in shock as Gretel removes her hand from the bark of the tree it's sitting on. It flies into the air, lecturing her for disturbing its rest.

"Hurry, girls, we have to get to the town." Bauer pulls ahead of us, leading the way now that he's certain the trees are slowing the guards down. In the distance, I hear calls for the witch's head.

Gretel is breathing heavily, and I slow our pace. Bauer realizes we're lagging and slows as well, knowing we can't tax the girl before her mission. Each time she uses her gift, she depletes some of her power until she can recharge. Small tasks like bringing dying plants back to life in the bakery hardly affects her but rearranging an entire forest and now creating a wall of trees within two days will certainly take its toll on her—I can't let her do anything else until the mission has been completed or we risk putting her in danger without being able to kill the king.

Bauer guides us off course, looping around toward the outside of the forest. Releasing Gretel's hand, I wrap an arm around her waist to help support her as we slow to a quick walk.

"I'm fine," she puffs in response. She's anything but fine.

"We need to get out of the forest," Bauer informs us, looking back. "We've lost the guards thanks to Gretel, but now they know we were there and will be searching the woods for you both—for all of us. We have to get you around people."

"You want us to blend in?" I ask.

Bauer nods. "You need to belong to whatever town you find yourselves in. We'll move quickly to get you to the palace district, but it's going to involve a little waiting while I clear the area before I bring you out in the open."

I study him as we move. I can tell he's nervous. His gait is stiff, though, I suppose that could be from discomfort since he isn't walking with his fake limp at the moment. Slowing again, he pauses until we catch up and slips his arm behind Gretel, under her arm, to help support her with me. The more we can do for her now, the easier it will be later.

"Hansel is going to kill me for this," Bauer grumbles.

"Probably," Gretel offers meekly. I blow air out of my nose instead of laughing to let her know I got that she was joking, but I'm too tired and too focused on our movements to offer a real laugh.

"Not much farther, girls," Bauer adds softly. "Once we reach the tree line, I'll get you two hidden, and I'll make sure the guards have already swept the area. Then I'll come back for you two."

"Okay," I agree quietly. I've done far too much running the last two days, especially for a baker who focuses on building muscle through lifting heavy bags of cooking ingredients.

"It looks like that's the town up ahead." Bauer nods forward.

If I strain, I think I can hear music coming from the streets of whichever town we've stumbled upon—possibly Gimpenlaug or Perihausen. If the music is so loud, that has to be a clear sign that the guards haven't left yet.

"There," Bauer says, pointing. "There's a large cluster of trees growing together. You can rest there and use the tree to hide yourselves if need be."

If we must, I'm sure Gretel could cause the five trees to swirl together, locking us inside until help can come, safe from whatever guards we might run into. We'll have given ourselves away, but at least Gretel will be protected until then.

I guide my charge to the trees, helping her to sit in the makeshift seat the trunks have formed. Glancing around, I make sure no one else is near, even though Bauer swept the area before he disappeared through the trees.

"Are you all right, Gretel?"

"I'll be fine," she murmurs. "This running thing is for the *guards* though. No one else should be subjected to this nonsense."

"Your brother trained you." I give her an incredulous look, "There's no way he didn't teach you how to run."

"Oh, I can run, Annika," she grumbles. "I just don't like it."

"Well, I can't say I blame you there. How long are you going to need?" I pray she doesn't need more than a few days to recover from using herself up over this.

"I'll be ready," she answers.

I sidestep as a cricket leaps past me, frightening me enough that I gasp—I forgot they like to act like rockets being shot at neighboring countries this time of year. It pings against a branch as it lands.

"I hate those things," Gretel voices my own thoughts. "I'll be ready, though, Annika. You don't have to worry."

She sounds stronger and less winded, but I know it's an act—like one of my illusions. It's a pretty façade to put people at ease. I've even done it to keep others calm around me. Poor Hansel has been a victim to my charms a time or two.

"We're going to be okay," she says, taking my hand. "You'll get me where I need to go, I'll do what I need to do, and we'll handle the rest of it. It will all work out, you'll see."

She's wise not to give any details of our plan while out in the open, but she's Hansel's sister so I should expect nothing less.

"Any chance you still have some of that peanut butter fudge in your pocket that you slipped my brother earlier?"

"Sorry, dear. We can make more later if you'd like." It wouldn't be terribly hard to make more of Hansel and Gretel's favorite candy. I know the recipe by heart these days.

"At least Hansel will know how to find us," Gretel changes the subject. "Good thinking on using the fireflies."

"We might have to use yours soon, too, if we go any further."

Gretel reaches to tap on the pouch on her hip just as the explosion goes off. I drop to the ground, pulling Gretel down with me. Overhead, a firework crackles in the bright blue sky.

"What in the name of lollipops is going on here?" Gretel's face scrunches up as we try to see through the trees.

"I don't know," I respond.

It's hard to see the colors in the light of day, but the remnants of the white glow slowly falls down from the sky. A second screaming collision with the air frightens us again. I lurch back against the tree, trying not to be too obvious about jumping.

"If the lanterns meant something—even if it *was* Bauer—do you think these fireworks mean something?"

"We have to assume that it does, but this time, Bauer hasn't had enough time to reach the fireworks at the center of the town. Something else is going on here."

I listen for the sounds of music coming from the town, but it's strangely silent. A third firework goes up in the air. Peeking around the tree, I look for signs of life along the edge of the town, hoping someone might be walking by and I could gauge their reaction to the fireworks. No one is there.

Another minute passes before I hear it—the sound of screams.

"It must be the guards," I whisper. "They've probably caught someone."

"What should we do?" Gretel struggles to turn around so she can see toward the town as well. I wrap an arm around her waist as she leans to the other side of the tree.

"Stay hidden, Gretel." I pull her to my side and she sighs.

The wind kicks up, knocking leaves off of the trees. They cascade around us like yellow raindrops. The rustling covers up the sound of crunching leaves for a moment—just long enough for us to lose our edge.

We turn at the same time, hearing the boots stomping through the woods. Gretel's face pales. She reaches out, getting ready to hide us if need be. I grab her hand, pinching it tightly—she can't do anything else to conceal us, or the assassination attempt is over before we've been able to do anything, and since *I* don't have time to make a *real* cake now, the king will probably have me executed.

Still holding her hand between my fingers, I flick my other wrist, causing a shower of illusion leaves to fall between the men and us—they likely won't notice fallen leaves disappearing as much as they'd notice tall trees suddenly poofing out of existence when I get too far away, so I don't create any illusion trees for the moment.

As the shower of greenery continues, I pull Gretel toward the town. We're going to have to face the guards in the town if we want to escape the ones we're leaving behind, whose sole attention would be on the two of us in the woods—I'll take a distracted guard over a group going after two lone women in the woods any day.

We stumble the first few feet, but the buildings are close enough that we dart behind the first one while the leaves are still coming down in front of the king's men. Glancing around, I assess the situation. Gretel clamps down on my hand, as she's been trained to do so we don't lose her in a situation like this. Our jobs have always been to protect her; Gretel's job is to make sure she doesn't get separated from us.

The buildings have a pink tone here, and while there are a variety of bright colors—pink seems to be the overwhelming hue of this street. Even the glass in some of the shops is tinted with rose. Doors slam shut all around us, though they aren't closing because of us—they're afraid.

I have to find somewhere to hide Gretel. Not knowing who we can trust, I put an illusion over us, changing our appearance so no one could find us.

"That was bold," Gretel chirps at me.

"We don't have time for subtleties right now," I growl back. I didn't mean to sound so harsh, but I left all my sugar back at the bakery. "There."

I haul the girl across the street, nearly colliding with a man and his son as they maneuver away. He curses but doesn't stop.

The old woman who waved me across the street can barely hold up the cellar door for us, but she waits until we're safely inside before letting it slam shut. I climb down the stairs, refusing to relinquish Gretel's hand.

Once on the dirt floor, the old woman points to where she wants us to go. I can't question it; we're underground, and the old woman only wants to be safe too—she doesn't mean to harm us.

She nods to the wall as she runs her hand over it. It clicks, revealing a hidden door. Just as she pulls it open, a firefly slips from Gretel's pouch, blinking in the dark cellar. The woman's head snaps over to the bright light.

My hand lashes out, concealing the device.

"I got it," I whisper as if I'd killed the bug. Holding my hand closed tightly, I try to block the light and conceal it behind my back. When the woman turns away, I slip it into Gretel's pouch. She tightens it so the rest can't escape to do their jobs.

The room smells like damp earth, but the woman touches a switch and a dim blue light fills the room, just enough to give us limited visibility.

"What did you see?" the woman asks. When hiding from the guards of Candestrachen, information is coveted and often the only means of survival.

"Nothing," I inform her. "We weren't here when it happened. Do you know what the fireworks were about?"

"You weren't here, and yet you're here, girlie. Where were you?" She doesn't answer my question.

"We were in the woods, collecting firewood. What were the fireworks about?"

"The guards found some rebels, I think." She waves her hand, referring to the resistance—she must not be one of us. "Whether they are or not, I'm sure we'll have an execution. Levin will be thrilled."

It's strange to hear her refer to the king without his title, but I like how it removes some of his power. I might have to try that sometime.

She eyes my new, curly red hair.

"Are you two sisters? Surely you aren't mother and daughter."

"Sisters," I inform her, picking up Gretel's hand. "We live with our mother over—"

My words are cut off as the heavy sound of a body trying to break through a door fills the space we just left. The guard pounds again on the outside cellar door.

"There's another way," the woman whispers. She hobbles across the blue-lit room. Opening another door, she motions us through. Maybe she is resistance. From the corner of my eye, I see her shutting the door behind us. "Go to your mother."

I try to protest, but she stays behind, shuffling back across the room to save us. Knowing we can't stop, we press forward, groping the walls to figure out where we're going in the dark.

"Ow." I gasp as I run into the bottom step of a staircase leading upward. Gretel bends down to feel what's ahead of me.

Carefully, we climb to the top, looking for a latch that will let us escape. "The firefly," I remind her. She pulls one of the tiny devices out of her bag and holds it between her hand. Every time it blinks, we search for the way out.

Finally, the door clicks. Gretel puts the firefly away, brushing back her now-brunette hair—a new illusion I cast meant to keep people from asking too many questions. This time, I look old enough to be her mother, and Gretel looks at least a few years younger than her age.

She nods, and I crack the door open to see what's outside. The street is quiet, so we hurry outside, closing the door behind it—it blends in perfectly with the side of a stone wall.

"Let one of them go," I instruct. "He's never going to be able to find us at this rate."

Gretel follows my command to leave a trail for her brother as I notice a pile of stacked logs at the end of the street, nearly on the corner. If we can hide behind it, we'll be able to see through the logs but won't be likely to be seen. I'll have to watch for snakes hiding in the firewood, but they're our least dangerous enemy at the moment.

This street is filled with colorful pastel houses, each boasting awnings and shutters of different colors. As we reach the end of the street, I try to determine if we're about to enter a pit of vipers more deadly than the king's guards, and then we duck behind the wood.

Through the holes in the cut fire logs, I can see out onto the street. It seems strange now that the fireworks have stopped—though they stopped before we ran into the cellar—and the sound of footsteps is overwhelmingly loud next to us in the explosions' absence.

The guards pass by, oblivious to two strange girls on the ground mere feet from them. The logs protect us from view, giving us the advantage. I eye the top of the stack, trying to decide if any of the pieces could make a good weapon.

When the street is quiet for a moment, I add a few illusions to the stack of wood, making faux pieces stick out farther than the rest to keep passersby at a distance. Gretel fidgets nervously beside me, and I wonder if that's what she does when I force her into barrels and that wooden cake meant to take down the king of Candestrachen.

The noise flairs up again down the street. With the logs sticking out perpendicular to the street, I can't see anywhere but straight ahead, leaving me to guess what is coming. Someone is struggling against the guards, but the shouts of the men overpower the person being dragged down the street.

A young boy is pulled past us, kicking and screaming. He lifts his feet off the ground, hoping to drag the men down with the sudden shift of weight, but he's small and doesn't carry the weight he thinks he does. Gretel tugs at my sleeve, but there's nothing we can do.

The boy's hat falls off and is quickly trampled by another guard. The man shoves the boy as he dangles in the air between the other men. The child kicks his legs as if he's running, trying desperately to find any kind of traction with which to turn himself around to confront the older man.

Gretel buries her face against my arm, not wanting to see the boy in the light blue shirt and suspenders dangling in the air. He looks to be around her age, and I know this is the image she will carry with her as we wheel her into the palace in a few days.

The boy shouts as the older men yell over him, taking him further down the street. Just before my line of sight is cut off, I see the far guard angle himself—they're turning. Throwing my hand out to the side, I nearly collide with Gretel as I force an illusion of darkness between us and the street we just vacated. The guards pass by without seeing us.

A few agonizing minutes later, we hear the wails of townspeople, pleading with the guards. I hold my breath, knowing the sound that's about to fill the air. A tear slips out of my eye as the poor boy dies from the small charge they tied around him somewhere a few streets over.

"We need to go, Annika," Gretel says, tugging on my arm. Her voice has a hard edge to it. "We need to go home."

Before she can do anything else, more footsteps approach. Gretel leans back against the side of the building, not wanting to see this time. A few women's dresses swish by us in a rainbow of colors. They hurry ahead, not wanting to slow in front of the guard coming our way.

Their ankles twist as they look back to see the men approaching, but they don't lose their step. Their words mesh together as they speak, but I hear something about a rebel leader.

"Make way," a guard calls. His voice is deeper than my father's was. It's startling to hear. I've always associated my father with the deep tone of his voice and the scent of cinnamon, and the sensory connection is so strong, I can nearly smell the spice in the air.

More people walk by, and I realize they aren't trying to escape at this point—they're following orders. This is a parade.

They've caught someone.

Legs position themselves in front of the openings I was looking through, so I scoot down, trying to get a better line of sight. Gretel follows, curiosity getting the better of her.

It's easier to see around men—they have wide stances, but the women's dresses make it impossible to view anything. Judging by the number of people I can't see around, I'm guessing there's at least fifty people out there—it's enough for us to blend in. The guards have someone in their grasp, so they shouldn't have time to bother with the likes of what appears to be a mother and daughter mixed into the crowd.

"Blend in," I hiss, poking Gretel until she moves.

Once in line, we hover behind a man and woman, trying not to look as nervous as the young girl standing next to them. Guards pass by, weapons ready as they glance over the crowd, eyes glazed now that their job is done and they've chosen a victim.

"Get back, you swine," the deep voice calls again. I search the crowd for him, bobbing around heads as they move in and out of my line of sight.

Someone is kicked. Air rushes from the man's lungs as he crumples back into the crowd a few yards down. A log flips as he grabs hold to steady himself, sending it flinging into the street nearly colliding with a guard. The king's man pauses, glaring at the man who stumbled. One of the other guards whispers something into his ear, and the angry man looks away, letting the townsmen live another day.

The group sways, forcing their victim forward. I can't see around the tall guard standing in the front, his uniform blindingly bright.

Gretel wraps her arm around my hip in case we need to run. I wish I could brush back her blonde hair, but my illusion has covered any trace of the girl we raised to be an assassin. Gretel has always looked like an innocent child, but the dark hair similar to mine makes her look even more angelic.

The mass of guards steps closer, yelling about what happens to rebels and traitors when they're caught by the king's men. The speech is different than the usual one—though perhaps that's because we're in a different town and the guards take a different tone here.

"This man is accused of leading the rebellion against His Royal Highness, King Levin and his armies. You know what happens to traitors and liars, but this man is worse than any treacherous scum slithering through our streets of Perihausen! He is the leader of all of the rebels and charges have been brought against him by one of his co-conspirators for plotting to destroy the king and his kingdom!

"He is being taken to the palace where he will be brought before the council and justice will be leveled upon him. King Levin will decide how to handle this kind of atrocious behavior and this man will pay for his crimes, as will the sniveling rat that pointed him out to us."

The guards sneer around him in response.

I'm sure the man who accused the leader was only trying to survive, but it backfired on him, and now two men will die instead of one—both a bigger spectacle than the guards had thought.

The tall guard moves, swaying to reveal the rebel leader behind him. Gretel nearly falls next to me, clutching at me to hold herself up.

Bauer.

Our leader fixes his eyes straight ahead, refusing to look to the left or the right. He's adopted his limp again, heavily leaning on one of the guards each time he steps with that foot. His shoulders are back, and his head is held high as the guards parade him through the streets.

Unlike the young boy earlier, Bauer will not die today. He will be put on trial and accused of whatever the younger man blamed on him to escape death and anything else the king hurls at him to put on a good show.

His death will be far more complicated than an explosive wrapped around his mid-section in the center of town, standing on a platform for all to see the spectacle. No, Bauer's death will be a celebration unlike anything we've seen in Candestrachen.

A firefly takes off through the crowd, rising above the heads of the men and women forced to cheer the death of someone they'd rather help save—no one knows who Bauer is, but if the king wants him dead, they assume he must have done at least something to help the people of Perihauser in their minds.

I turn to Gretel to see if the firefly is hers as it flies through the crowd. A deft nod is my answer, her eyes fixed in horror on Bauer as they lead him past us. The mechanical firefly blinks in front of Bauer, almost as if it knows him. The man flinches for the first time, and I can tell by the tiny tick in his neck that he almost turns to search for us. He forces himself to stay still, refusing to accidentally give us up.

If Gretel weren't with me, or if I didn't need to finish the cake and take it to the palace to complete our mission, I'd risk myself and create an illusion to distract the guards, kicking them or pushing them long enough for Bauer to have a chance at escaping. I'm not alone though, and I know what Bauer would command me to do—protect the mission at any cost.

The guards harass him and the other man as they walk by. People scream insults at the two traitors, knowing what is expected of them. They try to hide the defeat and sadness in their voices so they aren't called out as sympathizers.

As soon as they round the corner, people turn back, peeling away from the group. Much like they do in Leipden, they run into homes and businesses, trying to stay out of sight. I move with the flow of the group, pulling Gretel along behind me. She matches my pace, never stumbling—I wonder if she's regaining her strength or if it's fear pushing her forward for the moment. It's often in moments of great weakness that we find our deepest wells of strength and do the impossible, at least, according to my father.

When we reach the end of the street, I slip into the shadows. It's still day, and while the shadows aren't dark enough to hide us, they offer us at least a little concealment, and we move. It's cooler in the shadows of the buildings than it is in the sun and I suddenly realize just how strong the wind is.

Leaves gather around our feet as I slow us, trying not to draw attention by running now that we're away from the crowd. Each step elicits crunching noises, and I worry we might be overheard.

The edge of the town is quiet, but people still loiter around as if the guards hadn't just been there. The men aren't using their brains, but if they want their heads on a spike, that's up to them.

Before stepping out, I cause a fountain to appear on the far side of them. Water bubbles up from the ground, slowly at first—enough to go unnoticed—but once it's a few inches high, it starts to get attention. The men turn, trying to figure out where the water came from.

With their backs turned, I point Gretel to the woods. I entice the illusion water higher—knee level, then up to their waists. As they reach out, I cut it off, pausing for a moment before it springs up again. Gretel guides us to the safety of the woods while I distract the men who could possibly turn us in later on if they think it might save them when the guards inevitably find them out here. When we're far enough away that I'm straining to see, I cut it off, leaving the men confused.

"I know," I cut Gretel off. "We'll figure out how to get Bauer back."

"No, we won't, Annika. The mission is in one week. If you think the king won't kill Bauer as part of the celebration, you're crazy." She sounds like her brother—practical, logical, mission first.

"We can complete the mission *and* save him."

"*No*, Annika, we *can't*. We both know it." Gretel's arms shake once as if her entire body wants to convulse but can't because she's holding her muscles so tight. She swallows, breathing heavily. "Think this through—what is he going to do?"

She's not talking about Bauer; she means the king.

"He will move up the event because you're right, he *will* want it as part of the celebration, but he also doesn't let his enemies live long. He will move the ball up to match the execution."

"Which means we have to go back," she whispers. "We have to follow the markers, Annika. We can't stay."

I close my eyes, taking a deep breath. I'm supposed to be the logical one here, and yet, I'm being emotional. Of everyone who was willing to die for this mission, I didn't expect Bauer to be the one to actually make the sacrifice—he wasn't even supposed to be in the palace. Frankly, I assumed it would be me—Hansel and his sister are far too resilient to die at the hands of King Levin and his whims.

"There," I point, catching sight of a glowing blue dot in the distance.

We make our way through the trees, walking at a normal pace. There's no need to exhaust ourselves yet. We've got a few hours before darkness falls and if we arrive late, the guards will likely have left my little bakery home, giving us time to make preparations for the new date the king is bound to shift to.

If my calculations are correct, we'll have no more than three days until his tolerance gives out and he wants to end Bauer. Our leader, on the other hand, will hold out until his dying breath. He will never give us up, but he'll hold out long enough to give us time to get everything into place so when we come to his funeral-masquerading-as-a-ball, we'll be ready to kill his executioner to prevent it from ever happening again.

The walk is long, much longer than the run. The wind gusts around our clothes and I realize I can drop the illusion I've been holding around us since we were in the town. My pink dress moves around my ankles, picking up stray leaves and pieces of debris.

We walk in silence—there's nothing to say. Bauer will die. We'll have to work night and day on the cake to be ready. Hansel will find us eventually. The king will die—there's nothing we can change until he does.

Another blue firefly blinks ahead, hovering in a bush. I open my hand, picking it up and returning it to the pouch on my hip. By the time we find the next two, the weight of the day has crashed over me, and I feel exhausted.

"Are you feeling any better?" I ask softly.

"I'll be fine," she replies. "Even if it moves up, I'll be fine."

She will have to be.

I didn't realize how far we'd traveled until it took half an hour to locate the next firefly. We nearly took the wrong path, but Gretel saw it blink in the distance on the opposite side of the fork. I have to squint to see it as she points.

Another twenty minutes and we find the next firefly, its blue glow bouncing off a tree as the sun shifts in the sky. The clouds take on a pink light, tinging everything a strange shade of red-gold.

"Annika!" Hansel's voice startled me. I jump, spinning to face him. I hadn't heard him approach, though, no one ever does if he doesn't want them to.

"Hansel."

"Hansel!" Gretel charges past me toward her brother.

Aurik stands next to him, Brahms just behind. All three hold axes in their hands—innocuous enough to be played off as if they were leaving work, but deadly enough to take down anyone who got between them and Gretel.

Hansel steps forward, dropping his weapon to the side. Gretel throws herself against her brother, and he wraps his free arm around her.

"What happened?" he demands.

"Bauer showed up," I inform them. "The guards were on their way, and he came to get us out."

"There were guards in the woods," Gretel continues. "They came for us."

"We made it to Perihausen. A woman hid us, but it didn't last long. We hid in the crowd and discovered that someone had turned Bauer in as a rebel leader. They have him, Hansel."

His face pales. Tension lines form around his eyes as he drops his arm from his sister's waist.

"They'll move up the ball," I say.

Hansel nods. "We need to get back. The bakery is fine—no one was there when we arrived. It looked like they did some damage to your cover story supply though."

"The cake?" I inquire. I'm terrified if they found the extra food, they might have also found our delivery method.

"You did a good job hiding it." He nods to Gretel.

"What did you do?" I turn to the girl. She hadn't had enough time to hide it when Bauer came in.

"I slipped a few of your plants in." She tries to shrug casually.

"She covered it with greenery like it was a massive plant stand." Hansel chuckles.

"She even added some trays of bread to it as if they were cooling there," Brahms adds.

"It was pretty inventive." Aurik cocks an eyebrow, shooting Gretel an impressed look.

A worried look fills Hansel's face when I glance at Gretel. She stares back at me defiantly.

"What did you do?" Hansel's voice comes out as a whisper.

When Gretel doesn't speak, I answer for her. "There were guards in the woods—apparently there are *always* guards in the woods now—and Gretel moved the trees again."

"But we didn't see anything shift." Aurik's statement comes out like a question.

"Further down," I inform him. "It wasn't the entire forest this time."

"Hansel, you've been holding out on us about your sister," Aurik protests good-naturedly. "We could have borrowed her last year for that big project—"

"No, we couldn't have." Hansel silences him. "She has a bigger purpose, and we're dangerously close to having that opportunity destroyed."

They grimace at his protective tone. Stepping away from the other men, Hansel pulls Gretel aside, whispering harshly. "How bad?"

She murmurs but I can't hear her reply. Aurik and Brahms glance at me uncomfortably—none of us like being caught in a sibling argument but there's nowhere we can go.

"We can't risk it," Hansel argues, still whispering loudly as if we can't hear him. Gretel quarrels back, crossing her arms over her chest. After a moment, she flings her hands out to the side, catching herself just before she shouts.

"Okay, that's enough," I interrupt. "We need to get back to the bakery. We have to replenish whatever the guards ruined and finish the cake because we all know Levin is going to move this stupid ball up and we'll all be in trouble if we're not ready on time."

The three men look taken aback when I use the king's name without his title. I like their reaction to it.

"She's not ready—" Hansel protests.

"I'm fine!" Gretel shouts, disturbing two birds sitting in different trees. They flap their wings at the same time, taking off in a similar direction.

"It doesn't matter," Brahms interjects. "Annika is right. We have to get back; we can handle this discussion there, no matter what we choose."

Hansel broods as his friends start to walk away, guiding us back to the bakery. I take Gretel by the arm, spinning her to follow them. After a moment, I hear Hansel's footsteps crunching behind us in the fallen leaves.

He stalks behind us for a few minutes, but eventually lengthens his stride and takes his place by Gretel's side. Hansel glances over Gretel's head to make eye contact with me. He clearly isn't happy, his narrowed eyes are a clear indication of that, but he softens his gaze, silently asking for my opinion on his sister's condition.

I think about it for a moment. If Gretel is sure she can handle the mission, we have to trust her. I understand why Hansel is so worried —I'm worried too—but this has to be Gretel's choice. She knows herself better than we do.

Gretel barely comes up to my shoulder, so I'm pretty familiar with the top of her head. Her hair parts in the middle, cascading down into long white-blonde strands on either side in a shiny curtain that protects her from the world when she hides behind it like I used to as a child. Somehow, looking down on her at this angle makes her seem even younger.

I nod.

Hansel purses his lips and nods back, closing his eyes for only a moment—he trusts us to make this decision, even though he doesn't like it.

The rest of the walk back to the bakery is quiet, comprised of stiff steps and dark moods.

The outside of the bakery is just as I left it earlier today, though it glows in the setting sun. I anticipate the fireworks display will be brighter and longer tonight in celebration of Bauer's capture. Brahms informed us that the fireworks earlier were also to announce a capture, this one in Gimpenlaug, though we haven't discovered who the king's men caught yet.

We trudge up the steps, and I want nothing more than to lean against Hansel's arm and let him drag me up the stairs to the bakery. He's too busy keeping Gretel upright.

The moment we get inside and close the door behind us, Hansel takes her upstairs to rest. Brahms and Aurik look to me for instructions.

"We're not going anywhere, so you might as well put us to work,"

Brahms says.

"He meant *you might as well feed us,*" Aurik corrects.

"You can have whatever the guards didn't take." I make my way to the back where I had set everything out of sight.

The room is practically empty. While they didn't tip anything over or destroy it, the guards helped themselves to the sweets and treats laying around the bakery. I'm sure if the king's cake had been baked and ready to go—assuming it was a real cake—they probably would have devoured that without a second thought as well, leaving me to take the fall if I didn't recreate it in time for the ball.

"Looks like there's some bread and cookies over there, boys, help yourselves." I wave at the remnants of the trays. It's a shame Bauer hadn't delivered that massive fake flour order I had placed yesterday…I have a feeling I'm going to need it to replace everything.

"Where do we start, Annika?" Brahms asks softly, touching my arm like Hansel might have before we became close.

I sigh. At least they're willing to help.

Pointing things out, I set them to work collecting materials for me while I walk into the other room to start the ovens. I don't bother playing with the fire, knowing Hansel will be down momentarily to start it.

As if on cue, the fireplace lights up, casting the room in a deep orange tint. Sidling up behind me, Hansel wraps his arms around me.

"Hansel, what if they see?" I shrug him off, attempting to slip away. He catches me by the hip and spins me, pinning me against the oven.

"Those two?" He grins, cocking an eyebrow at me. Hansel leans toward me. "What do you care? Let them find out."

"Find out you two have been making out for weeks?" Aurik walks into the room, arms full with bags of flour and sugar.

"Oh, whatever will we do when we find out *that* news?" Brahms asks innocently.

"Why, we might just die of shock." Aurik continues, setting down the supplies on the large table.

"Wow, really?" Hansel retorts. He wraps his arms around my waist. "Fine, if there are no secrets here…"

His lips touch mine softly, which is shocking considering the force with which he moved toward me. My hands rest on the crooks of his arms, and I let him kiss me publicly for the first time. The men ignore us for a moment before telling us to knock it off.

Hansel brushes back a strand of my long hair.

"I like not having to hide," he whispers just loud enough for me to hear. "And apparently, we were terrible at keeping it a secret anyway."

"*You* were. *You* were terrible at it. *I* had no one to keep it from."

Since I lost my father, all I've had was Hansel and his sister. Bauer too, I suppose. If anyone gave our secret away, it was Hansel.

"I think Gretel knows, too," he murmurs as he kisses me again.

"Oh, she knows."

"We *all* know," Aurik snaps. "What we *don't* know is how to bake this stuff. A little help here, Annika?"

The two motion at the table littered with supplies. I pull away from Hansel and start to direct the baking efforts. Once I have Aurik and Brahms settled, Hansel wheels the cake form out for me to begin my work. He leaves me alone to complete my task and takes his place alongside his cohorts.

I open and shut the lid a dozen times to make sure it will work. It doesn't so much as creak. When I'm satisfied, I begin to circle the wooden cake, formulating a plan for decorating it.

From the corner of my eye, I can see the three men watching me as I stalk around my project, but they don't say anything as I work. My hands reach for the fondant.

I smooth every bit of the fondant over the cake form, leaving only the top uncovered. It only picks up bits of light over the carvings I created on it earlier, the rest is so dark that it almost looks like I pulled night from the sky and whipped it into the fondant.

The fireworks explode outside as if the king knew what I was thinking. Pink fills the sky, radiant and bold, as it announces Bauer's capture. Reds sparkle after it, followed by screaming white blazes of light. The show would be magnificent if it weren't so murderous.

We make our way to the porch to watch it in case anything is different about it. Like every night, the fireworks glitter in the sky, reflections bouncing off of the pointed rooftops.

Minutes go by and the show proceeds as normal, the only variation is the colors and styles of fireworks the palace and towns shoot into the sky simultaneously. Hansel rests his hand on my shoulder as I lean against the porch railing. I can smell the scones inside and turn to go and check on them. Hansel's hand trails after me, but he doesn't take his eye off the skies above us.

I duck into the bakery and remove the tray of scones from the oven. Setting them on the table to cool, I glance around to see if anything else needs to be attended to.

"What is *that*?" Aurik's voice fills the room.

"It can't be," Brahms responds, panic in his voice.

"Annika!" I run to the door when I hear Hansel's harsh call.

In the sky, an orange fireball curves up into the air. I exit the bakery only a moment before it transitions from a streak of orange with a long tail into what looks to be a fire with a tail of blue and purple, almost like the wick of a candle. When the light hits it, it changes again, becoming a white glowing cloud trailing after a tiny spec of orange as it continues to arc up into the night sky.

"What is it?" I ask.

"It's a rocket, Annika." Hansel sounds breathless. It's terrifying.

As if totally disjointed, the rocket separates, leaving the thick trail of clouds behind, only a thin line of almost-blue clouds connecting the now-white glowing circle to the tail end of its streak.

"Where is it heading?" Aurik murmurs. I have a feeling he already knows.

Suddenly, it's as if the rocket explodes, a large cloud of pulsing blue frills out from it like a petticoat some of the towns ladies wear under their massive skirts. It swirls around the glowing streak as it changes its trajectory, beginning its descent.

Another moment goes by and none of us speak, fixated on the rocket sailing through the night sky. Behind it, fireworks continue to go off as normal in greens and yellows. The clouds from the rocket suddenly widen, becoming a solid wave rolling off the bright white light guiding it through the air. Something flickers behind it, leaving the secondary glowing object to pulse out strangely-shaped clouds in two different directions as it keeps up with the part of the rocket in the lead.

Pieces of the rocket break off, drifting quietly to the ground, glowing just as brightly as the main rocket. The entire glowing mass tips down, propelling itself quickly toward the ground before I realize what's happening.

"Hansel, is that—"

"Perihausen." He confirms my suspicions only moments before the rocket collides somewhere beyond the trees. Small ripples can be felt in the floorboards under my feet, but I likely wouldn't have noticed if I hadn't watched the rocket slam into the ground as it wreaked havoc on the city where Bauer was captured only hours ago. I hope the old woman who helped us is safe.

The vapor trail still glitters in the sky as smoke drifts up above the tree line to meet it. The fireworks finish their explosive show, the last of the finale sparkling away in the cool night breeze as we turn to go back inside.

"At least it wasn't here," Brahms says, breaking the silence.

"The king wouldn't hurt his precious cake." I didn't mean to lash out.

"He didn't touch Leipden, at least," Aurik adds.

"But he destroyed Perihausen," I protest.

"We don't know that for sure yet." Hansel tries to calm me. "We'll find out tomorrow."

"You know he did," I say under my breath as I return to my cake.

The dark colors inspire me, and I set to work decorating the device that will deliver death to King Levin.

It's late morning when I finally wake up, no longer perched against the chair I was leaning on while icing the wooden cake. My blanket is warm around me, demanding I stay in place longer.

The floor is cool when my feet touch it. Hansel must have carried me upstairs after I fell asleep, but there's too much work to be done to stay in bed any longer.

Opening the curtains, I find that the daylight is unaffected by the spoils of last night's attack. Opening the window, I can faintly smell smoke, and I'm sure once I reach the first floor and can see out another window that there will be a dark trail of black smoke from the charred ruins of whatever remains of Perihusen.

Candestrachen lost a fine town last night to the king's whims.

Downstairs, Gretel is awake and working over the stove. Bacon, eggs, and French toast scents fill the air. Aurik stares in Gretel's direction hungrily. Brahms looks up as I approach.

"You shouldn't have let me sleep so long."

"Thank your boyfriend," Aurik calls over his shoulder.

"Boyfriend?" Gretel snaps, turning to look at me. "Is that what we're finally calling it?"

The front door swings open, revealing Hansel. His frame fills the doorway, backlit beautifully by the sun. His blond hair takes on a golden sheen as the breeze moves a few strands. The girls in the town have been throwing themselves at him for years…if only they could see him now.

"You're up," he mentions, moving across the floor. He kicks the door closed behind him, cutting off the sunlight.

"What did you find out?" Brahms asks.

"The ball has been moved up."

"To when?" Brahms inquires.

"Tomorrow." Hansel sounds grim, his face showing the wear of the day, dragging down his features.

"Tomorrow?" I gasp.

"Tomorrow?" Gretel's terrified voice jerks us all into action. We leap toward her, ready to comfort her. I reach her first, wrapping her in my arms.

"You'll be okay, Gretel," Brahms promises her as Hansel reaches us.

"We'll take care of you," Aurik adds. "No one will hurt you."

"Will you be ready, Gretel?" Ever the big brother, Hansel sounds as if he's ready to carry her off to safety right now and call the entire mission off.

"Can you get me out of there, Hansel?" she asks.

"Always. I will always get you out of bad situations."

"Than I will do this," she announces, gathering her confidence around her like a barrier between her and the world. "Annika, can you finish the cake?"

It's as if Gretel has suddenly been possessed by the girl in the mill, ready to take down the king. I have no doubt that she can kill the king and escape.

"I can finish it, but you have to promise not to do anything today, Gretel. You need to be as recharged as possible when we put you in that cake tomorrow morning."

"This is nearly a week before we expected it to be," Hansel responds. "We need to make sure everything is in order and that we don't forget anything when the time comes. We're rushing, and that makes me nervous."

"I can work on a list while I'm sitting around since I'm not allowed to help." Gretel side glances at me. She adds quickly, "It will give me something quiet to do so I don't have time for my brain to stress out about everything."

"I'll get you some paper." I move away to find a notebook and pen for her.

When I return, I find her in a chair near the wooden cake—we'll be able to chat about the list while I work. Hansel stands behind us, observing the dark cake for a moment.

"Did he ask for that?"

"No." I shrug. "He said he wanted a cake to celebrate Candestrachen. What better way than to bring in the elements of the cities?"

"I don't see how—"

"You will," I interrupt him. "Now, go. You have work to do."

Aurik slips out the front door to prepare the other men for the change of orders. I have one day to complete this cake—in the morning, we have to deliver it to His Royal Highness.

"What *is* your plan for that, Annika?" Gretel asks as her brother steps away.

"The king is so fond of his candy-shaped rooftops and glittering light displays. I'm going to bring them to life on the cake."

"And his fondness for *death* will be included on the inside?" She smirks like her brother does.

"Yes, my dear, his death will most certainly be on the inside of his precious cake."

I lift the icing bag and begin to swirl large strands of bright pink frosting around the base of the cake. Walking around it, I cover it evenly with smooth lines of sugared perfection. After a while, I set the pink down and pick up an icing bag with white icing. Tracing along the same path, I mimic my motions, adding a thin white line next to each pink stripe.

Gretel mutters in approval, glancing up from her list for a moment before looking back down. I catch her staring at the cake when she doesn't realize I'm looking. I'm sure she's worried about everything, but the moment I look up as if I might glance over, she goes right back to work—I hope I'm helping keep her mind off of tomorrow.

In just over twenty-four hours, she'll be springing from the cake, prepared to touch the king of Candestrachen's hand. She'll pull the life from him, taking on every bit of darkness and soul inside of him. It will flood her over, threatening to break her.

I've seen her do it before—take life. Each time, it darkens her eyes, leaving her looking cold and lifeless. Though I've only ever seen her do it to plants, I know the toll it takes on the young girl's mind and body.

Hansel will not only have to pull her to safety once the guards realize what's happening, but he will have to use his power over light and *light* to pull her back from the evil she will have to take on. He's the only one that has the ability to rescue her and share the burden.

Along the top tier of the cake, I drizzle an off-white liquid icing, allowing it to dribble down the sides of the top tier of the massive cake. The droplets fall down, some reaching the top of the next tier, others ending relatively high.

I hand a bowl of sprinkles to Gretel. "Here, I know you were looking forward to this."

She grins and tosses a few handfuls at the drying icing. Most of them stick in place. I walk around, adding the colorful sprinkles to the sides she can't reach from her chair.

"So much for not working." Hansel snickers at us. Without missing a beat, Gretel tosses a handful of sprinkles at her brother's face. He reels back in surprise.

I join the young girl, tossing the tiny candies at Hansel…I'll regret it when I have to clean it up later.

Aurik walks in just in time to see Brahms and Hansel team up against Gretel and me. With a flick of my wrist, I transform the entire room into the candy-world illusion I had cast a few days before. The room springs to life with candy chandeliers and chocolate fountains. Swirled candies cover the banisters, and the fire pops in delight as I string illusion hard candies up by their wrappers from one edge of the fireplace to the other.

Brahms looks shocked as he turns to explore this sudden new world, eyes wide with delight. Aurik picks his jaw up and grins, frowning only when he realizes illusions aren't edible.

"Cruel," he comments.

"Isn't *everything* we're doing these days?" I counter.

"As delightful as this is, I have news," Aurik redirects us. "Bauer is to be executed at the ball tomorrow."

We grow somber as he explains the new plans for the party.

"The guards will be coming for you tomorrow morning, Annika. They'll escort you and the cake to the palace to see that nothing happens with it. I lied and told them I was your brother and that I would deliver the news of the rush order to you so they wouldn't come here themselves."

"At least you didn't say you were her boyfriend," Brahms jokes, glancing at Hansel.

"I would have turned him over as the witch they've been searching for if he had," I say sweetly, batting my eyelashes.

"I knew I liked you," Hansel adds, throwing an arm around my shoulder.

"You like me for my peanut butter fudge and my pastries."

"We've established that," Hansel replies, "but I like you for other reasons, too, like your quick sarcasm."

"It's her lips," Aurik jumps in. "Don't deny it. You're in it for the kissing."

"And that's enough of that, thank you," Gretel says shrilly. "We need to get back to work."

Aurik quickly relays the rest of the information he and his team found out, and we all settle back in to complete our tasks—the boys baking up our alibi, Gretel ensuring we won't forget anything, and me sugarcoating King Levin's demise.

"Open by order of the king!"

I wheel around to face the door. My hand dances in the air, concealing the scones, cookies, breads, and pies Hansel, Aurik, and Brahms had created. The candy-world illusion drops immediately, taking the sparkling sprinkles with it. Another flick of my wrist conceals Gretel behind a false wall with Aurik and Brahms as her protectors. Hansel is at the door before I can drop my hand.

I nearly drop the icing bag as I try to look natural as the guards force their way in.

"Where is the baker?" one demands.

Hansel looks to me.

"I'm the baker," I answer softly.

"By order of King Levin, we are to deliver you to the palace." The guard eyes me carefully, slowly dragging his gaze over my dark red dress.

"I assumed as much," I reply, motioning to the cake. "I need a few more hours to finish the decorations."

I lean toward the cake, ready to continue my work. The guards grumble.

"Surely you don't mean for me to leave with a half-finished cake. What will His Majesty say?"

The guards protest rudely, but Hansel silences them. "The lady says she's not done, and your job doesn't require you to escort us there until the ball tomorrow. If you want to go out and have fun this evening, go. You don't need to babysit us while we're icing a cake. Come back tomorrow to collect us."

"Fine, finish the cake. We can go in the morning."

"We'll bring the vehicle first thing."

Strange, they didn't seem to have brought a vehicle to transport us this afternoon. Perhaps they were anticipating finding me flustered without the cake ready and thought they'd be taking me to be punished instead of lauded for my magnificent sugar creation.

They stalk out of the bakery and down the steps. The snake that chases them is my own design, slithering after them as one of the men screams long enough to make Hansel snicker beside me. The snake hisses, lashing out, only to disappear as the men run off.

"Testy now, aren't we?"

"I didn't like them." I eye Hansel. "They were planning on hauling me to the palace to stand trial."

"Ah, you noticed that too, did you?"

I drop the illusion as we turn back from the doorway.

"It's safe," Hansel announces. "We need to get this finished and ready to go, though."

"Did I hear you invite yourself along on the cake delivery?" Aurik asks, stepping away from his place along the wall.

"Better than trying to *talk* myself in," Hansel retorts. "The two of you are on watch duty tonight. If those guards come back, we have to be ready to get Gretel into place before they make it up the stairs. You can take turns standing watch while the rest of us sleep."

"We should stay down here by the cake," I comment, pushing back my hair. I wind part of it around my finger in a loose curl.

"Agreed. But first, we need to actually finish it." Hansel takes my elbow and turns me back to the cake covered in candies, swirls, and sugar designs. He whispers into my ear. "After you, mistress baker."

"It's a good thing you all need me tomorrow, or I'd have to end myself right now after a sappy line like that." Gretel pretends to gag. "Now fetch me a snack. I'm hungry, and I'm not supposed to do anything for myself."

She plops herself back down on her chair and waves for her brother to bring her a pastry.

"This only lasts until tomorrow, little sister," he warns her playfully.

"We'll see," she retorts, waving her hand again. "I'm killing a king, after all."

"You're rescuing Candestrachen," I add, holding the icing bag that I just scooped up out to her waiting finger. "Killing the king is just the method that gets us there. Don't forget that."

Hansel looks surprised, lips slightly parted as he returns.

"Don't ever forget that," he says seriously to his little sister, turning to her. It's important we protect her from what she's about to do—taking a life, even to save thousands, is a devastating, life-altering situation to be in. I imagine the poor girl will have a hard time coping with it after.

"Got it." She licks the white icing off her finger, making a popping sound for emphasis.

"Now let me see that list while Annika finishes this monster up." He kneels down beside Gretel, eyeing me from under his long, dark lashes. I turn away, not needing the distraction.

"Are you ready?" Hansel asks as we lean against the railing. Brahms and Aurik sit inside, giving us a few minutes alone on the porch to decompress before we turn in for the night.

"The cake is ready," I answer. "I *think I* am. I'm nervous. What if I can't hold the illusion long enough?"

"You can," he promises, taking my hand. "You've held massive illusions for very long periods of time. All you have to do is keep the three of us from being recognized once we get inside. The rest is up to Gretel and me."

"I'm nervous about that too," I confess.

"You don't think I can get her out of there?" I can hear the frown in his voice. The fireworks display has long since ended, but I almost wish Hansel would add a little lighting out here for us to see by since the moon is hidden behind the clouds.

As if reading my mind, a string of lights snakes its way around the column next to me, adding a soft glow as Hansel turns me toward him. His touch is warm against the coolness of the breeze.

"You're the only one that *can* get her out, Hansel." I sigh. "I'm just...I'm worried that something will go wrong. Our entire plan had to be rearranged and pulled together in one day. There are so many ways it could fail."

"We're going to be fine, Annika." He lifts the necklace off my neck, twisting it in his fingers. "I've always been able to find you by this when you were wearing an illusion. It has always been the *key* to reuniting us."

A lone cricket chirps in the yard somewhere. I nearly glance toward it, but I know we're having an important conversation.

"I'll be able to find you tomorrow, no matter what. And because of you and your necklace, I'll be able to find Gretel because of her necklace too. No matter what happens, no matter how many illusions you pull, I'll be able to recognize you."

I raise my hand, touching the gold trinket on the end of my mother's golden chain. It's a key with a burst of sparkling light at the top—a perfect representation of the lights Candestrachen is so obsessed with. In the palace, they'll catch the light and sparkle—even across the room, anyone who is specifically looking will notice it.

"I'm changing the plan, Hansel."

"What?"

My wrist brushes against the skin on his cheekbone, lightly brushing over his face as I move strands of his hair back from his eyes. He leans into my touch.

"I know we had planned to make Gretel a brunette and younger, but there's a better way now—the guards have handed it to us."

"What do you mean, Annika?" He reaches up and takes my hand, turning his face to kiss my open palm. It burns through me as if I accidentally touched the wire rack in the oven while adding a tray of uncooked muffins.

"The guards want a witch...we'll give them a witch. It won't be a tiny girl betraying the king, it will be the haggard old woman they saw in the woods that day. We'll give them their greatest nightmare—the woman who destroyed the forest and cost men their lives. They'll search for her until the day they die, but they'll never find a little blonde girl living with her brother in Leipden."

His lips are on mine as he mumbles, "You're brilliant." His fingers scrunch through my hair as he focuses on our deep kiss. I don't bother to stop him, even though our friends are only feet away inside the house. After an intense moment, I pull away.

"We should go in."

"Should we?" He grins.

"We need to sleep, Hansel. Tomorrow, we go to the palace."

He lets me lead him inside, holding his hand behind me with my arm stretched out as he pauses long enough to let me know he wants to stay.

Scooping up an apple from the table, he hands it to me as Aurik heads outside to take the first watch. Hansel sinks along the wall, waiting for me to join him a few feet from the cake form. I nestle against him, leaning against his shoulder and chest as I take a bite of the apple.

"It's always amused me how someone who bakes all these sugary treats could prefer healthy food like apples."

"A different kind of sweet, my friend."

"Well, I prefer your kind of sweet." He kisses my lips again. "Maybe apples aren't so bad after all."

"Annika, it's time." Gretel shakes me gently. "Help me into the cake, Annika."

The room is deathly quiet aside from the snap of the fire and Gretel's tiny voice. Hansel and Aurik lay sprawled out on the floor, sleeping in different corners. Brahms stands on the porch, a sliver of his arm and side visible through the window.

"Wake up Hansel, and we'll help you—"

"No."

I blink at her.

"I will not say goodbye to my brother. I won't do it. I'll see him after, and that is that. Now, help me in before they wake up. We need to be ready when the guards arrive."

"Did you even eat yet?" I rub my eyes.

"I'll eat inside. You can hand me some snacks before you close it and add the final layer of icing." She tugs at my hand. "Please, Annika, I need to do this before I lose my nerve."

"Okay, okay." I stumble to my feet. "Go get whatever snacks you want, and I'll create the ladder."

I poke at my eyes again, trying to see straight. Blinking, I force my curls back. Separating my feet, I find my balance and stare at the cake. Terror washes over me—this is it.

My hands move slowly as if I'm conducting musicians. They flow through the air gracefully, and I picture the strangest set of stairs that lead from the floor, around the side of the cake in a wide arc. Railings appear on either side of the steps, swirling around the edges of the king's cake. I douse the entire thing in what looks to be pink swirled frosting and rock candy lollipops.

Gretel smiles softly as she returns.

"Gretel," I say, taking her hand as she sets her treats on the chair next to me. "I know you wanted to look a little different for this, but we've come up with a new plan—one where they'll never have any hope of finding you."

She raises an eyebrow at me.

"Gretel, you're going to be a witch."

"What?" She raises an eyebrow, her voice flat.

"From the woods. You're going to be the witch that rearranged the forest. A haggard old thing. When they come looking, they'll never expect to find a child."

She cringes as I use the word *child*, but she nods in understanding.

"I'm already the witch that rearranged the forest."

"But now you'll look like her."

"It's a shame not everyone has gifts like we do. It would make all of this a lot easier."

"It's a glorious thing that we are unique in this, Gretel, or we'd never pull this off—they'd be watchful of everyone. Besides, can you imagine what King Levin would do if he had the ability to do more than create fancy clothes with his gift?"

"He would be so jealous if he knew you could create illusions." She giggles quietly. "If he knew about you, you'd be stuck by his side for the rest of your life, transforming his little parties into even-more-grand events."

"You're probably right. Good thing he'll never find out." I take a deep breath. "Are you ready?"

She nods. Her eyes dare me to try to say anything that remotely sounds like a goodbye.

"Once you're inside, I'll seal off the top." I escort her to the first step. She places her hand on the rung of the railing and lifts a foot daintily. "You'll know when it's time to come out.

"I'll leave you in this form until we reach the palace and then I'll give you the illusion of an old woman. The ride will be long and probably bumpy, even with the motored machine. Try not to crash into the sides of the cake. If you need more air, you know what to do."

She nods, taking the next step.

"Try to focus on your surroundings. I'll be in the vehicle with you, so listen for my voice."

"I doubt they'll let you speak." She takes another step, allowing her to look down at me. My heart hammers in my chest with every step she rises into the air.

"Than just know that I'm there. Focus on every sound you hear. You'll be able to hear Levin's voice when he gets close enough to cut the cake.

"Be careful of the knife in his hand when you come out of the cake form. You're going to surprise him, and he might lash out. You need to be quick about it."

Gretel nears the top of the cake form, dressed in dark-colored clothes. She looks like an avenging angel.

"Do what you need to do, then get out of the cake, Gretel. Run. Hansel will find you, and I'll block however I can."

"I know."

"I'll find you when it's over, Gretel," I promise.

"I know you will, Annika. You've always taken care of Hansel and me." She takes the final three steps, tipped down into the cake form. My fingers move, adding a few steps that disappear as she takes her foot off of them until she's standing up to her chest inside the wooden contraption. "I'll see you after."

She taps the sparkly necklace on her chest, and I tap on mine. Hansel will be wearing something similar on his coat pocket as well. All three charms shiny and noticeable, but nothing that can tie us together.

I hand the food to her and Gretel closes the lid, settling into the cake. I turn to find Brahms staring in the window at us. His eyes are glassy. He tips his head toward Hansel, eyes squinting as if asking why we didn't wake him.

I clutch my necklace in my fingers and smile. Nodding, I assure him it's okay, this is what needed to happen. Brahms sighs and turns back to his post.

I double and triple check my work once the top of the cake is concealed. When Brahms and Aurik switch places, I drag Brahms over to check my work.

"It's fine, Annika. You did good work."

"I'm sure it's fine," Gretel calls from inside the cake, her voice muffled by layers of fondant and icing.

"Aurik and I are going to try to rescue Bauer," Brahms confides in me quietly. "Hansel and Gretel will be our priority, of course, but if they don't need us, we're going to try to prevent the execution. We're hoping it takes place after the cake."

"You don't think he will use the cake to celebrate?" I frown. "And *you're* not even supposed to *be* at the palace."

"I'm sure he will, but maybe you could make something flash on the cake to keep drawing his attention all afternoon so he can't take his mind off it and he'll do it early."

"We have no idea when he will use the cake, Brahms."

"It's our best shot. Maybe we can get Bauer out in the chaos."

"Okay, I'll try, but I can't do anything to compromise Gretel."

"I would never ask you to." He touches my elbow.

"Thank you for risking yourself to try to save Bauer. You and Aurik could be safe in all this, but I'm really glad you're going to try."

"You three shouldn't be the only ones taking a risk today." He pats my hand. "Now, wake up Hansel and let's get ready. The light is peeking up, and I imagine the guards will either show up incredibly early or incredibly late."

"Gretel," I say a bit louder so she can hear me. "It's time to wake your brother up."

I want to give her as much time to prepare for his reaction as possible. Walking over to Hansel, I kneel down and touch his arm. He blinks awake, smiling for only a moment as he sees me before he remembers what day it is. He sits up quickly.

"Are they here?" He tosses a blanket off of himself and jumps to his feet.

"No, not yet." I take his hand. "We need to eat before they arrive though."

His eyes sweep the room.

"Where is Gretel?"

"She's ready, Hansel." It takes a moment before he catches on. His muscles tighten as he stalks toward the cake.

"Hansel, don't you dare upset her," I snap at him, whispering so Gretel can't hear. "She didn't want some big goodbye scene to throw her off. Tell her good luck and come outside to yell at me."

Hansel stares me down for a moment, jaw clenched. Glancing at the cake, tears fill his eyes. "I'm not going to yell at you," he whispers.

He looks like he's being torn in two, like some machine the guards use to torture people is shredding him right down the middle. I wish I could protect him from this like he's protected me so many times before.

"You good in there, Gretel?" he calls, gaze fixed on the floor off to the side.

"I'm fine," she calls back, sounding stronger than Hansel looks at the moment.

"Okay, I'm going to get something to eat and then I'll be back to walk through everything with you."

"Okay," she calls in reply.

I step forward and take Hansel in my arms—I know how hard this is for him. He lets me hold him for a minute, transferring his worry into our embrace. If I can carry even a little of it for him, I will.

His breath is shaky when he pulls away, but to his credit, his body doesn't show any signs of shuddering. He takes both of my hands in his, holding them near his chest.

"It will be okay, Hansel. We'll get her out of there."

"I know." He pulls away from me, sauntering over to the table for food. He picks up a palmier and holds it in his hands. After a moment, he takes a bite, looking like he might be sick. For as terrified as I am, it's so much worse for him with his little sister putting her life at risk.

"They're here." Aurik slips into the bakery from the porch.

Hansel swallows the rest of the sugary treat.

"Did you eat?" He shoved one at me. I gratefully devour it, wiping my hands on a towel before running over to the cake.

"Ready, boys?" I ask as Aurik and Brahms shove themselves against the back wall. I put an illusion wall between us as Hansel helps me move the cake. "Time to go, Gretel. We'll be with you the whole way. Just watch for the pendants."

She stays quiet, knowing her mission has started.

The motor on the vehicle roars loudly as the guards pound up the steps. I open the door before they can knock, inviting them inside. Before we went to sleep, we put away all of the extra pastries so the guards wouldn't see them, leaving only a tray out for us to eat this morning. I motion to it, inviting the guards to partake.

Hansel instructs them on how to help move the cake. Together, the three men lower the cake down the stairs and wheel it toward the brightly colored vehicle. Leave it to the king of Candestrachen to go overboard on the decorations on a motor vehicle.

The taller guard lowers the back, pulling down a ramp. The entire vehicle lowers to the ground, leaving the ramp as a mere decoration. Had they tried, they could have easily just lifted the cart with the cake into the vehicle.

As the men assist him, I take a small magnetic device and push it against the underside of the wheel well. Hansel reprogramed his fireflies to work in unison, so as we make our way from the palace after the assassination, we'll be able to easily find our way back to territory we know, no matter what happens.

The guards instruct Hansel to push the cake inside, nearly touching the seats in the front. From the sides, the men pull down extra seats and demand I get in. I climb up next to Hansel, taking a seat opposite him, positioning ourselves between the guards who follow us in and the cake.

A third man drives, steering us away from the bakery. Once they're sure we're gone, Aurik and Brahms will race through the woods toward the palace, slipping onto paths the vehicle can't take. They won't beat us, but it won't be more than an extra half hour until they arrive—it will give us enough time to be turned away from the palace and use illusions to slip back in, that way, in the aftermath, the baker can't be blamed because she was back at her shop, making pastries.

The road is less bumpy than I thought, the vehicle stabilizing us each time we hit a dip in the road. The cake is barely jostled as we move. If I didn't hate things the king oversaw so much, I might actually be impressed with their ingenuity.

Hansel watches me in the bouncing light of the vehicle. The sun shifts and changes as we drive under trees and around corners, casting long shadows at strange angles. He locks eyes with me, stretching his foot out quietly to touch mine, calming his nerves as much as mine.

I wish I could see out of the back of the motorized transportation, but there are no windows on the back doors. It's probably for the best —the guards can't accidentally see our fireflies and grow suspicious— but I wish *I* could check on them.

The journey stretches out, simultaneously taking forever and no time at all. The guards comment crudely as I step out of the vehicle to allow them to assist Hansel. Making sure no one is looking, I pull the magnetic container off the car and toss it away.

The men maneuver the cake out of the vehicle and onto the ground. They instantly wheel it up onto a marble ramp, taking it into the palace.

"Thank you," a woman with folded hands and a high collar says from the platform. "You may go now."

I start to protest, but she holds a hand up. "You are dismissed, young ma'am."

I blink. I hadn't anticipated being turned away so quickly.

"You don't want to come in here," she adds quietly. "This is no place for a pretty young thing like you. You will leave immediately. You've been thanked for your service, now go."

Her words leave no room for argument, but I've heard they prefer men take the accolades and praise inside the palace—I suppose this wise woman is why. I appreciate her looking out for me, but I value her unexpected part in our assassination plot even more—she has no idea she's giving me an even better alibi for the murder. At least I didn't have to come up with a reason for them to keep me out.

The woman hands me a few coins, not nearly enough to cover the cost of the cake if it had been real. I pocket it and turn to go. With the guards inside guiding the cake, Hansel and I are left to walk all the way back to the bakery.

Once we're out of sight, we round the corner to the front of the palace where large groups of people wait to get inside. Dignitaries hover near the front, flanked by townspeople doing their duty to show up to the frivolities.

My fingers dance, dousing me in shades of green. I release my hair from its bun and let it fall down to my waist. Hansel's breath catches as I look up. He's suddenly clad in an illusion dusty blue suit, with a long jacket reminiscent of the one Bauer was wearing when he was captured. I change Hansel's hair to a shocking red-colored that will ensure he is noticed in the crowd. My own hair morphs into a light brown that's not quite light enough to be blonde, but not dark enough to be brunette.

"I'm amazed at how stunning you look, even in different forms."

"You'd rethink that if you saw my haggard look from the other day," I joke. "Now, go get yourself into the palace. Good luck."

"Are you sure? That might be your best look of them all." He kisses my cheek, grinning. "After you, madam."

I make my way into the crowd, looking for an opening. If I can find a family or group, I might be able to sneak in at the end of their party without the guards noticing an extra person. The townspeople huddle together, acting like they're having fun, but there is nervousness in the depths of their eyes, and they quickly look away when I accidentally make eye contact with them. I hope they all make it out when the chaos erupts.

A group of men and women hover at the far edge, and I make my way over as the line shifts, allowing people into the palace. Slowly, I inch toward them. One step at a time, I get closer.

Suddenly, they sidestep, walking into the palace through a second door the guards open—I missed my chance.

"Well, what do we have here?"

I look up into the eyes of a guard towering over me.

"I'm here for the ball," I reply, batting my eyelashes. One of the perks of an illusion is that I can fix up my lashes when I need to.

"Are you now?" he asks. "Are you on the list?"

"Do I need to be?" I ask breathlessly. I could gag.

"That depends," the guard steps toward me.

From the corner of my eye, I catch sight of Hansel's illusion-red hair. He tries not to look horrified, but I can't miss his wrinkled nose and tight brow.

I take the guard's hand holding the list and stretch on my toes to lean over his arm. Pointing at the list. "There I am. Though, I'm not sure I'll be able to stay for the entire ball. If you see me coming out of those doors a little early, well, don't you fret. I just needed a little fresh air."

My toes curl in my shoes as I realize just how bad I am at flirting. I bat my eyes again, hoping to distract him from my ridiculous words.

His hand drops from the list as he transfers it to the one with the pen. It finds its way to my backside. "I'll keep an eye out for you."

I spin away, rushing toward the open palace door as he laughs behind me. Without bothering to wait for Hansel, I scurry down the hall to find my place in the throne room where the cake will be waiting.

If the outside of the palace was impressive, the inside is *inspired*. For as stunning as my candy-world illusions are, the interior of King Levin's palace is more spectacular and encompasses everything I created without any reference to candy.

Large columns shoot up from the floor covered in hand-carved vines and flowers. The marble floor is tinged pink and laid with small rivers of sparkling gold that course throughout the entire room. Chandeliers grace the ceiling every few yards with one massively large one hanging in the center.

Floor-to-ceiling windows allow the sparkling light to bounce through the diamonds placed into the crystal glass. Along the tops of the walls, there is a runner of precious jewels in every color, acting as a border for the room.

The cake sits by the throne—a massive silver thing made of arrows and dark metal. The king hasn't arrived yet, but once his crowd fills the room, I'm sure he'll make a grand entrance—he'll probably fly in on the back of a golden swan if the rest of this room is any indication of the lengths he will go to in order to impress people.

"Are you okay?" Hansel whispers harshly as he slowly walks by.

"Fine," I mumble—we can't be seen together. "Go away."

He steers himself across the room, positioning himself a dozen people away from the cake in the second row of the crowd. Pedestals with roses under glass cases dot my side of the room, and I pick a place next to a dark red one. I can tap it with my elbow if I need something to anchor myself to as I focus on everything around me.

Using my sleeve to hide my movements, I wave my fingers at the cake, adding a few small sticks around the tiers. If I need to get the king's attention, this will be how I do it.

The room grows louder as more townspeople enter. The dignitaries and visitors from other lands take places near the throne and in the stands off to the side left for guests of the king. Music swells up, and a number of couples dance as if it's their job—I'm sure it is—to make outsiders believe this is something we revel in every week. At least the king enjoys himself at these parties.

Heat creeps up my neck into my cheeks as more people fill the room. They mumble about Bauer out in the courtyard, locked in a cage with a rope around his neck, waiting for his execution. The dignitaries discuss it so loudly from their places in the stands that I can hear them taking bets on how the king will murder my friend.

The room feels like it's moving around me, but it's only overwhelm messing with my perception. A few deep breaths and I calm myself. I hope Gretel is staying focused inside of the cake. I move my fingers, transforming her into the old hag that claimed the forest as her own.

As her dress grows dark, and wrinkles form on her skin, I add a small piece of candy into her hand to let her know it's done. She can't eat it, but it will make her smile and give her a reason to relax. I picture her tucking her now-gray and matted locks behind her ear as she arranged her witch's dress to accommodate the space around her. We were only separated for a few moments, but she must have been terrified to be on her own with no protection or backup.

An hour goes by as more people file into the throne room. The noise is louder. Each breath makes it hotter. I lock eyes with Hansel once and his lips part, but I look away.

The world stops as Levin, King of Candestrachen walks into the room.

Levin struts into the room, a gold crown rests on his dark brown hair. Like me, he's wearing a green outfit, complete with a cape. For a moment, I consider giving Gretel a cloak with a hood to add to the witch's character, but the crowd needs to see she's old and a hood would cover that.

The king takes long steps through the center of the room as the crowd parts, bowing as he passes. He holds one arm behind his back, shoulders straight and head held high as he surveys this tiny sample of the kingdom crammed into his spacious throne room.

Slowly, he takes the steps up to his seat. Spinning quickly, he makes a few women nearby gasp in surprise as he faces the room. The man sits, resting his hands on the ends of the armrests of his silver chair. One side of his lips tick up in a sickening smile and the crowd cheers.

Music pours out from the instruments in the corner of the room, the people playing them intentionally precise about every note. The chandeliers sparkle and I wonder how much Hansel is itching to change the colors of the light in them to shock the king.

The king waves his hand, and the dancing begins. People whirl around the room as I try to hide behind the glass-encased rose. Eventually, a man offers me his hand, and I have no choice but to allow him to lead me to the floor.

As I swirl, I try to find Hansel. Instead, the eyes I find are far more sinister—King Levin. He watches me for a moment as I dance. I try not to take notice, but it's hard to rip my eyes away from his piercing gaze. Does he remember me from outside Bauer's shop? He can't in my altered state, but I feel as though he knows everything about our plan as if he can read my mind.

The man swirls me one last time and I hurry off the floor with the crowd and Levin looks away, locking eyes with another girl and grinning wildly—no wonder the woman with the clasped hands warned me off. I huddle next to the rose again, watching the cake closely, but no one seems to be bothering it.

The king eventually gives a speech, ranting about the rebels and how easy it was to catch Bauer. He still doesn't know our leader's name, so he assigns one that doesn't fit Bauer at all.

The list of crimes is long, but we knew it would be. Outside, fireworks go off, giving me an idea. If I need to distract the king, now is the time for it.

I brush my thumb and pointer finger together as if I were snapping, brushing the skin together enough that if I were in a silent room, I'd hear a quiet swish. The sticks I had placed in the cake earlier spring to life—sparklers—emphasizing the king's words just as he gets to the part about moving outside for the execution. He's picked a particularly painful way to kill Bauer, and if I can give him even the smallest chance of escape, I have to try.

Levin glances to his right toward the cake. If he wasn't so distracted by the sparking dessert, he might have spotted Hansel with his illusion-red hair glaring at him in the background.

For a moment, hope swells in my chest, and I actually believe we can do this—we can assassinate the mad king and take our country back. But then the king takes a step off of his platform toward the crowd.

"I'd like to thank you all for joining me today," King Levin addresses them, holding his hands out in front of him benevolently. "I know you weren't expecting to be here until next weekend, but with the rebels quelled here in the glorious kingdom of Candestrachen, I couldn't help but share my joy with you."

He takes another step, and several stewards rush forward to move the cake as Levin barely moves one finger toward it.

"Given this entire event has been rearranged, I think perhaps we should toss aside tradition on this momentous occasion and celebrate first—perhaps even *during* the execution of our enemy. Let him see us reveling in the life I've created for this kingdom—a life of happiness and generosity. Let him see what he tried to destroy and what he shall never have for himself. What do you say?"

The crowd cheers on command, raising hands into the air. A man starts a chant. The crowd picks it up, praising Levin and his wondrous works.

Men wheel the sparkling cake from its position off to the side to where it can be seen in front of the king, closer to the far side of the crowd as they wait for him to call it forward.

Any normal person would have noticed the sparklers should have gone out by now, but I hold them in place, sparking and glowing for the king as he monologues. He never even considers the sparklers wouldn't bend to his will.

Suddenly, the sparklers glow brighter, as if an entire cloud of light surrounded each of them—Hansel. I find him in the crowd, but his eyes are trained on the cake as they should be.

"Even our cake knows we've earned our treats today!" the king jokes as the sparklers glow, transitioning to a red glow. "I've never seen a cake so beautiful—just look at it! It's Candestrachen in cake form!"

He uses the words he sent to me when he requested the cake be made and I feel as if I've done my job well. It may be a fake cake, but the outside was crafted to perfection. Dark icing with pink and white swirls and streams of icing flowing down the sides mixed with sprinkles—the architecture of the kingdom ready to bite the king when he least expects it.

"Ladies and gentlemen," he continues. How can one man speak for so long? "Today we celebrate the quick thinking of our guards. We celebrate the takedown of a rebel leader who never stood a chance against the *greatness* that is Candestrachen. We celebrate a cake that represents the *greatness* of this nation, but first, we celebrate the death of a traitor."

He lifts the hand near my side of the room, and the doors fly open as guards stomp into the room. The cake keeps sparkling as everyone turns. Trapped between several of the king's men is the man who turned in Bauer.

They force him several steps into the room before kicking the backs of his knees, making him drop to the ground. A guard pulls a sword—a weapon I've never seen any of the king's men use before—and swings it at the man before any of us can react.

I've witnessed men and women being blown up by explosive devices before, I've even seen them being pulled apart in different directions, but I've never seen one die like this before—it's archaic and grotesque. Blood pools out, reminding me of the icing I dripped on the cake less than a day ago. People push back to avoid it touching their shoes.

"And now...cake!" the king proclaims. I turn back to find him grinning, looking every bit the madman we know him to be.

The group turns in horror toward him. Several women blanch, fighting to keep their hands by their sides instead of clutching their chests. Children fidgeted against their parents' legs, trying not to react.

I've heard stories about time slowing down when major moments occur in one's life—every sense becomes sharpened, every heartbeat is felt, everything is experienced in acute detail. That doesn't happen now, but I wish it would so I could be more aware of everything going on around me—it would let me protect the people I love easier.

The guards wheel the cake forward in front of the mad king, sparklers still spraying small sparks everywhere. Even if the king got close enough, the illusion wouldn't burn him.

The executioner walks up from the back of the room, drying off the sword on a piece of material he found somewhere. I wonder for a moment if the king planned it this way—he probably did.

Once the blade is clean, he hands it to King Levin with a slight bow. This wasn't a part of our plan—he could run Gretel through with that sword, and she has no idea the king is holding it. She likely doesn't even know how the man was killed across the room.

"Darkness once overtook us," Levin says, slipping back into his speech as he points at the black, fondant-covered cake. "But *I* have brought the light."

I twist my fingers together again just enough that the sparklers expand with his words as if on cue. I can see Levin's eyes widen in surprise, but he grins as if he knew it was coming.

"I've brought life back into this nation and have given it a reason to thrive. We live in a land of luxury that cannot be found in any of our neighboring kingdoms." He turns to his guests. "We welcome you here, my brothers. There is none greater than Candestrachen, and your friendship is welcome here."

He glances around to his guests, selecting which will be honored. He nods to an old man with a gray beard reaching halfway down his chest. The man returns his nod, lips tight.

Levin turns, his green jacket and cape moving gloriously behind him. A piece of his long, brown bangs flips in front of his eye, and for a moment, he almost looks like he could belong in the towns of Candestrachen, selling wares in a shop, attending parades, and courting young women. His sneer morphs his face into something dark and twisted, though, as his evil side creeps out.

The side of the top tier of the cake unlatches, moving just enough so I can see it. Gretel has clicked the button on the inside of the wooden cake form as she prepares to launch herself at her target.

I slice my hand through the air at my side, killing the sparklers on the cake as Gretel in the form of the most decayed old woman I've ever seen flies from the top of the cake. Her face droops, skin sagging off her shallow bones. Deep recesses under her eyes demand the light create shadows there. Her hands, while fast, show the wear of years, and her veins protrude deeply.

Tight sleeves wrap around her wrist, pointing down toward her fingers—a feature I'm sure the king would appreciate had he had time to see it. Black and gray lace swirl over the dark fabric of her dress. Her bodice matches the sleeves, flowing into a skirt she can easily pick up to run in.

Gretel's face shows no emotion as the king attempts to reel back in surprise. The sword catches on the bottom of the cake form. Instead of slicing through it like it would with a normal cake, it scrapes up it harshly, sticking before it reaches the middle layer. It tumbles from his hand, crashing to the floor, point still stuck in the wood of the cake form.

"The witch," he cries, his words loud above the quiet crowd.

Gretel reaches out, catching his hand in hers. She leans forward, squinting into his eyes. The more hers close, the wider his grow.

She mumbles something at him as he pales.

Everyone watches in horror as the king begins to fade. It happens so quickly that his guards don't know how to react. As if transforming into a male version of Gretel's witch form, the king begins to hollow, his face growing slim and skin sagging off his bones. His once-brown hair turns a vicious gray moving out from the roots to the tips.

It looks like he shrinks before our eyes, caving in on himself as Gretel pulls the life from him, leaving only the decay of death.

She doesn't move as she works, focusing solely on her victim. Hansel is fixated on the young girl in disguise, so I take up the responsibility of watching the crowd. No one moves...except the guard who brought the king the sword.

The king falls to his knees; Gretel leans forward with him, but the approaching guard moves faster than she expects.

"Look out!" someone in the crowd cries, warning Gretel.

A woman screams, distracting a few people. The guard isn't deterred though. I rush forward as our plan goes sideways.

The man in uniform pulls the king away, tossing him on the ground, half dead. Pulling the sword from the cake, he reaches for Gretel. I throw my hands out, creating a barrier around the girl. The wall snakes around people, forming an oddly-shaped room and a maze-of-a-hallway leading out of the throne room. People jump out of the way as the barrier races at them. I slip inside the wall before it races past me and I barrel toward Gretel.

She's in a daze, not moving. I try to pull her from the cake form, but she's trapped in a world of death and Hansel isn't here to pull her back from the horrors she's committed. With no other choice, I leap over the bottom tier of the cake form and push it down the corridor I've created.

Tears burn against my eyes as I realize we've failed and now the only way out is through this maze I've built us. Even if we escape it, where can we go? How can we escape the palace? If I extend the escape outside of the palace walls, they'll just follow it and catch us when I lower the illusion wall. We have no hope and no means of finding freedom.

"I'm so sorry, Gretel." My words come out mixed with tears.

At least I can hold Hansel's illusion until he can escape. He'll be devastated over the loss of his little sister. I'm responsible for her death now.

"Get out of here, Hansel," I will him, whispering as guards pound against the wall, some nearby. "Don't be stupid. Go get Aurik and Brahms and leave. Come back and kill the king another day."

I can't believe we had come so close only to have him be pulled out of Gretel's grasp before she had ended him. She only had him under her control for a moment before the guard interrupted her, but it wasn't quite long enough. It was much easier for her to create life than death.

"Gretel? Gretel, I need you to come back to me," I beg, but I'm not Hansel and I have no control over life and light.

I wheel us around a corner, trusting the illusion walls to take us out of the palace by way of the main entrance—it's the only way I knew to get out.

Maybe, by some miracle, I can reach the end before the guards do and transform Gretel back into a young girl, fulfilling her request to look like me. And if by some miracle, I can, maybe Hansel will be there to pull her to safety.

I have to hope.

Light starts to filter into the tunnel I've created, and I assume we're reaching the end, but the noise behind me assures me I'll never make it—the guards have broken in and are running behind us.

Tears blur my vision as Gretel stares back blankly at me. Then, she blinks.

Perhaps she's coming back.

Moving my wrist to take the pressure of pushing the cake, I wiggle my fingers at her, dropping the illusion I'd placed over her. Her skin bounces back, tightening. Brunette locks color in the gray mats as Gretel returns to me.

But two women entered the tunnel—one of them was a witch.

The men gain on me. Another few steps and they will know.

I do the only thing I can—I transform.

I cover the tunnel in candies of every color as I work to change everything the guards will see. I bring my candy-world to life again, hoping to distract them. At the very least, I hope they trip over some of it.

A man slams into me, knocking me to the ground. Gretel careens forward, slamming into the wall that turns at a ninety-degree angle, jutting out into the courtyard. I kick the man off me, scrambling to reach Gretel. My screams fill the hollow hallways, echoing out into the courtyard.

Hansel has one chance of saving his sister, and it's now.

I drop all of the illusions but the ones that cling to my body and to Hansel and Gretel. The walls disappear, but the candy bounces on the ground around us, reappearing. Brunette-Gretel—nearly unrecognizable—sits in a pile on the ground, free from the cake debris. Somewhere, Hansel is in his illusion form, looking for a way to us. Light floods around us and I squint.

"The witch!" one of the men shouts.

"She put a girl in the cake!"

"How did she get her?" another shouts.

People pull at Gretel, trying to get her away from the evil witch rising from the ground. Hands pull at her, and I want to stop them, but I can't draw extra attention to her.

"The witch was trying to eat the child!" someone screams. "She couldn't have the king's soul, so she tried to take the little girl's!"

"Stand back!" A man's voice shouts. It's familiar. "She'll steal your souls too!"

Bauer rushes toward Gretel and pulls her from a woman's hand. The boys must have been able to release him in the chaos of the king's almost-death. I move my fingers, concealing our leader in an illusion so the guards don't recognize him. He nods once to me, reinforcing the decision I made. Someone will pay the price, and it's going to be me.

Aurik and Brahms stand off to the side, trying to assess the scene. They haven't caught on yet, but they watch Bauer—they saw him transform, so they know I'm here somewhere—and take his lead as he clings to Gretel. They know the brunette girl isn't me, but they haven't figured out I switched places with the girl yet.

The guards draw their weapons, kicking the illusion candy out of the way.

"You can't kill a witch, you fools," Bauer shouts. The boys echo him, realizing where I am as they try to spare me an immediate death.

The crowd is fearful of me, holding their children behind their backs, trying to move as far away as possible without catching the attention of the men wielding weapons. Any movement toward or away from me could be taken as a sign of their involvement—either to help the witch or run from their crimes connected to the hag that tried to kill the king and nearly sucked the soul from a small girl.

A guard calls to me, trying to talk me into kneeling and giving up. As long as Hansel isn't here to save Gretel, I can't give up yet, no matter what that means.

Searing pain rips through my arm as one of the guards shoots at me. It tears through my flesh, and blood spills out, dousing my black lace sleeve. Better me than Gretel.

Bauer pulls Gretel deeper into the crowd. She steps back with him, but she's still not with us.

"Witch!" the deep-voiced guard calls to me, reminding me once again of my father's voice. "You are accused of trying to kill the king of Candestrachen. The punishment is death."

Oddly enough, I'm about to take Bauer's place. At least the resistance has their leader back—I'm of no use to them anymore now anyway—we've played my card.

A flash of red grabs my attention—Hansel is here.

I look him in the eye and tap my necklace. He registers my height—much taller than Gretel—and realizes that I'm taking her place. He locks eyes with me and his face falls. Hansel shakes his head once, begging me to find another way, but I can't; not from this.

"Witch!" the deep-voiced man calls again. "Give up."

I dip my hands to the sides, stretching out my arms, but I say nothing. Hansel's gaze follows my more emphasized arm to where his sister's necklace gleams in the light. His pendant glints as he rushes to her side.

Bauer says something to Hansel, letting him know he's in an illusion, preventing him from ripping his sister away unnecessarily. I see them as I slowly spin in a circle, taking in the crowd.

This is the last time I'll see the sun or breathe the fresh air. It's the last time I'll feel dirt under my feet, and the final time I'll see people. I take it all in. Closing my eyes for a moment, I inhale, filling my lungs.

When I open my eyes, I complete my circle. I stare down the guard, daring him to come for me. I don't speak.

He takes a strong step forward, thinking I'll balk. I don't.

"You'll die for this, Witch. You'll be taken before the king. You'll pay for this."

I wave my hand and the candy littering the courtyard disappears.

I'm sure I will pay for this.

At least I'll get to see what has become of the half-dead king in person. I'll know how soon they'll all be safe from him in his weakened state.

Weapons are raised in my direction again, but the guard instructs them not to kill me yet. The king, of course, will want his say in the matter.

"He's alive, Witch. You didn't kill him, but you knew that, didn't you? That's why you stole the child."

With all eyes on me, I drop Hansel and Gretel's illusions, leaving them in their true forms. The little girl the witch tried to devour is no more—they'll never find the brunette again.

The guards run at me, tackling me. Screams rise up in the crowd as they kick me, mingling with my own. I'm wrenched backward, onto my knees to face the crowd.

"This is what happens when you come against the king!" He rips my hair back, tears pressing against my open eyes as I snarl. I must look hideous in this form when I make that face.

Hansel looks devastated, hands wrapped tightly around Gretel as if she's the only thing anchoring him to this world. He rocks on his feet, leaning forward with her. She's the only barrier keeping him from running to save me.

Aurik places a hand on Hansel's arm, ready to make the decision for him if he needs to—escape comes first. Bauer prepares to back him up if necessary.

Gretel blinks, slowly coming back as Hansel pulls her back to us. She'll register what's happening in a moment. She doesn't need to see this, and I silently will Hansel to run. I don't want her feeling responsible for me. He can tell her I was lost during the escape, but not how it came to be—he'll protect her from this, but he can't if she sees with her own eyes.

Hansel's beautiful hair falls over his face, catching the light just enough to make him glow, but then, Hansel has always been full of light. He radiates everywhere he goes and illuminates the path for every life he touches. I regret not spending more time with him earlier on.

He's breathing heavily as he watches me. A tear slips down his cheek. His lips part in a silent prayer.

I try to smile. I want him to know I'll be all right. I want to do this for them.

He shakes his head, disappointed that everything crumbled around us like a candy house smashed by a child's errant fist. Tears stream down his face—he knows there's nothing he can do.

Bauer tugs him back—it's time for them to go.

I nod and blink back tears.

Bauer and Aurik pull Hansel back, fighting him. Brahms wraps Gretel in his arms and pulls her away just as she comes out of her trance. He shields her from the horrors around her. Hansel strains against his friends. Giving up, he finally bows his head, a complete wreck.

"I'm sorry," he mouths to me, disappearing in the crowd as they force him away. He reaches for me, hand disappearing behind the crowd.

The guards beat me, forcing my body to jerk in different ways until they lift me off my feet.

Hansel and Gretel will try again. Bauer will come up with a new plan. The bakery will likely be taken over by one of the other girls in our group of rebels that can pass as me, but I doubt Hansel and Gretel will ever set foot in it again. Life will go on without me for the rebels and for Hansel and Gretel.

My fate is uncertain. Should the king lock me in one of his prisons before my execution, I'll decorate it in illusions and slip away in my mind, oblivious to what will happen to me. If he kills me on the spot, it will all be over. The fireworks this evening will signal the destruction of the witch that kills kings and eats the souls of children.

I was never a witch, but if I must take the fall to protect Hansel and Gretel, I'll be whatever kind of monster Levin needs me to be.

I contributed to the cause, and now the king is aged so dramatically that even if the resistance fails again, Levin only has a few years at most. Our people will see his candy-colored world crumbles around him, even if I'm not here to see it through.

I wave my hands at the sky, setting off illusion fireworks that end in shattered pieces of candy bouncing off the rooftops of Candestrachen—my final goodbye to the world I'm giving my life to protect.

I can't sugarcoat their world anymore.

ABOUT K.M. ROBINSON

K.M. Robinson is a storyteller who creates new worlds both in her writing and in her fine arts conceptual photography. She is a marketing, branding and social media strategy educator who is recognized at first sight by her very long hair. She is a creative who focuses on photography, videography, couture dress making, and writing to express the stories she needs to tell. She almost always has a camera within reach. Visit her at her website for free books and exclusive samples: www.kmrobinsonbooks.com

CONNECT ON SOCIAL MEDIA

facebook.com/kmrobinsonbooks

instagram.com/kmrobinsonbooks

twitter.com/kmrobinsonbooks

youtube.kmrobinsonbooks.com

Get free books and excerpts of other K.M. Robinson books at excerpt.kmrobinsonbooks.com

ALSO BY K.M. ROBINSON

The Golden Trilogy

Book One: Golden

Forged: A Golden Novella

Book Two: Locked

Book Three: Edge

The Complete Series Boxset/Omnibus with exclusive bonus novella, Tempered

The Jaded Duology

Book One: Jaded

Book Two: Risen

The Complete Series Boxset/Omnibus with exclusive epilogue

The Siren Wars Saga

Book One: The Siren Wars

Book Two: Darker Depths

Book Three: Beyond The Shores

Origins of the Siren Wars: Prequel Novella

The Legends Chronicles

Along Came A Spider: A Prequel Novelette

And They'll Come Home: A Prequel Novelette

The Archives of Jack Frost Series

The Revolution of Jack Frost

The Redemption of Jack Frost (TBA)

Virtually Sleeping Beauty: A Novella Retelling

The Goose Girl and The Artificial: A Novella Retelling

The Sinking: A Novella Retelling

The Boy Who Cried

by Helen Vivienne Fletcher

You probably think you know my story. You've probably already judged me, decided I got what I deserved. You're not alone. That's what most people think. My story is told as a cautionary tale, even.

You know what happened to the boy who cried wolf mothers say, when they catch their children lying. But there's one piece of the story you're missing.

I didn't lie.

There really was a wolf.

"Billy, get up!"

I groaned, and pulled the ragged blanket closer around myself. The afternoon sun streamed through the window, but I squeezed my eyes tighter closed, ignoring it.

"Billy!" My mother ripped the cover off me, slapping the back of my head with the flat of her hand.

I cracked my eyes open.

"Get up, you lazy boy!" she yelled again.

I swung my legs over the side of the bed, and rubbed my head, ruffling up my hair.

My mother's face softened. "I've made you some breakfast. It's on the table."

She left me to get dressed. I pulled on my warmest woollen coat, watching through the window as the sun crept down behind the hills. Last night the farmer hadn't returned until mid-morning, so I'd not got to bed until noon. Mother may like to blame laziness, but these days I got less sleep than her.

She'd left a bowl of oatmeal on the table. I picked up a spoon, diving it into the gloopy mixture, then letting it fall back into the bowl in globs. Breakfast was not quite the same when you were starting your shift at 5pm.

From the stove I could smell a stew slowly cooking. She would try to save some for me, but if the little ones were hungry after they'd eaten their meagre share, she'd be hard pressed to keep it from them. Usually their starved cries got to her, and she'd dole it out between them. On those mornings, she'd give me a hard-faced shrug when I returned home, unable to feel another layer of guilt on top of the ones she already carried with her daily.

I didn't mind really. Since living with the sheep, I'd been less and less inclined to eat meat. And besides, I knew she deprived herself far more than any of us. Her cheeks had grown hollow, the lined, wasting of her flesh caused by more than just age.

She pulled a hat down on my head and over my eyes. "Be careful out there tonight, Billy."

I pushed the hat back, so I could see. "I always am."

She stared at me, the guilt spilling over again. "It will only be for a couple more months. He'll be home soon."

She turned back to the stove, stirring the pot. It didn't really need it; the stew was more liquid than substance. She muttered to herself as if she could conjure a meal with mere words.

She'd been saying my father would be "home soon" for nearly a year. He went out in search of better work months ago, and we'd heard little of him since. I'd found a job helping a farmer watch his sheep overnight in the hopes that we wouldn't starve before my mother accepted that my father was gone for good.

I touched her arm as I got ready to leave. She looked up at me, the dark circles under her eyes matching the ones under mine.

"Get some sleep tonight, Ma." I gave her thin arm a squeeze. She nodded, though I knew she wouldn't. In the months since my father left, she'd been possessed with a nervous energy that left her pacing and restless. I could see the exhausted madness growing behind her eyes, just waiting to spill over.

"Try bringing home some wool," she said.

I nodded. The snags I pulled from the bushes wouldn't amount to much. She had dreams of spinning it, as if the small income she would get from selling it would make a difference. I didn't tell her otherwise. Everyone needed a little hope.

The farmer slapped my head when I arrived, in much the same way my mother had.

"You're late," he said. He gave me another clip on the ear to emphasize his point. I wished I could do the same to him when he returned late to the meadow in the morning, but that would do worse than just get me fired. I smelt alcohol on his breath already, and he hadn't even left his post for the day.

"I'm sorry," I said. I hung my head, in what I hoped would look like contrition.

The farmer grunted, buying it I guessed. He grabbed my chin suddenly, forcing my face up.

"You tired, boy?" He studied the circles under my eyes, and there seemed no point in lying.

I shrugged instead of answering.

He pushed my face to the side, though not roughly, and dropped his hand. "Don't go sleeping on the job, you hear?"

I nodded, again recognizing that silence was my best bet to avoid violence with him. He shoved a pan and spoon into my hands, the tools of my trade, then left with just a grunt aimed my way in parting farewell.

I settled down on the grass once he'd gone. I hadn't forgotten my promise to check the bushes for wool, but I wanted to make sure the farmer was really gone first. If he caught me taking wool, he'd claim I was stealing from him, though he never bothered to clear the bushes himself, and would have no use for the snags even if he did.

I yawned. The sheep's bleating made a soft, comforting soundtrack as they settled down to sleep. They were timid, backing off a few paces if I got too close, but they weren't really afraid of me, not now that I'd been among them for months. Perhaps my mop of dark curly hair had fooled them, and they'd accepted me as one of their own—a tall and strangely lacking-in-wool friend.

I liked their company too. Here I seemed to fit in with an ease I didn't around humans. People always spoke of black sheep as ones who were different—ostracized. That seemed to me a much more human mentality. Sheep weren't as quick to judge.

One of the older ewes settled down next to me. I wanted to reach out and stroke her wool, but I knew they weren't quite that comfortable with me yet. She looked so soft though, like a comforting pillow. I daydreamed about curling up next to her, laying my head against her back and letting her warmth cradle me, as together we slipped into sleep.

I woke with a start. The blanket of darkness and the number of stars above told me I'd been asleep at my post for far too many hours. The ewe was still beside me, but she was no longer settled, ready for sleep. There was movement in the flock, a discontented bleating working its way through them.

I scrambled to my feet, looking for the source of their distress. I could smell it. The musky odour of danger—of wolf—mixed in with the acidic scent of their fear. I spun around, searching for it, until I caught a flash at the edge of the bushes. Eyes.

Sweat dripped down my neck. This was what I'd been waiting for. This is what the farmer paid me for, night after night, but now that the moment was here, I felt sick.

I stepped forward, hoping my height would be enough to make the wolf wary of coming any closer. Instead, it moved forward too, eyeing me like it was curious as to what I would do next.

"Shoo!" I yelled, flapping my arms in front of me. "Shoo!"

It tipped its head to the side, studying me.

"Shoo!" I yelled, louder this time. "Get gone! Go!" I moved forward, and this time the wolf seemed to take offense to it. A low growl started in its throat, and its hackles came up as it dropped into a crouch.

"Get gone," I tried to yell again, but the words disappeared on my lips. I stood frozen, my eyes locked with the wolf's. A stillness seemed to fall over both of us. I was aware of the sheep shifting, their cries growing as they moved behind me for protection, but the wolf and I were still caught in silent communication. I knew it could smell my fear. Somehow the growl seemed like less of a threat, more of a warning.

"Shoo–"

The wolf leapt.

I screamed. So did one of the sheep.

"No!" I dived back, stumbling out of the way as the wolf attacked. It caught one of the sheep instead, tearing into her throat.

"No!" I screamed again. I leapt onto its back, pulling it from the ewe. Its weight caught me off guard, and we fell backwards, tumbling like children play fighting.

A snarl told me I was far from the truth in thinking that. I threw my arms up, protecting my neck as the wolf lunged for me. I felt a searing pain at my wrist.

"Help! Help!" It was all I could do to find the air to scream. I felt myself go weak as I started to pass out.

One of the ewes cried out again, and the wolf's attention snapped away from me, returning to the more appealing prey. It backed away from me, dropping low and stalking the sheep.

I struggled to sit up. The wolf glanced my way, its eyes meeting mine and taking in my flailing movements, but it no longer seemed interested in me. I fell back, giving up. Exhaustion and adrenaline fought for their place in my system, making everything swirl, but I felt something hard and cold under my head. The pan.

I scrambled up, finding the spoon, and striking the two together as hard as I could. The sharp metal clang broke the night.

"Hey!" I yelled. "Hey, hey, hey!" I hit the pan each time I yelled, my voice finding renewed strength suddenly.

"Hey!"

The wolf started at the noise. Its head titled again, the look of curiosity growing once more.

"Hey!"

The strike of the spoon was louder than any sound I could produce myself, but I kept yelling anyway, hoping to attract attention from the town. The wolf wasn't afraid of me—I could see that, but the noise was confusing it. I hoped I could keep it distracted long enough for help to arrive. I hit the pan again.

The wolf stepped towards me. There was something in that moment that raised a similar curiosity in me. We stared at each other, like we'd done before it had attacked. The low growl started in its throat again, but it didn't sound like a threat.

"Hey!"

The farmer's shout startled me. He hit a larger pan, making a louder sound than mine.

"Hey, hey, hey!"

I was aware of other voices joining the farmer's. Other towns folk coming to help him in warding off the wolf. The wolf's eyes stayed locked on mine for a second longer, then they flicked away, taking in the crowd moving toward us. The wolf seemed to shrink. It slunk lower and crept toward the bushes, disappearing into them.

I sunk to my knees, whatever had been holding me up evaporating now. I saw a flash of light catch the wolf's eyes, between the bushes, then it was gone.

I closed my eyes, as the crowd surrounded me.

The farmer's wife, Martha, took my hand firmly in hers. "Let me see."

I raised my arm, suddenly aware of how painful it was now that everything was quiet.

She sniffed. "That'll need a dressing."

Her manner was brusque, but she cleaned the wound gently, taking care with me.

I'd never been in the farmer's home before. The kitchen alone was half the size of our whole house, and I couldn't help but stare at the shelves filled with fresh food surrounding us.

"You did good, boy," the farmer said. Martha nodded her agreement. I ducked my head as I felt my cheeks flush.

The farmer made a noise in his throat, which might have been a laugh, and he ruffled my hair. "Don't you go getting a big head, mind. Back here on time tomorrow, you hear?"

I smiled. The chastisement more comfortable and familiar than praise.

Martha gave me a piece of bread and cheese. My stomach rumbled, but I folded the food into my handkerchief to take home. Someone had called in on my mother to tell her what had happened. She hadn't come though. She would likely have been awake, wandering the house in the night as she often did, but the children would have been asleep.

"Not hungry?" Martha nodded to the parcel of food in my lap.

I shook my head, but my stomach growled again, giving me away. She eyed my thin arms and wasted cheeks, then turned away, cutting more bread and cheese. The farmer grunted as she did but made no real objection.

She put the food in a basket for me, then unwrapped the piece I'd placed in my handkerchief. "Eat," she said. "You'll take the rest home with you."

My mother took the basket, her face conflicted at doing so. In the past, she would never have taken charity, but we were all so hungry she couldn't afford that moral high ground anymore.

She winced as her eyes traced over the bandage on my wrist.

I shook my head. "It's nothing, Ma. Just a scratch." My hand throbbed as I said that, but there was no use in both of us feeling the pain of it.

"I told you to be careful, Billy." Her voice was tight with reproach, none of the praise the farmer or the rest of the village had given me, but I knew it came from fear and guilt rather than any real reprimand.

I nodded, unsure how else to respond. "I need to get to bed," I said. "I can't be late again."

I slept deeply, despite the pain, and despite the noise from my brothers and sisters waking and playing. They were too young to think outside themselves, too young to realise my staying up all night was the only real income we had, so day after day they woke me despite my mother trying to shush them.

The wolf followed me into my dreams. It wasn't a nightmare, at least not at first. It didn't attack, just watched me, the low growl rumbling in its throat and its eyes flashing with the light. I stepped towards it, reaching out a hand in greeting as if it were a dog. It stepped forward, raising its head to gently headbutt my hand.

And then its teeth flashed.

I woke with a start, my hand searing as if the dream-wolf had reopened my wound. I touched it gently. My skin was hot under my palm. In fact, I felt hot all over, and my throat burned for water.

I started as something shifted. My mother stood watching me from the other side of the room. She eyed me, her expression hard to read.

"I'm okay, Ma," I said. "Just a nightmare."

She didn't respond, continuing her silent staring. I glanced at the window. It was early afternoon, I guessed by the light. If I wanted, I could curl up and go back to sleep for another hour or two. Something in my mother's stare told me not to.

"I'm going to head up to the farm early," I said. "Don't want to be late again."

My mother studied me for a moment longer, then she gave a quick nod. I waited for her to tell me to be careful, or to offer to make me breakfast, but she said nothing.

"Bye, Ma," I said.

She didn't reply.

I was feverish by the time I reached the meadow. The sheep were more anxious than usual, shifting and bleating as if it were early in the day, rather than time for them to be settling down to sleep. I suppose that wasn't surprising. They had lost one of their own, and they were probably just as afraid as I was.

The farmer eyed me as I arrived. I'd never been early before, but I don't think that's what he was worried about.

"You alright, Billy?"

I nodded. The farmer never called me by my name, only "boy" or "you". I must look worse than I thought.

He took my wrist in his hand, examining the wound. He grunted. "Come down to the house in the morning. Martha will redress that for you."

I nodded. I wasn't sure how much difference a new dressing would make, but I didn't want to rebuff his rare kindness.

I settled down on the ground as the farmer left. The ewe who'd slept beside me yesterday was nearby, but she didn't come close tonight. In fact, none of them did. They were giving me a much wider berth than usual, and very few of them had laid down, preferring to stay standing.

"It's alright," I said to them. "The wolf is gone."

A small slither of fear crept its way into my stomach as I said that. I hoped the wolf had been driven off, too frightened by the noise and movement of the townsfolk. But doubt filled me, making it hard to swallow.

I shivered. The night wasn't all that cold, but I was definitely running a temperature now, alternating between overheating and chills. My arm underneath the bandage was burning, growing hotter with each passing minute. I tried to stay awake, but the fever and exhaustion got to me. I lay down, hoping I would wake if the wolf returned.

It was the growl I heard first. Last night it was the bleating of the sheep, but this time I felt the wolf's presence before they did.

I jumped up, scanning the bushes. Eyes glinted back at me, giving the wolf away.

"Shoo!" I yelled. "Go! Get away now!"

I felt braver this time, knowing I'd chased it off the night before, but the growl grew louder, echoing until it seemed like it was right beside me. I covered my ears, cowering against the volume. The sheep's bleating rose too, the sounds melding and clashing together.

I forced myself to look up, to face the wolf. But there were more eyes, dozens of them, peering out at me from behind all of the bushes. They blinked, their glinting light flickering as they moved forward.

"No!" I grabbed the pan, beating the spoon against it as hard as I could. "Wolf!" I yelled. "Wolves! Help!"

The eyes closed in, all of them trained on me. The growls grew again, the sound seeming to press against my skin like it would crush me.

"Help!" I sank to my knees, cowering as the wolves surrounded me. "No ..." The word disappeared into a sob.

"Hey! Hey, hey, hey!"

I didn't look up at the farmer's shout. I kept my hands over my face, shaking too much to look until the wolves were gone. The townsfolk's voices joined him, calling out and stomping their feet to help drive off the wolves.

"They're in the bushes," I yelled. "Everywhere! They're everywhere!" I still couldn't look, but the glowing eyes found their way behind my eyelids, taunting me. "Please ... please just make them go away."

"Billy ..."

I heard Martha's voice, but I couldn't look. She gripped my arms, pulling my hands back from my face. I fought her, even though the wound burned as I did.

"The wolves!"

She took my face in her hands, forcing me to meet her eye. "It's all right, Billy. It was just a dream."

"No, they were here. I saw them!"

She bit her lip, her eyebrows drawing together as she stared down at me. She exchanged glances with her husband. Something was wrong. The townsfolk weren't calling out or stomping anymore. Instead an unsettled quiet had fallen over them, broken only by the cries of the sheep.

I looked at the farmer. "I swear I saw them."

He cleared his throat. "I told you not to go sleeping on the job, boy." His voice was gruff and he didn't meet my eye, embarrassment on my behalf written across his face.

I forced myself to look up at the people gathered around. They shifted uncomfortably, muttering to each other. I couldn't hear the words, but the meaning was clear.

The bushes were empty. The eyes were gone, and so was the sound of the growl.

"I – I'm sorry," I said finally. "I thought …"

The farmer grunted, but Martha just shook her head. "It's alright, Billy. You had a fright last night is all."

The crowd started to disperse, their mutterings growing louder as they did.

"I'm sorry," I called after them. "I didn't mean to …"

It was clear they weren't listening. Most didn't look back, and those that did shook their heads in an angry, jerky way.

"I'm sorry," I said again, though it was more to myself than to them. The farmer walked away, checking the sheep it seemed, but I could tell it was more out of wanting an excuse to avoid me. Martha stayed by my side, watching as the last of the crowd dispersed.

One girl hadn't turned away. She stood staring at me, her head tilted to the side, the unabashed curiosity in her eyes making me want to squirm. I ignored her, laying my head in my hands as I tried to slow my breathing.

Martha sent me home early. The farmer grumbled about it, but I was too tired to care. I expected my mother to tell me off, but again she just stared. I fell into bed without speaking to her.

Over the next couple of weeks, I saw the wolves again. Or rather I saw their eyes. Sometimes it was just one—a large male wolf crouched at the edge of the bushes, waiting for its chance to pounce. Other times there were hundreds of them. Glowing spots surrounding me, always accompanied by that low rumbling growl.

I tried not to cry out, though some nights it would get the better of me. Each time I did call for help fewer and fewer people would come running. Those that did came slower. The farmer docked my wages for the false alarms, and the boys from the town—my former classmates—ridiculed me every time they saw me. *Billy, the boy who cries over nightmares.*

The wolf wasn't my only concern. The wound on my hand still hadn't healed, and the fevers were getting longer. Sometimes I seemed to lose time within them, waking in a different place to the one I fell asleep in.

One night I woke standing in the kitchen, having stolen food from the stove. The stew had only been half cooked, but I'd eaten it anyway, piling the raw meat into my mouth. When I came to, the pot had been empty, gravy strewn across my face and hands, and my mother stood watching me from across the room. I'd tried to apologise–to tell her how sorry I was for taking food from her and the children's mouths, but she'd turned and walked away without hearing me.

It was a few days after that I saw the wolf again. I was wide awake, too scared to fall asleep now. I'd been gathering wool from the bushes, like my mother had asked. Not that she'd brought it up again. In fact, she'd barely spoken to me in days.

I was focused on collecting the snags when the wolf slipped from between the trees. It wasn't until I turned around that I realised it was there. This wasn't like the dream wolf. It didn't have glowing eyes, and it didn't growl. It just watched me.

"Shoo," I called, but my voice didn't have much power. I knew I needed to cry out–to alert the farmer and everyone else to come help drive it away. But I thought of the nights when I called them because of my dreams, and the words crumbled in my mouth.

The wolf's attention flicked away from me. It eyed the sheep.

"No!" I yelled. "Leave them alone." I hit the pan, but even as the first clang sounded I knew no one would come. "No," I tried to yell again, but somehow the word didn't form. All that came out was a growl.

The wolf looked up at this, its interest piqued. I tried again, and again no words formed. All of them replaced with a low guttural sound. The wolf stepped towards me, hackles raised. Glowing eyes appeared in the bushes, hundreds of them all trained on me. But this time I wasn't afraid. I wanted them to come closer.

I stalked towards the wolf. We circled each other, spiralling in, ready to attack. The eyes were on my side, I realised. Watching me, ready to give me power.

My stomach rumbled, echoing the rumble coming from my throat. The wolf's eyes flicked away from me. I followed them to one of the ewes, her scent appealing suddenly.

I stepped forward, my movements sleek and stealthy. There was a beat in the air, a pulse. It was coming from the ewe, I realised. Underneath her wool, blood flowed. I could taste it at the back of my mind. One bite, and I would taste it on my tongue too.

The wolf crept forward, its posture matching mine. I felt its intent, felt our minds and bodies syncing together. We moved as one, stalking the ewe. The sound in my throat changed, becoming a snarl.

I woke with blood on my hands and face. The ewe lay dead beside me, her throat ripped open. I crouched beside her, my breath catching as I took in the wound.

"It wasn't you."

I started at the girl's voice. She sat on the ground near me, the sheep bleating their discomfort at her presence. She was the girl I'd seen in the crowd, the one who hadn't turned away.

"It was me," she said. "You didn't kill her."

"You?" I took in the slight figure in front of me. My hands were trembling. I tried to wipe the blood from them, but it clung, thick and viscous.

"You tried to stop me. That's why you have blood on your hands."

I remembered stalking the ewe, the wolf and I moving as one. I remembered the eyes from the bushes giving me power.

"I thought it was taking over," she said. "But you fought it at the last minute. Came back to yourself and tried to fight me instead."

I nodded, though I couldn't make sense of her words.

She was admitting to killing. I should be afraid of her, but I felt strangely calm. The girl shrugged, as if she wasn't sure how she felt about what she was saying–whether she was angry or impressed that I had tried to fight her.

No one had come to drive off the wolf, my false cries in the previous weeks too much for me to be believed. They would believe me now, I thought wryly, when they came back in the morning and found the dead sheep... or would they? I stood, backing away. Some of the townsfolk thought I was crazy, and blood on my hands was hardly going to calm those thoughts.

"You won't have that after you turn completely." The girl gestured to my hands, as if she'd read my thoughts. "The blood will stay with the wolf form."

I nodded again, though she still wasn't making any sense.

"My name's Maryanne, by the way." She reached out as if to take my hand, then stopped and withdrew it, remembering the blood.

"Billy," I said. I was shaking badly now, though I couldn't tell whether it was from the cold or from shock. I stared down at the bloodied sheep, still trying to make sense of it. Maryanne had killed her. That part still didn't feel true, but I was puzzling over something else as well now. I didn't feel the revulsion I should at the sight of the wound. There was something else stirring inside me instead–a feeling or instinct I didn't quite have a name for. It was similar to what I'd felt when I joined the wolf in stalking the ewe.

"You still don't understand, do you?" Maryanne asked.

I didn't reply. If the answer wasn't obvious, it wouldn't be helped by my ignorance being spilled out,

"There's no wolf," she said.

"There is!" My voice cracked as my frustration from the last few weeks spilled out. I wasn't making it up. I didn't know how to make anyone believe me, but I had seen the eyes in the bushes. I had seen the wolf stalking the sheep.

"It's inside your head, Billy. The wolf is inside you."

"It's not! It's–" I cut myself off, her meaning suddenly becoming clear. "I'm insane," I said. Somehow it didn't feel like as much of a shock as it should have. Instead a feeling of resignation spread through me, mixed with something else. Relief, as I could finally let go.

She shook her head. "No, but when I tell you, you might wish that's all it is."

I didn't answer. I was sick of her riddles and couldn't handle her drawing this out any longer.

"I'm a werewolf," she said.

That should have been a shock as well, even more so than the idea that I was losing my mind, but again a strange calmness spread over me. I stared into her face, into her eyes. The same eyes that had stared at me with such curiosity that first night I saw the wolf.

The calmness spilled over into anger. "So it's been you taunting me this whole time!"

"No." Her head jerked into a shake, emphasizing that as firmly as she could. "Just that first night. I came to find you, but the wolf took over and I couldn't control myself."

"I don't believe you."

She had been there those other nights, hiding in the bushes and slipping away before anyone else saw her. Making them doubt me.

She sighed. "The last few weeks … You never properly saw the wolf, did you? Just its eyes? It was like that for me too."

"You're making this up."

"The wolf you've been seeing–the eyes–it's the other side of you. It won't be able to get out until the full moon, but it wants to. It's waiting."

I found I didn't have an answer for that, so I nodded again, as if it made perfect sense. Something she'd said niggled at me, and I focused on that because it was easier. "You said you were looking for me."

She dropped her gaze. "Yes."

"But ... why?" We'd never met before that night, I was sure of it.

"Your father sent me."

"My father?"

She wouldn't meet my eye, keeping hers on the ground. "I met him nearly a year ago. He startled me, and I bit him." She looked up, her eyes full of sadness, begging me to understand. "I didn't mean to, it was an accident," she said in a rush. "He couldn't come back, because ... but he asked me check on you. I was supposed to come in human form, but it was too close to the full moon, and I didn't expect to find you outside in the middle of the night."

"I was working," I said.

She nodded. "Your father didn't know the farmer had hired you."

"What did he expect?" I spat the words out. "We would have starved by now if I hadn't found work."

Maryanne was quiet for a moment, then she reached out, taking my hand despite the blood. "He left a hole here, didn't he?"

I didn't answer. A hole was too mild a description. Our lives–my mother–had been falling apart since he had left. He'd gone off looking for better work, a way to provide for us. In the meantime, we were scrambling, trying to support ourselves through my meagre wages.

"You're struggling to survive," she said.

I nodded. The way things were going, the farmer wouldn't employ me for much longer, and we'd be left with nothing. My eyes welled up again. I didn't try to stop the tears this time, just let them fall.

She stepped forward. "Then come with me. Once you turn."

"I can't." I shook my head. "I don't want to."

She tilted her head and studied my face. "You don't want to come with me, or ...?"

"I don't want to turn into a werewolf!" I realised in saying that, I had accepted her story. My voice shook from the fear building up inside me but I said it as firmly as I could. I had to make her understand I couldn't do this.

She made a huffing sound, which might have been a laugh. "You don't get a choice, Billy." She didn't continue, but I thought I could fill in the part she wasn't saying. She wouldn't have become a wolf herself if she'd had a choice.

She sighed. "But it's not so bad. Once you learn to control it, you can live a normal life. You only *have* to be a wolf on the full moon. The rest of the time you can choose."

I shook my head again. "I can't leave my family."

She dropped her gaze, and I could finally think straight without those curious eyes watching me. "Your father is your family too," she said quietly.

"He was. Then he left us." All of my bitterness from the last few months slid out in those words, but as soon as they were out I regretted them. He hadn't left us on purpose.

She didn't answer, just stared at her hands.

"I can't leave," I said again. "My family will starve without my wages.

"They're starving now!" Her eyes shot up to meet mine, her stare intense.

I reeled back at her words. I thought of the food I stole the other night, of the money the farmer was refusing to pay me. Most of all, I thought of my mother's hollow cheeks. My brothers and sisters were healthy for now, but only just, and only because my mother and I were wasting away to save them.

Maryanne's face softened. "Remember how they rewarded you after you chased off the first wolf? They'll reward your family once you're gone. They'll feel guilty for your death."

"My death?!" My head shot up, but Maryanne met my shock with laughter.

"That's what they'll think when they find you gone and the sheep dead. That the wolf carried you off, because they didn't come to help."

She seemed to find the idea amusing. Imagining the townsfolk–my mother–believing me dead didn't bring me any joy. Sure I was angry at them for not trusting me about the wolf, but I'd never want to cause them all that pain.

"I can't."

Maryanne was quiet for a moment, then she swallowed. "There is another way."

"What is it? I'll do anything! I won't turn into a wolf."

Maryanne flinched at my words. She shook herself slightly, as if brushing them off. "Kill me," she said

"What?" I stared at her.

"Kill me–kill the one who bit you–and you'll be human again." Her voice was flat, no emotion either way.

"I – I can't do that." I'd been willing to kill her in wolf form – I'd called for the townsfolk, knowing that if we couldn't drive her away, then they would help me kill her to save the sheep. But now? Knowing who she was, it was different.

Maryanne shrugged. "I'd understand if you did. If I'd found the wolf who bit me, I'd have done it."

I didn't know how to answer that. She studied my face. "It's your choice," she said quietly. "Kill me and return to human form. But you'll always be struggling for work and food, and you'll never see your father again." She squeezed my hand, holding it between both of hers. "Or become a wolf, live with us, and have your family taken care of when you're gone."

She made it sound simple, but there was a lot she was leaving out. Having to hunt for food, and being chased off by people every time we did. Everywhere we went, people would fear us, and I would never see my family again.

Maryanne stood, turning towards the bushes. "You have until midnight, tomorrow night to decide."

Tomorrow night–the full moon.

"Once you turn, the decision is made." Maryanne gave a strange smile. "And you'll need to kill me when I'm a wolf, so come prepared if that's what you decide."

She disappeared into the bushes, slipping back into wolf's form as she did.

I washed the blood from my hands before the farmer arrived in the

morning. I noticed as I did that my wound had stopped hurting. Yesterday it had still been an open sore, but now the skin was meshing together. I doubted I would even have a scar. I covered it up with the bandage regardless. It was easier than facing my own confusion.

When the farmer arrived, he stared at the dead ewe – at me standing beside her with the pan and spoon in my hands.

"You didn't come," I said. "I told you there really was a wolf."

The farmer shook his head. "Billy–"

"You'll pay me my full wages from now on. No more docking my pay."

The farmer stared at me, then nodded once. This would be as close to an apology as I would get from him. I dropped the pan and spoon, and walked past him, heading home.

The house was strangely silent when I got there–no sounds of the little ones playing, and there was nothing cooking in the kitchen.

"Ma?" I called.

"Billy?" My little sister, Louise, came running out to greet me. She was crying.

I picked her up. "What's wrong, Lou Lou?"

She buried her face in my shoulder. "Ma says we can't talk to you anymore. She says you have to go away like Daddy."

"What?" I craned my neck to look at Louise, to check for signs of mischief, but her tear-stained face told me she was telling the truth.

I set her down. "Where are the others?"

"Ma said we had to stay in our room until you were gone."

I shook my head. "It's okay, Lou. You don't need to hide. Tell the others they can go play outside."

I found my mother hiding in her room. She clutched a broom and swiped at me with it when I came through the doorway. My fear that she was losing her mind bubbled up as she cowered away from me.

"Get back!" she hissed.

"Ma, what's wrong?" I held up my hands, trying to ward off another smack of the broom.

"You're like him, aren't you? One of them." Her eyes flashed. "I saw it in your father before he left. It's in you too now, isn't it?"

"What are you talking about?"

"The wolf."

"Ma ..." I wanted to tell her she was wrong, that it was lack of sleep and she was imagining things. But those two words cut me short: *the wolf.*

"You know what happened to him? To Dad?"

She gave a fierce shake of her head. "Happened to him? It was always in him, lurking. He said it was the bite, but I knew it had always been there."

She had seen my father after he turned? Maryanne had said he couldn't come back, but she hadn't said why.

"You knew all this time? You knew, and you just kept saying ..."

She'd lied to me, over and over. Every night when she told me I'd only have to keep working a little longer, until my father returned. She'd known he couldn't come back. She'd known *she* was the reason he couldn't come back.

"It's not like that, Ma. He only has to be a wolf on the full moon. The rest of the time–"

She smacked me with the broom again. "He's got to you. *Poisoned* you. You get away. I'm not going to let you steal another one of my babies." She broke down crying.

I touched her shoulder, but she flinched away from me, returning to her cowering. "It's okay, Ma," I said. "I'll go."

I left the house, stopping briefly to watch my brothers and sisters play outside. Louise was no longer crying, her earlier fears forgotten already in the way that's only possible for the very young.

I went up to the farm house. Martha was in the kitchen, cooking. I knocked on the door, and let myself in. She seemed surprised to see me, but then smiled, ushering me into the room.

"I wondered if you could look at my arm again," I said. The wound was all but healed now and didn't need attention. I just wanted an excuse to speak to her alone.

She frowned, then nodded. She removed the bandage, gently cleaning my arm. Washing away the last visible evidence that I had ever been bitten.

I glanced around the room. There were no signs of children, no pictures or toys scattered around. As far as I knew she and the farmer had never had any–perhaps they couldn't–but it still seemed strange. Martha was a natural mother.

"My mother ..." I said.

Martha looked up at me sharply. Perhaps she had already heard stories of my mother wandering in the night. I was sure the town must be beginning to suspect something was wrong.

"She's not well. I ... if anything happens to me ..." I couldn't quite get the words out. Saying something felt like too much of a betrayal.

Martha stared at me, then lowered her gaze. "You're worried about your brothers and sisters," she said.

I nodded. She was silent for a moment, then cleared her throat.

"There's no need to be, Billy. Those children will always have someone to watch over them."

She squeezed my hand. I squeezed back, pouring all of my gratitude into the gesture.

"Thank you," I whispered.

That night, the moonlight washed over me, and I saw the wolf beside me, the one with the glowing eyes that had been haunting me for the last month. I met its eye, knowing this would be the last time we would be face to face.

Maryanne crept out of the bushes. She was in human form, but she seemed blurred at the edges; her wolf forming an aura around her.

"You didn't tell me it was my mother," I said. "The reason my father couldn't come home."

Maryanne shrugged. "He didn't want me to. He didn't want that to colour your decision."

My father stepped out of the bushes then. He was in wolf's form, but I knew his eyes.

"Dad," I whispered.

He lay down, responding to the name and showing me he was no threat.

When I looked back at Maryanne, she had moved into wolf form too, and stood watching me. I sniffed the air, the scent of the sheep strong suddenly. But no ... the sheep were my friends. I sniffed again, and caught traces of other animals. Rabbits, rats, beavers, deer. I felt the grumble in my stomach, and I realised with relief this would be the last time I would feel it.

Maryanne didn't seem afraid. She'd given me the choice, freely told me she would understand if I chose to kill her, but she padded across the grass towards me, her eyes full of curiosity rather than fear. Perhaps she knew my decision was already made.

I threw my head back and howled. The spirit wolf beside me threw its head back too, its call echoing mine.

When I looked back, the wolf with the glowing eyes was gone. No, not gone, just no longer beside me. For better or worse, the wolf was inside me now, and I was a part of Maryanne's pack. My father's pack.

Maryanne responded to my call, tilting her head back and letting the sound echo around us. My father howled too, our calls melding together into one.

I heard welcome in their voices. I heard family.

ABOUT HELEN VIVIENNE FLETCHER

Helen Vivienne Fletcher is a children's and young adult author, spoken word poet and award-winning playwright. She discovered her passion for writing for young people while working as a youth support worker, and now helps children find their own passion for storytelling through her work as a creative writing tutor. Overall, Helen just loves telling stories and is always excited when people want to read or hear them.

CONNECT ON SOCIAL MEDIA

helenvfletcher.com

facebook.com/Helen-Vivienne-Fletcher-Writer

twitter.com/helenvivienne

ALSO BY HELEN VIVIENNE FLETCHER

Broken Silence

Underwater

Hunter's Truce

by Elle Beaumont

Someone shook me violently by the shoulders—the sound of my name on their lips seemed so distant—but as my eyes opened a bright frantic face peered down at me.

"Niki, wake up, wake up!" the tinkling voice pleaded.

A groan escaped me as I began to roll over again, fingers trapping the fabric of the blanket; the little demon was trying to yank it off of me.

"Don't you dare! Wake up!"

A small fist connected with my shoulder and I quickly sat up, offering a mock glare as the lithe redhead tumbled on her backside.

Liesel, my little sister, offered a scowl in return, promptly sticking her tongue out at me.

She brought in the scent of blood—there was always a copper tang slithering through our home—mostly because we lived above a butcher shop smack dab in the middle of Walddorf village. We didn't always live here, but it had been home since I was four, and Liesel had been born in this very house.

Sleep still clung to me, even stretching out did nothing to shake it. Eyeing my pillow, I had every intention of hugging it and rolling over once more, and yet, Liesel had a different idea.

She still sat on the floor and shot me an accusatory look. Her round, freckled cheeks were puffed out indignantly and her yellow eyes darted to the door.

"Well, are you going to sit there or are you going to spit it out?" I questioned as I tossed the blankets off of my figure and went about making my bed.

"It's my first hunt today, Niki." She sighed heavily and stood up.

Wolves, that's what we are. Werewolves to be exact. Supernatural predators in the world.

Today happened to be Liesel's twelfth birthday, two years overdue for her first hunt with our small pack, but there was a reason behind it. One our mother was never keen on elaborating, but of course, I knew.

"No, it isn't," I teased her and began to walk past her.

She was tiny for her age, and where she was round in features like our mother, I had all sharp angles, however, we shared the same eyes, freckles, and red hair.

"Niklaus, are you teasing your sister again?" Mother called up the stairwell.

I shot Liesel a look and arched my brow before I ruffled her long red hair.

"Yes, but she knows it," I retorted. "You should, anyway. Do you think I'd forget your birthday, LiLi?" I bent over and scooped her up into my arms, twirling her around.

Four years separated us and I still remembered the day she came into our lives, wriggling and tiny.

"Well, come down here, Lu needs a hand in the shop. We'll leave after you're done."

Lu was the man who graciously welcomed us into his home. Long before he and my mother became an item, he saw a pregnant woman and her son in need. He didn't know what we were and yet he welcomed us, gave us a place to rest our heads and food to fill our belly. When he discovered what we were he didn't seem alarmed.

Walddorf had always held strong ideas and beliefs in regard to our kind, even though wolves ran rampantly through the kingdom of Abendrot. The humans always believed this village was somewhat of a sanctuary for their kind, as if we were all ruthless creatures, as if the kingdom wasn't founded by our species centuries ago. Pigs sat on the throne now, selfish, greedy pigs.

"Coming."

When I released Liesel, she darted by me and hopped down the stairs two at a time in a manner that one could describe as *spritely*.

My mother pulled her short, cropped hair back in a swath of cloth before she bent over to tend to the food in the oven. The scent of apple pie wafted through the house and it mingled with the scent of blood and death.

Since the butcher shop sat so closely to the house, the scent could be unbearable in the summer months. However, as we grew, our noses opted to become blind to the stale fragrance of death.

"Ma said you needed some help," I called out and stepped into the room. Laid out on the table, a half-butchered pig glared up at the ceiling. For a moment, I simply looked at it and found my hand reaching for a nearby cleaver.

Never once did I shed a tear or even flinch as the life fled from an animal's eyes. I was born different, so my mother said, and I knew a part of me was missing.

A grunt came from Lu as he strung up some sausage links. "Did she now? Ah, sure, finish that pig off, will ya? I've got to get to the smoker. Lars will be coming in to pick up that order any time." He jerked his head toward the door and slid out the back.

Methodically, the cleaver became an artist's tool, cutting and slicing through meat and bone until all that remained of the pig was its ugly head and hooves. Those wouldn't be discarded, we didn't believe in waste. Some people thoroughly enjoyed pickled pigs feet. They weren't on the top of my go-to list, but they weren't bad either.

The bell on the door tinkled when it opened, the sound of heavy boots falling on the floor made my attention snap to it.

My fingers were finishing the ties on the last wrapped portion of meat. "He's outside," was all I said.

A grunt came from Lars as he lumbered his way toward me. His hair was salt and pepper, eyes an eerie shade of hazel. Short, stocky, he wasn't as tall as me. Lars also wasn't keen on me and never was. Not that I really cared.

"Go get him," he said.

Shrugging a shoulder, I piled the meat carefully and looked at him squarely. A smile formed on my face. "No," I began. "He's busy and I'm here to—"

"To what exactly? I don't trust you. I don't like it… your mother should have…"

Red spilled into my vision, my knuckles turned white as I gripped the edge of the counter, two seconds away from jumping it, but I reeled myself in—it would do no good to chase off one of Lu's customers.

Lars muttered something under his breath, human ears would have missed it but I wasn't human. Not at all.

I hopped the counter in a swift motion, curled my fingers around the collar of his shirt and slammed him against the wall. "You can hate on me, you can say whatever you'd like about me, but leave them out of it." No need to tap into the beast that lay beneath my skin, the point was clear.

Lars must have realized his error and the fact he was spitting hate when a cleaver was inches away from my grasp. I would have gladly chosen my fists over a knife any day, it was more gratifying feeling the snap of bones when your knuckles connected to flesh.

"You are the devil's spawn," he spat out, his eyes flicking toward the knife, it was clear that he was warring with pushing me over the edge.

A wolfish grin pulled at my lips as I looked down at him. "Papa sends his regards, pay up and be gone."

Easing up on him, I moved to the side and motioned toward the counter where his order was. I didn't feel inclined to help him, but I did feel inclined to take his money and shove it into the drawer.

Lars' face looked as if it would burst it was so red, which pleased me to no end. I waved my hand at him to leave, blood flecked my skin from carving up his order.

Moments later, Lu came back inside, his brows lifting in question as he looked at me and the empty room. "Lars came already?"

Soap coated my hands as I washed them in the basin, my back

turned to Lu. I simply nodded and watched the white suds turn to pink as the blood ran off.

"You going with your ma and sis?"

Finishing up, I grabbed a hand towel. "Of course, it's dangerous out there and besides that, it's Liesel's first hunt."

He knew what we were and yet he didn't care, it was a testament to how good he was. Lu could have been afraid, he could have viewed my mother as some demon-spawn but he didn't. Instead, he not only welcomed us into his home, he didn't bat an eyelash at what we were either. He was the only father Liesel ever knew, and it was better that way.

His face became unreadable, top teeth biting down on his lower lip. "Be careful out there, the hunters have been out in full force."

It was well known the humans hunted our kind, it was easy enough to differentiate between a wolf and a werewolf. Werewolves were the size of a large pony with shaggier hair, intelligent, otherworldly eyes, and our howl was deeper. There were poachers who dedicated their lives to taking out werewolves, and though it wasn't outright illegal, it was highly frowned upon.

One of the many things the crown had never seen to, filthy pigs.

Liesel chirped by my mother's side, beaming up at her. "I am so excited!" she whispered, but her body shook with glee.

A hum coursed through the air, tension as thick as a cord. Not the kind that set any of us on edge, but it was all of us honing in on our senses.

It wasn't safe here, not in the village, and so we wound our way down a path until we met the thick woodlands. The pine trees stretched toward the sky and peppered the earth so thickly that it gave the woods a claustrophobic feeling.

The sun was blocked by evergreens and in between sturdy oaks as well as bramble ensured that only stray fragments of light entered.

Ravens perched in the trees protesting our arrival; they could sense it and what we were—natural predators—and it went against their instinct.

Initially, the change was uncomfortable, especially the younger you were, but as werewolves aged and grew, it became a seamless process. Bones shifted, skin stretched and rearranged as we took our other form.

Instead of three red headed humans standing, there were wolves.

My mother and sister nuzzled me and I shook my head. Simply because we were wolves did not mean we lacked intelligent ways of communicating. We could speak through our minds.

"Are you ready to tear into your first hide, Li?" I asked my sister, tongue lolling out of the side of my mouth.

Her small red figure vibrated with euphoria and instead of yipping, she let a small whine out, knowing better than to alert the woods that we were there.

In spite of this being her first hunt, Liesel knew how to stalk her prey and how to move so the pads of her paws absorbed sound. I had shown her the best ways, after all.

"Are we ready, my lovelies?" Mother asked.

Flicking my gaze to Liesel and then back to my mother, I cocked my head to the side. *"Readier than Liesel."*

A joke of course, because my sister had been counting down the days until this hunt, nonetheless she nipped at a tuft of my fur as punishment.

Beyond the thicket, we maneuvered, a clearing came into view and with it, a gift of a young buck. Easy enough for one of us to take down given our size, but this was Liesel's first and my mother and I would only be there as support. Liesel would be taking the kill as a trophy.

"Nik, you know what to do and I'll only say this once— do not take your sister's glory." She shot me a look that left no room for an argument.

As if I'd steal Liesel's glory.

On cue, mother and I spread out wide, trapping the creature in the clearing while Liesel crept up from behind. Mother and I went wide to the side, letting the birthday girl do most of the work. We were there for support and if she needed another pair of snapping jaws—but this was her moment. Liesel crept forward, using the cover of the woods as she approached the unsuspecting creature, its ears twitched but it continued to graze without pause. My muscles twitched as I watched a few opportunities slip by and just as I was beginning to think that she was overwhelmed she moved into action.

She began to move wide, too, and went around the backside—right in the animal's blind spot—and when she was ready, she pounced into action, leaping at the buck's haunches.

White fangs snapped at the flesh, finding purchase on the thick muscle and the buck swung his head as he began to kick out. She lost her grip on him as he launched another kick, his head swinging toward her with antlers primed for attack.

A snarl left me, the only thing cementing me in my spot was mother's rumbling from a distance.

Liesel dodged a blow to her side and quickly recovered before she launched at a leg, chomping down on the slender limb. She tugged and ripped her mouth away before doing the same to a hind leg. Each time she injured the buck and each time he grew more tired.

She wore him down until he was ready to flee, his legs gave out from under him and Liesel let out a victorious yip before she launched on top of it. Proudly, she began to feast on his soft belly.

Our bellies were soon full and if we didn't have to move swiftly, a nap would have been in order, but it wasn't safe for us to dally. Just because we were deep in the woods didn't mean they wouldn't brave the darkest parts of them.

"Congratulations, Li, you did great," I offered, nuzzling her bloodied maw with my head.

"You did a great job, sweetling," Mother chimed in and licked at Liesel's mouth.

Death hung heavily in the air, which made the forest sound all the quieter. The birds had long since silenced their chattering and had flown away, the rodents had made themselves scarce and it was relatively peaceful.

Except, the sound of fluttering wings and a cry of warning had the three of us snapping to attention.

"Move," Mother demanded, and we didn't hesitate.

As we ran, I grabbed Liesel's scruff and pulled her ahead of me, shoving her when it was necessary. Mother was behind us, shouting orders as to where to turn and duck. Changing wasn't an option, they were already too close, and by the time we were finished shifting we would have been more vulnerable than what we were now. Teeth, claws, and thick hair would give us more of an advantage than what flesh would.

I hadn't smelled it in the clearing, but I did now; the stench of humans invaded my senses. The sound of a bow's string creaking caught my attention and when I turned back to look at my mother, panic filled her yellow eyes.

Poachers were here, and they knew *we* were here.

"Run!" she cried out.

As if we hadn't been running before, our lives depended on it and so we began a mad dash through the woods— ducking under bushes, leaping over fallen logs, taking the beatings from the briars that cut along our faces.

An arrow zinged by my head, whistling its murderous song and sunk deep into a nearby tree. My attention was on the arrow, so I nearly missed the sound of a boot crunching down on twigs. It struck me as odd, hunters prided themselves in remaining stealthy.

Another creak of a bow and the twang of it seemed to echo around us, mingling with the panting breaths we took.

I dipped my nose and pushed Liesel through a tunnel of briars, my heart pounding in my ears. It took me a moment to register that mother was no longer trailing behind us.

Slowly, she limped her way forward, gulping down air. *"Keep going Nik, go!"*

So I did. I kept pushing my sister forward. The sound of the boots crunching were distant, but they were there, and when the arrows seemed to cease, I finally let up in my running.

I recognized the tang that filled the air. Dread coiled deep in my stomach. I snarled and turned to Liesel. *"Stay!"* I barked at her and frantically looked around for our mother, I couldn't see her body or hear her labored breathing. I shot one last look at Liesel before launching myself into a steady run *back* to where we came from.

Winding my way through the brush, I made my way to where my mother's body lay.

Her ears laid flat against her skull as she looked up at me. *"Stubborn boy, go. They're coming."* She wheezed, there was an arrow jutting out from her rib cage and I knew it had caused irreparable damage.

My mother was dying.

"Go, Niklaus, I love you. Remind...remind Li this is not her fault."

Fury bubbled up inside of me. Everyone always talks about seeing red, but I didn't see red. My vision almost blacked out and I felt my body pulse with white hot fury and the need for revenge.

Willing myself to calm down, I opened my senses, drinking in the surrounding scents, listening for the faintest sound. Some poachers had grown smart enough to disguise their heartbeats. Through rigorous training their heart rates had slowed dramatically, they knew how to breathe and control the beats even while on a hunt. Not all of them knew how to do this, but every seasoned poacher knew how.

I shifted into my natural state, my hands cupping my mother's furry face. "You can't die," I murmured and stroked her face.

"But she is, Niklaus," a voice said from behind.

The light faded in my mother's eyes as she exhaled her last breath, her chest moved purely out of muscle memory. The words the familiar voice uttered were not ones I wanted to hear, because now I had to tell my little sister that our mother was dead, and this jerk was so matter-of-fact about it.

"What are you doing here?" I snapped at my father.

"Taking care of the human scum, of course. She may have been your mother but she was my *mate*," Gregor growled his words.

Only when it suited you, I thought. Releasing my mother's face, I stood up and turned to look at the man who sired me. "Get out of here!" He was not welcome here and if there had been a word strong enough to describe how loathsome of a being he was, I would have hurled it at him. As it was, my body shook all over and I felt my fingers curl into my palm, sharpened nails digging into my flesh.

"Niklaus—" he began.

Cutting him off, I glared. "Do *not* speak my name, you have no right." The only thing he had done was sire me and my sister. He was abusive toward my mother, and sought to whisk me away from her countless times. Liesel didn't remember him. Nor had she the misfortune of ever meeting him. I wasn't so fortunate. I had seen the bruises on my mother, heard the horror stories and it was enough—enough to drive me further into a blind rage.

Gregor was a knight in the royal army, but it meant nothing. If he thought he was an honorable man, he was even more warped than I was. At least I didn't claim to be honorable.

"I am your father!" he bellowed and started forward.

It was the wrong time, the wrong moment, and I launched myself at him, taking him to the ground. I saw red and I saw black. Every ounce of hatred I had for him poured out of me as we grappled. He took the revenge I sought away from me, he took advantage of my mother, he hurt her, and for that, he would pay.

"Where were you when they were hunting us? Where were you when they put an arrow through her heart?" I shouted, not caring who heard me.

Guttural growls left him and the scent of blood filled the air anew, it belonged to him, my fist connected with his nose and blood poured from it.

He went to pin me onto the ground as he rolled us over, but I snatched up one of his blades that was strapped to his waist. I pulled it out in a smooth movement and as he went to punch me, I embedded the blade deep in his chest. I don't think he was anticipating me killing him or that I would have the balls to do it. He also didn't know *how much* I hated him.

He gawked at me and ran his fingers along the hilt of the dagger, yanked it out and the sharp lines of his face contorted in not only pain but fury.

"You son of a—" he coughed out the words, blood flecking his lips as he crawled after me.

Scooting back and looking for a weapon I could use, I opted to pick up a rock, lobbed it at him, and when it distracted him, I dove at him again.

The blade in his hand scraped along my torso but didn't bite in, still, I felt the sting just the same. I wailed on him with everything I had, wasting time and tiring him out until the fatal stabbing I had incurred on him bled out sufficiently.

Gregor grew weaker and more blood bubbled from his mouth as he began to sway on his feet. "You… you're more mine than—" He paused and coughed up a mouth full of blood. "You will ever know." Gregor fell to his knees, a twisted smile on his face before his lifeless body collapsed to the ground.

When it was done, I sat back and glanced down at my blood-soaked hands. My knuckles split open when they collided with my father's face and scraped on the ground. A form of misery bled into my soul—I wish I could have cried or felt anything remotely close to what a normal being would have felt in this circumstance.

Empty, that was what I felt, a heap of nothing. No, that wasn't true, I was pissed off; both of my parents were dead now and only one made me want to howl.

At the thought, I heard a quiet 'woof' in the distance.

Liesel.

I wished I could spare her this, but I couldn't, and I knew she needed to see our mother for that closure. "Liesel," I called out, rising from my spot, blood sticking to my hands, face and clothing.

Just as she was ready to emerge, I held up a hand and quickly ducked down. My fingers curl around the discarded knife, muscles twitching in anticipation of having to launch into action again. However, as the figure emerged my muscles relaxed only slightly.

"It's not a good time, Sabrina," I growled. Sabrina Seidel was a frequent customer at the butcher shop and she was currently standing with her arms folded across her person. Alarmingly, the sight of the two dead bodies didn't seem to bother her.

"I see that," she remarked and swept her bright blue eyes along the body. "There is a trail of death following you, what the hell did you do, Niklaus?"

"It wasn't me and now is really not a good time," I began to say and was cut off as Liesel burst from the wood line in her human form, tears streaming down her face as she ran over to our mother.

"No!" she screamed, clawing at the limp form on the ground.

I grit my teeth and looked up at Sabrina, ultimately it wasn't the time for me to bite her head off and instead I knelt down next to my sister, stroking her back. There was nothing I could say to comfort her, no words could bring our mother back.

For all that she knew, the man behind us was the one who did it and I was fine letting her believe that. He might as well have been.

After a time, I sent Liesel with Sabrina to return back home and trusted that Sabrina would be the one to break the news to Lu. I glanced around and took stock of the woods around and wondered how the hell I'd get us back home. When we died we didn't shift back into human forms—we remained as wolves. At this point, we weren't too deep in the woods, and I recalled that on the edge of it there was a horse. If I could make a sled out of pine boughs and use the horse to pull her we'd eventually make it home.

That was exactly what I did. My sire's body could rot where it lay.

When I got home, Lu had already pulled himself together, his face red from crying, and Liesel locked herself in her room. She needed the time to herself and so I didn't bother her, but Lu pulled me in for a bear hug and gave my back a sturdy pounding.

He didn't say anything about the blood coating me, he likely assumed it belonged to my mother. As for the blood coating my side, I pulled my jacket over it, hiding it.

"I know you tried, Nik, I know you did. I couldn't tell you guys to stay in, it's not fair and I'm not your keeper, but gods..." He ran a callused hand down his face, biting back the tears.

"I know." I sighed quietly and turned on my heel. My lips pressed into a grim line as I walked out the door and raked my fingers through my hair.

Sabrina sucked in a breath and lifted her eyebrows. "You all right, kid?" She motioned to the wound.

"Mad as hell," I said, gritting my teeth as I glared in her direction.

"I gathered that, given the state of the man you butchered." She didn't seem taken aback, but she did seem impressed. "Is it bad?" She motioned to my side for the second time.

"Heh, you think it's funny?" I looked down at my ribs and shrugged. "Not that bad."

"No, killing people isn't funny, Niklaus, are you psycho?" She wrinkled her nose up and slid her hands into her back pockets.

"Depends on who you ask, but generally I'd say no."

Sabrina's face lost the light that was there a moment ago. "Meet me behind Stein's tomorrow at five in the evening, we have to talk."

Was she going to turn me in? Or talk to Lu about what I had done in the woods? I didn't think he would have blamed me, I had heard him mutter his wishes over the years and his only regret likely would have been it wasn't him delivering the blows to Gregor.

"What is this about, Sabrina?" I squinted at her, not trusting her even though I had known her for most of my life. She was still human and it would have been foolish of me to fully trust her.

"I'm not going to rat on you, kid. I do have a proposition and it's going to wait until tomorrow. Whether you think you need it or not, you need some time, and if you don't… your family needs you." She nodded her head toward the house and turned her back to me, walking away.

"I'll see you at Stein's then," I offered.

"Behind Stein's, Niklaus."

As it turned out, my mother was more loved in the village than I had thought. Everyone adored her because she was generous, and of course, being the village medicine woman, she knew a lot of people, and had cared for them, too.

That didn't mean I wasn't taken aback when we had the funeral the next day. Word traveled fast in our village and people came to pay their respects to Heidi Bintz, offering their condolences and gifts to us.

We didn't offer the truth to them of how she died, they just knew she had passed away from natural causes. Death was natural, but murder wasn't.

"Li, come here," I murmured as I walked over to my sister, she was staring at my mother's headstone. Countless times I had reassured her that it wasn't her fault, it wasn't because of the hunt, it had everything to do with the hunters.

"We knew the risks, it just… I never thought it would happen to us, you know?" She buried her head in my chest and I combed my fingers through her hair to reassure her.

Sighing heavily, I lowered my head to kiss her temple and stared at the stone with our mother's name on it. "I know." Pulling back, I looked down at her bloodshot eyes and blotchy face, wishing I could do something for her. "I have to go soon, Li, Sabrina needs my help near Stein's."

Lu and Liesel knew me well enough to know I dealt with things differently and if I needed to escape the area, then that's what I needed. Although, that had nothing to do with it and everything to do with the way Sabrina was acting yesterday.

Sabrina was in her early thirties, I had known her since we moved to this area and while we weren't close to her, we were friendly enough.

"Tell Lu I'll be back before dark." I nodded my head and gave her one last kiss before I headed off to Stein's.

The smell of wheat, barley, and hops tickled my nose. Stein's specialized in beer—it was quite pungent. Amidst the sour smell was a sweet one, the fragrant cider that I had no qualms with partaking in. My mouth watered at the idea.

"Behind, Niklaus," Sabrina teased as she slunk from behind.

Not bothering to turn around, I contemplated purchasing a

tankard of cider, it was the perfect occasion for one. Grunting, I turned on my heel and offered her a bland look.

Dressed in black leathers and two hunting knives on each hip, Sabrina looked like a force to be reckoned with and as far as I knew, she was. There was a new light in her gaze today and it was one that told me whatever I knew of Sabrina was what she allowed me or anyone to know, and there was a whole other twisted side to her.

"Behind," she repeated and jerked her thumb toward the back of Stein's and moved behind the building.

What did it matter if we were beside or behind? The question must have been plastered across my face because she smirked at me as she pulled her auburn hair back from her face.

"It doesn't actually matter if we're behind it, but we're walking this way," she said as she pointed to the wood line. "So it's just easier being behind it."

"That clears everything up," I sniped and rolled my eyes. "You wanted me to accompany you on a jaunt through the woods?"

"Wow, the attitude! No, I saw you and what you did to that guy in the woods. Plus, there was that trail of dead bodies you left behind. You're welcome, I cleaned those up." She shot me a smirk and fluffed her auburn hair. It was an odd gesture because Sabrina was feminine in appearance but not the air around her. She was more likely to pummel a guy into the ground than I was.

"That wasn't me, that was him—I only attacked him." Shrugging, I stepped under a low hanging limb and lifted my head to see Sabrina staring at me.

"Your father? I'm guessing because—"

"I'm the spitting image of him, got it, thanks."

She only nodded as she drummed her fingers against her thighs. "I watched you do it, you didn't blink, you didn't care...You just did it."

Of course I wouldn't, it was hard to blink when I lacked the ability to feel *most* things. I should have bawled my eyes out over my dead mother's body, I should have screamed and howled at the sky, but I didn't. I was angry, but that was it.

There was no use in commenting on what I already knew, but

Sabrina knew how to talk or at least hold up a one-sided conversation.

"That's when I saw it and knew you had the capability to do what I need from you." She locked eyes with me, blue eyes full of intensity. "Nik, I want you to be part of a league I'm building. My brother and I haven't begun recruiting—you'd be the first recruit and since we know you, it's less pressure on us, too.

"We're hired killers," she paused and waited for a beat, but when I said nothing she continued, "and we need more blades than what we currently have."

"Which is?" Likely not the response I should have uttered, or in the very least, what she had been expecting.

"Two. Lukas and me."

Running my hand down my face, I considered her words carefully. "What am I supposed to do?"

"Learn from us and when you're ready, take on assignations we will give to you. It's remarkable how much people are willing to pay to kill someone."

Money was a necessary evil. The butcher shop was the only one in the village and therefore people always flocked to it, but it by no means ensured that my family was of wealth. What would it be like to not have to worry about money? Or to see Liesel buy whatever she wanted and not have to consider where the money would be better spent.

"Okay, I'll do it," I said, turning my gaze on Sabrina as I nodded and continued down the path.

"Wow, not going to ask how much you could be making?" She snorted and swept a hand to the side. "A pound of gold is the least amount I've received for one hit, by the way, so imagine the possibilities."

"I did, which is why I said I'll do it," I replied flatly.

Sabrina gaped and then snorted as her hands moved toward her side. "I should have known you'd be so calm about it." She didn't offer any more than that, but she didn't have to.

There was little in life that made me take pause or gave me goosebumps. Even my mother's death just left me angry, my father infuriated me and killing him was a cinch— mostly because I knew the truth behind the conception of both myself and Liesel— and that felt like serving justice more than anything.

At sixteen years old, I should have been worrying about what career I'd take in life and perhaps what pretty little girl would be mine to wed. Although, I never cared much for mingling with my peers and while girls were certainly nice to look at, it wasn't my main goal.

"So, it's settled then? That's that, I'm in?"

She considered my words and nodded. "Yes, you're in. Of course, there will be rigorous training and you're expected to follow *our* rules." She eyed me closely as she emphasized *their rules.*

Waving my hand in front of me, I wrinkled my nose. "Is there some kind of contract I have to sign that has these so-called rules?"

A laugh escaped her and she pinned her intense blue eyes on me. "Oh yes, which is where we're currently heading."

I assumed that we were heading to her house but I was wrong. As we cut through a clearing, a massive establishment came into view. It was the largest log cabin I'd ever seen in my life and more akin to what a duke would possess. Three stories high with the second story boasting a wrap-around porch— the windows were strategically placed so that while they offered sunlight, it didn't allow a glimpse into the building so that anyone could spy in.

The front yard had a clearing, somewhat like a courtyard, and stone steps led to the front door which was just as impressive as the rest of the house. A large oak door towered over me. I must have had a strange look on my face because Sabrina nudged my ribs with her elbow—lucky for her it wasn't my sore side.

"Pretty impressive, huh?" She grinned and opened the door which offered me a glimpse inside.

"Shit," I muttered, stepping inside and looking around. It wasn't just the outside that was impressive, the inside was too—high, open ceilings with exposed beams, prized taxidermy decorated the wall, and as if that wasn't enough, the chandelier that hung from the ceiling consisted of a tangle of massive antlers.

"Lukas said it was a bit much, but we had more than enough to throw into it, and it took years. He was thinking too small, I want this to be extraordinary."

"Yeah, I can see what he meant…" Spinning around I took in everything and shook my head.

"Eventually, I'd like to see more people milling around here-—this will be the headquarters, where everyone is trained, and all the contracts pour in. Oh! Speaking of which, follow me." She walked down the hall which had numerous doors along the way. Sabrina motioned with her thumb toward one. "Bedrooms for overnights, or permanent residents." Eventually the hall led toward a staircase which wound its way up to the second floor.

I followed, taking my time as I absorbed every little detail. Upstairs was grand, the windows offered a bird's eye view of the forest around and into the backyard which was set up like a training ground. Targets littered the yard and I had an itch to go outside and try my hand at some of them.

"In here," Sabrina called out.

Following her voice, it led me into the main office, the smell of leather tickled my nose and I spied her reclining in an oversized leather chair. She pushed a piece of parchment toward me and nodded her head.

"Read it over."

It was straight forward. I had the right to name what my refusals were for assignations, I was not allowed to break their rules or the penalty would be great. I had to take up a code name, and above all, I was not allowed to discuss *The Huntsmen.*

"The Huntsmen?" I asked. A laugh made my voice quaver.

"It's what we are and what we do; we hunt people, we take them down, the end of their story." She shrugged her shoulders and waved at the paper. "If you agree, sign, and we'll discuss what you're willing to do and not."

Nodding, I took up the quill pen and signed my name. Maybe somewhere in me I expected to feel dread creep over me. I didn't, I didn't hear the devil snickering, I didn't feel any god's disappointment wash over me, there was just a whole lot of nothing.

It was done.

"Welcome to the Huntsmen, Niklaus. I will give you two weeks to mourn with your family, but after that, I will see you here to begin training. Now, let's discuss what you're not willing to do, because I have a feeling that list will be shorter." She smirked and sat back in her chair, fingers steepled.

Two weeks and I'd be training to become an assassin. Life certainly did have peculiar twists and turns.

In the two weeks that passed, it was clear there was a hole in our family now. The scent of minced meat pie was missing, the humming in the kitchen was gone, and the gentle chiding that always came when I'd tease Liesel wasn't there.

Liesel still wept herself to sleep, so did Lu. Sometimes it was frustrating not being able to express or feel things like they did. I missed her, I mourned her, but in my own way.

There was no need to sneak out of the house, Lu never pretended to be my keeper and he simply nodded at the door as I left the house.

The trail toward the Huntsmen Headquarters was fresh and easy to follow. Somewhere, halfway to the establishment, I caught the scent of something—or someone. My head snapped to the side too late and a blade nicked my throat before I landed on my backside in a swift movement.

I coughed, the breath whooshed out of me and before my mind knew what my body was doing, it sprung into action. Except, a punch to the side of my face stilled my movements.

Sabrina lowered her hand and let out a laugh. "So, you're not made of iron." She flexed her fingers as she smirked in my direction.

"Is that a new way of greeting me?" I spit blood on the ground, my canines chewed up the inside of my cheek when she threw the punch. I could have retaliated but given the sting of the cut at my throat and the throb beginning on my cheekbone, I'd say that Sabrina had a good chance of handing my ass to me.

A snort came from her and she crossed her arms over her chest. "You're a wolf, I didn't know that before two weeks ago. This explains a lot and it'll make some of your training easy. Your secret is safe with me, only Lukas will know." She lowered her arms and jerked her head toward the path.

By the time we made it to the headquarters, Lukas was waiting outside with his arms folded, his piercing blue eyes pinned me where I stood or at least they would have if I was impressed by his stature. He was taller than me, thicker too, not in a bumbling oaf fashion, but more of a professional fighter way. That wasn't too far off the mark now that I knew what they did for a living.

"Sabrina, did you hit him?" His nose scrunched up as he stalked forward and eyed the bloom of color on my cheek. "He's a kid!" Lukas' eyes dropped to my neck for a split second before he glared at his twin.

My guess was that Lukas wasn't thrilled about me being on board to begin with, at sixteen I was more than capable of making decisions but in the eyes of a thirty-year-old I wasn't.

His fingers combed through his dark hair as he turned toward her.

"This *kid* is a recruit and if he can't handle a punch, he should go home," she snapped at him.

"I've had worse," I interjected, not bothering to brush my fingers against the growing bruise. Being a redhead in Abendrot wasn't uncommon, red hair was in an abundance here for whatever reason, but my smart mouth usually landed me in a world of trouble. There was one scuffle I got into that had my ribs bruised to the point I couldn't breathe properly. Thankfully, my mother knew how to wrap them and rubbed essential oils on my bruises to ease the pain.

Lukas huffed a breath, his hands on his hips. "All right, head out back and you'll see where you need to go, I'll be there in a moment."

I did as I was told, moving around the building, and as I rounded the corner, I could hear the screaming match begin between the siblings. A chuckle slid from me as I waited for it to end.

In the meantime, I picked up a bow and nocked an arrow. This was nothing new, I knew how to hunt as most of the villagers who didn't depend on Lu's shop did. Lifting it, I eyed the target in the distance and let the arrow whistle through the air. It bit into the target, off-centered, but if it were an animal or individual, it still would have been a lethal hit.

"Not too bad," Lukas offered. "It could be better. You should know to draw back quietly, prey can hear and they itch to run." He selected another arrow and took up a bow for himself. "Like this," he said, and nocked an arrow. Slowly, he drew the arrow back, the string didn't so much as creak, and when he exhaled, the arrow pierced the air and struck the target dead center.

He was right, of course, I should know the subtle sounds would trigger prey to run, and so I mimicked his actions. Instead of being so intent on releasing the arrow, I focused on the target, focused on my breath, and when I exhaled, my arrow bit into the material next to Lukas' arrow.

"Just like that. I don't think you'll have an issue with a bow, it'll be more about honing the skill you have."

Sabrina snorted. "He's good with a knife, too, I've seen it. He just needs to learn to maneuver himself appropriately."

She *had* seen me fight with my father, saw how I took him to the ground and pummeled him into the dirt. I handled knives on the daily at Lu's, knew where the vital organs were on a person and animal, but I'd need to perfect how to move my body, how to flow in a fight rather than let my adrenaline kick me into a blind fury.

For the rest of the day they, ran me ragged, had me wield several weapons, and they saw what I was made of—or at least a glimpse.

The next several weeks passed in a blur and no matter how much sleep I got, I couldn't seem to catch up. One morning, Liesel came in as I was pulling a shirt on and she gawked at me.

"Where did those come from?" she asked, pointing at my stomach.

I slid a hand to my stomach, roughened fingers dragging over the tender muscle there. "I lift heavy things," I supplied with a grin.

"No, Nik." She insisted and walked up to me, pulling my shirt up to spy the bruises. "These!" Her face crumpled into a mixture of fear and anger, her cheeks flushing with color.

"Li," I began, taking her hands in mine.

"No! I never see you anymore. I'm worried, Nik, I'm worried about you and what you're up to, but you won't tell me. You don't tell me anything."

Chewing my bottom lip, I began to nod my head. She was right, I didn't tell her anything and it was safer for her that way. Liesel didn't know what I was training for, what took me away from her and the shop, what distracted me, what would soon pay a handsome sum and supply her with a life I knew she was worthy of.

Instead of arguing with her, I wrapped my arms around her small frame. "I'm okay, it was just a friendly match. I got sloppy, I promise that is it. It was Lukas Seidel, okay?" I dropped his name, because Liesel trusted the Seidel siblings and she knew they were good—or at least good enough—he would never intentionally hurt me in her eyes.

I hoped my sister would never change, the world needed more people like her to counteract the ones like me. Gritting my teeth, my eyes squeezed shut as I hugged her a little tighter. My lips brushed against her temple and I pulled back to look into her eyes. "I'm going to try to make a difference today, got it?" Tweaking the tip of her nose, I dropped my arms.

The King of Abendrot had decided to open the floor to citizens, this was our annual chance to make a difference in the kingdom, for our voices and our problems to be heard by the king specifically. I had little faith in him, but what could be done other than trying? At least I could be satisfied that I'd speak my piece to King Ansgar.

"Okay." She huffed and scrubbed at her eyes. "I'm going into the village with Lu for the market, please be careful in the city." She clung to me again and I gave her one more tight squeeze before sending her off.

I made certain any weapon I'd grown used to carrying was left behind. No hidden knives in my boot, no weapon in my pant's pocket, anything I wore on my person would be stripped away and I'd likely be accused of trying to maim the king or one of his children. I really didn't want to end up in the stocks or worse.

Our closest neighbor was heading into the city of Sorensberg to attend the open forum and so I bummed a ride with him. Fortunately, he didn't like talking and in that we shared a meaningful ride in silence.

Growing up, I never had cause to venture to the city, this was my first time here and it was overwhelming. The buildings were on top of one another, attached even to its neighboring business, and people littered the streets. There were several shops in a row and some were two stories tall—this was strange to me, for in Walddorf, we had tiny shops or simply just vendors peddling their wares in the street.

They weren't as openly friendly here, either. I saw it written on their faces, saw it in the way they charged ahead of one another; there was no polite conversation at every turn, but there was almost a scowl at every turn.

I hopped out of the wagon and nodded to my neighbor before I pushed my way through the crowd. If no one was going to get out of my way, I was going to *make* them.

Beyond the twists and turns of the city, the castle came into view. It was impressive—I had seen the tower from the distance but up close, it was something else entirely.

Encased in green vines, Sorensberg Castle stood proudly against a backdrop of massive pine trees, the dark bricks lent the structure an eerie appearance. Of course, the fog that rolled in from behind it didn't help. I hoped that the sunless sky wasn't foretelling of how this day would transpire.

Pushing my way through the crowd, I was forced to stop as a guard pushed my chest. I scarcely rocked on my heels as I eyed him.

"No closer, kid."

Flicking my gaze upward, I noticed that the king and his two daughters sat on the first landing. Stasya, the eldest, and Edda the youngest. It wasn't the unruly, curly-haired, bright Edda that caught my eye, it was her sister. Stasya's hair was as pale as the full moon. She sat composed, hands folded in her lap and her lips pressed together in a thin line. Edda must have said something to her, because her shoulders shook and her face contorted as she withheld a laugh.

The crowd around me quieted and soon the king began to speak. I found the interaction between the two sister's fascinating. Even as the king spoke, the younger sister tried her best to get her older sister to squirm. Thrice she had to bite her bottom lip to keep from cracking a smile.

My attention slid to one of the city folk as they began to offer up their complaints and what they thought would solve it. It was mostly about taxes, about restrictions, and while some offered up grand ideas on how to better businesses, it didn't touch on the lives that ran the businesses.

"I have something to say," I spoke at last, someone thought they'd cut me off. "No! I have something to say. What of the wolves of the kingdom? Will you offer protection to the kind that founded this country?" My eyes flicked toward Stasya for a moment and she flinched. "Every day, the poachers sweep into the woods and kill werewolves. The sheriffs turn a blind eye, the *crown* turns a blind eye. What of the lives that have been lost, the families that suffer?"

Around me, I felt people move away, there were some who echoed my sentiments, but for the most part I found myself in a clearing, alone.

This was personal, but more than that, it affected a grand portion of the kingdom.

King Ansgar ran his fingers along his tidy beard, considering his words carefully before he spoke. "It is not condoned by the crown to be hunting wolves."

"It isn't illegal, Your Majesty," I said in a clipped tone, curbing a good portion of my attitude. "And with it not being illegal, people will continue to hunt werewolves. It is *murder*."

"And we frown upon murder." He lowered his voice, narrowing his dark eyes on me.

Color rushed into my cheeks, my hands balled up at my sides. Nothing would be done, murder was *frowned upon,* like it was akin to belching at the dinner table. Or one of his daughters being too forward with a male. It was frowned upon. What it came down to was that he was more concerned with businesses thriving and putting coin in his pocket. I spared one more glance at Stasya, the king had just sealed his fate. If he would not help the other half of the country, then matters would be taken into my own hands.

The king wasn't the only useless one, if his daughters cared anything for the country, they'd speak up, they'd try something, anything to convince the wicked pig wearing the crown to do *something.*

A sneer contorted my face as the king swiftly moved onto another topic, but it was Stasya's green eyes that focused on me as if trying to convey a message. I didn't linger to find out, she was a blasted swine just like her father and before long, I promised that I'd come knocking on their door a second time.

This time when I barreled my way through the crowd, people moved. None could confirm that I was a werewolf, but if I was a sympathizer, it branded me in some way. If I was willing to defend them, I might as well have *been* one. That was Ansgar's first chance, he had two more and that would be it. Something had to change.

I bit my tongue and walked away from the gathering, but not with my tail between my legs. No, I vowed that I'd have my revenge against the useless king and while I was in the city, I would make the most of it, it was time to make some acquaintances here.

I found myself standing outside of a shop, arms crossed against my chest as I stared through a window that specialized in hunting gear. Striding inside, I took note of the compound bows that hung on display, knives and axes, spears. But it was the hunting arrows that I honed in on.

Black arrows, with a broad silver head caught my eye. Gleaming in the afternoon sun on the wall, I walked over to it and ran my finger along the sharpened tip.

"It'll drop a bull moose with ease," the shop owner offered. "New to the market and not popular yet."

Considering his words, I picked up the arrow and felt the weight in my hand, it was well-balanced, well made, too. "Locally made?"

The shop owner grunted. "Yeah, all by the same kid, Raif. I bet he's about your age, lives on the outskirts of the city."

Interesting, I mused and lifted the arrow. "I'll buy one to try out." Digging out the money in my pocket, I paid for it.

"You fancy yourself some moose?" He cackled as he slid the money into a drawer, eyeing me up and nodding his head. "Huntin' is good for the soul, boy, enjoy that and let me know how it is."

He had no idea how good hunting truly felt. One whiff of him and I knew he was only human. I nodded my head toward him and left the shop. Raif was about to get a visit from me and an offer he couldn't refuse. I'd catch flack for it from the Seidel siblings but they could bite me—this was too good of an opportunity to pass up.

On the edge of the city I caught sight of the smoke billowing from a shop, the sound of a hammer striking metal caught my attention and as I approached the building, I saw a bundle of frizzy, brown hair pulled back into a bun. A muscled arm continued to pound the heated metal into the desired shape. I watched somewhat fascinated and moved around the caramel-skinned individual.

"What are you making?" I caught him off guard because he startled, his green eyes narrowing on me before he repositioned the bandana around his hair.

Instead of responding to me he just stared and squinted his eyes.

"What. Are. You. Making?" I asked again. Maybe he didn't hear me.

He lifted the metal, shrugging his shoulders, and it was my turn to stare at him. I wasn't sure if he was all there or if he was born with something different about him.

"An arrow," someone said from behind him. It was a woman's voice. "He's making an arrow, and he heard you. Raif can't talk and I doubt you can sign." Fire blazed beneath her words, daring me to contradict her, daring me to step into the snare she laid out.

Well, she was right about that, I definitely couldn't sign aside from flipping someone off. "Gotcha. Is this his work?" I lifted the newly purchased arrow and Raif grabbed my hand to tug me back to him, because I wasn't expecting it, I moved with him, *allowed* for the other wolf to yank on me.

Raif nodded his head, his intense gaze locked onto mine and I roughly pulled my arm away from him. He sighed through his nose and gave up on his current project before he turned to the female and signed to her.

Waiting was the only option allotted to me at that moment.

"He says it's rude to talk like he can't hear you, he's perfectly capable of hearing—just not speaking." The female looked to be around his age, they had the same tone of skin and same bright green eyes.

"Your brother, I'm assuming?" I thought it was a fair enough question, but Raif didn't, he took his hands and shoved me hard enough so that I stumbled back. I caught my balance by leaning forward and glared at him. "Hey! I was asking a question!" I bit out. I hadn't been expecting it, but I wasn't pissed off yet either. My gaze flicked between him and his sister.

He signed rapidly, glaring down at me as I stood upright.

"Don't talk like I don't exist," she repeated his signs.

"You exist, so says my tender skin, but I was asking your *sister* a question." I muttered a curse under my breath. This guy was like a massive bull ready to go on a rampage and he was built like one, too.

"Listen, he's used to people assuming he's stupid or deaf, don't take it personally. The shove was for his own amusement." She snickered.

Brilliant, so he was a regular comedian. I shot him an icy glare, contemplating smacking the arrow in my grasp across the smug look on his face. I let the image play out in my head and relaxed the grip on the metal in my hand instead.

"I wanted to compliment you on your work. I also wanted to know if you had any contracts with anyone." I eyed his workmanship that hung up on various racks outside and let out a whistle as I hoisted a mean looking arrow tip into my grasp. It wasn't attached to a shaft like the others, this one was created to spin and dig into flesh.

This time, I didn't turn around as his sister began to talk. I watched Raif, watched the expressions shift in his gaze instead of ignoring him and honing in on his sister.

"No, I don't. Like she said, most people think I'm dumb." It was his sister's voice but Raif's words.

"But that clearly isn't the case, Raif." My gaze swept along the finished pieces, each one a handcrafted marvel. Each one had a piece of Raif's blood or sweat fused into the piece. The guy was talented, that was for certain.

"How do you know his name?" she snapped, suddenly defensive.

"The man in the center of the city who's selling his stuff ratted Raif out. What's your name anyway? And don't hit me again, Raif." I added in the last part with a scowl in Raif's direction.

"Kina." She didn't offer her hand in greeting, she purposely folded her arms across her chest.

"You're a friendly bunch." Luckily, it didn't matter. Sticks and stones, all of that, one thing was for certain my bark wasn't worse than my bite. My bite was worse. I weighed the arrow in my palm, lips twisting as I considered my next words carefully. "I need a dozen of these, and those arrow heads."

"That's great, but we need a down payment from you *Red*. No payment no product. Deal with Raif by yourself." Kina rolled her eyes as she walked back into the shop.

Raif surprisingly didn't follow suit, he stayed put and considered the offer. His hands moved quickly, too quickly for me to even try to piece together what he meant. I squinted and pointed to the arrow head and the arrow in my grasp.

He nodded and snatched a piece of parchment paper, scribbling a date and price on it. Once he was done, he pressed it into my chest, eyeing me levelly.

A snort came from me as I peered down at the figures, it wasn't ultimately my money to spend but maybe the Seidel's would find this interesting, it wasn't as if they were suffering money wise.

"I'll be seeing you soon, Raif." I jerked my chin toward him.

This time, he signed with a single finger, and that one I knew quite well.

On the trek back to Walddorf, curses frequently fled my mouth like they were songs of praise for the twisted gods that ruled above. One thing went smoothly today, at least, and that was meeting Raif, if one could call it smooth. However, the more I thought of Ansgar, the more my blood boiled.

It didn't matter if he outlawed hunting werewolves, there would still be poachers lurking around the corner, waiting to off one of us when we least expected it, but at least there would have been retribution. There would have been some action taken against murdering a wolf in cold blood.

As it stood, there was none; everyone turned a blind eye and I imagined they secretly rejoiced that another wolf bit the dust, and in their mind, the world was a little safer for it.

Halfway back home, someone cried my name and I spun around to face the direction it came. The impact against my chest caused the air to rush out of me and rather than scowl, a chuckle slipped out. "Nice to see you too, Li." My fingers scritched at her back before I pulled away.

Liesel grinned as she moved back, motioning to Lu. "We had a good time at the market," she offered, but her face soon crumpled. "What happened?"

"That's good." Shrugging my shoulders, I looked away from her and at Lu, nodding my head. "What? Nothing, nothing happened."

She pointed at the arrow and pressed her lips together. "What's that then?"

"Are you going to keep me hostage with the questions? I bought an arrow." Lifting my hand, I opened my fist and balanced the arrow there before flicking it so it spun.

Liesel frowned, clearly not pleased with that answer and she moved to snatch the arrow. "But what happened?"

The arrow ceased spinning as I clutched the shaft in my hand and lowered it. "Absolutely nothing. Immovable as always, I don't know, Li, I'll try two more times, next time I'll be more prepared." All that we could hope for would be for the king to expire and maybe, just maybe Stasya would lead the country as it ought to be. Although, I wasn't about to hold my breath.

Liesel chewed on her bottom lip and peered up at Lu as he approached.

"One day it'll be better," he said, leaning down to kiss the top of Liesel's head. His arms looped around her front as he playfully tugged her into his body. "Am I right?" He tickled Liesel and chuckled.

"Yes! Yes!" she cried out and squirmed in his grasp.

Maybe Lu was right, but I didn't for a second believe that everything would miraculously be fixed in the future. It wasn't just going to fall into place, someone needed to change it, someone needed to get their hands dirty.

"Niki, can we go blueberry picking tomorrow?" Liesel asked.

The twins would likely have something in store for me tomorrow, but my sister rarely asked for anything. Training could wait, even if the Seidels would argue, they could kick my ass another day; tomorrow Liesel would have my undivided attention. "I'll see you at home."

Winding toward the Huntsmen Headquarters, I stopped at the edge of the woods. It would have looked abandoned if it weren't for the newness of the logs or the manicured property. No one was milling around, there wasn't a sound to be heard except for the forest which teemed with life.

In the weeks I had been trained, I learned a few things, which was not to trust the stillness of the environment, so as a rush of air went sailing by, my hands gripped a pair of slender shoulders so I could use the momentum to pull them over. I stood with a relaxed posture and a cocky grin plastered across my face.

"You're lucky I didn't use the arrow to stab you," I offered as I peered down at Sabrina.

She sneered. "Not like you'd succeed."

Quickly, her prone form turned into a weapon, her leg swung out and collided with mine which sent me off balance. That was all the window of opportunity she needed—she advanced on me and kicked at my shin which further set me off. Nimbly, I recovered, held up my hands, and shielded my face before she fancied hitting me there.

I should have guarded my ribs, because she landed a roundhouse kick to them which sent me to my knees. She relented—which was a sign of mercy—but mercy had no place amongst assassins. I launched at her legs and yanked her to the ground; she writhed around like a woman possessed. Clambering on the ground we grappled until she tapped out.

"Not bad," she panted as she spoke and rolled over onto her knees, grinning. "What do you want?"

Nostrils flaring, it took a few moments to regain my breath enough so I could talk without gasping. "This," I said, pulling the arrow from my back pocket, which thankfully hadn't pierced my hide or fallen out and stabbed me—or her. I'd wager Lukas would put a target on me if that came to pass.

Sabrina took the arrow and examined it carefully, her blue eyes training on the tip. "Where did you get this?"

"In the capital. There was a shop and he said it was new. I found the kid that makes them." I paused and pulled the scribbled piece of paper out. "We chatted." If one could call it chatting.

She made a noncommittal noise in the back of her throat, took the note, and began to walk away. "I'll talk to Lukas, mind if I keep it?" She didn't stop, just continued walking away.

I didn't need the arrow. "You can put that on my tab!"

She laughed and disappeared behind the front door.

As per promised, blueberry picking came the next day, Liesel's bright yellow eyes gleamed in the sun as she joked about having eaten more blueberries than picked.

"Quit eating them, Li, we're not going to have any left over for that pie you promised." In the past weeks, she had taken over the role of piemaker in the house. The scent of the baking pies had been absent, and both of us had missed the scent of mulled spices and buttery crust. The first few pies had been full of her tears. Gradually, the act of baking them seemed therapeutic for her.

She huffed in my direction, to which I replied with a puff.

"We will have plenty, it's a full moon tonight and we'll both be hungry after it."

That was true, Lu was dreading it, but he knew he couldn't keep us cooped up in the house, where we'd be caged in our rooms and liable to tear it apart, only to escape into the night in spite of his efforts.

"That doesn't mean much—I'm always hungry." Shrugging my shoulders, I took a handful of berries out of her basket and grinned wolfishly.

"Niklaus!"

A smug look crept over my face which didn't last for long, because she had a fistful of berries that she slapped—or rather smooshed—against my face. Sticky, sweet smelling fragments of the berry dripped from my face and plopped on the ground. Staring dryly at her, I rubbed my cheek against the arm of the shirt I wore.

"Dirty fighter."

When we finished picking an adequate amount of berries, we maneuvered our way back to the house, only one of us was still happy enough to bounce their way home.

Lu heard Liesel's laugh ring out and he stuck his head out of the shop. "Nik, Sabrina is here, mind helping her load the wagon? Another customer is lined up."

Giving nothing away, I nodded my head and handed Liesel the other basket of berries. "It's all you from here." Moving away from her, I sought out Sabrina who sat casually on the bed of the wagon.

"Where's my order?" She raked her gaze over my face and snickered. I couldn't say I blamed her, covered in blueberry guts and my face stained with juice, I must have been a sight to see.

"Should I snap for the genie express?" Snapping my fingers, I rolled my eyes and headed inside to grab the crate that held her order. Carrying it outside I plopped it down inside her cart. "Happy?"

"Absolutely. I wanted to let you know Lukas was impressed with your friend's talent. We're willing to pay and we'd like to meet him."

This didn't exactly come as a surprise—Raif was talented and knew his way around forging. Besides, those arrows were a nightmare.

"Go clean yourself up, be careful tonight, and I'll see you tomorrow."

Heading back inside, I did just that and enjoyed the scent of blueberry pie baking. It took all the strength I had not to devour an entire pie before the evening, that coupled with the threats gifted by my sister held me at bay—only barely.

By nightfall, the sky burst with life, stars shone brightly in numbers that were too high to count, and the full moon hung against the backdrop. We both felt it, the tug and the itching of our skin as we traipsed into the woods.

Two full moons had passed since my mother died and Liesel hadn't seemed to lose the anxiety that came with each shift now. The killers had stolen that from her, and it was unforgivable in my eyes.

"I won't let anything happen to you," I murmured and kissed the top of her head.

"I know, but what about you?" she asked softly, wearing on her lower lip.

A laugh tore from me and it shouldn't have, but I let out a playful growl as I hugged her. "They'd have to catch me first." I winked at her and heard the sounds of bones crunching. Shifting—no matter how many times it occurred—broke bones. They snapped, shifted, realigned as our bodies became something other. Luckily, with age, it became seamless and less painful. The pain that came with shifting was dull, at least to me, my sister never handled it well.

Liesel shook her head, licking her chops, more than ready to begin a night of hunting.

It was quicker for me, the snapping of bones, the way my skin grew fur and bones elongated. Claws jutted out from my fingertips, and in a blink, I stood in my wolf form. Burnt red, not so unlike the color of my hair. Liesel was a smaller twin version of me.

Lifting our muzzles to the sky, we let out a howl to the mother moon, deep and mournful. One glance at one another and we were off.

The hunt was on and we didn't return home until our bellies were satisfied.

Long before the sun rose, I woke. I scribbled a vague note for Lu to let him know when I'd be back and then I was off to train.

It was funny—Lukas typically went easier on me—I was a kid in his eyes—but Sabrina viewed it more practically. If this was the life I chose, I needed to be prepared and in the heat of an altercation, someone wasn't going to step back and shout, "Damn, he's only a kid!" And so she threw everything at me, things I wouldn't expect, things I might expect, she made my muscles scream, drew blood and almost made me regret my decision.

Almost.

Truth be told, I would always enjoy the work, the pushing my body to extremes, it was one of the few things in life I garnered joy from.

As I rounded the corner of the building, I caught a familiar scent, one that hadn't been here before. Standing with his arms folded and his back toward me, Raif stared at Sabrina. Instead of having his hair pulled back into a tight bun, it was loose and wild, which lent him what I imagined to be a terrifying look.

Sabrina eyed me briefly, moving her hands to sign to Raif rather than speak out loud, which told me she didn't want me to be part of the conversation. Or maybe it was that Raif wasn't comfortable with it. Whatever the reasoning I cemented myself in the middle of the conversation, watching their fingers move. Clearly, I needed to add this to my bag of tricks.

"Staring is rude, Nik," Sabrina said with a smirk.

"Bite me." I paused. "Are you in?" The last of my words were aimed at Raif and when he nodded a 'yes,' I grinned. "Wait, in-in?" This time I looked at Sabrina who nodded her head as well. Not just a smithy but a trainee, too? Squinting my eyes, I took a good, hard look at Raif and wondered if he had it in him. There was an underlying tension about him, although he wore a mask of calm, something told me it was just that— a mask.

"Lukas will be handling him today, you're lucky enough to have me all to yourself, Niki."

"Don't call me that," I snapped. It was a rarity that I snapped at her. "It's Nik or nothing." Niklaus meant I was in trouble and Niki was a term of endearment she had no place using.

The look on her face said she considered furthering the teasing but she pointed to the circle in the backyard. "Get in and warm up."

"Wait, I have a request." She turned to me and waited, cocking an eyebrow. "I want to learn how to scale a building quietly. How to get past guards."

A muscle twitched in her jaw, but she didn't ask why or where such skills would be used. Instead she agreed. "Warm up, and we will begin."

That was how the next several weeks went—warm up and begin. Lukas handled Raif and when we were both done, to-the-bone tired, Raif would sit with me and patiently teach me how to sign. When I'd mess up, which was quite often, he'd sign with a rude gesture.

It turned out that Raif was a natural when it came to the business of fighting, but there was more to this than just fighting for practice, it was a job, too.

"I think you're ready for your first assignment," Sabrina said one day, holding up a paper in her hand.

My stomach twisted in anticipation."What is it?"

"A known poacher, targeted a family, and they know for a fact it was him because he boasted about it. As your first assignment, this one could be felt personally, I'd like to see if you can continue to keep yourself detached from those feelings."

Maybe she expected another reaction from me, but all I did was smile and take the paper in my grasp. Details were written down— where he lived, who he lived with, and something I hadn't been anticipating: how he should die. "They dictate how they want them to die?"

"Some do, not all, but those who don't want to get their hands dirty want it done how *they* would do it, like they're living through you."

"I'll do it." This assignment couldn't be personal, but Sabrina knew that it was on some level. They had been the reason my mother died and this was a test. A test to measure how I kept my head on a job, if I could reel myself in and simply just *do the job*. It was easy enough to say that I could, but it'd be harder in the heat of the moment, especially since most of these poachers had either a military background or had been trained by one who did.

Zeroing in on the date of the assignment, I lifted my eyes and laughed.

"What do you find so funny?"

"It's on my birthday."

"Is that a problem?" There was a hint of a challenge in her tone and she arched a brow.

"Not at all, it's just a unique present, I guess."

"Happy birthday," she offered dryly.

There was a particular bite to the air on the evening of the assignment. My breath billowed out of me in white clouds and the moon was still bright. One of the perks of being a wolf was our ability to see more clearly in the dark—it made us the ultimate predator, and in this case, only aided in my ability to take this poacher out.

The sun had set a little over a half hour ago, it was amusing that the individual who sought out the hit had done his recon for us. He had followed this man, had watched his every move and learned his habits enough to know what he'd be doing at this time of night.

Outside, next to the barn, my mark filled a bucket of water for the livestock. He muttered something to himself as he walked inside and I waited. The animals would give my presence away, wolves unnerved them and I had no desire to give him a head start. I waited until he was done with the water, the distinct sound of the wheel turning on a barrel caught my attention and I knew it was time.

Launching myself from the cover of the bushes, I rushed forward just as his body twisted to dump the barrel. A flash of silver in the moonlight caught his attention, but it was too late as I jabbed it into his side. He groaned, swore, and twisted to face his attacker with a scowl on his features.

He wasn't slow, not as he launched at me in return, his fist almost connecting with my ribs. If I had been stupid enough to leave the blade in his side, he would have used it on me, but I had no intention of offering him a weapon.

Drawn out—that was what the contract had said—he wanted this drawn out and he wanted the man to suffer. I could do that; I could give the man that peace of mind.

I slid low, low enough so that my dagger pierced his pants and bit into the back of his leg right near a precious artery. His fist connected with my back moments after and I sucked in a breath. Instead of cursing, I laughed.

"You little s—" he began to curse at me but stopped as he barreled forward. I used his momentum to pull him to the ground, keeping my own weight low and centered.

The scent of his blood wafted in the air, his movements were slowing and I took advantage of the opportunity to leap on him. He was too focused on one of the blades in my hand to realize there was a twin until that one nicked an artery in his arm. One cut at a time, he would bleed out, slowly and surely.

He grabbed my hands, trying to use his brute strength to cause me to drop the blades, but Sabrina had killed the nerves there during training. Time after time, my knuckles collided with tree bark until the nerves in them dulled. I may not have understood then, but I certainly did now.

Finally, he managed to dislodge me, his hands groping for my quick figure, he managed to ensnare my ankle, and as he moved his other I knew at once what he was about to do—he wanted to snap my ankle.

In a lightning quick movement, I twisted around, my other foot connecting with his face as he began to retaliate. I felt my tendons stretching. With no other option, I twisted forward, hand moving downward before I thought of it. Somewhere I must have actually thought it through to adhere to the contract, because as the blade penetrated his flesh his movements ceased at once, but he did not die.

"You bastard," he said with panic in his tone. "I can't...I can't feel my hands. My legs!" His eyes widened as he realized that the lack of feeling extended to his feet. He lay there, paralyzed and bleeding out.

Leaning forward, I took the knife out and cleaned it on his shirt. "Don't waste your breath, you're dying." I gave him one last look over, secured my blades and headed off into the woods with a limp.

It was late and my ankle was swollen by the time I made it inside. Sabrina sat waiting in a leather chair, her blue eyes taking in the limp, the dirt and blood. "Sit, now," she ordered and stood from her chair. She grabbed a towel, some herbs and made her way to me. "Congratulations, you're not dead."

I chuckled and regretted it, my ribs complained. "Better than what I can say for the mark."

She unlaced my boot unceremoniously and rolled my pant leg up so she could access the ankle. Bruised, throwing off heat and definitely ugly, she wrinkled her nose and emitted a hiss.

"He wrenched it, that's all."

"Not bad for your first go, he didn't get you anywhere else?" she asked as her fingers probed the area. When it was certain there was no break, she lathered the herbal remedy on the swollen area.

"My back and ribs," I offered and propped my leg up when she prompted me with her hand.

"Well, use this on them, I'll rub your ankle but that's as far as I'm going, kid." She arched a red brow and tossed the jar in my direction.

I snatched it out of the air and nodded, feeling exhaustion take over. There was still a long trek back home ahead of me and on a bum leg to boot.

"Don't even think about it, you're staying the night. I'll have Lukas run a note over so Lu doesn't panic," she offered.

I had no energy in me to disagree, so I nodded my head and let sleep take over, plunging me into darkness.

The sound of someone plopping into a chair roused me, the scent of apple streusel enough cause to open my eyes. Raif sat with two plates resting on his knees and he lifted one. Nodding, I grabbed it and began to greedily eat the delicious treat. Humans were odd—they could eat dessert for breakfast, whereas us wolves preferred hardier things such as schlackwurst, bacon, pretzels and jam.

I lifted the plate and nodded at him.

"How's your ankle?" He signed slowly so that no words were confused or lost.

"Feels better, I wouldn't run to the city on it, but I'd walk." A perk of being a wolf—we heal faster—still hurt like a mother, but it wasn't swollen any longer. However, when I sat forward and shifted the wrap on my ankle, a deep bruising glared at me angrily.

"I have to go out tonight, wish me luck." Signing, his shoulders moved as he silently chuckled.

"Very little of the act has anything to do with luck, Raif. Be careful, be smart." Somewhere amidst the discussion, the streusel had disappeared and I sighed, it was barely enough to touch the pit that was my stomach.

Raif signed something and I managed to catch the tail end of it which made my nose wrinkle. I had missed something, but I let it go at that. Whatever it was, he sure was amused. Ass.

The streusel would be enough to hold me over until I got back home to gorge on real food. Leaning forward, I tugged each boot on and stood up, the weight on my bad ankle was surprisingly not bad. Testing it without pushing it too far, I found myself pleased that I'd definitely be able to walk back home without issue.

Raif looked lost in his world, perhaps he was wondering about tonight or maybe he was worried. Who could say? I knew he'd pull through and more than that, I knew he'd go above and beyond. No one who was *that* meticulous crafting could be sloppy when it came to other aspects in their life.

"Go home, Nik." He jerked his head, staring at me with those intense green eyes. "Home." He repeated the motion and let his fingers linger by his temple.

"Yeah, yeah, I'm leaving." And I did, my boots hit the ground and I didn't bother to look back. As it was, Lu and Liesel were probably worried enough.

By the time I reached home, Lu was outside, the lines in his face tight as I approached, coupled by the leaping muscle in his jaw, I knew he was mad, but I was old enough now he wasn't going to bark at me. Not to mention there was always this weird boundary he never dared to cross, like he knew not to growl at me.

"Your sister was worried about you," he said, turning his blue eyes away. It was his way of saying he was too.

"Lukas left you a note? I couldn't walk home last night." Assuming he read it, Lukas had told a half-truth—I hurt my ankle in the woods while helping them cut down a few trees and had to stay the night. But by the time Lukas had reached the house, it was too late to knock.

"Yeah," he grunted his words, scratching at his cheek as he moved away.

Good talk, as always, I thought, and pushed my way into the house. The scent of minced meat pie made my mouth water at once, and when I stepped into the kitchen, I was bombarded with memories. A redhead stood at the stove with her hair in a bandana, humming a song and I could have sworn it was my mother, but it wasn't. Blinking, I shook away memories of Liesel when she was just learning to walk and me dancing with her.

"Figured the smell of pie would bring you home," she sniped, not bothering to look at me as she took the pie out of the oven. It went without saying that I wasn't to touch it, that was our mother's rule and it was now hers.

A smirk formed on my face as my shoulders lifted in a shrug. "You got me there."

"Well, since you weren't really around yesterday, I didn't get to tell you. Today Princess Stasya is visiting Bromiel," she began to say.

Liesel barely finished before I interrupted. "As in, she's touring? For what reason, and why Bromiel?" It just so happened to be the neighboring town and one that was known for being the poorest in the country—the sort of poor that everyone frowned if it became known you were from there.

"If you'd let me finish... yes, apparently the king wants her to grow used to it if she is to be crowned queen one day." This time she did look at me, hope daring to spark in her eyes.

Thoughts ran rampantly through my mind, if I could get there and speak to her privately without guards lingering around, perhaps there was a better chance at one of the royals listening.

Liesel turned to look at me, her pale face full of concern. "That's good, right? Another chance to change something?"

"Maybe," I said quietly, because I didn't know. There was something about Stasya that set her apart from her family and maybe that would work in our favor.

"Then eat before you go—I'm sure you didn't eat enough yesterday. The Seidels have human stomachs." She laughed and flitted about the kitchen to grab me some food before my trip.

With a full belly, it was time to go, luckily, we lived right next to the road that led to Bromiel.

The surrounding forest was so thick that the sun scarcely shown through the treetops. Even in the middle of Bromiel, the sun seemed to shy away, which gave it a macabre vibe. As if it wasn't dark enough, several smoke stacks from nearby buildings expelled smoke, and whatever light may have filtered through the treetops seemed to be extinguished.

Typically, the streets were barren, but today they were lively, no doubt the town was attempting to create the deception that it was better than what it was. Most individuals suffered from depression, drank themselves to death and never attempted to move away, as if they were cursed to live and die on the soil they loathed.

"She's here!" a young girl shouted, perhaps only a year or two younger than Liesel.

Dragging my eyes toward the approaching carriage I made the decision to begin moving closer. Flanked by guards, it made it impossible to move in close enough to speak to her—now wasn't the time anyway.

Princess Stasya emerged from the carriage, her pale head bowed as a guard helped her down. "Thank you," she murmured demurely and cast her otherworldly eyes on the crowd before her. She searched it as if looking for someone and finally settled on a small girl in front. "Hello." She offered her hand in greeting and looked at the troubling sight before her.

The houses here were built mostly out of sticks and resembled shacks instead of the cottages in Walddorf. They were rickety and were a testament to how much they were in need of assistance or some kind of break in taxes.

"Watch it," a man grumbled as I moved forward.

I slid my gaze toward him and offered a glare. He muttered an obscenity but backed away.

Stasya, still flanked by guards, was led down the row of buildings, letting the townsfolk speak to her plainly of what required the most work, what they thought would help the state of their town and people.

"Perhaps if people turned their eyes to us, then we could begin logging, it would help the state of our town and bring light to it once more, in so many ways," an older woman offered, her worn fingers gnarled and wrinkled.

That was one of their many issues, they had resources but no one paid them any heed because… well, because it was Bromiel.

"We have so many trees to offer, surely we could begin sawmills, we have talented woodworkers if only people would remember us."

I grimaced. It was sad to hear the desperation in their voices and to Stasya's credit she didn't school her face into an unreadable mask. No, she let her concern and consideration wash over her face—as if she were truly listening to their plight.

The crowd grew thicker, which made the guards tighten their security and it made me consider the surroundings. Nodding to myself, I kicked a vat of bacon grease over a fire, which caused it to burst into a flame. The crowd panicked and I seized the moment, grabbing Stasya and ushered her through the writhing mob of people while the guards were preoccupied trying to keep them at bay.

Stasya thrashed in my grasp violently and I easily hoisted her up to avoid kicks to my shins. Screaming, she flailed harder, trying to capture the attention of her guards, yet they couldn't hear a damn thing over the cries of the people as they threw dirt over the fire to contain it.

Thrusting her into a vacant hut, I slammed the door shut and locked it. "Stop!" I barked out at her, huffing as I stared at her. "I'm not going to hurt you."

"Really?" she spat out and then jerked backward as recognition dawned on her.

At the same time, my eyes widened as I realized what set her apart from her family. "You're…"

"Don't say it," she snapped, scowling at me.

I didn't have to say it, I could smell it rolling off of her—she was not human. I laughed at the irony of it all and only ceased chuckling when I felt the cold sting of a slap against my face. Shaking it off, I turned my full attention on her. "Well, Princess, I'm not. I'm giving your family a second chance to change the way this kingdom is ruled. For too long, the wolves have been hunted and nothing has been done about it. This was *our* kingdom first and it was only because your grandfather *murdered* King Raul that the humans ever inherited the throne." A snarl ripped from me and before I knew it I was standing in front of her, gritting my teeth.

To her credit she didn't back down, instead she snarled right back. "I am not to blame, and believe me I understand the plight and wish to do something of it, but do you think for one moment my father would allow for that?"

"So you're in agreement that he's allowing this to happen?"

"Of course I am, I'm not blind nor am I stupid! He hates wolves, so if you have any attachment to your head you'd stay *away*!"

At that moment Stasya gave herself away entirely, for I never once said I was a werewolf, and to any human I looked just as they did. This made the entire predicament far more interesting than it had been, which caused a smirk to curl my lips up.

Unfortunately, I had less than zero self-preservation skills. Running my hand down my face, I considered what she'd said. "So he is behind the killings?"

She said nothing and I took it as an answer in and of itself.

"Return home and speak with him, or I will, and you won't like how I do it, or maybe I'll talk to Edda."

"Do not say her name." A growl rumbled in her chest and she looked poised to launch at me.

I was certain the only thing that kept her rooted where she was were the etiquette classes that had been drilled into her skull since childhood. There was something rather intriguing about Stasya, the lines in her face, the way she held her lips. It was wholly strange, because I had never been so focused on each feature of a girl before.

"I'll give you a month, only a month, before I come knocking for the third and last time," I said.

"You can't—"

Guards shouted outside, searching for Stasya, and as she moved her head, I reached out to wrap a strand of her pale hair around a finger. Silvery as the full moon. "Has it always been this color?" I mindlessly asked, mesmerized by the way it cascaded down.

She pulled away, still uncertain if I was going to harm her and I couldn't blame her. "No, it changed."

"When you were bitten?" I asked bluntly.

It wasn't hard to deduce and the way she glared before her green eyes softened told me I had hit the mark. Folding her arms across her chest, it looked as if she were contemplating whether or not to tell me. This was at least an upgrade from wanting to claw my face off. "I was blonde before and when I was bitten it changed. One strand at first and then several others. In a year's time it was silver."

"It suits you."

Her face soured as she looked at me, refusing to utter the words 'thank you' in the bizarre circumstance.

"Unless you want to be stabbed, I suggest you open that door and let me go; we're done here." Stasya motioned toward the door, where guards were no doubt milling around in search for her.

"If I open that door, I will be stabbed." Upon entering the hut, I had observed the escapes we could use, and the window toward the backyard would suffice. Pointing toward the window with my hand, I opened my mouth to speak except no words came out.

“I won’t go through a window, my dress won’t fit.” She moved her hand toward the wide skirt. It wasn’t as wide as most because this one was meant for traveling as opposed to milling around a court. The dress, however, was still heavy and cumbersome.

I eyed the layers of fabric, it was certainly bulky around the bottom but the top clung to her slender figure where that wouldn’t be an issue. “How many layers do you have on the bottom?”

“Excuse you!” she cried out.

“How many?” I asked again.

“Enough,” she replied and snorted, folding her arms across her chest stubbornly.

Whatever she had been thinking, surely she hadn’t anticipated me moving forward and kneeling before her.

“Don’t you dare,” she hissed and lifted a foot as if to kick me.

I grabbed the foot in between my hands and lifted a brow, applying just enough pressure as I spoke. “If you dare, this will go a whole lot differently. Stand still,” I ordered, she stilled, and I lifted my hands until I felt the hem of one of the layers. I tugged until it tore away, then did away with the next layer until there was only one. Bundling the fabric up, I shoved it into the small hearth against the back wall. “Now you can.” I thumbed toward the direction of the window.

Pushing open the window, I climbed out first and helped Stasya through as well. She stumbled into my chest. If it weren’t for the close proximity, I wouldn’t have seen her pupils blow wide. My hand instinctively went to her back to steady her but she didn’t pull away. I smelled the subtle change in the air and felt my gut twist, I couldn’t be sure of what *that* was, but judging by how her mouth gaped open, she caught it, too.

She sniffed the air, silver brows furrowing, and eventually she stepped back.

“I’m glad you didn’t bite my jugular.”

Her head jerked in my direction, a quizzical expression on her face. “What?”

"I'm just saying you looked poised to bite."

"No," she said breathlessly, blinking rapidly.

We were running out of time and as much as I wanted to inquire as to what the hell that was all about we needed to move. Bending down, I scooped up some dirt, and while Stasya wasn't paying attention, I rubbed it on her cheeks and then arms quicker than she had time to react.

She huffed again and looked down at the filth in disgust. "Really?"

"Gotta make it look convincing, there is a pig slop over there if you feel so inclined to roll in it?"

"You disgusting…" her words were cut off as the guards hollered.

"Now or never…" I scooped her up into my arms, her face inches from mine and composed into the most sumptuous scowl I had ever seen in my life.

Stasya was quick-witted to understand that I meant for this to look like a rescue. She ran her fingers through her hair, mussing it up and lowered her eyelids to make it look as if she had been put through the ringer.

"Hans, over here," she shouted, motioning to the head guard.

Rushing over to us, he picked her up and apologized profusely to Stasya. He never once thanked me for the safe return of the princess. He did, however, glare at me as if I were a savage.

"Hans, he was the one who found me, you would do well to thank him," she said in an attempt to smooth things over.

I lifted a brow as Hans finally regarded me with a nod; that was as close to a thank you as I'd be getting from him and I'm certain it hurt —judging by the way his lips were tightened. I winked at him and turned my gaze toward Stasya, mouthing 'one' to her before I slipped into the calming crowd.

In one month, I'd be visiting the royals again and if nothing had been done, *something* would be done. If I had to prove a point to light a fire beneath the ass of the king, then I'd do it. One wolf did not paint all of them bad, and I had a feeling there was more to Stasya's story. While it was none of my business to know it, but perhaps it'd clarify things, mostly as to why her father hated *all* of them so much that he would sit on his hands while hundreds of lives were lost in a year.

When I returned back home, Liesel had run off to deliver a package to one of the elders. I was grateful she wouldn't be there waiting for the recountings of the events in the village. Some were not worth it and others were not necessary to relay.

Lu was there and he knew where I had run off to, he didn't prompt me verbally but his brows lifted as if to say "Well?"

"I doubt anything will come of the chat, but we will see and I don't doubt for a moment that by next year something will change." Of course, I knew this because I'd be doing something about it. I was done lingering in the shadows, the third and final visit would be one where something would be done.

Later that day, Lukas emerged from the woods, his blue eyes transfixed on the axe in my grasp. "Time to change things up," he said.

Eyeing him, I spread my feet apart and cocked my head. "How so?" Was he going to attack me here and test me? Idly, I wondered if Raif made it out okay, too, if that meant I needed to pick up his slack because he died on the job.

"Raif is fine." He motioned with his hand to follow him.

I dragged my gaze to the house and dropped the axe on the trunk I was using. "But?"

"Just shut your mouth and follow."

"Pardon my inquisitive nature, Lord-Master," I sniped and ducked as a fist came flying my way. Just as I was lowering my body, a leg swept at my legs. I rolled off to the side, begrudging the fact I left the axe on the stump. Launching myself upward I used my preternatural strength and speed which took him off guard. My arms wrapped around his neck, and I used his momentum to flip him onto his back, finger pointed at his chest as if it were a blade.

A grunt escaped him. "Well done, but that's why Sabrina is done with you. As strong as she is... she's a vital piece and I can take more hits than her."

"Can you? She seems to be highly capable," I replied dryly.

"Shut your mouth and let's get back to headquarters."

Lukas didn't seem keen on offering a real explanation why, although I figured it was something along the lines of him wanting to push me in physical ways that Sabrina wasn't able to; he wanted to test me and what my instincts could offer. Perhaps he simply didn't want his sister at the mercy of my self-control, perhaps he didn't trust me altogether like Sabrina did.

When we arrived, he didn't bother to offer any explanation, he simply came at me and both of us gave it our all. The only difference was that I was naturally more nimble, stronger, it didn't mean that I had the upper hand. He knew how to use his body and how to use my movements against me.

More often than I'd care to admit, I crashed to the ground with a grunt and he demanded I do it again.

I huffed and puffed, hands on my knees as Lukas stood upright, scarcely breathing, as heavy as I was. "Point taken," I said after a few sharp intakes of breath.

He dusted his hands off and shrugged his shoulders. "Not bad, actually. Guess you really are a big bad wolf." It was the first time I'd seen him crack a smile. "Tonight, you'll be visiting Amschteg, go clean up and change your clothing, then I'll tell you more of it."

I cleaned the dirt and blood from my skin and dressed in the black attire I had grown used to using when on a mission—black boots, pants and a long-sleeved shirt. Attached to it, a half mask slid up over my mouth just beneath my nose.

Each mission, I wore a different utility belt, depending on what weapon I'd be using. This one called for twin blades which hung on my hip.

Striding out of the room, I entered the office and plopped down in the leather chair, feet lifting to hang over the arm of it.

"In Amschteg, Lord Gustaf Pinzer has a bad habit of dabbling with young girls." He eyed me pointedly and I arched a brow. "Yes, exactly what you're thinking."

"Any guidelines?"

"None, get creative. The pay is a surprise."

"You mean it's a freebie," I offered dryly.

"Quite the opposite… I mean it's more than we've seen come through here before. I'll surprise you with the figure once you've made it back."

"The timeframe?"

"None. You can be home for supper if you'd like."

"Living arrangements?" There had to be some information on him, I wasn't going to walk in blindly without some knowledge as to his lifestyle.

"Alone, he's sixty years old, no kin and no wife. He terrorizes his female staff, and frequently disturbs the ones at court affairs." Lukas pinched the bridge of his nose and sighed. "Just do what you're good at, here's the coordinates to his mansion."

Snatching up the paper, I glanced down at the address and snorted. "Fancy little twit, isn't he? Well, it's time he learned what it is to be terrorized, and face judgment."

Amschteg was opulent in comparison to the capital city, whereas the capital housed the growing businesses and massive markets, Amschteg housed the wealth of the country. Pristine was a way of describing it, but it was all a farce. This place might have looked as if it had been carved from heaven but the refuse lurked in the shadows.

Buildings stretched toward the sky and massive mansions sprawled across manicured lawns. Iron gates ensured that no wandering unsavories would be able to step foot on the green grass; it struck me as odd. Yesterday, I stood in the poorest town and today I stood in the richest.

Lord Gustaf Pinzer's mansion, at first glance, was ostentatious and at second glance, it was even more so. Brick upon brick was stacked for two stories until it met the next portion which was timber painted white.

No one milled around his yard and perhaps the gate would ward most people off, but I wasn't most people. Hopping the gate, I tugged the half mask into place below my nose and strode toward the house.

A young servant, not much older than Liesel, emerged from around the house, her eyes widened as she caught sight of me and as I lifted a finger to my mouth she nodded her head, understanding in her gaze as I approached the back.

"Get him for us all," she whispered. "He's in his study." She shifted away but not before I was able to catch sight of her rounded belly.

"He's a bad wolf, he is," an older woman said by her side.

"I'm not afraid of the big bad wolf, not today."

I heard her last words as I wound my way through the house, it was quiet and most of the other servants were occupied in their quarters. I smelled tobacco and it only grew stronger as I grew closer to the study. Gustaf was chuckling as he ran over his figures, muttering something occasionally. I watched his antics before the grossly overweight male had disgusted me enough.

"You have a choice—easy way or hard way—decide now." My hands hung by my side, loose and yet ready to spring into action.

"Well, who the bugger are you! And why are you in my house? I'm not giving you a dime, you wretched…"

"I said decide."

"Screw you."

"I was hoping you'd decide the harder way." Unsheathing one of the daggers at my hip, Gustaf's eyes widened but he seemed to think that this was a bluff, which it was not. I drew out the movement and he sat smugly in his chair, until I launched the blade at his writing hand. I didn't miss my mark and it bit into his hand.

Blood began to seep from the wound as he howled in pain, spittle flecked his lips and chin as he panted. "You monster!"

"No, no, that is your title. You've been harassing enough women." I drew my next blade and sauntered toward him casually. "You're thoroughly finished."

"I'll have your head for this, you have no idea who I am."

"Sure I do, Lord Gustaf Pinzer. Owner of the bank of Amschteg, highly esteemed by King Ansgar... "

"You don't think the king would notice my death? You're wrong." A mad laugh escaped him, clearly he thought himself the victor in this.

"No, I am counting on it, as a matter of fact, and I hope to achieve quite a bit once your eyes glaze over."

I relished the sound of his cries as he yanked the blade from his hand, the scent of his blood lingering in the room. There was a reason why Lukas sent me on this mission and it had everything to do with the fact it was a trigger for me. Waving my dagger, I motioned toward the other in his grasp. "Are you going to use it on me, porky?"

"Damn right, I am." He hissed as he wrapped his kerchief around the bleeding hand and came my way, charging like a boar intent on goring.

His blade went in for a blow, but my arm came down on his, and with my free hand, I twisted his arm around and bumped it up until I heard a satisfying pop.

Another cry rang out from Gustaf and I relented only because I wanted to prolong this dance. As his limp arm dangled by his side and he panted heavily, I snatched the blade that was nearly falling out of his grasp.

"What else?" I teased.

"No more," he pleaded with me.

"Now, that… that is amusing, because I'm sure you've heard that before."

And so it went for an hour, until the man was gurgling in a pool of his own blood, rasping.

"Who are you?" Blood poured from his mouth.

The memory of the girl and woman roused and I replied, "The Big Bad Wolf."

It went like this for a month, one ruthless mission after the next and the country began to whisper about the shadow known as the *Big Bad Wolf*.

It was a month to the day when I stood outside the castle, the torches blazing to illuminate the structure even in the absolute dark. There was no moon this night, entirely absent, but the stars winked down silently, offering me all the light I needed.

All of the guards I had located were human and therefore wouldn't scent my arrival—that would make this easy. I pulled myself up the wall and ran a distance to where there was a gap in patrol and let my form plummet ten feet down. I landed quietly and wove my way around to the vine covered siding. The black garb I wore allowed me to move freely, but also unseen even when the flames shifted and cast light on where I was.

Hopping through an open window, I took in the surroundings, it was the end of a hallway, no guards around this wing. There were several drapes hung along the walls which could be used as cover as I advanced down the hall.

A familiar laugh bounced along the hallway and I quickly darted into a room, it didn't sound as if anyone was in it but as I closed the door and spun around, I discovered I was wrong.

Edda.

Her mouth gaped open and her throat worked as if she wanted to scream but couldn't find her voice to do so.

"No, shh, listen," I began, "I'm not here to hurt you." I wouldn't, but she didn't know that—especially in my current attire.

"What do you want?" she whispered softly. "My jewels are over there on my dresser, I don't have any coin on me."

"I don't want that." My eyes flicked to the door and I planted a hand on it as footsteps neared.

"Edda? Can I come in?" Stasya called out. She didn't wait for her sister to reply and instead tried the door. "Edda, what are you doing?" she asked with a laugh.

Grumbling, I opened the door and yanked her inside and brought a hand to her mouth. "Don't."

"You!" she spat out.

"I'd say it's a pleasure, but considering no advancements were made in a month, it isn't, is it?" Narrowing my eyes, I made no indication I was willing to move away from the door.

"Stasya, what does he want?" she asked worriedly.

"It's okay, Edda, he's not going to hurt you." She sent a fiery look in my direction, taking no issue with approaching me swiftly. "You won't."

She was right about that, I wouldn't and had no desire to, but for my cause, I'd certainly pretend I had every intention in killing her.

"This is how it's going to go, you're both coming with me, Edda you'll be in front of Stasya, and Stasya, you will be held hostage. We're going to pay your father a visit." My tone brooked no room for an argument, especially as I unsheathed a long dagger from my hip. "Walk," I ordered.

Outside of the room, the girls moved without complaint—mostly. If Stasya could, she would have spit venom in my eyes, but as I brushed my thumb along her jaw it was a reminder that while this may have been an act, I still had a blade against her neck. One wrong move on either of our parts and she would bleed.

"Lead the way."

"There are guards all over," she began. Edda turned to look back at us and she huffed.

"They could very well snag Edda, but you, Stasya, are the one being held." In fact, I almost hoped they would snag Edda and whisk her away so the dramatics could be amped up.

Stasya's hands clenched by her sides, as if she were contemplating moving away or even trying to attack me, but even as she breathed, the blade pressed against her throat, and even with the slightest pressure, a trickle of blood ran down her pale skin. She hissed as it did.

"I wouldn't."

"Yes, or else this will go in a very different way, wasn't that it?"

Apparently, she wasn't fazed by the notion of being held hostage. "Exactly, maybe you ought to hold your tongue, too, Princess."

A sound of disgust came from her as we walked down the hall, and before long, a guard came into view. He cried out and rushed forward, my lips twisting behind the mask. "Don't, one wrong move and she'll be dead, isn't that right?" I cocked my head so my breath tickled at her ear.

Strangely, I felt her shudder against me but it wasn't fear I scented. Turning my attention toward the shouts in the distance, I heard them order to hide away the king.

"No, don't. Let us talk to him," Stasya began to reason with the guards but they were not listening, they were trained to protect the king.

In the corridor, as we advanced down, Edda began to wander forward a little too much, which allowed a guard to sweep her away from the danger. It would be easier this way.

"No, Stasya!" Edda cried out as they pulled her down the hall.

"Where is his room?" I asked her calmly.

Stasya's limbs tightened as Edda began to cry, yet she didn't halt. "Down the hall on the left. You can't miss the carved oak doors. Would you loosen the blade?"

"Not happening. Move."

And she did. The guards were collecting, shouting orders and servants froze in place as we made our way to the king's bedroom door. Two grand doors glared at me and I used my foot to kick at it. "Your Majesty... I think you'll want to open the door and let me in," I growled.

"Unlikely. Who are you?" he spat out. "However you got into my castle—"

"—is really of no consequence at this point. Let me in. Let. Me. In."

"Please, Father," Stasya pleaded with him.

The doors flew open. He stood in his nightdress and stumbled backward as he saw the severity of the situation. He didn't know it was staged, and didn't know that I wouldn't hurt her. Of course, he did see the blood trickling down her throat which sold the current situation all the better.

"Let her go!" His eyes widened and he lifted a trembling hand. "At once, you let her go!"

"You're in no position to make demands." I used my foot and kicked the door shut. One arm slid around the front of Stasya while I held the blade against her neck. "We have something to discuss."

"What, what could you possibly want to discuss?!"

"Werewolves."

A disgusted noise left him and I felt the princess stiffen against me. "What of them?"

"Would you at least listen to him, this pertains to me as well."

"You are not a werewolf! You were cursed!" He spat out, lifting his hands as he grew enraged. "You were bitten by an infected handmaiden, it wasn't your fault."

"Neither was it theirs. I should have known better than to approach her, but I thought it was fascinating and she turned on me. I never blamed her, but you killed her and you've signed up thousands to die, too."

"There is nothing I can do, I cannot call it off. I made a bargain, Stasya, and I cannot go back on it."

"What do you mean? What did you do, Father?" Stasya whispered harshly.

Somewhere along the way, I let the blade drop from her neck and relaxed my hold on her, she didn't bother to move.

"He is called The Hawk, but there are many he refers to as his "flock" and they do his bidding. No one knows who belongs to it—it could be anyone! A few years back, the kingdom fell into some trouble, he's a wealthy man..." the king began to say.

"So you sold out half the population of the kingdom, by allowing him to murder the founding species?" I snapped. "My mother was one of your victims."

Stasya moved her head to look up at me, frowning, but said nothing.

"If she was a wolf, she deserved it." He sniffed haughtily and that was all it took to send me after him.

Launching at him, I pushed his frame to the floor and slammed his head against it. "I will end you in a blink!" Fury swept through me like wildfire, and at that moment, I was unsure if it had more to do with my mother's death, or the fact Stasya was a werewolf, too. He would dismiss his daughter so readily simply because of what she was?

"No! Please, no. Don't!" Stasya cried out. "Stop! Father!"

My hand worked its way around his neck, clamping down as he pawed at me to get off, but I was beyond reasoning and my vision was turning black. Ansgar deserved to die for slaughtering so many, for being so careless when it came to his daughter.

Stasya shoved my shoulder and caused me to rock but I was fully intent on killing him.

"Stop! Please!" She fell to her knees and began to punch me.

Stasya could throw a punch, but in my blind fury it might as well have been straw raining down on me. Working my jaw, I released my grip only slightly. I didn't trust him to not retaliate.

Stasya blurted her words. "I… I have a proposition. I want to hire you to take out The Hawk, if I do that will this end? The killings and threatening my family?"

"Stasya, no! You're not hiring filth!" Ansgar tried to cry out, but my hand stopped his words prematurely.

"We have no choice, he is the only one who can stop him. He is the shadow the kingdom whispers of."

The king was silent for a moment, and then realization dawned on him. "He...he's the Big Bad Wolf?" Ansgar asked, his voice raspy.

A growl tore from me as I glared down at him, squeezing tight again. "I am." I released my grip and stood to my feet, folding my arms. "If I agree—and that is a big if—will you swear on your daughter's life that you'll protect wolves from here on out?"

"Absolutely not."

"Then you forfeit your daughter's life. Who is to say that one day one of those birds won't come after her?" In his delusional mind, the king likely saw his daughter set apart from the society of wolves, but she was one of us and if he valued her life as he said, he would obey.

King Ansgar's bottom lip wobbled as he mulled over the facts. "What have I done?" he murmured and covered his face.

"Will you swear on her life?" I prompted him.

"Yes." He slid his gaze toward her. "You must believe I never meant for you to be in harm's way…"

"I know, but I am a wolf and there is nothing we can do about that. I've tried reasoning with you, why is it only now that my life hangs in the balance that you're considering it?"

"Because… He sent me a missive, and he knows. He knows what

you are, and if I should go back on our agreement, he will have your life as payment, Stasya."

Shaking beside me, Stasya's green eyes hardened. "How do I finalize the contract?" she asked.

A moment went by and I considered my words carefully before I spoke. "I will take your life as payment."

"You wretched…" The king moved forward, poised to attack.

I stood with my arms crossed and hip cocked, my cold eyes locking onto his being. "I am not the one who unwittingly placed a hit on my kin, am I? I will have your daughter's life, but not as you think. She knows how."

I had seen it flitter across her face, had seen the way her pupils blew wide in my presence and although I wasn't the best when it came to tuning in to another's emotions, there was no mistaking the bond that longed to be locked into place.

To her credit, Stasya didn't flinch, only nodded. "It is fair and he is right. He wishes to protect the wolves...not obliterate them." She turned to me, still a spark of mistrust and perhaps loathing in her gaze as she regarded me. "I promise myself to you."

"This is all my fault," Ansgar mumbled. "You are to be Queen one day, and he…" His words died out before he finished, which was in his best interest.

I turned to face him. "It sure as hell is, now go out there and tell them it's safe." Moving toward the side, I waited for him to open the door and announce to the guards the coast was clear. Nevertheless, the guards rushed in and escorted Ansgar away.

Stasya bit her bottom lip and fiddled with a strand of her hair, it was uncharacteristic of her—at least from what I had seen. "I know why you suggested that."

"Do you?" I asked quietly, moving the bottom of the mask down around my neck. I was amused by the sudden change of topic.

"I know what you are," she began.

I teased her. "Yes, I'm a wolf, we clarified that previously."

Perhaps she wasn't ready to endure the teasings, her face crumpled in frustration and she looked away. "Yes, the Big Bad Wolf, who comes huffing and puffing at our doorstep."

"I don't huff or puff," I said casually and looked down at her.

Stasya's cheeks reddened and I opened my mouth to say something else, but soon her mouth was on mine. My brows furrowed in question, but as she grew more confident in the kiss, I returned it. Her lips were soft against mine and spread heat throughout my body. The noises she made only encouraged me to deepen the kiss, my fingers spreading across her back so I could tug her closer.

I had kissed girls before, but none had felt like this, and that was the strangest thing of all—I felt something. She tasted like cinnamon and it left me craving more.

We were mates, destined to be together.

In that moment, I felt it, we both did, we felt the call and the desire of a bond that would last a lifetime, but this was not the moment to discuss it. Pulling back, I lifted the mask into place, winking at her. "I'll take what payments I can get for now. Stasya, stay inside, and do not venture out—none of you. Not until I contact you again."

I swung out of the bedroom window and climbed down the vines before I became one with the shadows.

Who's afraid of the Big Bad Wolf?

The Hawk definitely should be.

ABOUT ELLE BEAUMONT

Elle was born and raised in Southeastern, Massachusetts in a little farm town by the harbor. She grew up fascinated with all things whimsical and a strong love for animals.

As she grew so did her passion for reading and writing. Although she prefers devouring all genres she largely enjoys dark fantasy.

She is married to her best friend and has two lively sprites who inspire madness, love and a sense of humor in her. They also have a menagerie of animals, two dogs, three cats and a horse. In her down-time, Elle enjoys creating candles, crocheting, horseback riding and running.

CONNECT ON SOCIAL MEDIA

ellebeaumontbooks.com

facebook.com/ellebeaumontbooks

instagram.com/ellebeaumontbooks

by Lou Wilham

From the lowliest of urchins to the most powerful of kings, there are two things that are true of every being under the sea. Every creature has at least a drop of living magic in them, and each being is born with a soulmate. That link to another being's soul can change a creature and the magic living inside of them. In some cases, it can make their magic more powerful. In the cases of heartbreak, their magic can warp itself into something dark and twisted.

I, Irsa the sea-witch, am no different. This is the story of how I became the vile and hated creature that I am today.

In spite of what the stories may say, I didn't rise from the deep dark depths of the sea to wreak havoc on the kingdom of Alon. No, I was brought into this world much as you may have been, thrashing my flippers and screaming like mad in a small village on the outskirts of Alon. I had a mother and a frequently absent father. My father happened to be absent on the day of my birth, leaving Mother to name me. Much to his chagrin, I was a bouncing baby girl, instead of the strapping son he'd always wanted.

Mother dubbed me Irsa, after my grandmother, which only proved to make Father even more irritated with my very existence.

To be quite honest, it wasn't the name I would have chosen for myself, but this is the name I was given. As with most things, I either grew into the name, or the name grew into me. So much so that by the time I was old enough to change it, I couldn't.

A fortnight after I was born my mother's best friend also gave birth to a baby girl, her name was Aislin, and we were instant friends. It is said that the moment we were placed in the kelp lined crib together our chubby hands found one another, and our fingers linked rendering us inseparable.

I suppose that was when all of this started. It had to have been because I do not remember a moment in my life when Aislin was not by my side. Nor a moment without her when I didn't feel the subtle tug of her presence calling me to her.

We grew up there chasing each other through the streets in the small village of Glassvik. Glassvik was made up of small huts built from pale shimmering shells held together by mortar made from magic sand. Aislin always seemed to glow a little too brightly there.

How could she not? Aislin, with her shining jade-colored tail, and beautiful hair. She always stood out. Aislin—or Ace as I'd taken to calling her early on when her name was too hard to say—was a burst of color and light amongst a village of muted shades and shadows. I stood out in a different way, where many of the mer surrounding us were the usual shades of blond and brunette mermaids, I had pale grey hair, a blue tail, and black eyes.

In our minds, we were everyday little mer-girls laughing and playing in the streets of our village as children are wont to do. Now and then, one of our neighbors would remark on what a strange pair we made, but we paid them little heed and went on with our games—carefree and happy, until the day of the trials.

When merfolk reached the age of sixteen, it is a tradition that they participate in the trials. During which the mer-child is taken out into the open ocean and tested to see how much magic lives in their blood. You see, magic is a commodity in the sea, this rite of passage determines the rest of our lives. What happens during the trials, no one knows, as a spell is cast to block the memories but based on the result of the trials a child is then apprenticed to a master or mistress of the appropriate occupation. In our kingdom, occupations ranging from seafloor sweepers to shopkeepers are all decided within the span of a few minutes at the age of sixteen

As children, we are told not to worry about the trials. As children we are told what will be will be. Most don't worry about the trials, in fact, they spend much of their time not thinking of it at all. For me, all I could feel was the pressure which compounded as my birthday steadily approached.

On the day of the trials, Aislin and I were sitting on the soft seaweed of my bed as she slowly brushed through my hair. She wasn't worried, but then she never was. I, on the other hand, was a complete wreck.

"You worry too much, Irsa. It's not like there is anything you can do if you *aren't* magical, so why worry?" Her point was sound and logical, we both knew that. However, it didn't make the feeling of a million tiny minnows in my stomach go away. My hands fell down to try to get them to be still, but they stubbornly refused. "That makes it worse." It came out more like a petulant huff than I meant it to, and she rewarded me with a firm yank on my hair to try to get me to calm.

"No, it doesn't." She snorted and rolled her bright green eyes. "What if I haven't any? What if I'm going to be a-a-a-a *seafloor sweeper* for the rest of my life?"

Another snort, eye roll, and small yank on my hair. "Irsa, you are not going to be a seafloor sweeper. Calm your clams."

A soft grumble left me as I brushed a piece of loose hair back from my face. I needed to get my mind off of everything. I needed to think of something else. So instead of another worry or grumble, I asked, "What do you think you'll be assigned?"

I didn't see it so much as hear the smirk in her voice when she said, "I'll be a princess, and then Queen of Alon, obviously."

Now it was my turn to snort, and I did so involuntarily. We all knew that royalty was not a job that was *assigned;* one was simply born into it, or, if they were fortunate enough, they married into it.

"What?" Ace asked, clearly offended. She dropped the brush, and it floated to the bed beside us as she crossed her arms over her chest. "Every little girl in the ocean wants to be a princess."

There was a much sharper tug on my hair and I yelped before turning to swat her back lightly. Ace was ready for me with a pillow in her grasp. She smacked me with it. Soon we were giggling—for the moment, I forgot my trial later that day.

That evening, there was no escaping my worry and fear. There was no sweet, sassy Aislin to take my mind off my troubles, no silly topics to discuss, or time to daydream about princes. It was just Mother and me in a carriage that rocked back and forth slowly as the seahorses dragged us out into the open sea.

Once we arrived, I remembered swimming from the carriage out into the open water—it was so quiet there, without the ambient noise of the village around us. The water was still, and there was nothing... nothing to greet me except two mermen in long, hooded cloaks. I bowed my head in respect, and they nodded in return. I couldn't remember what happened next.

A time later—how long I'm unsure—I returned to the carriage with no recollection of what had happened. Although I knew that would be the case, it still felt strange to have time missing from my memory. I turned to Mother, my face feeling pale, and settled into the seat beside her waiting for the carriage to begin moving once more.

"I-I don't remember what happened," I whispered softly, trying to push the words through the haze that had become my mind. The world around me was in soft focus, and I found myself lilting a little as I leaned into my mother.

"That's how it is meant to be, darling. Just try not to think too much about it." Her long fingers stroked my pale hair to try to soothe me, but I found it was only making me sleepy.

I didn't want to sleep—I didn't want to drift off. I wanted to think about this and understand what had happened to me out there. However, it seemed that the harder I thought about it, the more it evaded me—memories slipping through my fingers the way fish do when you try to catch them without a net, constantly eluding my clutches.

"What if I didn't do well?" The question was loaded with all of the terror that was slowly building back up in my stomach. "Nonsense, darling. I'm sure you did just fine." She leaned in to press a kiss to the crown of my head. "Either way, we'll know this time next week."

A week! I didn't think I could wait a whole week to know what my fate was. "What if you're wrong?"

Mother merely shook her head. "I'm not." Her words were firm as she pulled me into a tight hug and continued to stroke my hair as I let my mind wander. As it wandered, I began to prepare for my inevitable march towards anonymity—in so many words, I was sixteen; I didn't actually know what mediocrity meant.

I let the sway of the carriage soothe my body as my mind wandered. My eyes closed for a moment before jerking open once more at a sudden jolt to the carriage, yanking me from any thoughts of a boring life. That's when the shouting started as a small band of high-seamen ran the driver of our carriage through with a dagger before ripping open the door to pull Mother out onto the sandy seafloor.

Everything happened in a flurry of bubbles and loud commotion. They wanted Mother to give up her jewelry, not that she had much as it was, and she refused. Something flashed in the light filtering through the water, and I realized perhaps a little too late it was a blade as blood began to stain the water around us. Suddenly, there was screaming coming from someone, ear-piercing screaming.

I didn't realize at the time, but it must have been me. With the screaming came the glow of magic. A pulsing, bright, living, thing was fluttering to life and taking form in the water as the tentacle of some great Kraken-like creature.

It slithered across the sand to wrap itself around the man holding the blade, and then it began to squeeze. The man let out a choking sound, but the magic refused to release him. Instead, it squeezed ever tighter. I wasn't sure what was happening, but in some strange, distant way, I knew that glowing purple strand was a part of me. It felt oddly familiar in a way nothing else ever had before. In that same strange and distant way, I wasn't sure how to stop it, nor that I actually wanted to.

"Irsa, no," came the faint, quivering voice of Mother as I moved to take her hand. Her long, lean fingers curled around my smaller hand, and she looked down at my clenched fist. "You have to let it go."

My head shook in one quick, vigorous motion. I didn't *want* to let it go. I wanted to hurt him, the same way he'd hurt her. There was no fixing my mother—I knew that—I couldn't put her back together again no matter how much magic I had in me. What I *could* do was hurt *him*, and that would have to be enough.

Mother shook her head back at me, her weak fingers desperately trying to peel my little fingers open one by one. "You can't... it'll taint... taint your magic," she said in between labored breathing. "Death will... will ruin this." She finally peeled my fingers open, forcing me to release the man who'd hurt her. He fell to the ocean floor, choking and sputtering, but it was my dark eyes that were burning with tears as they met Mother's. "This is pure and wonderful." She coughed softly. "You must not let anyone ruin it. Promise me."

I nodded, unable to say the words as the men made away with what they'd stolen and the last of my hopes for revenge. It mattered little because the damage was done—Mother was dead, or soon would be.

"Promise me," she repeated sternly, pulling me from such dismal thoughts.

Pale gray brows knitted together as I met her eyes again. I knew I couldn't really promise this. My magic had a life of its own—it would do as it wished—but I knew I had to give her this. Instead of arguing, I merely nodded and whispered, "Promise."

She faded with her hand still in mine. I sat there for a long while, sobbing, as I tried in vain to get a hold of myself. Eventually, I got enough control of myself to free one of the seahorses from its harness and steered it back to one of the outposts surrounding the kingdom. There, I found two soldiers and told them what had happened. They headed out into the sea right away to help, but I already knew Mother was gone and that there was nothing they could do to help.

"It is quite the thing, you know. The whole sea-witch community heard about your trials and is saying you're the strongest sea-witch they've heard of in nearly a hundred years," Janette chattered on as she spread some fish egg butter on a stale seaweed cracker. I watched her wondering idly how she could eat quite so much when she never seemed to stop talking. Janette was a little put out when the only reaction this statement garnered was one quirked brow. "You don't believe me?" she asked, sounding affronted as she buttered what must have been a fifth—*I'm not quite sure, I'd lost count at some point*—cracker.

"No," I said in return. What else was I to say? I had never shown a spark of magic before the trial and then last week, and Father had forbidden Mother from taking me to see any of the sea-witches, so I knew nothing of what their magic even looked like. The most I had seen was some minor kitchen magic when Mother made a pot of tea, but even a jellyfish had enough magic in its body to do that.

"No, she says," Janette muttered to herself as she buttered another cracker shaking her head. "Well, it's the truth." Her tone became quite prim as she pursed her lips and sat up a little straighter. "In fact, they're all fighting over you. Every sea-witch wants you as their apprentice. Even the ones from the next kingdom over! Granted, King Hemnes would never let such a talent just up and move to Vassviken. You're quite something, missy."

I still didn't quite believe her, but I let her chatter on and on about this witch or that who'd vied for me as their apprentice. I supposed I'd find out who my master or mistress was to be soon enough, so there was no point in listening to gossip.

The deliberations must have taken some time, for it was a fortnight before Janette was back with more news. In the meantime, we had Mother's funeral—which unsurprisingly the entire village attended—and Aislin had her trial. Ace was assigned to work as a seamstress at a shop in the town neighboring us. It was a good position; she wouldn't be too far from home, and there was more room for her to grow there.

Then, one morning as I ate breakfast alone—as Father had been mysteriously even more absent since Mother's funeral—there was a knock at the door. Upon opening it, I found the bespeckled face of Janette once more. The girl was practically bobbing in her excitement as she squeezed her lips shut, perhaps trying to keep the words in.

"Would you like to come in for some tea?" I asked, mostly hoping she'd say 'no' and we could get this whole thing over and done with.

Janette nodded yes, and I let her inside without another word. It wasn't until we were set up at the small kitchen table with a plate of kelp crackers and manatee cheese before us that Janette finally opened her mouth to let it all spill out.

"You've been assigned!" She practically squealed as she spread the smooth cheese across her cracker. I did my best not to cover my ears to try to muffle the sound in surprise, but it was a very near thing. "And you've been sent to tell me to whom," I guessed, already feeling my patience wearing thin. It was not but a week ago that we buried Mother and I was more than happy to go back to my bed and think no more of magic or sea-witches.

Janette nodded quickly, her muted blue hair floating around her as her matching eyes sparkled in delight at being able to be the one to tell me such news.

"Am I to guess? Or are you going to tell me?" I couldn't help myself, it was irritating, and I was ready to have this new life begin so maybe I could escape the stifling sadness of my current situation.

There was a bark of laughter as she went for another cracker, and I thought vaguely that surely if this girl were to stay any longer, there would be no food left in the house.

"Well?" I asked trying to prompt her into action as she seemed reasonably happy to hold me in suspense. I had never done well with uncertainty.

"It is the Lady Calypso!" She squealed in excitement once more. The expression on my face must have been one of bland interest because Janette let out a soft huff of indignation. "Really child, do you know nothing?"

I shrugged a little, taking a piece of cheese to cover my awkwardness.

"The Lady Calypso is the highest ranked sea-witch in all of Alon! She is perhaps the most powerful witch in the entire ocean! The King Hemnes himself has tried on numerous occasions to get her to come to the palace and work for him as his royal witch, but she refuses. Girls *dream* of being Calypso's apprentice." At that moment I was sure that Janette had dreamt of being Calypso's apprentice and hadn't made the cut. I felt a little bad, as Janette clearly had spent her childhood dreaming of being a witch, and I had merely fallen into the vocation.

"Oh." It came out of my lips sounding a little less enthusiastic than I meant it to. A part of my mind told my lips that this was something Janette was excited about, so I should feel honored, but I couldn't make myself.

"Oh. *Oh!* Calypso hasn't taken on an apprentice in nearly two hundred years! You should be ecstatic! Are you not honored?" Her eyes were on fire now with the emotion she felt, and I had to bite my tongue to keep from laughing. "I suppose I am," I said uncertainly. I wasn't honored because I didn't know at all what any of it meant.

From there, the conversation dissolved into more gossip, and the demolishing of the plate of manatee cheese and kelp crackers.

As I escorted Janette out, she stopped suddenly in the doorway and turned to me. "I forgot one more thing!" She waved her hand in the water, a flicker of electric blue magic lighting it up before a slip of parchment appeared, and she held it out to me. "This is your assignment. You're to pack your things and be there within the month. Lady Calypso is expecting you, and I would not keep her waiting."

I nodded dumbly looking down at the paper, and when I looked up once more, Janette had disappeared. Nothing but a flurry of bubbles remained in her wake. I was sure she had just swum off at the same speed she seemed to speak.

Packing up for my apprenticeship was easier than I'd thought it would be. I had spent my entire life in one place, and yet packing it all up didn't seem to take me any time at all— even with Aislin there to distract me.

"So, Calypso is whom you're apprenticed to?" Ace asked perhaps for the third time as if to verify she'd heard me correctly.

"Yes," came the tired and somewhat annoyed response. "We've been over this a half a dozen times already."

"And I still can't believe it." There was a look of awestruck amazement in her eyes that I'd never seen before and a hint of jealousy.

"How do you even know who she is?" I asked as I stuffed my hairbrush into a netted bag, the hard-shell case clicking against the mirror already inside of the bag. I was fairly sure Aislin had never even mentioned any witches to me, much less famous ones, so where had she come across this seemingly vast knowledge all of a sudden?

There was a huff, and I looked up just in time to find a clam shell floating through the water aimed right at my head an arm's length away. I ducked out of the way and sent her a dirty look. "The question, *Irsa*," she began, clearly irritated, "is how have you *not* heard of her?"

I shrugged my shoulders, a gesture I seemed to be growing quite fond of these days as I felt like I knew absolutely nothing anymore. "You know Father doesn't like witches."

A snort left Aislin and she rolled her eyes. "Your father doesn't like much of anything. Except for little miss Lansa, who he's been seen swimming through the market with of late."

"Ace, that's nothing but gossip, and you know it." It stung a little—no, it stung a lot—to know that Father had moved on so very quickly after Mother's death. It felt as if we had only just had her funeral and already he was being seen places with other mermaids. It left a girl to wonder if perhaps he'd been seeing them all along, but I refused to go down that path.

"But sometimes gossip is true." She shrugged a little herself rolling over on the tiny bed to look up at the ceiling.

"I know," I mumbled quietly as I turned back to the small dresser where I'd stacked many of my things and continued to stuff them into the bag. We were silent like that for a long moment, as I let the thought of Father and some other mermaid drift away on the tide.

"I'm awful glad you're not going too far, though. It's a blessing Calypso is kind of a hermit. It means you won't be too far from me!" She sat up quickly to grin at me, all pearly white teeth. "We can still visit."

I nodded. "Yes, we can still visit."

I couldn't imagine my life without Aislin in it. She had been a part of me for so long, I was sure without her, it would feel as if I were missing a fin.

We finished packing up what was left of my things just in time for the carriage Calypso had sent to arrive. It was a glittering, gilded beast of a contraption complete with a well-dressed footman, and driver no less—both of which came to help me load up my luggage.

"Great Poseidon, look how pretty it is!" Aislin gasped, taking a quick swim around the blasted thing to drink it all in before coming to a stop beside me once more.

I snorted softly, trying and failing to bite my tongue as a sarcastic comment surfaced. "Yeah, what do you think the old witch is compensating for?" The remark earned me a light swat. Aislin cut me a look from the corner of her eyes. It was then that I looked around and realized that my little entourage was drawing quite a bit of attention. No one in our small village had ever seen something so grand before, and people were beginning to crowd around the carriage. "Great, just what I need, gawkers," I muttered as the footman took my last bag and strapped it to the back of the carriage. "I better hurry up and get out of here before they think to throw me a parade." There was a snicker from beside me, and I looked over to see Ace covering her mouth and trying to hold back a laugh. I nudged her with my elbow, making the laughter worse. "Sorry, sorry," she choked past another chortle. "Sure you are. Alright, I'll see you so—" the words were cut off as Ace pulled me into a bone-crushing hug, and then shoved me up into the carriage before any more could be said. Father wasn't there to see me off—not that I'd expected him to be—but as I leaned out the window to blow Aislin a kiss, I realized it didn't matter. She was my family, and she was there; nothing else mattered. I did, in fact, get a parade. The people of the village followed us all the way to the edge, and the children even followed us out into the open ocean for a little bit. All the while, I felt the tug of loneliness as it began to sink in more and more that I was leaving my friend behind, at least for the moment, which left me feeling strangely incomplete.

The first few months with Lady Calypso were what can only be described as a whirlpool, chocked full of events to attend, lessons to be had, and people to see. It was as if she were showing me off like some prized seahorse to all of her friends—rubbing it in their faces and laughing that *she* had the new toy. While all of this was going on, Calypso was nothing but kind to me. Our lessons went smoothly enough, and I found I was happy in my position there, if not a little lonely. Aislin was still back in the village and wasn't due to start her apprenticeship for a while, so I had time to settle into my new life. When it was finally time for Ace to move to the town of Trysil and start her apprenticeship, I asked for the day to go and help her get settled. Calypso granted me that much with very little fuss. Aislin arrived at the small manor house of "The Lady Calypso"—as people always seemed to call it, which was needlessly snotty in my opinion—bright eyed and flippy tailed, and with a hug waiting for me. The moment I opened the door, she launched herself at me, hugging me tightly, and I had to admit I felt a part of myself sigh in relief. "Come in, come in! Klimpen has made us tea!" I ushered her inside and back to the small nook just off the kitchen where Calypso and I usually took our breakfast, albeit at different times. The little nook was furnished with soft kelp cushioned chairs, and a small two-mer person driftwood table perfect for breakfast for two. "Tides, this place is huge." She gasped in awe as her bright green eyes grew wide and looked around. My own dark eyes flicked around to drink in the smooth opalescent mother-of-pearl walls with fresh eyes, trying to see it how she saw it. I remembered the first night I had been there and how hollow the place had felt with the big open foyer complete with wide, winding halls, and lush kelp carpeting. It was beautiful and extravagant, but it had always been quiet and lonely until Calypso and I settled into a nice rhythm. "I suppose it is." My friend laughed as she nudged me gently and we headed back to tea. It had been three months since I'd seen Ace, and something about her had changed over the time. It was as if the little girl who'd always been my best friend was suddenly now a grown up. I wondered if I too looked different, but I didn't think to ask. The tea was waiting for us on the little table set for two, and I swam over to pour us some, my magic weaving its way through the water as it held the liquid in the cups. Every sea creature, especially merfolk, had enough magic in them to keep the liquid from spilling out into the sea, and untainted by the salt of the water around us. A loose strand of silvery hair fell from my braid in the process and tickled my cheek before a pale, freckled hand lifted to brush it back into place. It was a strange movement, but we've been close for so long that it wasn't entirely out of place as she smiled at me. "So, where are all of your things?" I asked as I finished pouring the tea, taking a seat across from her. "I mean, you *did* move with things, didn't you? You don't expect to buy all new clothes now that you're here." Ace laughed as she took a sip from her cup. "No, I brought things. They're just all already there. I figured I'd come and see you before we got to the grueling work that is unpacking my closet. You know... have breakfast first," she teased with a twinkle in her bright green eyes as she brushed her vibrant hair back from her face. "Oh, well, thank you very much for deciding I'll get a last meal before I resign myself to my fate," I teased back laughing a little to myself. Her tail flicked out to smack me under the table, and then we were both laughing, the unsettling moment forgotten.

When I returned home from helping Aislin unpack her ridiculously large closet, I was tired and worn out, but there was a note waiting for me, pinned to my door. Scrubbing at my face, I squinted a little to make out the almost illegible scrawl that was Calypso's handwriting to see the words 'in ... study... now.' There were some words in between I couldn't read, but I got the general gist. Running a hand through the silvery locks that had all come free of my braid at this point, I took a deep breath and did an about-face spin in the water. Upon reaching Calypso's study, I found her bent over a spell book, and the room lit only by the lime green of the magical orbs burning away in lanterns. I knocked lightly on the door, just to be sure she meant for me to come in. The door swung open wider, and Calypso looked up from her book motioning for me to come in. "You wanted to see me, Mistress?" "Sit," the raven-haired sorceress commanded pointing to a chair in front of her desk. A chill ran through me at the way her mouth twisted with the word, but I swam forward to sit in the indicated chair even still. Once seated, I was pinned to my seat with a glower. "You will not be seeing that girl again." My dark eyes went wide at the words, and I felt my face pale even further, if that were possible. "I'm sorry, Mistress?" I asked in confusion, which only seemed to enrage her as the lamp lights blazed brighter. "I saw the way that you two looked at each other. I know what is going on there. You're distracted and we can't afford that." "I don't know what you mean. Aislin is my friend. We've been friends since we were born." I tried to reason with her, hoping maybe she'd see that this was ridiculous. Aislin wasn't a distraction. "And now that friendship will cease." The edge to those words could have sliced through coral. Her eyes narrowed further, the magic blazing behind them with her fury. "We have far too much to accomplish for you to start floundering now. The entire sea is watching us, Irsa; we will not disappoint them."

Our world is watching her because of me...if I slip up, they'll turn away from The Lady Calypso. This is about her reputation as a teacher and a great sea-witch.

"You will put a stop to it now." My dark eyes widened as I looked at her. She couldn't possibly be serious, I thought. She couldn't possibly mean that, but from her knitted eyebrows to the turned down corners of her too-red lips, there was nothing but seriousness written on her face. I shook my head thinking maybe it would change her mind. Maybe she would see how wrong it was, but there was no softening of her features.

Taking a deep breath, I swallowed a hard lump in my throat and sat up straighter in the hard chair. "I will not," a firm voice came from somewhere deep inside of my chest as my fingers began to glow with the soft light of my magic. I didn't recognize it, but it still felt like that familiar, powerful, firm voice. Calypso jerked back as if I'd slapped her, her face shifting to something more akin to shock. "What?" Tightening my jaw, I rose to my fins, and took another deep breath. "No, I will not. Aislin is my friend, and she will remain so. Now if you will excuse me, it is rather late, and I will be going to sleep." Turning my back on her, I headed to the door. There was a loud crack as a flash of lime green magic slammed the door shut. "Excuse me?" Her voice slithered through the water to my ears. My shoulders tightened as my back straightened further, but I didn't turn around. "Look at me, Irsa," she hissed. Slowly, I turned in the water to meet her dark green eyes which seemed to glow with the rage and power boiling within her. I knew it was insolent, I knew it would only further enrage her, but I couldn't stop it as my brow quirked insolently. "What?" "Do not test me, child," she warned, wanting my full attention on her and our work. A little smirk tugged at my lips at the warning. Calypso needed me—I had learned that during all of those grand balls and council meetings. I gave her an air of notoriety she'd been lacking as of late. "Or what?" She moved so quickly that I didn't see her swim up over the desk towards me before the sting of a slap landed on my cheek. "I can make life very uncomfortable for you here, Irsa," she threatened. Resisting the urge to rub at my reddened cheek, I shrugged. "So be it." "You may change your mind, but I will not let up. Make your choice now." "I will not abandon my friend." I felt a certain amount of power in my stubbornness. She could tell me what to do, but she could not take away my will not to listen. Let her make my life miserable. Let her do her worst. "Then, as you say, so be it."

Calypso held good to her word, coveting the looks people gave her because I was working under her tutelage. In the morning, my things were moved out of the lavish bedroom I'd been given upon arrival to a small room just off the kitchen. The servants watched me with pity as they swam my things down the curved stairs of the foyer, and through the clatter of the kitchen to the little room. I sunk down on the hard cot made of driftwood and seaweed, and let myself think for a moment. Surely, my apprenticeship could not be much longer—a year, at most. I could survive in that cramped little room for a year. If Calypso thought this was going to make me change my mind, she was sorely mistaken. I had lived without the softness of a kelp mattress, and the beautiful colors of a painted bedroom all of my life. What were a few more months? This was less a punishment than she thought it was. What I hadn't anticipated was what would happen later that afternoon when it was time for our lessons. The training room was on the third floor of the manor, far enough away from everything else that our magic couldn't ruin anything. "How are you liking your new room, Irsa?" Calypso asked me as she settled into a chair in the corner, her hands folding together in her lap. I bit my tongue for a long moment to keep from responding with some snarky remark before saying, "It is fine, Mistress." "No complaints?" "No, Mistress." I swam to the center of the room and closed my eyes to begin to call upon my magic. The living thing inside of me seemed more willing to come out when I was in emotional distress, so it generally took me some time to awaken it when I was calm. My Mistress said nothing more as I concentrated on connecting myself with the magic, but I could feel her eyes upon me. Those dark green eyes that were so sharply contrasted with Ace's vibrant green ones were cutting into me critically, the way that they always did when we trained. "It shouldn't take you this long. Your magic should be awake and ready." Her tone was as sharp and cutting as her eyes. She'd never said any such thing to me before. During our training, she had always been kind and encouraging, though at times she could be a little critical. "Wh-what?" My dark eyes opened to meet her's, breaking my focus. "I said, this is ridiculous. We've been at this for months now, you should be able to just reach for it, and it should come to you." Swallowing roughly, I forced my face to remain impassive. "I'm sorry, Mistress. I will do better." A derisive scoff left her before she said, "You had better. Begin again." Nodding, I ducked my head, and closed my eyes once more to reach for the soft glow of my magic. I willed it to reach back to me—to come when I called it—but it felt as though there was a barrier between myself and it. A thin piece of glass separated us as we reached for one another that only became thicker as Calypso tapped one long red fingernail on the arm of her chair before letting out a loud, impatient sigh. I reached further and pushed harder. Finally, it came to me, filling me with the familiar glowing warmth. I lifted my head, opened my eyes, and smiled a little at the feeling. The room filled with the sound of an exaggerated clap as my mistress merely eyed me sardonically. "Took you long enough. Now let it go and begin again." I jerked, feeling as if I'd been slapped, the shock registering on my face. Usually, once I had reached my magic, we just began the lesson, but not today. "What?" "You heard me." Her red lips twitched as a smirk threatened to take over her face. I knew at that moment that this was just the beginning. The hours ticked by, and I was made to let go of my magic and reach for it over and over again. Each time, it felt as though the glass between myself and the glowing light got thicker and thicker. Each time, it took me longer and longer to reach it. We worked through lunch and did not stop until Klimpen knocked on the door to let us know that supper was ready. After eating, I poured myself into my bed, completely exhausted, and let sleep take me.

Calypso's new teaching method went on every day for months on end, leaving me no time to have a life or to visit Aislin in spite of her being nearby to Calypso's manor. I lost track of time before Calypso announced that she would be going into the city the following day to see to some business, and I decided to take my chance to go visit my friend. I pulled on a long flowing black cloak, hoping to keep anyone from recognizing me as I swam my way through town. I didn't want anyone to tell Calypso that they'd seen me, so I headed out the back door just off of the kitchen and out into the streets of Trysil. Aislin was apprenticed to the seamstress a few streets over, and I made my way through back alleys the whole way there. A little clamshell chime tinkled over top of the door when I ducked inside. I pushed back my hood, letting out a sigh of relief that I'd made it the whole way to the shop without anyone recognizing me. "We'll be with you in a moment," a voice rang out from the back room that must have belonged to the owner.

Then Aislin's head bobbed around the corner, her face lighting up with a smile the moment she saw me. "Irsa." She giggled in surprise as she threw herself at me to pull me into a bone-crushing hug. I sank into the hug, letting the warmth she provided spread through me and heal some of the exhaustion I'd felt every day for how long I didn't know. "Great Poseidon, it's so good to see you." I sighed hugging her back. When she finally pulled back from me, her green eyes widened as they fell on me and her mouth fell open in shock. "What's happened to you?" There were no mirrors in my little room now—no way to see what I looked like—so I'd just tied my hair back into a braid and headed out. "What are you talking about?" Frowning deeply, Ace took my hand and pulled me over to one of the full-length mirrors, holding onto my fingers. My dark eyes fell upon a mer who looked wholly unlike myself. She was pitiful and drawn. Her cheeks had hollowed out, and there was darkness ringing her eyes. I hadn't noticed it until that very moment, but even my tail looked thinner. "Oh." I gasped softly, lifting my hands to cover my mouth, untangling myself from her grasp. "What has she done to you?" Aislin demanded, pulling me over to a stool to sit me down. "You looked so happy and healthy when I saw you a couple of months ago." I shook my head as my arms curled around my middle self-consciously. I didn't want to tell Ace that Calypso had done this to me because she didn't want us to be friends anymore so I would focus on my work. Instead of asking again, Ace pursed her lips and told one of the other girls to make me some tea. A few minutes later, there was a hot cup of tea in my hands, and Aislin was sitting on a stool next to me, gently stroking my back. She waited until I'd had a couple of sips of tea before asking, "Now, what happened?" Taking a deep breath, I dove into the whole story. I told her about what Calypso had demanded, how I'd defied her, and how I was having so much trouble reaching my magic now. "I just... I feel like it's so far away now. Like it's leaving me." Aislin was silent for a long moment, seeming to process everything that had happened. All the while, her hand continued to rub my back soothingly. I was almost sure she wouldn't say anything at all—she was quiet so long—but when she finally did speak, it seemed sudden. "She's done something to you. We have to get you out of there." In all of the years that we had been friends, it had always felt like I was protecting Aislin. I had stood up for her when the other children in the village had teased her, and when she had first been learning to ride a seahorse, and it had bucked her, I'd been there to treat her wounds. Now it seemed that Aislin was the one protecting me. "I'm going to get you out of there," she said firmly. I was shaking my head before she even told me her plan because I already knew it was going to cost both of us more than we had to give. "No. You can't. Whatever you're thinking, no." Ace turned to me with one brow quirked, wrinkling her freckled forehead. "You don't even know what I'm thinking." "Well, whatever it is, it can't be good." "Trust me. We'll sort it out. Can you get away tomorrow evening to talk?" I knew I didn't have much of a choice. Ace had made up her mind, and she was a stubborn spit of a thing, she wasn't going to change her mind just because I didn't agree with her. We made a plan to meet up after I finished my training with Calypso the following day.

Sneaking from the manor in the dead of night was no easy feat. Calypso had put up wards to keep merfolk out, but they did a damn good job of keeping me in as well, and after a day of reaching for my magic which seemed to get more and more distant, I was exhausted. The only thing that drew it closer was the image of Ace waiting for me in the tavern where we'd agreed to meet. Thinking of her always seemed to awaken the magic inside of me more easily, and I was able to work my way around the wards. However, I didn't allow myself to breathe until I was swimming two streets over. Once I reached the tavern, I let my hood fall back from my face, and my shoulders relax. Ace was there, sitting at a table in the back corner of the tavern. She'd left the seat open for me against the back wall so I could watch the customers milling about the tavern, although I was sure Calypso wouldn't be joining us. "Alright, what's this grand plan of yours," I asked as my fingers drummed on the coral table nervously, my dark eyes flicking around the dimly lit tavern. "We are going to get you a position in the palace." Her words were excited as she smiled to herself. She'd thought this up all on her own, and clearly, she was quite pleased with herself. I, on the other hand, was skeptical. "I'm sorry... what?" The whole idea sounded entirely preposterous. The royal family hadn't had a sea-witch in hundreds of years, and everyone knew that. Just like everyone knew that Prince Tynan did not believe in the use of sea-witches. He much preferred to get his way via negotiations. "The royal family is hosting a ball. I'll go and request an audience with the prince. Then I'll ask him for his help. Prince Tynan is a good man and he'll want to help." I blinked at her—mouth agape—Aislin had always been a dreamer, but she'd never said anything so ridiculous in all of our lives. "The prince is not going to give a flying fish about me and my problems, Ace. Don't be silly." Her freckled hands reached over and grasped mine in earnest. "He will, Irsa, he will. I promise I'll make him care." "Why would he care?" Ace smirked a little, her bright green eyes twinkling with some dirty little secret she obviously had been keeping all of this time. "Because King Hemnes hates Calypso." I felt my jaw drop open, my eyes flying wide in surprise. I'd heard so much gossip, everyone I'd spoken to had always said that King Hemnes had tried to bring Calypso on at one point. It was the thing she prided herself most on, that she—*The Lady Calypso*—had been asked by the king himself to come to work in the palace. Although, I began to realize that what she'd always failed to mention was how he'd reacted when she'd denied him. Ace was nodding, her lips stretching into more of a smirk. "When she turned down the position at the castle, it infuriated the king. Since then, he's exiled her to Trysil—that's why she's here." The smug look of satisfaction on Ace's face was only paralleled by the flutter of hope I felt well up inside of my chest. "You'll need a dress," I said after I let everything sink in. She let out a girlish giggle, lifting my hands to her lips to brush a soft kiss to my knuckles which only made my cheeks flush hotly. "I will." "How long do we have?" "A month." "Will you have time to make yourself something?" "I'll figure something out," she said unsurely. I nodded as my mind began to wander. "I can help. I can get you a carriage." It was the least I could do. If Ace was going to put her neck on the line to try to save me from Calypso, then my magic and I could get her a dress. Another giggle permeated the water around us, and I found myself smiling for the first time in months. This plan could work—we could *make* it work. After we left the tavern, Aislin dragged me back to her tiny closet of an room for a cup of tea, and some *real* food. She sat me down on an old couch and began to swim quickly about the tiny room making tea and a clam sandwich for me. "You don't have to do this," I protested weakly. It wasn't as if Calypso had been starving me, in spite of how I looked. "Nonsense." Ace would hear none of it, and in a few minutes, I had a drink and food shoved into my hands. "Now, eat. I'll work up a design for my dress." "What about fabric?" I asked setting the plate aside as I took a sip of tea. "I'll have it before the week's out." She didn't even look up from her sketchbook as she made quick work of designing a dress with squid ink. "I'll just have Tarva order it tomorrow, and it'll be in by the end of the week." She shrugged a little. "Can you afford that?" The conversation of money hadn't come up before, but now I was thinking about it, she would ultimately have to pay for the fabric, and I didn't know how much money she actually made in her apprenticeship. There was another shrug of her dainty, freckled shoulders. "It'll be alright. Don't worry about it."

True to her word, before the week was out, there was a note waiting for me on my cot one evening. There was no indication of how it had gotten there. Perhaps Ace had paid one of Calypso's staff to bring it in for her, or maybe she'd winked at the stable boy, and he'd brought it in. Either way, there it sat. Swimming to my hard cot, I settled onto the rough seaweed quilt and snatched up the note. As I opened the parchment, my lips spread into a soft smile at the sight of Aislin's neat scrawl. A warm feeling began to grow in my belly that hadn't been there before, but I brushed it aside and focused on the words. The note read simply, 'You're coming with me.' My dark eyes blinked down at the words before I noticed the little envelope that had been waiting beneath the note. Once opened, the envelope revealed a second dress sketch, this time of what I could only assume was a dress for me, and a fabric swatch in a deep sapphire color. There was another little note on the sketch that said, "I'll see you in two weeks." Between training, and the distance Calypso seemed to be putting between myself and my magic, the two weeks seemed to drag by. When it was finally time to meet Ace at the tiny room she rented above the seamstress shop, I was so exhausted it didn't take much to pretend to be ill so that I could sneak out. I looked so ill, in fact, that Calypso didn't even bother to question it. She just told me to keep my sickness to myself. Sneaking out that evening was easy enough—the first time I'd escaped, I'd created a hole in the wards for myself. I tugged my cloak around myself to make sure no one would notice me —just as I'd done so many times before—and made my way to Ace's room. "Irsa!" Aislin shouted as the little clamshell chime over top of her door sounded, and she swam over to me at breakneck speeds. It had been weeks since we'd seen each other, but she hugged me as if we hadn't seen each other in years. Just as before, I allowed her warmth to permeate the cold that seemed to have settled into my bones over the months of training with Calypso. Ace pulled back to get a better look at me, and her face fell a little as her eyes flicked over me. Her teeth began to wear on her red lip, as she held in the words she wanted to say. "I know, I know. I look tired. But come on, we have dresses to try on." "Right, and makeup to do." She nodded firmly, a smile tugging at her lips. Her hands reached down to take mine, and soon I was sitting before a mirror as she set to work applying makeup to my face. My eyes were lined in squid ink, and my lips were covered with jellyfish jelly. Her fingers made quick work of my hair, tying it up into an intricate braid. Once finished, she shooed me from the seat and settled there herself. "Your dress is in the closet, go try it on." I floated there for a long moment, watching Ace as she pinned and clipped her hair up into an elegant twisting pattern with a few wisps of hair brushing down along her long elegant neck. Swallowing roughly, I nodded my head before turning to go look in the closet. The door opened to reveal a long flowing dress in sapphire blue so beautiful it brought tears to my eyes. A soft sniff left me, and as I lifted a hand to scrub at my face, Aislin let out a soft hiss. "Don't you dare." I laughed loudly as I turned to her. "It's perfect." Ace smiled widely at me in the mirror. "Of course it is, I made it for you. Now go on; get changed. We don't have all of the time in the world. The carriage will be here in an hour." Turning from her, I headed into the small washroom to slip into the dress. The length of it felt strange to wear something so long, but looking in the small mirror in the washroom, I could tell that the color looked beautiful against my skin. "Well? Let's see it," Aislin demanded. As I came from the small room to show her, she gasped loudly. "Great Poseidon, Irsa... you look..." She gestured wildly unable to even tell me as her cheeks flushed red. I laughed a little, doing a twirl in the water, bubbles fluttering up around me. "Completely ridiculous?" "No. Never." Ace shook her head, moving to me to take my hands. "You look stunning." She leaned in to press a quick kiss to my lips, without even thinking, and my heart gave a harsh twist. "We're going to knock 'em dead," she whispered, her lips still so close to mine that I could feel her breath in the water. "Yeah," I agreed, not paying much attention to what I agreed with at that point. The rest of our preparations for the ball went by in a whirlpool of fluttering fabric, and happy laughs from Aislin as my mind remained firmly planted in the moment of that kiss. I could still feel her lips against mine as we loaded up into the carriage to head to the ball. It wasn't until we actually reached the castle that I was pulled back into the strange excitement of the evening. Somehow, Aislin had procured two invitations to the ball, and these were handed to the guard at the door before we were allowed into the castle. "Where did you get those?" I whispered as we swam down the hallway. Ace's bright green eyes shimmered, and she winked before tapping the side of her nose. "That's for me to know, and you to never find out." I scoffed, rolling my dark eyes and vowing to get the answer from her at some point during the evening—I couldn't do it as we were being asked our names so that we could be announced. The overstuffed tuna-of-a-merman sniffed indignantly at us, but turned to declare our entrance to the room all the same. From there, the evening seemed to melt into delicious food, shimmering orbs of magic, and the fluttering bubbles that could only be caused by merfolk dancing. I couldn't seem to help myself, and I got swept up in all of it, so much so that I found myself smiling from ear to ear as Aislin and I danced, sang, and ate until we couldn't swim anymore. When it was finally time for Aislin to have a dance with the prince, he came over to her. His electric hair and tail reminded me very much of an eel, and everything from his posture to his expression made me feel as if he thought himself better than all of us. I sat at our table, giving my fins a break, as I watched them both move across the dance floor. Aislin had always enjoyed a good dance—at that moment, she was in her element. Her lips were split in a wide smile, the dress she'd sewn for herself flowing out around her as the prince spun her around. All the while, his eyes were sweeping the area around them, noting how the other merfolk in the room were beginning to form a loose circle around them. My eyes flicked around, seeing that all eyes seemed to be on them. When the dance ended, there was a round of applause like I'd never heard before. The prince swooped in to give Aislin a quick kiss to her cheek before releasing her so she could head back to our table. I swallowed down any irritation I had, brushing the whole thing off as a show. Everyone in the ballroom was watching, so the prince had put on a performance. "So?" I asked when Ace returned to me. She settled into her seat, taking a moment, perhaps, to catch her breath—but more likely just to draw out the suspense. Her freckled arm reached out to take her goblet and she took a sip of her drink. She laughed when I huffed in annoyance. "He will see us after the last dance. We are to meet him in the courtyard before meeting our carriage to head home. Don't you fret, Irsa, I will take care of everything." Her hand stretched out beneath the table, where no one could see, and gripped my pale one. She offered me an encouraging smile and gave it a squeeze. "I know you think this is going to work, Ace, but..." I started to say that there was no way this would work—that she'd lost her mind thinking that it would—but I couldn't. The way she was smiling at me, the way she was holding my hand—she wanted so badly for this work, and I wasn't going to be the one to dash those hopes. "But I guess we'll see," I finished lamely. "It will work, Irsa, I swear," she promised me, her voice full of nothing but certainty and her chin held high. She knew without a shadow of a doubt that this was going to work, and I found myself believing it too. We sat there for a long while, just holding hands, and silently praying to the great sea god that this would all work out in the end. The ball around us began to die down, and soon it was time to go and meet the prince. A servant came to escort us to the courtyard, his face drawn down in a scowl of disapproval of what was going on. Once there, we were told, "Wait here. The prince will be with you shortly." It seemed like forever as we waited for the prince to finish up his goodbyes. The entire time, my stomach writhed like an eel, and Ace swam up and down the length of the courtyard. When he finally showed up, his chin was tilted up and there was a smooth smile on his lips as though he'd arrived exactly when he'd meant to, obviously caring little for how long we had been kept waiting, or the fact that we both had to be up early in the morning for our jobs. "I don't believe we've been introduced," Prince Tynan said as he turned to eye me thoughtfully. There was no attempt at an apology—no *sorry to have kept you waiting*—he just moved on with business as usual. I found myself disliking him from the start—there was something so arrogant about him—like a blue tang with too many yellow stripes. I had to bite my tongue to keep from snarling at him, thankfully Aislin was there to swoop in and save us both. "This is my friend Irsa. She's the one whom I told you would make an excellent royal sea-witch." One brow quirked as he looked me over once more. He didn't say as much— there was no need, the way his blue eyes flicked over my small frame told me he found my very existence inconsequential. After the months of working myself to dead exhaustion with Calypso, he would be right—I didn't look like much. "I am Prince Tynan, son of King Hemnes and heir to the throne of Alon," He announced. My pale grey brows raised, and I wondered if I was supposed to bow. The answer to that particular question came in the form of the jab of an elbow to my side as Aislin bowed. "Of course, it is a pleasure," I said keeping the sarcasm from my tone by some small miracle. "I'm Irsa, Calypso's apprentice." I righted myself and met his sharp blue eyes with my almost black ones. If he thought I would be cowed by such a pedigree, he was wrong. "So your friend says." I got the distinct impression he didn't care much for me, nor did he want to chat at all with me, but here we were, nonetheless. "Your beautiful friend has taken care to provide me with all of your information and informed me that if I were to bring you on as the royal sea-witch, it would enrage Calypso to the point of madness." This seemed to please him, for his lips turned up ever so slightly at the corners. "Her name is Aislin," I found myself saying without much thought. I hated the way he was talking about Ace like she wasn't there, or as if she were some inanimate thing that merely recited information. Ace jabbed me again with her elbow. A wry smirk tugged at Tynan's lips. I wasn't sure if I'd amused him or irritated him. "Very well, Aislin," he said with a nod and shot Ace a charming smile which she only returned with an awkward smile of her own. "While putting a jelly-fish in Calypso's bonnet would certainly suit me just fine, I feel that's not quite enough of a reward for the havoc she could very well wreak on Alon." My heart sank like an anchor. Surely, that meant he would not be bringing me on as the royal sea-witch. I realized for the first time in weeks that I'd begun to count on this to work. It had been the thing that was keeping me alive, and without it, I didn't know that I would survive any more of Calypso's torture. "But... Your Highness, I assure you—" Aislin started to argue in my defense, and I sent up a little thank you to Poseidon for her. She was an angelfish if I'd ever seen one. The prince raised his hand to silence her—a gesture that was surprisingly effective considering how much Aislin liked to talk. "But, I am a man of negotiations, and I can be persuaded. I have a deal in mind." If my heart had sunk down to the very tip of my fin, I was sure now it had sunken to the ocean floor, for there was a glint in his eyes that told me that I wasn't going to like this deal, and Aislin wasn't likely to either.

"Anything," Ace said before I could stop her. That handsome face stretched into a smirk of triumph. "Then in six months' time, you will be my wife Miss Aislin, and you will bear me a son. In the meantime, I will give your friend the position of Royal Sea-witch." "I…you…she —" The words all seemed to struggle for dominance as I tried to tell him that it was impossible and that Aislin was meant for no one else but me—something I'd only just realized—and I wasn't willing to share her with him, even if it meant my own safety. I wouldn't allow her to sacrifice that. Aislin had fallen unusually silent beside me. She'd reached out to take my hand and grip it hard before nodding slowly. "Very well." "Ace, no!" My protests were met with a mere shake of her head. "Very well then. In the morning, I will be by to collect you both. Aislin, you will begin your lessons here as a princess, and Irsa you will move into the chambers left aside for the Royal Sea-witch. Now, you both best get home. I expect to see you both bright and early." Then he spun in the water before heading back into the castle.

I don't remember what happened after that. In fact, the entirety of it seemed blank until we were back in the carriage headed back to Aislin's small room. "I can't believe you just agreed to that," I growled at her suddenly—the anger I'd felt at the prince even asking such a thing welling up and spilling over. "How could you?" Sighing, Aislin reached over to take my hands once more. She lifted them to her lips to brush a kiss to each knuckle before she spoke. "I have six months to think my way out of this. A lot can happen in six months. But for now, you're safe." "And *what* do you plan to do to get out of it?" I asked incredulously. Of course, she thought she could get out of this. *Of course,* she thought she could outsmart the prince. "Well, I have a little money saved, and you'll be making quite a lot as the Royal Sea-witch. We should have enough in a month to run away." The way Ace said those words—as if they were the simplest thing in all of the world—made me feel like maybe it was possible. She'd believed with all of her heart that she would be able to convince the prince to take me on, and she had. Why couldn't this work too? I nodded slowly. "Then you'll... swim away with me?" I had to ask the question. We both knew what she was saying, but I needed to hear her say it anyway. The truth was that I had loved Aislin from the moment we'd been born. She was a part of me—one half of the whole— and I couldn't live without her. "Oh, you stupid girl." Aislin laughed and leaned in to kiss me once more. This time when our lips met, she didn't pull away quite so quickly. This time I felt my fins curl with the heat of it. I lost myself to Aislin—her smell, and her taste—so much so that I didn't even realize the carriage had stopped until the footmen banged on the door to let me know that we had reached the edge of the wards at the manor. "I'd swim anywhere with you," she whispered softly against my lips. I let out a youthful giggle and practically fell out of the carriage. "I'd run anywhere with you, too." Ace watched me make my way through the wards on the window, a wide smile on her lips. I turned back right as I reached the edge of them and blew her a kiss which she caught with much show. As I lay in bed trying to sleep, I could feel her lips burning on mine still. We would make this work.

I had dozed off for an hour before a loud commotion somewhere in the manor woke me. Swimming carefully from my room, I peeked around the corner of the foyer to find Calypso and Prince Tynan facing off. Tynan bobbed casually in the water, his posture relaxed, and an easy smirk on his features, while Calypso was struggling to hold her magic in as it raged against her. "You can't just decide you're going to come and take my apprentice," Calypso's voice carried low and dangerously across the foyer. "She is not ready for any such occupation, not to mention it is illegal. An apprentice cannot leave their apprenticeship without their master or mistress's approval." For a moment, it looked like perhaps Calypso had won. Her chin tilted up in victory, and a slow smile spread across her lips. At least, she *thought* she had won. The prince held out his hand, and one of the servants that was accompanying him placed a neatly curled scroll in his hand. He unfurled it in one well-practiced motion, electric blue eyes flicking across the page for show until he "found" what he was looking for. "Ah, here it is. Sanction 916." He cleared his throat before he began to read. "In the event that it is brought to the attention of the ruling party of Alon that an apprentice has been mistreated under their master's tutelage, it is within the ruling party's right to remove the apprentice to find them a more appropriate place of employment." A little smirk tugged at his lips as he finished, and Calypso's hands fell to her sides, closing into tight fists sparking with the green of her magic. "Now, it was brought to my attention just last night that your apprentice has been vilely mistreated, and I feel that given the strength of her magic, an appropriate place of employment can only be the castle." "Irsa," Calypso called as if she'd known I'd been floating there all along. I swam around the corner but refused to meet her eyes. "Yes, Mistress?" I asked softly my head bowed to look at the plush carpet of kelp in the foyer. "Have you been mistreated here?" The question was loaded, we both knew that it was. If I were to say yes—go away with the prince this very morning, and make an enemy of Calypso forever. If I were to say no—I'd stay here and allow myself to waste away to nothing in a matter of months. Her hope had to be that I was more afraid of her ire than of death—she was mistaken. Maybe before last night, I would have been, but now, I had Aislin to live for, and one day we would run away together to live our lives together with no more interference from Calypso or the Prince. So instead of saying *no* meekly as she hoped I would, I responded with a resounding, "Yes." It didn't take but a moment for Calypso to swim over to me, swing back her hand, and smack me with all of her strength, leaving a long cut along my cheekbone. "How dare you, you insolent child! I have given you everything, and this is how you repay me?" She swung back to smack me once more, but one of the servants had moved to grab her wrist. "I've seen quite enough. Irsa, go and pack your things; I will wait here." The prince's words were final. He motioned to one of his servants to follow me, and between the two of us, we had everything I owned packed up within an hour including the beautiful dress Aislin had made for me. Once we were done, I was loaded up into the carriage alongside the prince, and he gave directions for us to go to Aislin's seamstress shop. Prince Tynan said nothing to me as the carriage rocked along the ocean tides, but I noticed we were gathering a bit of a following as we made our way through the town. When we reached the shop, the servants bobbed on either side of the unfurled carpet to keep the onlookers at bay as the prince went into the little seamstress shop. I hadn't been told so, but I knew I was meant to stay inside of the carriage, out of the way. I had to watch everything from the window of the carriage. I sent up a silent prayer to Poseidon that Aislin would make a good show of this whole thing. After all, that was what the Prince wanted. I knew that was the only reason he had made the deal in the first place—because all of the people in the ball had seemed to love Aislin. Who wouldn't love her? She was beautiful, elegant, and everything that was kind and wholesome. Ace's personality perfectly contrasted that of the prince, and I knew that they were all thinking what a wonderful queen she'd make. There was a loud squeal, and a murmur from the people outside as I watched Aislin bobbing happily in the water and accepting the prince's ring. In a whirl of bubbles, they were back up the carpet and had joined me in the carriage. Ace settled in beside me, giving me a little wink as the carriage took off once more. "Well, now that that's settled..." the Prince said as he leaned back in his seat with a yawn, looking quite bored with the whole thing. "Your training begins in the morning, Aislin, and I'll be by this evening with a job for you, Irsa." No more was said as the young merman across from us dozed in his seat, completely uncaring of his guests.

Settling into the expansive chamber I was given inside of the castle felt strange. There was so much space for the few personal items I had, but I was sure over the coming months, I would be able to build up a collection of books. Although, I told myself that perhaps I wouldn't want to build up too much of a collection as I would be leaving them behind inevitably. That evening, the pretentious sea-urchin-of-a-prince joined me in my office as I sat behind the desk just trying to grasp the day's events fully. He didn't bother to knock; he just swam into the room unannounced and took up residence in one of the chairs on the other side of my desk. "I see you have settled in," he said in a tone that said he didn't care one way or the other if I had. "Yes, Your Highness." The term of respect came out a little begrudgingly, and I had already decided I didn't much care for his politics. We had come here as a means to save my life, but I was sure we would leave as a means to save Ace's. "Is there something I can help you with?" "Yes, I need a spell to ensure that Aislin bears me a son." I choked a little at the abrupt words and frowned at him. "What?" "I assume it will take you some time to think of something, but I will need it for when we're married when she turns seventeen." He was saying all of this so casually, as if it were the most normal thing in the ocean as he sat there examining his fingernails. "Spells like that can be dangerous," I warned as I felt my stomach twist. I wouldn't—*couldn't*—do anything to put Aislin in danger. "Then I suppose you ought to find a way to make it safe, shouldn't you? You have six months to do it, that should be plenty of time." He lifted his eyes to look at me, as if he thought perhaps I'd tell him no. I wanted to. There was nothing in the ocean I wanted more than to tell him no, but I knew at that moment that I didn't have much choice. "And if I don't?" I felt like I had to ask, even though I knew the answer deep down. The over-inflated pufferfish was no one to be trifled with. For all his self-importance and blustering, he did actually hold my life, and Ace's, in his hands. "Then I'll find someone else. My father won't give me the crown until I have an heir, and I'm sure Calypso would be willing to risk your friend's life to get me what I want. Especially after you betrayed her as you did." He shrugged, his eyes nonchalantly flicking over my face to judge the impact of the words. I must have looked like I wasn't going to agree in order to save Aislin, because he added, "Or, perhaps I need to sweeten the deal for you?"

I watched him for a long moment as he thought about this. His fingers were drumming on the bend in his vivid blue tail. The young prince was silent as his mind worked over all of the possibilities. He was a negotiator, after all, surely he could offer me something that would get me to do as he asked. "What if I were to promise to let you both go when she bore me a son?" The words made my heart stop as my dark eyes flicked to him to try to understand what he was saying.

"Did you think I missed the way you two looked at one another? I know very well that Aislin does not love me, and that at the first chance she gets, you two will run away. All that I ask is that she provide me with an heir first and we'll come up with a story for her sudden disappearance later." "You'll... let us go?" It didn't seem possible. We could have everything we'd ever wanted, and we could be free of Calypso, Tynan, and Alon. "I'll let you go with enough money in hand to keep you both comfortable for the rest for your lives," he promised. "And what will you tell the people happened to your queen?" His lips turned up in a little bit of a smirk. "I think I'll make quite a charming widower king, don't you?" This was a deal unlike any we'd ever be offered again— I was sure of that. This was our opportunity to leave Alon behind us for good. There was no way I could possibly turn that down, so I stretched out my hand to the prince. "You have a deal." Those handsome features split into a wide smile, and he reached across the desk to shake my hand. "Good. Then you have six months." I nodded.

Six months seemed like a long time when I'd made the deal, but the truth was that it flew by. Ace's time was full of training and fittings, while mine was full of meetings, and odd jobs for King Hemnes. The only time I was left to work on the spell was in the evenings, and then sometimes that time was taken up by Aislin joining me in my office, during which time, no work got done. When the wedding date was a week away, the prince appeared in my office once more. I had spent the evening in the gardens, hand-in-hand with Aislin, and returned to find him sitting in my chair behind the desk looking ever the self-important blue tang that he was. "To what do I owe the pleasure, Your Highness?" I asked, opting to float behind one of the chairs on the opposite side of the desk instead of sitting. He looked up at me over steepled fingers and smirked at me. "I'm just here to remind you of our deal, Irsa. I need an heir. My father will not step down as king until I have one, so this is of vital importance." "Of course, Your Highness." Tynan rose from his seat and swam towards the door only to stop just as he reached it and looked at me over his shoulder. "One more thing, Irsa." I turned to look at him, brows drawn up in question. "Yes, Your Highness?" "You have three tries. If Aislin does not have a son by the third pregnancy, I *will* get someone else to do this for me, and you will be exiled. That is all." The young prince turned back to the door and disappeared through it with a flick of a bright blue fin.

We didn't, as it turned out, have enough money to leave the prince before the wedding— although, we had tried valiantly. I had saved every clamshell I made, and Aislin had hoarded items she thought we could sell, but it wasn't enough. Somewhere deep down, I supposed I'd known it wouldn't be, which is why I'd made the deal with the prince to provide a potion to help Ace give him an heir. It wasn't a perfect system, but it would have to do. The wedding was a kingdom-wide event; merfolk from in the city were even invited to a floating room only row. Prince Tynan, it seemed, wanted to do everything in his power to gain the approval of his people, and Aislin was just one more piece in the puzzle that he seemed to be putting together for himself. Thus, the wedding was what little mergirls' dreams were made of, and everyone who was anyone was invited. I managed to swallow down my distaste for the whole charade long enough to get through the wedding and was there waiting for Aislin in her dressing room after. "So, you're officially a princess now," I teased as she swam into the room, her long train trailing behind her. Ace shook her head and swam to me, settling herself on my lap. My arms wrapped tightly around her by instinct, and I let out a soft sigh at how good it felt to hold her. "We'll have to start trying for an heir tonight," she whispered in a small voice. My lips tugged down into a frown as I squeezed her a little bit tighter. "I know, love, I know, but I've worked up a spell, and hopefully, you'll have a boy very soon. Then we can leave." There was that crazy thing again— that hope blossoming in my chest. Even in an impossible situation, it seemed like maybe there was a way out as long as Ace and I were together. We sent up our prayers to the Great Poseidon and hoped he would bless all of us with a boy.

Aislin became pregnant right away, a blessing we were both grateful for. It meant that she and the prince would not have to continue to try. Every day, she visited me in my offices, and every day I administered a tonic, and a spell in the hopes to ensure the child inside of her grew into a healthy baby boy. "Great Poseidon, I'm so fat," Ace whined as she flopped down onto the chaise lounge in my office one day towards the end of her pregnancy. She'd been miserable almost the entire time with horrible morning sickness, and various other aches and pains. I'd done the best that I could to make her comfortable, but it was no easy feat. "Not much longer," I promised as I brought her the tonic which she drank down in a single gulp. "What do you think I should name him?" She was looking down at her belly now, her fingers dancing along the bump as she smiled a little. She hadn't liked being pregnant, but I could tell from the look she was giving the bulge that she'd make a good mother. "I'm sure the prince will have some ideas about that." I wondered idly if Aislin would be able to leave once the child was born. She'd bonded so much with it already, and maybe she wouldn't be able to. However, I didn't say as much because doing so would likely only add stress to her and the child, and that was not something I needed. "Oh, I'm sure he will." Ace snorted softly rolling her eyes. "He'll probably want to name it after his father or something equally uncreative." I shrugged a little, and she let out a soft laugh.

When the baby finally came, the labor was no easy thing. Between myself and the midwife the prince had brought on, we had managed to help Ace through the birth, but afterward, she was weak. The midwife announced the child to be a girl, and our hopes were dashed, at least for this time. I had two more chances, and it took Aislin a little while to recover from the first child, giving me time to rework the spell.

When at last she was fully recovered, we tried again. This time, Aislin seemed less miserable throughout the pregnancy. In fact, she seemed to be glowing. I wondered if maybe this meant the spell had worked. Maybe this time it would be a boy, and we could leave. "I can feel it, and I want to name him Aries," she told me as she took her tonic a broad smile on her face. "He likes you. Every time you're around, he wiggles." Ace was giggling, and I couldn't help myself but smile with her. There was hope growing inside of me once more, in spite of the real chance that this time wouldn't work either.

When it came time for her to give birth, it was with me and two midwives this time. The sounds of distress coming from Aislin and the child tore my heart open. She was in pain—they were both in pain —I could feel it. One of the midwives held up the child and announced it to be a beautiful baby girl once more, and my heart sank. Aislin let out a cry of anguish and rolled over to sleep. As the midwives excused themselves with the baby, I floated down to curl up next to her on the bed gathering her in my arms. "I will do better next time," I promised, and kissed her shoulder softly. "You're doing the best you can," she whispered brokenly in reply as she snuggled back into me. We fell asleep that way, curled around each other. I woke long before she did, and snuck from the bed to head back down to my office. I vowed to not leave that room until I had perfected the spell that would give Aislin the one thing she wanted above all other things—our freedom.

I spent countless hours in that room working as Aislin recovered—

sleeping very little and begging my magic to cooperate with me. At some point, it seemed as if my magic and I had come to an agreement. Both of us wanted to save Aislin, and there was only one way to do that. Once Aislin was better, we tried once more. I administered a tonic, and spell before she and the prince were to try to conceive, and it seemed to work. Aislin became pregnant right away. This pregnancy seemed worse than the first, and she was put on bed rest soon after she began to show. I visited Ace every day, giving her the tonic and curling up beside her in the bed to soothe her into sleep. Every night before bed, I prayed to the Great Poseidon that he would bring Aislin a son. The day arrived for her to give birth, and this labor was worse than any of the others. I feared for Aislin's life as I held her hand in mine and murmured soft spells to try to ease the pain. I didn't dare to hope or pray that it was a boy, I just held onto her and prayed that she would make it through the labor alive. By the time the child was born, Aislin was so exhausted that she promptly fell right to sleep, leaving me to receive the news that she'd had yet another girl.

Everything happened so fast after that. I returned to my office after a long swim around the gardens during which I tried to think of something else I could use to bargain with the prince. If I just had something to give him, then perhaps he'd let me try again. However, when I swam in, I saw that all of my things had been packed, and Calypso was sitting behind my desk, a self-satisfied little smirk stretching her full, red lips. "I told you that you didn't want to cross me, child." She didn't have to slap me this time—I felt her words as if she had. "This isn't over," I countered grabbing up my bag and throwing it over my shoulder. "Not by a long shot." "Irsa, it was over long before you even came here." Her raven head shook giving me a pitying look. "The wheels of fate had already decided what would become of you and your friend. Did you learn nothing under my tutelage?" I lifted my chin and pinned her with my dark eyes. "Fate doesn't always get to decide." Maybe I was right, and maybe I was wrong. Either way, I was not going to swim from that room with my head held down in shame. A soft snort left Calypso as she shook her head. "Oh child, you can't be that stupid." I said nothing more as I turned from her and swam from the room. A guard was waiting for me in the hall, and he escorted me from the castle and out to the edge of the city. I hadn't put much thought into what Tynan meant by exile up to that point—for of course, it wouldn't happen—but I realized as soon as I reached the edge of the city what he'd meant. Exile didn't just mean banned from the castle, it meant from the entire city.

It took me a few months to set up shop right on the outskirts of town in a small hut. The merfolk seemed to flock to me, wanting to see the strangeness that was a cast out sea-witch, not that I'd complain; business was good. I was still saving in the vain hope that maybe Ace and I would get lucky enough to run away as we'd been dreaming. I had just seen off a client who'd wanted a love potion when a young boy carrying a message arrived. I took the note from him and headed back inside. Floating down onto the chaise in the middle of my office that was covered in books, I opened it. Inside was the neat scrawl of Aislin. My heart warmed at the mere sight of it, just knowing that she'd been thinking of me enough to send me a note. My heart dropped at the first line, "The king is dead." The prince had never asked me to do anything about the king, but with Aislin continuing to give him only mer-girls I supposed he would have to do something to become king. It made sense that Calypso would aid him in this, as it would put her in the position of having some power over Tynan.

Irsa,

I begin to wonder if this was Calypso's plan all along, to earn favor with Tynan, but I've said no such thing to him. Meanwhile, she's given me a new tonic to aid in my continued trials to produce an heir for Tynan. It tastes absolutely awful and leaves me feeling quite ill after.

Reading those words made my stomach twist. I had been trying very hard to keep Aislin healthy while trying to get her pregnant with a boy, and I knew Calypso would offer no such care. All I could hope was that the old sea-witch wasn't vengeful enough to try to hurt me through Ace.

I miss you very much, the only thing that seems to help is snuggles from the girls. I wish you could see them now—they're growing so quickly. Soon, they'll be chasing each other through the halls just as we used to back home. Love, Ace

Leaning back into the chaise lounge, I let out a little sob as I rubbed at my face. Great Poseidon, how I'd missed her too. I had been able to keep myself busy and avoid such thoughts until that moment, but now they all came crashing down on me. I swam to my desk to write back, immediately. I did my best to express how much I missed her as well and hoped that the girls would keep her company in my absence. I promised to pray every night to Poseidon that he would bless her with a boy. Above all else, I warned her to be careful of Calypso for she could not be trusted.

Time wore on, and Aislin was pregnant thrice more in my absence. Each time it seemed that she grew sicker and sicker throughout the pregnancy. Each time she had another healthy baby girl. So with each healthy baby girl, Aislin lost more and more of herself and fell more and more in love with her daughters. She didn't say as much in her letters, but I could almost feel her growing weaker, leaving me with an ache for Aislin like never before.

In my next letter, I begged her not to try again. I promised that we would find another way. Perhaps we could convince Tynan to take on a mistress, and she would provide him with a male heir so that all of this could finally be put behind us. We would take the girls and leave, there had to be a way—the prince had no need for the girls. Ace would hear none of it, and she was going to try one more time before we had to think up another plan. I did not receive another letter from Aislin ever again. For that seventh birth was worse than all of the others combined, I could feel the stress through our bond, and then came the searing pain. I didn't have to be told what happened on the street the following morning; I already knew. For the moment Aislin had died, I felt the bond between us sever, and something in me died along with her. As I reached for my magic, I found that it had changed. That soft glowing warmth—which had always lived inside of me—had faded along with Aislin leaving the magic feeling colder and darker somehow. From that coldness, a dark and twisted rage grew. I knew exactly who was to blame for the loss of my Ace, and I would punish each and every one of them. Starting with Calypso. She would be the easiest to get to, as she was still spending much of her time in the manor of Trysil, and I had already proven on numerous occasions that I could break through her wards. So, on one particular evening, I snuck into the manor and made my way to her room. Once I reached that room and saw her sleeping, I realized that killing Calypso would not be enough. I'd have to do more. I had to keep her alive, but separate her from something she loved just as she'd separated me from Aislin forever. I gathered up all of the magic I had within myself and ripped her magic from her in a quick jerk that left her screaming in her sleep. I was gone before she could waken—the vibrant glow of her magic bobbing in a little vial at my side. The spell left me drained and tired, so I retreated once more to my little hut on the outskirts of the city. There I could regain my strength and plot my revenge.

To this day, I remain living on the outskirts—watching over her little mermaids and protecting my last living connection to Aislin, all the while trying to keep the darkness of my magic at bay as the loneliness and heartbreak of losing Ace threatened to swallow my magic and me whole.

One day the girls and I would have our revenge, we just had to bide our time.

ABOUT LOU WILHAM

Born and raised in a small town near the Chesapeake Bay, Lou Wilham grew up on a steady diet of fiction, arts and crafts, and Old Bay. After years of absorbing everything there was to absorb of fiction, fantasy, and sci-fi, she's left with a serious writing/drawing habit that just won't quit. These days, she spends much of her time writing, drawing, and chasing a very short Basset Hound named Sherlock.

When not, daydreaming up new characters to write and draw she can be found crocheting, making cute bookmarks, and binge watching whatever happens to catch her eye.

CONNECT ON SOCIAL MEDIA

louinprogress.com

facebook.com/LouWilham

instagram.com/lou.wilham

by Jalessa Bettis

The state of mind willing to take everything and bend it for control of another is a mind ready to open oneself to a mental state that is all-encompassing. If a willing spirit is all which is needed for such a state, what holds one back from reaching this?

Frowning, Cletus tossed his quill onto the recently written parchment. Theory reading was, at best, entertaining and, at worst, aggravating. Cletus only read such books to keep up with the scholars of the court. The old men who could not forget about their younger years and thought they were right because they lived so long. In truth, he could care less about what they thought, how they felt, or what they really wanted. The only thing he was really bothered about was his magical studies— which were going to lead him into becoming a very great sorcerer one day.

He wasn't trying to become the greatest or world renown. Like most magicians, he was very much used to his own company. Yet, Cletus was aware of the trouble he brought on himself by staying in his tower instead of trying to be public. Was it wrong that he was aware of the dangers of seeking the attention of the crowd or to know how much more laborious it would be to keeping his own company?

Picking up the quill, Cletus stared at the splattered ink spots left behind. Ezra would have a comment to say about the waste of the ink. His tongue ran against his teeth at the unbidden thought while his attention returned to the words instead of the ink spots.

A great deal of responsibility came with the magic he was willing to perform, and Cletus was smart enough not to take on more than what he could handle, if only to avoid having to deal with people more than necessary.

"And here I thought I would find you mixing some kind of concoction that could be smelled in this part of the castle for days Cletus."

"Not all my potions smell," he complained instantly before remembering whom he was speaking to and didn't even bother trying to finish the words. Ezra would ignore them because it mattered little to him. Clearing his throat and setting the quill to the side on a handkerchief, Cletus asked, looking at the other young man, "What do you want, Your Highness?"

The speaker—Ezra— the Prince Heir of the small kingdom Zif, flashed him a grin, taking the question as an invitation to approach the table. The corners of Cletus' mouth dipped at the sight of that easy-going smile.

As indebted as he was to him for taking a chance on him when his parents were killed in that highway robbery when he had been thirteen, Cletus disliked being around those with more power than he. Although, magically speaking, no one matched him, but being in court was a different matter. In that sense, he had some abilities as a Baron, but being the only royal companion, Ezra never bothered to officially name made things more entertaining when it came to gossip and why he had a harder time keeping to himself.

"What have you been reading to put you in a foul mood, my friend?" Ezra asked.

Cletus cracked his knuckles before answering. Eyes returning to the pages as if the words were going to read themselves aloud to him. "I am in the middle of a debate, and the direction the topic has taken leaves me with a headache."

With a little nod of his head, either in agreement or some other reason, Ezra held out a hand. "May I take a look?" Without a word, Cletus closed the book and handed it over.

With the book in hand, Cletus watched Ezra first look over the cover before opening to the first official pages. Being a much slower reader than he was, Cletus pushed the stool he had been sitting on back and rises, intending to clear the table of the books he had been using for preparation of his late-night debate.

The second floor of his single tower doubled as a lab, and a library with protection spells in place to protect the books. Making two trips to the shelf covered walls; the books were slid back into place before papers he had been writing on were separated into two piles. One pile was put into a folder to be viewed later. The other collection would be burned. However, upon seeing Ezra focused on the book, Cletus crossed to his fireplace with them in hand. Grabbing the poker, he stoked the fire and added another log to build the flames up. Once it was hot enough, he began feeding it the papers, one at a time.

"Even if this book is an interesting study, it is not good enough for you to look as if you haven't slept in two days, Cletus."

Facing the fire, Cletus swore mentally, his jaw tight against letting any of the words become vocal; ceasing the action of throwing the papers to be burned. Ezra was very insistent on the cleanness of the spirit and body. The closest Ezra ever really got to being able to preach about Godly teachings within Cletus' hearing without having to drag him before the priest. For this reason, Cletus never told him about the few times he mixed in lessons of the darker magic's.

"As much as you love your debates, they aren't enough to keep you locked up studying in this tower for two full days. What have you been up to this time?" Ezra continued, thoughtfully asking.

Cletus did not want to answer that question. "Perhaps not this time no, but does it really matter as long as it is not a week?"

"When it comes to you, it always matters, but I am glad you continue to take the King's decree seriously." Cletus could hear the cheer in Ezra's voice. What about his comment had put a smile on Ezra's face?

"Fine. You win. What are you here to ask of me, Your Highness?" Cletus asked, turning to face Ezra, his back to the fire. His face wouldn't be hidden. The windows were uncovered, and there were candles lit.

"Don't get all formal on me, we are alone, and I have done nothing to annoy you, my prickly friend. I have come with good news. The two lovely ladies of our youth, Davita DeCandia, and Chanah Luecht have returned, and when you come down for the weekly ball, you'll have some explaining to do to the both of them." For the first time since being bothered, Cletus grinned at Ezra's announcement.

The DeCandia and Luecht families shared neighboring lands, and, as such, the children had grown up together. When both ladies had reached the age of fourteen, they had been sent to the castle court to get the attention of a wealthy husband in need of a young wife. The idea was to have the possible husbands see them blossom into beauties over time until they would be formally introduced. Depending on who was asked regarding this decision heavily relied on the sort of answer one got, but in the last two years, neither lady had ever been formally spoken for. Cletus had an idea about Chanah's interests thanks to their relationship, but his attention was always for Davita—who refused even to think he was serious about marrying her. She belonged to him and she just wanted nothing to do with the topic.

For all her boldness in coming to his tower late at night, unchaperoned, and making sure she never took a step out of line in public, Cletus would not have thought Davita would keep making him put off the topic of speaking to her parents.

The reminder of Davita's stubbornness killed the grin, causing his lips to twist in distaste. "When did they return?" he asked.

Suddenly, as if he had said something wrong, Ezra seemed to find the cover of the book very interesting to look at. Cletus' expression shifted to contempt—mouth thinning into a straight line and a single eye narrowing as a brow lifted in question.

People really did have to learn better ways of breaking bad news—if this could be considered bad news. The ladies had to have recently returned, which would make their arrival either two days ago or yesterday since he would have heard about their appearance before then. Cletus had no idea what could possibly make Ezra not want to look him in the eye, but it had to be pretty big. With an exhale to show his exasperation, Cletus turned to the fire to stoke the flames so that he could toss in the rest of the unneeded papers.

"I know I should have come and gotten you as soon as the carriage had been spotted, but—"

Cletus tossed in one sheet before looking back to see what Ezra was going to say. He did not expect to find Ezra seated, his hands curved over his mouth as if he were about to bite his nails, looking down at the table.

"Ezra?"

Ezra lifted his eyes to him before letting the hand drop from his mouth to the table surface. Folding his arms, Cletus watched him lean against them as if he wanted to hug himself, but wouldn't allow it. A crooked smile settled in the corner of Ezra's mouth, letting Cletus know this was a false attempt of humor. He tossed another sheet of paper into the fire.

"It is not like you to be uncomfortable speaking to me regardless if it is truth or a lie." Cletus points out, watching the paper burn completely before adding another. "You're the one who is the public speaker after all."

"Yeah, you're right, I apologize. I just know how you are when it comes to the girls, but they arrived two days ago. In fact, I'm just as guilty as you in missing their arrival as I was in the middle of an important alliance—I might be making an official engagement."

Cletus' head turned towards Ezra as soon as the words registered. His eyes widened, lips parting as if it were going to fall open before he gained control and closed it with a jerk of his head. As a prince, Ezra would marry, it was guaranteed. Being the heir to the throne made that guarantee more of a question of when such a wedding would take place. In truth, Cletus thought the talks would happen closer to Ezra's eighteenth birthday than before it.

Ezra must have read some of his thoughts on his face. Very quietly, he says, "You knew this was going to happen, Cletus."

Now rolling his eyes to the ceiling, Cletus tossed the last two sheets into the fire. Not bothering to watch them, he turned his entire body to Ezra. "Of course, I knew that. Since Prince Nathan's death, I have known you would have to fill his role and that includes marrying a woman who would be the next Queen. I— I just thought you would be given more time."

Ezra made a despairing sound that seemed to come from his nose, getting up from the stool. "You don't think four years is long enough to prepare?" Cletus considered Ezra for the space of two inhales and exhales of air. Using the moment to realize they were too close to a still touchy subject.

"Who is going to be the future Princess Consort?"

"Later," Ezra announced, straightening his spine and lifting his chin, putting a command in the word. "I did not come up here to speak of her just yet. I came to get you and make sure you don't miss the return of the ladies and the weekly ball. Make sure to come to my room. I won't have you creeping in where no one will notice you."

The corner of Cletus' mouth twitched as if he wanted to smile. He would do just as Ezra suggested.

"As you wish."

When the sun began to change colors and set, Cletus went up to the third floor, where his bedroom was located. Going into his wardrobe cabinet, he picked his favorite two-piece attire colored in a dark shade of amber and ruby. Tying his auburn hair back into a ball at the nape of his neck, Cletus left his room to go meet Ezra as requested before going to the ballroom.

Making it to the suite in short order, Cletus found the doors unguarded. He wondered if the guards were on a shift change. For a second, Cletus briefly wondered if he should check for danger or assume Ezra sent them away. Deciding to play it safe, he knocked on the door once, paused then knocked a second time a little louder, just in case the entrance to the bedroom was closed.

Just as he was beginning to rock on his heels, the door was opened, revealing Jonah, Ezra's manservant. On seeing him, Jonah opened the door wider to let him in.

"Where are the guards?" he asked, stepping into the room, heading straight for the couch.

"They should be heading back now. I know how much you love having them around me at all times." Ezra called out from the other opened door in the room. With a brief glance at the ceiling, asking for patience, Cletus took a seat throwing both of his arms across the back of the couch.

"You know, they are there for your protection right?"

Instead of responding, Ezra steps out of his room looking every inch the Prince Heir. The change was remarkable as Ezra always wore gray and purple with no jewelry to confirm his status within the court.

"What do you say, Jonah? Who has dressed better tonight?" Ezra asked the older man with an affectionate smile.

"I would say both you and the Baron are out to make an impression tonight, Your Highness," the manservant says.

Cletus snorts, crossing his arms across his chest. He knew an evasive answer when he heard one. "You are playing it safe. You know that will not work with me."

Jonah bowed to the both of them before going back into Ezra's room, as if the attention of the both of them was too much to handle. Cletus watched in silence. Ezra *tsked* as if this were a tragic thing.

"Now look at what you did. You know Jonah dislikes being the center of attention!"

Cletus pointed at himself in question before twisting his lips and looking away. He had not been the one who first posed the question.

"So, have you prepared some entertainment for us this week?"

"Can I make a few people disappear?" he asked immediately.

"No."

"Can I make them unable to speak?"

"No." This time the word was drawn out as if Ezra were considering the thought—his smile looking almost crooked from the way he cocked his head to the side.

"Can I turn them into rodents?"

"You mastered that spell?" All the humor from Ezra disappeared at the question. Crossing the room, Ezra came to stand in front of Cletus, looking him right in the eye, as if he hoped to catch him in a lie, waiting for an answer. Cletus didn't squirm under the sudden scrutiny, but he did not have an immediate response to the question because he did not want to give one. "I'm not sure how to take you wanting to do physical harm to members of my court as entertainment, Cletus."

"You know I would not harm anyone who has not given me cause to do harm in return."

"Yet every suggestion you have made is a way to harm others. The entire court could not have possibly harmed you in some way."

"Clearly, then I am not going to be this evening's entertainment." Cletus' tone was as dry as leaves in the autumn.

Ezra threw his head back to look at his ceiling, jaw moving as he was grinding his teeth, hands coming to rest at his hips. "What am I to do with you? It is almost as if I am speaking to a completely different person at times."

Cletus did not know what to say. What could he do to convince Ezra that he hadn't changed, when he knew he had. It would be impossible to stay the same child who had become a ward of the court after being the only known survivor in a highway robbery gone wrong, mainly since he was no longer a child. He had to grow up—they all had.

Ezra lowered his head and dropped his arms with a heavy sigh. "For my sake, try to control that temper of yours. Now let's go." Turning away from him, Ezra went to the doors to open them.

Two guards snapped to attention. Only giving them a cursory glance, Ezra walked out into the hallway. Cletus stepped out of the room behind him, getting a more extended look at their faces before catching up to Ezra— who headed for the ballroom.

The weekly balls were not like the grand affairs given around holidays, royal birthdays or visiting dignitaries the royal family wanted to impress. They were like little treats given to keep things lively when the court could get weighed down by politics, gossip, and scandal. Everyone gathered in the dining hall to eat dinner, why not have a little dancing before and after in the ballroom?

With an absent-minded pat to the shoulder after greeting the King and Queen, Cletus left Ezra's side, allowing others to draw close to the Heir, either hoping to ask for a personal favor or merely seeking to catch his eye for the evening. Ezra needed no matchmaker for this sort of thing, not if he was nearly engaged.

With his mind only on one person, Cletus weaved through the crowds and around small groups, grass-green eyes sweeping the room— looking for the natural blonde curls of Davita DeCandia.

"It has been a long time, my lord Cletus von Rothbart." A silvery voice called out to him from behind.

Cletus had not planned on meeting Chanah Luecht first tonight— that honor had been for Davita— but the other woman was nowhere he could see. Beginning to feel aggravated, he barely remembered to place a smile on his face and loosen his shoulders, as he turned entirely to the petite, raven-haired woman.

"Formality, from you, Chanah? You have been gone for six months, not six years; you were the one who did not want titles between us…now you use them?"

The lady, who was not only his lover's best friend but also an aspiring sorceress, gave a twinkling laugh that did not get swallowed by the noise of the room. "Perhaps, I wanted to get your attention in a way you did not expect? You are looking for Davita?" she asked, holding out a hand to him.

His reply was to laugh a bit and take her offered hand to kiss. As he did so, he noted the dangling dance card on it. If he could have gotten away with frowning disapproval at her in such a crowd, he would have. She knew he hated to dance because he disliked the attention.

"Chanah..." he warned, not looking up from her hand, but he knew she heard him.

"Just for tonight, Cletus, please, and you will not get the request again from me." Her voice dropped even lower, yet he was still able to hear her. She was using a spell. He straightened and let go of her hand. She did not let it fall to her side. "I thought things would be a little different if I went away as I had, but nothing has changed. The men of the court still believe me to be too pale. How am I to find a husband if no one will even bother to dance with me?"

They have had this conversation before, but no solution had been found. Finally, Cletus took pity on her and slipped the band off her wrist. Taking the offered writing stick from her, Cletus signed his last name on the card twice before sliding it back into place. She smiled prettily at him before slipping around to take the arm he had not offered to her.

"Thank you. Now, if you are looking for Davita, I'm afraid you'll have to get in line. She's been very popular since arriving back," Chanah stated.

Something in her tone—jealousy, contempt, or anger—made Cletus give her his full attention. A flush, which did not become her, began to spread from her pale white cheeks down to her equally pale white neck. He could literally see her swallowing. It was almost as if he made her nervous, too.

"We have been here for two days with no appearance of you, Cletus. Most took it as a sign, thinking you were disinterested and began to try and court her."

In being tucked away out of sight, no one bothered to visit him and inform him of his lover's arrival. Interestingly, no one should have assumed him tired of her, not when Cletus never bothered to hide his protectiveness towards Davita when it came to other men. To keep others from noticing too much, Cletus kept Chanah around. He would have kept her around even if she wasn't his apprentice.

"So, she has been flirting as if I had tired of her. That sounds exactly like her," Cletus commented, dryly, leading Chanah closer to the walls of the room.

"I need to tell you something else. Davita's parents are coming to court."

Cletus did not think such words would make him genuinely smile, but they did. For that reason, he asked in one word. "When?" he asked, seeing Chanah's face had lost that horrible looking pink. Something in her features looked as if something had broken her heart.

"In three months they should be arriving. Davita admitted to me about wanting to be engaged by then or have the progress in the works."

Was she trying to make him work for her? The music changed

into the next piece. "Come, Chanah, I owe you a dance or two, and you owe me information."

"That sounds like a fair trade."

Later that night, a short hour or two after the party ended, Cletus sat out on the railing of his personal balcony tossing up magic into the air as if he were juggling balls. The only difference was the magic balls did not stay as balls in the air. Instead, they would pop and seem to give a little light show against the glow of the moon. All was silent. All was peaceful—only him and his thoughts. Or it *was* until four taps on the tower front door reached his ears.

If it were not for the spell to make even the softest tap sound thunderous against the thick wooden door, he would not have known anyone was there. On the other hand, if someone were to bang on the door as hard as they could, the sound would be nearly muted.

The only one who it could be at this time of night was the one woman who had avoided him all night. Closing his hand into a fist, Cletus rose from the railing, heading towards the door. Unlocking the locks the old fashioned way, he opened it just enough to peek and know it was exactly who he thought it was. The small blonde woman glided inside, barely missing getting the train of her dress caught when Cletus decided to slam the door closed.

"Cheri!" Even with her outright cry of shock and annoyance over his behavior, instead of turning on him, she whirled to check the train of her gown. She couldn't have been angry at him; she still called him by that nickname she thought was cute. In the time it took her to be sure nothing had been damaged, Cletus was able to see how she still looked as if she were ready for a ball. Satisfied her dress was all right, she whirled on him. "Is that any way to treat me after six months?"

He gave her a blank expression as if she should have known what would happen after avoiding him the way she had. "You stopped writing to me five months ago, neglected to inform me of your return, and then spent most of the night ignoring me." He pointed out, crossing his arms.

At his words, her face twisted as if she smelled something terrible. It was a face she only showed in private. Publicly she was the very picture of serenity. Usually, Cletus thought her very cute. There was just one little problem—he was not feeling very apologetic towards her.

"Is that why I haven't seen you for the last two days?" she coyly asked, lashes fluttering just enough to give the appearance of flirting. Her hands were drifting down the front of her dress from just under her breasts to her belly as if seeking to draw his attention to her body.

Well, two could play that game. Having not locked the door, Cletus proceeded to reopen that door and in a continuous motion, grabbed her upper arm and tossed her right back into the hallway. She knocked twice as soon as the door slammed in her face. Cletus did not move, standing there staring at the wood. As much as he cared about her, he would never let a woman rule him. Too many couples ended up giving one all the reins and that would not do.

The next time she knocked—the third time—Cletus opened the door wide enough for her to squeeze in. From her thinned lips, flaring nose and blazing eyes, Cletus knew he was drawing very close to angering her by his actions. Before she opened her mouth to say a single word, his own mouth covered hers as he grabbed her, spinning them both until he had her trapped against the door. Her hands pushed against his chest, a signal to tell him to back up. Cletus also took this to mean she did not want him so close to her.

He took two steps back. Feeling unbalanced from kissing Davita, Cletus closed his eyes to cool the desire that made him act rashly. When he opened them again, he felt more in control and was able to show his disapproval of her rejection. Yet, given her flushed cheeks, the way one of her hands rested against her abdomen, with fingers spread, and the quick rises of her chest, Cletus' disapproval shifted to smugness. This was why he wished she would agree to marry him. No other man would ever be as close to her as he was. Still, there was the matter of her actions earlier.

"Why have you come to my tower, Davita? If I am guilty of not bothering to learn you were here, you are just as guilty of not informing me of your presence. You clearly remember where I stay."

"Because we are friends."

"We are lovers, and that is the difference you keep forgetting about us," he corrected. There was no time for friends. The higher his power grew, even though he was young, the more projects he had. Besides, all friends did was keep you from focusing on what needed to be done in your life by drawing attention to their problems. Not even Ezra was a friend—despite their long history together.

Davita's face was half hidden in shadows created by candlelight, yet her blue eyes seemed to glow with that familiar passionate fire he had missed in the last six months. "We were friends first and always, Cheri." He could see she believed that. As if it were something she needed to believe in. "Lovers second."

He turned, going back to the balcony where he initially had been. This conversation was pointless. Davita's words dared him to speak of emotions he did not—and was unable—to feel. He could feel some emotions, just not all of them and to reveal the lack of what he did not have was to bring more attention than he needed.

Back outdoors in the moonlight, Cletus took his former seat on the railing. It took only a few minutes before Davita joined him, but instead of sitting, she came to stand in the middle of the balcony spreading her arms far enough apart to brace herself with her back to him. Seeing her silhouette in the moonlight made him want to touch her, to hold her close and ruin her hairstyle.

"At a time like this, a Gentleman offers a Lady a drink," she announced out into the open air, not looking at him.

"You are a Lady in name and training only, while I have never tried to be a Gentleman."

Her head fell back as she gazed at him out the corner of one eye with an impish grin. The effect would have had more reaction if her hair had been loose. The actual length was past her waist, and the sight of it was worth painting— if he could paint and if he could risk hanging such a painting around where it could possibly be seen. Just another reason for them to get married.

"I always wondered, Cheri, why are you still here— all alone in your corner, in your own little world, ignoring the court's many whispers about you?"

"You sent Chanah to keep me company," he said, as if this was the problem to everything between them.

The grin on her face vanished at the question while her body turned stiff as she looked away from him to the dark grounds below. Had he said something he was not supposed to? Folding his arms, he openly stared at her, willing her to turn around and tell him what was honestly going on.

"Cletus, take me to your bed," she finally said, turning only her head to him.

There was some hidden message in this— one Cletus was uninterested in uncovering. Raising one hand, he beckoned her closer with a finger. She did as requested, those eyes of hers blazing once again, only with desire this time. Once she was close enough, the same hand which called her over trailed down the front of her throat.

"Davita, I hate your games," was all he said.

"Cletus!"

There were only a handful of people who could get into his tower without needing the door opened for them. Chanah was one of them, but this was more from being his apprentice and Davita's friend than from the length of time they had known each other, so, her crying out his name did nothing more than make him glance up from the grimoire on his lap to the empty doorway. The problem presented itself when Chanah arrived. Cletus had been torn between wondering if there was some emergency and if he really wanted to be bothered before she appeared. Once she had, the very sight of her made him want to get to his feet in outrage and disgust. Only the fact that he held a priceless grimoire on his lap kept him seated.

With all her hair gathered on top of her head— her pale neck, shoulders, down to the swell of her breasts were exposed from the dramatic dip created by the top of her dark-colored dress. Cletus could not believe this was purposely done. There was so much of

Chanah's skin showing, all of it pale with no hint of color that Cletus could see the blue of her veins, and he could not stop staring. Chanah couldn't possibly think anything about this was attractive, could she?

"Cletus?"

He inhaled sharply, physically pushing backward to straighten his back, as if it were enough to make his eyes rise to her face. If anything, the action of doing so reminded him of the apple and dagger he held. Wetting his lower lip in what could be taken as a nervous gesture—although being nervous was the last thing he was feeling—Cletus set the half-peeled apple and dagger on a nearby plate.

"Cletus."

He looked at her, noticing how she was moving towards him with an expression that seemed confused and cautious. "Stop calling my name, Chanah, I heard you before you even came up the stairs," he grumbled, voice rougher than intended.

She paused, studying him, cautious now.

Cletus cleared his throat before asking, "New dress?"

Only training kept her from giving him a flat out rude look, but it was still a look only a stoic man would be unmoved by. He was aware of her displays of anger, but much like her friend, she could control them publicly.

"Yes, it is sort of a new dress, it is one I wouldn't dare wear to one of the balls, but Davita suggested I have it made." She looked down at herself, smoothing the fabric free of wrinkles with her hand. "What do you think?"

Davita, Cletus thought, *had done her no kindness in suggesting such a thing.* The dark sapphire color worked with her skin and ebony colored hair, but it only made her comfortable to look at— no color was added to her skin. Taking his feet down from the stool he used as a prop, he snorted dismissively.

"What I think is that it is a waste to wear here in my tower. You would be better off wearing it to one of the balls, then you wouldn't lack in dance partners, showing as much skin as you are. If you want a better opinion, you are better off asking Ezra."

"Ezra would not tell me the truth the way you would. He is a trained courtier." She came closer to the table.

"And I am not?"

Her dark eyes were cold as she assessed him. He closed the book on his lap, never taking his eyes from hers. Chanah looked away first, her throat moving as she swallowed. He closed the grimoire very carefully before rising from the table. She did not speak again until he was heading towards one of his shelves.

"What are you reading?"

"Transformation," he told her, stopping to gaze at her from the corner of his eyes. "How to safely transform the human body into an animal without having the body turning inside out when switching them back."

Ezra and Davita would have both asked him multiple questions, even if the likelihood of them understanding a word was not high. Chanah quietly waited at the table, watching him in utter stillness, waiting for what would happen next. Keeping eye contact, Cletus turned around and returned, going around the table so that it wasn't between them. As he drew closer to where she stood, Chanah's head began to tilt back to keep eye contact with him. Cletus handed the book to her. Taking it from his grasp, Chanah only continued to watch him, her chest rising and falling faster.

"Cletus, let's go out and experiment with this transformation spell. We can't do this spell here. The King would disapprove, not to mention the people whom would be the subjects of this project." Her words came out breathier than usual.

Cletus took that moment to consider what those words meant in silence. How unexpected he found the suggestion to leave when she had only returned. On the other hand, it was true—who would be upset if he practiced on the country folk or the wandering travelers? Who would miss them?

"Not a bad idea. One which would deserve some thought if my mind was not already made up. So my answer is no."

"Why, after how long we have worked together, do you not trust me as a partner?" she asked—no, demanded. Cletus laughed at such a claim. He would not have bothered to teach her what he knew if he hadn't had some trust in her. "Now, I feel as if you are teasing me, in the same way, those in court whisper about me."

He waved the comment away as if it were nothing to him. "I am not in a good enough mood to tease you." Bored at the turn of this conversation, Cletus went to one of his shelves and began looking around for another grimoire.

"Cletus!" she exclaimed, sounding exasperated. He ignored her; far more interested in finding what book came to mind. "Cletus, you didn't even act as if you had given the idea some thought."

"Because I did not need to think about it."

The slamming of a book against his table had him whirling around to see what she had done. With narrowed eyes and a straight mouth, he found Chanah breathing heavily, mouth partially opened, as that ugly color rose to the skin of her cheeks. His eyes drifted down to the swell of her breast, captivated by what was happening with every breath she took. With effort, his eyes went back up where he forced them to stay.

"You sorcerers are all the same." She sounded ready to hiss at him. Cletus wondered if she would dare, just like he wanted to ask what other sorcerers had she met.

"It is no concern of yours, but I don't need a partner in this, and in a month, I return to the Rothbart lands for my seasonal meeting with my steward." She did not say a single word to this announcement. "I trust that you will continue your studies while I am gone. The tower is at your disposal."

She seemed to stiffen at his offer. "Why would I come when I know you set traps?" She asked, turning on her heels and leaving before he could answer. A few minutes later, he knew she had left the tower. Cletus wondered for the first time if she might be more trouble than Davita.

True to his words, Cletus left the castle and the capital of Zif for the lands belonging to the Rothbart family, on what most thought to be an excellent four-day horseback ride. In the time it had taken him to pack and tell others of his plans for leaving— Davita continued to come to his tower at night, but their conversations slowly dwindled away to barely anything. Cletus wanted Davita to agree to his proposal and Davita— for reasons she never spoke of, no matter how much he asked— kept refusing him and insisted on encouraging the other noblemen. It had begun to become a problem. Then there was Chanah, who would appear during the day for lessons and be helpful in anything he wanted to do. At some point, on seeing them, Ezra had remarked how well they worked together— a fact Cletus dismissed as Chanah was not the one he lusted for.

She did not speak of going with him to his estates nor did she say what she would be doing while he was gone. Instead, she had taken to staring at him in curious silence at random moments of the day, almost as if she wanted to ask him what he was doing, but knew she would get no answer, something Cletus could deal with as he did not want to explain anything because there was a secret he hid on the lands, the sort of mystery that worked best when it wasn't shared with others.

Cletus arrived at the stables of the manor right when the sky was growing dark from the threat of rain. The head groomsman came out from somewhere and patted his horse before greeting Cletus. Cletus tossed him the bridle before getting smoothly off the horse he deemed as his favorite of the stock housed at the castle. Patting the side of the beast, he left instructions before getting his travel bags and heading up to the manor doors. The rain hadn't broken through the clouds just yet and continued to hold off until reaching his bedroom. Almost as soon as he dropped his things, he was greeted with a sound similar to water being poured out from a bucket. Crossing over to the large windows, he threw back the drapes to see.

A discreet knock came from the room door. "Enter!" Cletus called out not leaving the window. The door creaked softly before the familiar voice of his manservant cleared his throat.

"The flock will be arriving soon, my lord, did you wish to speak to them?"

"No, no, I will visit them tomorrow." Distracted by the rain, Cletus' words were almost drawn out. Listening to the rain was a great way to meditate. "Let them enjoy one evening without my presence being felt. You do allow them a cover of protection for this sort of weather correct? The last thing needed is for any of them to become sick."

"Yes, my lord."

"Good, then I will see them tomorrow evening. When my dinner is ready, send it up."

"Mister Huff will expect to see you at the table." His manservant stated diplomatically.

Cletus made a rude sound before letting the drapes go and turning to his manservant. He could not wait until he reached his majority. Then he would not have to answer to the steward appointed to watch over his lands and fortune by the King. At least the man never had anything to say about his decisions when it came to the punishments.

"Fine, bring water so I can wash and get the smell of horse off me."

The manservant bowed in agreement and left to do as told. Cletus exhaled loudly, irritated he would not have the night to himself. There was no keeping to himself until he was aware of all the affairs from his last visit— precisely three months ago.

An hour later, refreshed and in new clothing, Cletus went down to the small dining room where he was greeted by the steward, his wife, and children—a son around his age and a daughter only recently old enough to leave the nursery.

"Young Lord Cletus, how wonderful it is to see you!" Mister Huff announced in a happy tone as if they were in a room full of noisy people.

Cletus didn't wince, but only barely avoided doing so. The man was merely so happy and even-tempered that it was like finding the sun in your eyes when one could have sworn they were in the shade. For Mister Huff's benefit, Cletus gave a polite smile, heading over to shake the man's hand in greeting before moving down the line. Once this was done, they all entered the room to take their seats where the servants were waiting to begin.

"Well, Cletus, how goes things at court? Anything new to report that has not made it into the monthly newsletters sent out? Any new gossip?" Mistress Huff asked as soon as they were alone at the table.

"Nothing much, I believe the King is waiting for Prince Ezra to make an official announcement about his betrothal," he answers, not caring if this news was supposed to be a secret or not. Ezra had never given him the name of the lucky noblewoman.

"Betrothal!" Both the steward and his wife cried out.

Thankfully, when they both began pestering him for more information, Cletus had to spread his hands and shrug his shoulders after answering as many questions as he could. Once they saw he really didn't know much of anything, they settled down to return to their meal. A different topic was introduced after that between him and the Huffs.

"Cletus, did you know there is a nest of swans living at the lake?" the daughter, Ellette, asked him around dessert.

Cletus swirled the liquid around in the cup he held, smiling a bit at the question saying, "Yes, swans have always had a fondness of the lake here. My father says that is why the swan is in the family crest, but not in the family name. It is also why locals call it Swain Lake."

"I always did think that was a fitting name, especially when the current flock seemed to settle there almost— how long has it been? Two years?" Mistress Huff asked.

"Give or take," her husband muttered, looking oddly uncomfortable.

"Yes—yes, instead of migrating as most of those birds do," Mistress Huff says delighted.

"Yes, and that is why no one is allowed to hunt them," Cletus added, putting his cup to his lips.

The next morning, after breakfast, Cletus met with Mister Huff to get a review of all reports and records of the last three months. This was possibly the most tedious part of his visit because it was not as if anything exciting happened within the last three months. If anything, the whole point of this meeting was to make sure Cletus was aware of what things looked like normally so he could spot something unusual when it did happen.

By the time the sun began to set, Cletus was more than ready to get out of the office, and for once, out of the manor altogether. At the same time, there was something more important which had to be done, something that Mister Huff joined him for later once Mistress Huff and the children had been sent to their rooms for the night.

Needing horses, Cletus sent word ahead, and upon their arrival, mounted up and rode for Swain Lake, about an hour ride from the manor. Once they arrived, Cletus took the lead through the densely wooded area until the lake was before him, and there, floating on the surface were five swans swimming close to the shoreline. High overhead, the moon was coming out, shining its reflection and light on the swans. As one, they all raised their head as the water began to glow beneath them before shooting up to encase them in light. When the light faded, three women and two boys stood on the edges of the lake dressed in black and white, wearing a silver mask.

Cletus was impressed, as he was always, at the creation of his spell. He gave a clap of applause, drawing their attention as they were getting out of the water.

"Well done. Well done. It looks as if you have settled into your new life quite easily, Melody Warrick. I am sorry I missed watching the transition. Or maybe that was for the best." Cletus says, speaking to one of the smaller women, but with rusty brown hair. The other two were blonde.

Melody Warrick was his newest swan. Her crimes had been so troubling that none of the locals had wanted to decide her fate. Instead, they had taken her before his steward, who had her thrown into the dungeon for the locals to forget about her. When Cletus arrived a month later, he gave her the gift of a silver mask, telling her that wearing it would give her wings and she would be free of her charges.

"*You*! What must I do to be free of this curse?" She spat, stepping towards him, only to be held back by the others.

"Free of the curse? What curse is it that you speak of? I did not curse you. I only gave you a mask. You are the one who put it on." He told her mildly, a mock frown playing at the corner of his mouth.

No one knew it, but due to the nature of what he was trying to do, he had gotten creative with the transformation spell, and the key was the silver mask that covered the upper half of the face.

"You said...you said...you said I would be able to fly!"

Things might be omitted, but no lie has been told. Cletus's brows rose as he studied the girl, pointing out, "And so you have been able to do."

"Enough, Melody, stop trying to reason with the young lord. We are under his control, and as he has said, and as we have told you before, you are the one who put the mask on," One of the other women, Lynda Klein, says not looking at him.

The fight went out of his newest swan. Cletus' grin was cold and calculating as he applauded this too.

"Well, I have come to see what needed to be seen, good night to you all," he told them all as if they were all about to sleep. They wouldn't, being entirely nocturnal at this point, but it was polite.

Silently, Mister Huff and Cletus returned to their horses and back to the manor without a word said between them.

"Mister Huff," Cletus called after the very somber man. Mister Huff stopped and looked at him. "Is there anyone who would like a mask as a gift?"

"No... Not this time."

Cletus wished him a good night.

True to his Steward's word, nothing happened in the time Cletus was there at the estates. There were minor things here and there, but nothing which called on him to make any call of judgment. It was almost as if he were enjoying a little holiday from everything he usually did. Not directly a bad thing, if he had been older than he was. His age was one of the reasons why he did not return to the lands any more than four times in a year, because while he did have the title of Lord and Baron, all of it was name only.

As it happens, once Cletus was caught up in everything, and with nothing else to do, he began practicing the spell for reversing a transformation. He had no intentions of freeing his swans, but he instead thought it would be fun to see if he could turn into a bird of some sort and use wings as a form of transportation. With that plan in mind, Cletus often went out alone into the woods where no one could see him, doing so until it was time to return to the castle. No one asked what he was doing.

Five days before his return, Chanah reached out to him by water scrying. At the time, Cletus had been taking a break by washing in one of the nearby streams, but all Chanah saw was him standing before her wearing only his trousers. Her screech startled him enough to jump and send water flying.

"Chanah..." He got out once he was able to wipe his face and get his wet hair out the way. "Thanks, my clothes are wet now."

"Sorry, Cletus," she told him, yet she did not look very sorry. Instead, she looked as if she wanted to laugh. "It must be a hot day."

His lips twitched in disapproval before letting it go. Grabbing his hair, he took a seat on a stone to twist the water out. What point was there in getting mad? She could not have known he would be out. Back at the castle, he rarely went outdoors on his own.

"Why are you scrying from water?" he asked instead of commenting on the weather.

"You don't have your hand mirror on you."

Cletus grunted, realizing she was right. He had left it packed away in his room. Now that he thought about it, Cletus could not remember if he had done that on purpose or honestly had forgotten to unpack it. Letting go of his hair, he whipped his head back to have it out of the way.

"What do you want?"

She seemed taken back by the direct question. *Perhaps expecting to do more small talk before getting to the point,* Cletus thought, his attention on the spell.

"I just wanted to say that I missed you and I'm working on the transformation spell, too."

Cletus' tongue ran across his teeth as he looked away from Chanah's image to the surrounding trees. The best and politest thing would be to tell her he was not interested in her, but that was the thing, Chanah wouldn't listen to him.

"Davita— "

"Wants nothing to do with you." She cut him off quick.

Now it was Cletus' turn to look at her sharply as if she had said something completely out of character. If she had not stated it so matter-of-factly, Cletus would have continued to stare out at the trees, disinterested in the conversation. He had no time for what Chanah wanted and what he had no intentions of giving.

"She does not want you," Chanah repeated, "Not in the way you want her. Don't lie and try and tell me she does. She is my best friend. I have known her forever. Let her become someone else's problem, Cletus."

Tucking one foot under his bent knee, Cletus rested his arm on the bent leg, staring down at the watery image. His nostrils flared at the implied thought of him making verbal lies. Cletus' expression was grave as she spoke.

"And what of you? Do you hope to take her place, Chanah?" he mocked, a sneer appearing on his lips at the sight of the ugly shade of red on Chanah's cheeks. Nothing would ever make him like how she looked when she blushed—any emotion strong enough to make it appear was terrible. Blushing of any kind was not a good look for her. "Davita and I have the sort of relationship which does not need to be explained to others."

"I never took you for a fool," she told him. Her jaw was moving as if she wanted to grind her teeth. So, she hadn't been embarrassed, but upset.

Cletus got to his feet, jumping into the stream. Rage was overtaking him enough that he could not remain seated. Her image was distorted thanks to the splash, but she stayed connected.

"Enough! Forget your daydreams of me, Chanah. We are a teacher and student—partners only in magic and nothing else. Take it or take nothing."

She said nothing for a long moment, watching him as carefully as he watched her. Finally, Chanah closed her eyes, and her image disappeared from the water. Cletus stood there in the stream, eyes blazing at the moving water. His breathing accelerated the longer he stood there until he kicked out, sending water flying everywhere.

At the end of the planned fortnight, Cletus rode his horse the four-day journey back towards the capital of Fir. After making it on the grounds and leaving his horse in the care of the stable, Cletus entered the castle to be instantly greeted by Ezra.

"There you are. I was sure you slowed your horse down even more, making me impatient for your return."

"Careful, some of the spies might get the wrong idea about our relationship." Cletus pointed out, voice a little sluggish from the long ride.

Ezra waved this comment away as if he were shooing flies from his face. Stepping over to him, Ezra looked him up and down before saying, "Come with me. I have news, and it will not wait." Ezra stepped around him and walked right back outside.

If he had known how to do the emotion, Cletus would have groaned in complaint. It was two hours until dinner, and he wanted to rest a bit before then. Turning on his heels, he went after Ezra, who patted him on the back once he caught up.

"Stop frowning; you'll like my news. I wanted you to know before everyone else."

Both of Cletus' brows went up at this announcement, but instead of saying more, Ezra led the way toward the garden. When it looked as if they were in a spot where no one could sneak up on them, Ezra turned on Cletus with the reserved expression used for royal duties.

"Remember how I did not answer you when you asked who I was interested in making a marriage contract with? The reason I did not explain was because I had not been sure of her. More than anything, I needed to be sure she would not only make me a good wife, but she would be an incredible princess and a remarkable future Queen."

"With those qualities in mind, I would understand why you would take your time before the contract has been signed," Cletus replied carefully.

What noblewoman had Ezra found to fit? Cletus hadn't seen Ezra spend any extended period of time with any particular nobleman's daughter.

"Right, and she was right there, under my nose the whole time, Cletus, and all it took was a letter. Now she is to be my wife, my princess and my future Queen."

Cletus' gaze was dubious, but Ezra laughed good-naturedly, not the least bit bothered. It appeared that Ezra could not hold a serious expression when he was happy.

"Alright, what is her name?" Cletus asked, beginning to feel as if Ezra would not get to the point of this conversation.

Ezra grinned and said, "Davita DeCandia."

Later in the evening, Cletus stood in the doorway to his balcony with his hands behind his back. After the announcement, he had said and done something to show his approval to Ezra. Now was not the time to tell Ezra the truth. *Now was not the time to do anything at all,* Cletus had decided as Ezra told the tale of how he began writing Davita, but had misgivings at first.

"I knew you tended to be protective of her." Ezra had told him. *"I had even thought at one time you wanted to court her for marriage. Even when the both of us had joked about how their parents had sent the girls to court like prized bulls."*

As it happens, Chanah was the one who had asked Ezra to write to Davita, thinking he would help. To Cletus' horror and growing rage, before they left, Chanah mentioned how Lord DeCandia had an idea of marrying Davita to a man twice her age. The Lord would hold off such an idea if there were a possibility that the heir to the throne was interested in marriage. The Lord DeCandia wouldn't bat an eye if

Cletus were the one to write. Despite the logic, Cletus was not happy with Chanah.

"It was supposed to be a joke, you see. Nothing was to come of it because people don't fall in love over written words and nothing about Davita had interested me before. And again, there was you, but for all your attentiveness towards her, you never once acted like a man who was...in love."

If he had been able to do anything, Cletus would have punched a wall at hearing those words. Of course, he had never acted like he was in love! Cletus wasn't in love with Davita, nor did he love her at all. Yes, he did care about her, but the way he cared was the same way a man would care for his prized possessions. Cletus felt more lust for Davita. He wanted to own her, to possess her. Love had little to do with their relationship. Out of respect for their friendship, Cletus had held his tongue, choosing to listen to Ezra instead of speaking.

"Yet it happened, I found myself looking forward to her letters or her little notes. I don't know what changed. I look back at the letters and can't begin to tell you."

Ezra had wanted to tell Cletus earlier—both for an opinion and to see if something had been going on between Davita and Cletus. Instead, the Queen had stepped in and told Ezra to wait for Davita's return before saying anything, to anyone, and he had listened. This piece of news answered the question of why neither one of them had come to his tower for those first two days. The vague answers given then, now made sense.

As mad as he was at Ezra, the one Cletus blamed was Davita. She had known exactly how he felt and what he wanted from her from the very beginning. Cletus had never told her anything less than the truth. Why she never agreed with him, Cletus never learned, but if she really had not, why had she kept coming back to him? Cletus remembered how Davita had said they were friends.

She would pay.

Davita would come to him. She always did.

Moving away from the open doorway, Cletus began climbing the stairs to his third floor bedroom when the tapping came to the tower door. Pausing, Cletus turned back, trying to decide if he wanted to answer it before going to the door.

Davita stood there, hands clasped before her, looking very calm. Her serenity did nothing for his temper, his eyes coming down to narrow slits.

"Ezra told me he spoke to you. He had been waiting for you to return." Her voice had begun strong but had slowly become uncertain at the end.

Leaning a hip against the edge of the door, Cletus could feel his lips twist into something, not quite a smile. Given the way she seemed to lose some of her strong will, he was betting it was not an expression she was used to seeing on him.

"He did; caught me at one of the many doors leading inside. Did you expect me to hide in my room and sulk upon hearing the fantastic news, Davita? *To the point of missing dinner!* No, I had to be there. What sort of *scandal* would it have made if I had not shown up?"

Davita's face lost some of its color from the implied threat. Getting off the door, Cletus swept his arm out in a grand gesture for her to enter. Davita did not move. Cletus' head tilted up just an inch before coming back down. Dropping his arm, he took a step towards where she stood. She might have been strong standing there, but with that single step, she lost that bravado and stepped back. Cletus stopped, a low laugh coming from his throat.

"Are you scared of me, Davita?" He whispered, voice full of menace. Cletus liked the idea. Davita only scoffed, turning her head as if the very idea was ridiculous.

"Of you? Never!" She stated, gathering her strength in her spine and storming into his tower.

Cletus let her come in, watching as she stopped in the middle of the room and swirled around to face him. Making a dismissive sound, Cletus closed the door.

"I was never going to marry you," she began.

Cletus raised his head a fraction once more, this time to acknowledge hearing her words. No other body part moved. "You don't like me—you don't like anyone—you only want to possess me. How could I marry someone like that?"

"That is true, I don't like many people I come in contact with, but you, I like you just fine, Davita. I never once said I didn't like you. I said we were not friends." Cletus pointed out, his voice was dangerously low.

"One cannot like someone without being friends or be friends without liking someone," Davita countered, not hearing the warning.

"We are lovers, not friends."

"We are friends who were once lovers, but have returned to being friends."

There was an edge of possible hysteria to her words, almost as if she needed to believe them. Cletus' lips peeled back to show his teeth at that remark. He had no idea who would accept such a lie? This was all some sort of messed up game in her head.

"You don't believe that," Cletus announced, not bothering to hide his frustration from his eyes and voice. "I know you don't. Do you know why, Davita? Because when you returned to the castle, on your third night back, you came to this tower—to me—even though you had gotten Ezra to fall in love with you. I offered you marriage because I see what you try to deny every time." He went to her. Step by step, giving her the chance to back up.

Her bravery held fast, and she only moved her head back as he stepped closer. His voice changed to a seductive coo. "The fact is, I own you and the reason why I own you is because you come back to me...every...single...time." Cletus stopped directly in front of her. Her blue eyes blazed with anger and defiance.

"I left!" She shouted.

Cletus' voice hardened in anger once again. "Because of your parents! But you know as well as I that you have come back to this tower every night, like most nights, to get in my bed since you have returned. You come to this tower in clothes easy to discard, late enough in the night that only the guards could possibly see you if they so wished."

"I have always known what I needed. I have always known what I wanted. You don't fit either one of those categories."

Cletus laughed then, a laugh that came up from his belly, and hurt to release aloud and brought the provider no relief or happiness.

"Then go. Marry Ezra. Fulfill your every need and desire."

Even now, Cletus was impressed with how she did not run out of the tower.

A week later, a short note waited for Cletus after breakfast. On seeing the signature, his hand crumpled the note, more on reflex than what had been written. Chanah had not come to see him since his return. Cletus was of the mind that she was hiding—and she could have been —but she must have found some nerves because in the note, she invited him to meet her in the wooded area where there was a little meadow. Cletus grimaced at the thought of getting on another horse so soon, but an official announcement of Ezra's engagement was going to be made in two days. If they were going to talk, and if she wanted to have the conversation out where they could not be overheard, then he would take it.

Granted, Chanah was the last person Cletus wished to see, but Cletus had already set things in motion with Ezra. The final parts almost *depended* on Chanah. After sending a note back, Cletus went up to his lab to collect some vials.

An hour later, Cletus found Chanah speaking to one of the groomsmen outside of the stable. As he crossed the gravel, she smiled at him, as if she had done nothing wrong. Cletus frowned the rest of the walk over, coming to a stop next to her. Seeing Cletus' face, the groomsman muttered something before disappearing into the building.

"Chanah, I hope we have a chance to talk," Cletus told her, not hiding his displeasure. To his annoyance, she smiled again, instead of getting nervous.

"I thought I would have a little more time to get to the meadow before you came out, that way we would not need a chaperone."

"You and I have never needed a chaperone." He growled out low to avoid being heard.

"That is because no one wanted to go to your little tower. Ah, there is my horse. *Do* enjoy your ride, Cletus."

The same groomsman came back leading a light gray colored mare, Chanah called Sunkissed. Cletus watched her mount up and direct the horse on the path she wanted to take.

"I'll get your horse, my lord, be just a second." The groomsman told him before disappearing back inside.

Cletus only nodded as he watched Chanah get farther and farther away. Something was not right here. Between Davita and Chanah, Davita had the stronger will. She was the one who drew attention when they walked in the room. She was the one who went after what she wanted. Chanah had some strength, but in the time he had known her, this strength only showed sparingly. Cletus often forgot it was there, yet since her return, its appearance had been happening more and more. Now he was beginning to wonder.

The groomsman brought out his horse, and with a nod of thanks, he mounted. Going in a different direction, Cletus headed towards the meadow. The time would be used to figure out what else he had missed, which, as it happened, wasn't much, leaving him to ride and enjoy what the season did to the land.

Once he reached the meadow, Cletus found Chanah sitting on a large stone watching him. Keeping his own eyes on her, Cletus dismounted and made sure his horse was able to feed without wandering too far away. Slowly, he moved in her direction.

"An announcement will be made in two more days. A date will be picked soon after that. Will you finally let her go?"

"You forced them together to get me to let her go?" Cletus surmised, asking when he wanted to shout it.

Chanah shook her head, shifting on the rock, raising a hand to shade her eyes. The stone was shaded by enough trees to protect her skin. "No, I went to Ezra to help Davita. I did not expect anything to come of it, but I can't say I am sorry for it."

"Davita belongs to me." He flexed his jaw to keep from grinding his teeth.

"If she truly believed that, she would be bound to marry you instead." Chanah raised one shoulder as she seemed to examine him.

He had nothing to counter to this. Against all the odds, Davita had gotten away from him...or had she? There was something he could do and he needed a second person to do it. Cletus came to a stop a little more than fifteen steps from where Chanah sat.

"What do you want from me, Chanah?"

"Marry me."

There was no hesitation, no explanation. Chanah said the words and let them hang in the air. At last, they were out in the open. Cletus never wanted to hit someone as severely as he did her. His hands closed into fists, but he did not raise them. He would not hit her. He needed her.

"Let me make this clear to you, Chanah. I want only one woman. I will have just that woman, all others be damned."

Chanah leaned forward on the rock, her dark eyes hard and angry. "I will do everything in my power to make sure this wedding takes place." She snarled.

"Oh, a wedding will take place, but not the one you are thinking of."

Before she could understand or think to counter him, Cletus threw one of the vials he carried at the stone. When it burst open, releasing a large cloud of smoke, Cletus raised a handkerchief to his mouth and nose, retreating from the fumes. Looking confused, it took Chanah a second too late to move before her eyes rolled back in her head and fainted, falling to the ground. Waiting a little while longer, Cletus watched her before going over and making sure she hadn't landed on anything. Cradling her in his arms, Cletus pulled out the second vial and poured the contents down her throat, covering her mouth to make sure she swallowed. Once she had, he moved his hand and gazed at her with no heat of anger or sorrow or regret.

"I don't want you, Chanah." He whispered to her sleeping form. "I will never want you, but I will give you what you desire. You do not deserve it, but there is Ezra to also think about. I owe him a debt and this is the best way to clear it."

Cletus snapped his fingers in front of her face, and Chanah

instantly woke up. With a gasp, she choked and turned her head coughing. Cletus helped her sit up before letting her go.

"What did you throw at me?"

"Sleeping powder," he replied.

"I didn't know smoke had a taste! Why would you even be carrying that around?" she exclaimed, clearing her throat. Cletus did not respond to this, using the moment to rise to his feet and clean his pants. Once they were clean, Cletus went to his horse. "Where are you going?"

"Back to the castle; there is no agreement between us, so there is no reason for me to stay here."

"No! No, wait! I'll help you!" Cletus stopped, his back to her where she could not see his lips twitch. "I'll help you get Davita."

"Why?"

"Because she doesn't deserve to be the next Queen of Zif," Chanah told him before coughing once again. "*I* do."

Cletus looked over his shoulder at her. He didn't smile, but only because he was terrific at not doing so. Chanah got to her feet, looking as if she would take on the world to get what she wanted. She coughed again to clear her throat.

"Oh?" Cletus asked, mildly curious at what the potion was doing to her.

"Yes, I was the one who helped her write the letters."

A muscle in his jaw moved, but other than this, Cletus did not react.

"Good. We have a lot of planning to do. Let's get started," he said, turning back toward her.

Six Months Later

Cletus walked unhindered down the hallway leading to the room Davita and Chanah shared. There was a small smile on his lips as he thought of how ironic this was. Most of the time, Davita had been the one who traveled these halls to see him. Yes, his little blonde lady who swore she did not want him and insisted on marrying Ezra, still came to his tower late at night. Perhaps not as often as she used to, but she did. Her actions only proved how right he was in thinking she belonged to him and no other, and Cletus did not want Ezra to be married to a woman who could not be faithful to him. This showed how Cletus cared about Ezra. Not as much as when they were younger, but the bond had not been erased. Now Cletus considered this to be his way of returning the favor.

Making it to their rooms, Cletus gave a soft rap on the door. After a few minutes, Davita answered it, looking very awake for someone getting up before sunrise. Her eyes grew big and full at the sight of him. Cletus did not ask to come in, and it only took a heartbeat of hesitation before the door was opened wider. He slipped in.

"Cletus, what are you—?"

"Since you won't run away with me, I brought you a gift," Cletus told her, cutting off her words. He didn't need her to speak. In his hands, he held out a small rectangular box. Her wide eyes grew a curious light within them. "I know you will have a veil, but maybe you could wear this after?"

Removing the lid, nestled against black cloth was a silver mask. Davita's mouth formed a silent 'O' before picking it up, rubbing her fingers over the material.

"They say wearing one of these masks is like asking to never be the same."

Davita gave him a wry smile, tapping the mask against the palm of her hand. "So you have finally given up on me then?"

"Let's say I have arranged matters to become something I can live with."

The creaking of an opening door interrupted them. Chanah came out of her bedroom, frozen at the sight of them and didn't look as if she knew what to say. Cletus didn't spare a glance at Chanah.

"Calm down, Chanah. Cheri has come to give me a wedding gift. Look, a little mask to wear as the new Princess Consort of Zif." Davita waved the little mask in her hand for Chanah to see. Chanah appeared only capable of blinking. She opened her mouth then began coughing. Davita frowned, and grimaced. "I swear, Chanah, you just cannot get rid of that cough."

"Yes, yes, have you tried it on? The mask I mean," Chanah agreed, getting herself under control.

Davita looked thoughtfully at the mask. "It seems flexible enough for me not to need to..." Her voice trailed off as she took a more extended look. "But it couldn't hurt."

Even to Cletus' ears, Davita's voice began to sound somewhat distant—dreamy.

"Then put it on before everyone arrives to help you dress for your wedding," he prompted.

His words were all it took. Davita untied the ribbons attached and raised the mask to her face, tying the ribbons to hold it in place. As soon as her fingers let the fabric go, her mouth made a wordless 'O' at the same time the silver mask began to glow. Davita started trying to get the mask off, muttering words only she understood as the glow surrounded her. She fell to her knees, becoming encased in the bright light. When the light died, a swan stood where Davita once was.

"My god! It worked!" Chanah cried out, hands covering her mouth. "The transformation spell worked!"

Cletus snorted at Chanah's words, saying, "Of course. I would not have suggested it if it did not." At his feet, the swan—formally human—tried to take a step and fell over. Cletus looked at the bird dispassionately. Reaching into his pocket, Cletus pulled out a vial, holding it out to Chanah. "This is for you. It should also cure that coughing problem."

She took it from him, removed the cork and drank it without protest. She gave another cough and doubled over. Davita gave a rather loud honk of outrage. Cletus looked at her, giving her a smirk.

"I haven't hurt her. This plan was just as much her idea as it was mine. I just think you should be here to see it. Chanah wanted otherwise, correct?" he asked.

To his delight, Davita turned to look and began flapping her wings and carrying on for when she looked back to Chanah, Chanah wore Davita's face.

"She has seen me, now get her out! She's going to raise questions, Cletus."

Seeing the truth in her words, Cletus tied up the swan called Davita, and, using a "look-away" charm, carried her out of the castle. Getting his horse, he rode off of the grounds, out of the city, and into the countryside—only stopping once he arrived at a small pond. Untying her, he put her in the water.

"Now is the part where I am supposed to explain myself. Unfortunately for you, I don't have the time, but because I am fair, I will tell you this. I know who was writing those letters to Ezra. I know who Ezra truly loves. So let me explain the rules to you. From sunrise to sunset, you are a swan, able to travel as you will. By moonrise to dawn, you are human, confined wherever I so choose. I will give you a chance, one chance, to make it to Ezra's side in time for him to confess his loyal, undying love to you and you alone. If he does not, the spell will become permanent and you will belong to me. Ezra will drink a potion to make him grow feelings for Chanah. I will see you back at the castle, my lovely swan."

With a nod to her and a laugh, Cletus got back on his horse and rode off.

"Ah, Cletus, there you are! I have been looking everywhere for you!" Ezra announced, later on in the day.

Cletus looked up from the book he had been reading, resting a finger between the pages to hold his spot.

"I decided to hide from everyone until it was time for the wedding to start, that way I won't offend anyone." With everything going on, Cletus had decided to hide in the castle library instead of his tower. He did not want to be easily found.

"Look, I wanted to speak to you." Ezra pulled out the other empty chair, looking around the empty room as if someone were hiding. "I tried to find Chanah, but I guess she got grabbed by someone. Do you really think this is a good idea? You know, to say my own vows instead of what the priest says? It feels weird to do such a thing."

Cletus looked at the ceiling in exasperation. *Now was not the time for cold feet.* "Ezra, you speak of nothing but Davita's glorifying qualities—of how much you love her—to me. You should tell those who have doubts." Flipping the book over, page down, Cletus grabbed the jug on the table and poured the liquid in a second cup. "Here, drink. You get any more nervous, and you'll faint in front of the priest." He picked up the cup he had been using. "Listen, you are getting married today. To avoid getting all emotional, I'll just say that after today, your life will never be the same."

"Naturally, and you are next, my friend." Ezra teased, raising his cup.

"I have everything I want."

Cletus raised his own cup to toast, but even as he drank, his attention remained on Ezra as he drank the whole cup.

Cletus walked down the aisle next to Ezra in the decorated chapel. With the wedding set to begin at sundown, candles had been set up to provide light. What no one knew was that each candle had been dipped in a potion to make everyone more agreeable and just a little sleepy mentally. After all, it would be the nobles of Zif that would have to be convinced of the story Chanah and Cletus thought up. Chanah could not wear Davita's face forever.

Ezra took the two steps up to where he was to stand while Cletus moved off to the side. There, they waited until the royal family came into the chapel as well. Cletus hid his smile by looking down because no one realized the bride's family was not the DeCandia's. A hush fell over the chapel as the back doors opened revealing Chanah in the wedding dress Davita picked out, wearing Davita's face.

All day, the time had seemed to pass slowly, but in the same instant of seeing the bride, time sped up.

In no time at all, Chanah was on the platform standing across from Ezra. They held hands, looking nowhere else, but at each other. The priest began his sermon about faith, honor, loyalty, and trust. Nothing was said on love. Most of the nobility had not married for love. To speak of it would be pointless. As he sat there, hands clasped as if he were going to pray, Cletus lips very slowly moved, weaving a spell to cover the room.

"By the Father, Son and Holy Spirit, I, Ezra Siegfried Morando, do marry you, Davita Odetta DeCandia."

Cletus lifted his eyes to see something white fly past one of the windows. Still murmuring, he bowed his head to hide his expression of delight. *So, you have made it Davita, but it is too late,* he thought. There must have been some challenge in learning how to use the wings. The sermon continued after Chanah spoke, avoiding saying Davita's full name. Cletus wondered if his new swan would be bold enough to enter the chapel.

"I wish to speak my own vows!" Ezra announced. Cletus schooled his expression into surprise like everyone else, finishing the spell. "I know the vows are important, that is why I want to say my own. Davita, there are no words I can ever entirely say to explain all you are. You are the best thing for me, and the greatest treasure I could ever receive. All that you are, I love so much. I swear to you, from this day forth, I belong to you. I swear to love you and only you for as long as I live."

Lightning cracked across the sky outside. There was the faint sound of a scream. All the candles flickered then died as the doors to the chapel were thrown open by a strong gust of wind. There were different sounds of surprise and dismay before the priest asked everyone to remain calm. The doors were forced closed, and only the candles on the platform and around the couple were relit.

"Well, I would say no other vow can top that one. What do you say?" the priest asked to those in the pews, about to complete Cletus and Chanah's plan, under their spell. Some laughed. "Without further ado, I now pronounce you husband and wife. Your Highness Prince Ezra, you may kiss your bride—and the new Princess Consort—Her Highness, Princess *Chanah*."

Cletus used the distraction of the wind to leave the chapel. Outdoors, the wind had calmed, and the threat of a storm had passed. Following a magical cord, he created that morning, Cletus came to a stop at the sight of Davita crying on a bench, out of sight of anyone.

"Hello, Davita, my little swan." She instantly, turned her attention on him, hatred in her eyes.

"What have you done!"

"What I have needed to. You think I wouldn't have found out Chanah had been the one writing to Ezra? She might not have originally wanted him, and he did not either, but more than anything, she did want marriage. You, on the other hand, wanted me, but I am not rich enough for you." She got to her feet. If she could have, she would have stabbed him.

Cletus grinned pleasantly.

"Now, now, none of that, I told you, *didn't I*, but you didn't listen. You are mine. You belong to me, only me."

ABOUT JALESSA BETTIS

After many years, Jalessa Bettis is new to the world of publishing, editing, and now ready to tell everyone about the many characters who stop by for a visit and tell her their life story. These characters come in all ages, different genders, and many backgrounds. Every one of them enjoys telling her of happy times, troubling misdeeds, great sorrows, nail-biting adventures, epic romantics, and how stepping on the bad side can be the best idea they ever had. When she is not having such conversations, she can be found reading or listening to an audiobook while working on her latest craft project and playing video games.

CONNECT ON SOCIAL MEDIA

jalessabettis.com

instagram.com/jassa_jalessa

twitter.com/BettisJalessa

THANK YOU

Dearest readers,

Thank you so much for spending a little time with us in this anthology. We hope you enjoyed our dark, twisted villains as much as we do. Each author worked very on their individual stories and we hope you'll reach out to the authors you loved most to let them know how much you enjoyed their stories!

Special thanks to Jess P. for all of your hard work. We know this one was a lot more than expected and we could not be more grateful for your helpful eyes.

Thank you to Elle and Jess for all of your extra help too!

—the authors of the Blood From A Stone Twisted Villains Anthology

CPSIA information can be obtained
at www.ICGtesting.com
Printed in the USA
BVHW07s0937221018
530866BV00001B/44/P

9 781948 668125